Christmas at Tiffany's

Also by Karen Swan

Players
Prima Donna

Christmas at
TIFFANY'S
Karen Swan

WILLIAM MORROW
An Imprint of HarperCollins*Publishers*

CHRISTMAS AT TIFFANY'S. Copyright © 2011 by Karen Swan. All rights reserved. Printed in the United States of America. No part of this book may be used or reproduced in any manner whatsoever without written permission except in the case of brief quotations embodied in critical articles and reviews. For information address HarperCollins Publishers, 195 Broadway, New York, NY 10007.

HarperCollins books may be purchased for educational, business, or sales promotional use. For information please e-mail the Special Markets Department at SPsales@harpercollins.com.

First published in Great Britain as a hardback original in 2011 by Macmillan an imprint of Pan Macmillan, a division of Macmillan Publishers Limited.

FIRST WILLIAM MORROW PAPERBACK EDITION PUBLISHED 2014.

Library of Congress Cataloging-in-Publication Data has been applied for.

ISBN 978-0-06-236410-4

14 15 16 17 18   DIX/RRD   10 9 8 7 6 5 4 3 2 1

To Aason

For starting over with such grace

Christmas at Tiffany's

Prologue

Kelly Hartford looked out of the taxi window and scanned the horizon for a landmark—a loch or a folly or a particularly tall tree—that might give some clue that they were heading in the right direction. It was exactly ten years to the day since she had last visited, and she'd forgotten how far *beyond* the back of beyond her friend lived. Apart from a few tiny crofters' cottages on the moor, they'd not passed a house or car in over thirty miles. Kelly didn't know how Cassie stuck it.

A sunbeam streamed in through the window, dazzling her momentarily, and she rooted around in her bag for a pair of shades. She had also forgotten how much longer the days were up here in the summer. It was the end of August and just coming up to seven o'clock, but the sky was still noon-blue. It would be nearer eleven before the sun doffed its cap for the day and dropped behind the hills.

The taxi took a left fork in the seemingly endless road. Stretching her thumbs out the way her physiotherapist had shown her, Kelly resumed her speed-texting. But not for long. The car started hitting potholes and she had to grab the headrest for support.

"Jeez-us," she muttered as the overexcited suspension

tossed her about. "It would have been smoother coming by camel."

The dour driver said nothing, but she knew this pitted farm road was the landmark she'd been looking for. Up ahead, she could see the eagle-topped pillars and lodge house announcing the perimeter of the estate and the end of her long journey. She had been traveling for a full day now—having caught a connecting flight to Edinburgh at Heathrow—and she was desperate for a shower and a power-nap before the party kicked off. She knew she'd been cutting it fine catching the later flight. If she'd gone from Newark, she'd have landed three hours earlier and she could have rested all afternoon and caught up with the others, but who was she kidding? She was a JFK-only girl, and anyway, Bebe was going nuts trying to get the collection finished—she'd practically had a coronary when Kelly had insisted she really did have to leave her post to fly to Scotland for a *party*. They were in the final two weeks before the collections, and it had been the least she could do to stick around until the very last, hand-luggage-only, gates-closing minute.

The heather-topped moorland stopped abruptly at the gates as they swept into an avenue of towering Scots pines whose needles covered the ground like a carpet. Slowly the taxi meandered around high compacted banks of quivering maroon maples, purple rhododendrons, and springy lawns of magenta clover. The sudden riot of manicured color heralded the imminence of the great house, and as the car passed between a pair of gigantic domed yew trees flanking the drive, she thought it looked grander than she remembered—and pinker. Hewn from indigenous rock, it usually looked brown in the customary rain, but tonight, as it basked in the late-summer sun, it positively blushed with delight. Tall, with six gable ends as peaked as witches' hats, it had a sweep of stone steps up to the front door and heavily leaded windows, of which the centerpiece was a massive picture window that ran across the central facade, flooding the inner hall with light and affording a sensational view of the Lammermuir Hills from the minstrels' gallery within.

As the taxi slowed on its approach to the front steps, Kelly quickly turned the volume on her iPhone up to max— she didn't want to miss any calls once inside the enormous house—and purposely dropped her shoulders a good two inches from her ears as she took a series of deep yogic breaths. Bebe would be fine without her. She'd be back on the plane tomorrow night and straight into the office for Monday lunchtime. Most people took longer bathroom breaks than that.

The grandfather clock chimed seven times in the hall below, just as the champagne cork popped and Suzy poured them each a glass.

"Cheers!" Cassie beamed, her eyes glittering brightly as she tucked her legs underneath her on the bed. "To us."

Anouk tipped her head to the side. "Don't let your husband hear you say that," she teased in her silky French accent. "Strictly speaking it's to you and him tonight."

Cassie shrugged happily and sighed. Anouk was right, of course. They'd managed ten years together in a day and age when most couples couldn't manage two, and to celebrate they were throwing a huge bash that was as big as, if not even bigger than, their wedding. But even though Cassie was proud of their achievement—not least because it meant she'd upheld her side of their "agreement"—she was even more excited about the fact that it was the perfect opportunity to corral her best friends from their far-flung corners of the world. She knew that Suzy, Anouk, and Kelly all hooked up reasonably regularly. After all, London, Paris, and New York were practically commuter routes for them—but diversions up to the Scottish Borders? Not so much. This was the first time they'd all be together since her wedding—well, once Kelly got here.

Cassie watched as Suzy carefully lifted up a pale blue box with chocolate-brown polka dots from the far side of the bed. "Well, the champagne may be for you and Gil," she said, grinning, "but *these* are for us." Inside were four overscaled cupcakes, all frosted with the palest lemon icing and topped with a white rose.

"*Magnifique*," Anouk sighed, leaning over to pass one to Cassie.

"Oh my God—they're so cute," Cassie squealed, holding hers up to the sunlight. "They're like baby bunnies." Dundee cake was a far cry from the chichi delectations that flirted from the bakery windows in Pimlico, Cassie mused.

"They're *passion fruit*?" she asked, spraying crumbs everywhere.

Suzy nodded. "You like? I've been developing the recipe with the bakery for a wedding I'm doing. It's taken forever to get it right—one lot was too gloopy, the next not tangy enough. But I think it's there now—don't you?"

Cassie swooned in agreement.

"Is the bride behaving herself?" Anouk asked, reclining against the pillows and eating her cupcake in tiny little pinches.

Suzy rolled her eyes. "Do they ever? Just about the only thing she hasn't changed her mind about is the groom—and with a month to go, there's still time."

Anouk giggled, shaking her head. "I don't know how you put up with it. All that stress you're absorbing."

Suzy eyed her rounded tummy. "Well, I could do with absorbing a lot more. Why is it that my brides always lose at least ten pounds for their weddings, but I only ever seem to put it on? I mean, I'm the one with all the hassles—dealing with the florists, double-booked venues, unreliable bands, coked-up DJs, truculent vicars . . . You name it, I've dealt with it. You'd think I'd be the one losing weight."

Cassie sighed. For as long as she'd known her—which was since birth—Suzy had been permanently on a quest to make herself smaller. Already five foot ten by the age of twelve, with a build that had been athletic even at her thinnest, she'd always felt like she took up too much room, and the adolescent desire to conform had never left her—particularly, it seemed, as she now worked with diminishing brides on a daily basis.

Still, whatever Suzy felt about her weight, Cassie thought she looked better than ever—younger than her thirty years, for a start, with her velvety, rosy-hued complexion, her dark brown "Bambi" eyes, and a layered style she'd settled on that made the most of her too-fine dark blond hair.

Anouk, on the other hand, was Suzy's opposite in every way. Dark, petite, knowing. Her thick chestnut-brown hair was expensively cut in a long tousled bob that cut in perfectly beneath her pronounced cheekbones, her nose was straight and fine, and her full pout was tantalizingly offset by a hint of overbite. Compared with Suzy, she looked older than her thirty years, though not because of wrinkles or anything as bourgeois as aging—Cassie well knew that the contents of Anouk's bathroom would outstock Space NK and that she had a beauty regimen that would put Cleopatra to shame.

Rather, she had a worldly air, a sophistication that was rarely worn on such dainty shoulders but was more often seen on women ten, even twenty, years her senior.

"Honestly, I think living in these cities is bad for your health," Cassie said reprovingly. "From what I can see, it makes you all neurotic about your figures. No one thinks twice about things like that up here."

"Why not?" Anouk asked. "What's wrong with looking after yourself?"

"But that's just the thing. It's *not* looking after yourself. It's denying yourself. All of you always seem to be starving yourselves to some ridiculously low weight that just isn't sustainable. Everyone should just relax and . . . enjoy cupcakes," she sighed, taking the last remaining bite.

"That's what's so hateful about you," Suzy snarled. "You're slim without even thinking about it. At least I can take comfort in the knowledge that Anouk and Kelly suffer terribly to stay thin."

"I do *not* suffer," Anouk pouted, looking insulted that she should ever be thought to do anything so inelegant.

"Oh no? Then how come you get tinier every time I see you?"

"I am Parisienne, *chérie*," she shrugged, as if that explained everything. "It's in my DNA."

"Hmph, that old chestnut."

"What are you wearing tonight?" Anouk asked Cassie, still pinching away at her cake. "I trust you have frittered away the family trust on something fabulous?"

Cassie shook her head, knowing the consternation this would cause. "Afraid not. The shooting season starts next week and I've been up to my eyes in the kitchens, trying to get ahead. It hasn't helped that we had a bumper crop of damsons this summer and I've been trying to get everything off the tree and jammed."

Anouk dropped her hand in disgust. "You ditched a new dress for *damsons?*"

"It's never jam tomorrow in this house, is it?" Suzy muttered, rolling her eyes.

Cassie shrugged. "I've not been able to get off the estate for over a month now," she said, getting up and walking over to the wardrobe. "And anyway, Gil always liked this black velvet dress that I bought a few years ago for New Year's. I've probably only worn it three or four times." She held it against herself—knee-length, off the shoulder, with a velvet rose centerpiece. "It *is* Laura Ashley."

"Laura . . . ," Anouk mouthed, looking aghast at Suzy.

"Hey, I know it doesn't look anything on the hanger, but honestly, when it's on . . . " She caught sight of Suzy's skeptical expression. "Look, I'll put it on now. Then you'll see it's not so bad." She wriggled out of her dressing gown just as the door burst open.

Kelly took one look at Cassie in her once-white Playtex bra and baggy knickers and her jaw dropped. "Oh my God! It's worse than I thought."

Cassie shrieked and bounded over, swamping Kelly in a delighted hug.

Anouk picked up the velvet dress, grimacing. "It is *so* much worse than you thought," she said to Kelly, who was peering at her over Cassie's shoulder. She threw the dress down on the bed and lit a cigarette.

Suzy poured a fresh glass of champagne and sauntered over, waiting for Cassie to release Kelly. "You're still a stranger to color, I see," she tutted, handing Kelly the glass and kissing her affectionately. "And you've lost weight. You're too thin."

"There's no such thing," Anouk purred, holding her cigarette behind her as she kissed Kelly on each cheek.

"Exactly," Kelly agreed. They'd always been partners in crime and were both rampantly, defiantly single and at the height of their seductive powers. They even looked similar. Kelly was also a shimmering brunette, though her hair was reed-straight and longer than Anouk's, her nose more retroussé, her eyes hazelnut-colored and almond-shaped.

"I see I've come at just the right time," said Kelly, taking Cassie by the shoulders and giving her a Paddington Bear–like hard stare. "What the hell are you doing to Anouk?"

"What do you mean?"

"She's French, Cass. You can't walk around in underwear like that. She doesn't have the constitution for it."

"Well . . . I . . . But . . . ," she stammered, looking between her tragic bra and Anouk, who had one hand on her hip and one eyebrow raised to heaven. "Well, *Gil* doesn't mind," she blustered.

"Honey, right this instant, it's a *mystery* to me how you two have got to ten years together." Kelly took a sip of her drink. "You'd be kicked out of bed in Manhattan!"

"Institutionalized in Paris," Anouk drawled.

Cassie looked to Suzy for the final nail in the coffin. "Sorry, sweets," she shrugged. "Can't help you. London's definitely not calling."

"Urrrgh, you're a nightmare, the lot of you," Cassie said defensively, reaching for the toweling dressing gown heaped on the floor. "I'd forgotten how high-maintenance you all are. I don't know how your men put up with you."

She hated it when they ganged up on her like this. They might all live in different countries and be products of different cultures, but it seemed as though sophistication was an international language that linked her glamorous, urbane friends together. It wasn't as if their day-to-day lives overlapped: Kelly had her own fashion PR consultancy in Manhattan, Suzy was a high-octane wedding planner in London, and Anouk was a sought-after jewelery designer in Paris, who refused to sell through boutiques and would only accept new customers if they had contacts with at least three of her existing clients. And yet the three of them invariably used the same miracle moisturizer, carried the same Balenciaga bag, read the newspaper on their iPads, and minimized their bottoms in MiH jeans.

"Hey, chill—it's not like I'm surprised, or even disappointed," Kelly said, winking as she unzipped her overnight bag and pulled out a petal-pink, tissue-wrapped bundle. "Because I just so happen to have a little gift for you."

Cassie took it gingerly, looking slightly afraid of what she might find in there. She shook open the paper and a midnight-blue silk dress slid out. "Oh! What a beautiful nightie!' she exclaimed, running her hand over the fabric, her indignation instantly forgotten.

The others burst out laughing.

"Shall I wear it tonight?" she asked coquettishly, holding it against herself.

"Oh, you'll wear it tonight, all right." Kelly laughed. "But to the *party*. This ain't no nightie!"

"What?" Cassie said, alarmed. "But it's so . . . skimpy. Gil would be mortified if I . . ."

"*Au contraire*, Gil will be delighted to see his wife look so alluring," Anouk asserted. "Put it on."

Knowing she had no choice in the matter, Cassie slid the dress over her head. The silk felt exquisite next to her skin, and she noticed, now that it was on, two tiny lace peekaboo crescents arced over her hips. A tiny but incredibly sexy detail.

"Wow!" Suzy gasped.

"New season?" Anouk asked Kelly.

Kelly nodded. "Bebe Washington label. Gisele's walking in it in the show in a few weeks."

"I want it," Anouk purred.

"You shall have it. Got anything special in mind?" Kelly asked.

"Oh yes," Anouk said, refusing to elaborate.

Cassie couldn't stop looking at herself in the mirror. She looked so . . . different. Not like herself, somehow. She wasn't sure what Gil would say, despite the girls' assurances. She looked at the clock. Seven-thirty. Outside, the piper had started playing, beckoning the revelers toward the Lammermuir estate as he paced solemnly back and forth across the lawn.

She wondered whether Wiz would be able to get here early. She'd said she would try. Wiz'd tell it to her straight. After all, she was her go-to friend up here, her rock, her lunch companion and closest confidante—the one who'd taken her under her wing when she'd first arrived, not yet twenty-one, fresh from the air-conditioned climes of expat living in Hong Kong and new to the nuances of grouse-moor farming.

She looked down at the trio of childhood friends who were sitting together in a gaggle on the floor, examining a heap of shoes that had been upended from one of Anouk's many bags. Their friendship had been arranged practically before their births. Their fathers had all been CEOs of the multinational cosmetics conglomerate Neroli—Kelly's for the Americas in New York; Anouk's for Europe, excluding the UK, in Paris; Suzy's for the UK in London; and Cassie's for Asia in Hong Kong. Before the girls were even born, their mothers had all been good friends, meeting regularly around the world for coffee and shopping trips as they accompanied their husbands to annual meetings and conferences. And when the girls had been born, all in the same year—surely a collaboration by their mothers?—the friendship was handed down a generation as they shared crèches, rattles, and nannies. Their parents couldn't have been remotely surprised when, aged thirteen, the girls mounted a pressure group to be sent to the same boarding school in England, and they'd enjoyed five blissful years together, as close as sisters, sleeping in the same dorm, playing on the same lacrosse team, swooning over the same boys . . . until Cassie had blown it.

Perhaps "blown it" was too harsh, but she'd always had the feeling that by marrying Gil so early, she'd popped their sealed bubble. She'd met him at the Grosvenor House Ball in London and he'd swept her off her feet, not just with his extraordinary confidence and intelligence, but more particularly with his voice: crystal-cut with a whisper-soft burr. She would do anything for that voice—it had seduced her away from her virginity, taken her away from her friends, made her wait for the baby she yearned for . . .

There was a knock at the door.

"Cassie?" Speak of the devil.

Cassie's eyes widened in panic. He couldn't see her looking like this—half-dressed in a nightie over her grubby underwear with no makeup on.

The girls clearly had the same thought and sprang up off the floor to group around her like a footballer's wall, just as Gil peered in. He took in the scene of desolation—the empty cake box, the half-drunk bottles of champagne, the piles of shoes, the dresses on the beds, and the huddle of women, two of them in identikit toweling robes and hair turbans.

"I thought I'd find all of you in the one room together. Heaven forbid you should get ready in *your own rooms,*" he quipped.

He stepped into the room, looking relieved that everyone was "decent." He was already dressed for the festivities, wearing a bottle-green velvet smoking jacket and trousers in the family's dress tartan. His sharp, hawkish features— which always looked so intimidating in his barrister's gown and wig—were softened by the anticipation of the night's revelries.

"You've put me in the Faerie Room, Gil," Suzy said accusingly, hands on hips. "Don't think I've forgotten that's the one that's haunted. You weren't the only one who didn't sleep a wink on your wedding night."

Gil laughed softly at her allusion to the lap-dancing pole the girls had put up in his room. "I'm sorry Archie couldn't make it this weekend. It would have been good to see him."

"Well, you're not as sorry as he is," Suzy replied on behalf of her errant husband. "Camel racing with clients in Abu Dhabi is not his definition of a good time. The poor boy's terrified. I had to give him the beta blockers I keep on standby for my nervous brides."

Gil chortled and looked at Kelly, dressed top to toe in black—the only one who didn't look as if she was staying at a spa. "And how was your flight, Kelly?"

"Oh, you know . . . a supermodel in full tantrum in front, a drunk sleeping on my shoulder, and an air hostess with rage issues. The usual," she said drily.

He looked at the women clustered around Cassie, whose

blond curls were poking out from the middle of them. "Why're you all standing like that around my wife?" he asked suspiciously. "You haven't done anything to her, have you?"

"No. We're just getting her ready," Suzy said quickly.

"It looks like you've got her so drunk she can't stand."

"*Non!*" said Anouk.

"It's just bad luck for you to see her before it's time," Kelly explained.

"It's bad luck for me to see her in her wedding dress," he said, frowning. "Not at the anniversary party *ten years later.*"

"Pah! You say tom-*aaaah*-to, I say tom-*ay*-to," Kelly argued, making him grin.

"Fine," he said, holding his hands up in defeat. He stood on tiptoe, trying to catch sight of his wife. "Well, just so you know, darling, our guests are arriving."

Cassie nodded from behind the wall of friends. "Ten minutes."

"Uh-huh," he said knowingly, backing out of the room. "I'd like to see the odds they're offering for that." He shut the door on the telltale sounds of women in a rush—zips opening, wardrobe doors banging, the shower running. It was going to be half an hour, minimum.

Cassie was still looking at herself in the mirror when Kelly got out of the shower. "You can see my knickers through this dress," she hissed, panicking. She knew the girls were going to make her wear the dress, and that Gil would disapprove. The girls knew it too—why else would they have hidden her from him?

"Don't wear any," Anouk said across the room as she applied her eyeliner.

Cassie looked at her in horror.

"I've already thought of that," Kelly said, going over to her bag and throwing a plastic packet on the bed. "Flesh-colored too."

Cassie picked it up. "Spanx? What's that?"

Everyone rolled their eyes. "Sausage knickers, Cass!" Suzy said. "They hold your fat bits in and give you a smooth line under the dress. I make all my brides in bias-cut wear them."

"What shoes have you got?" Kelly asked, already dreading the answer. Don't say pumps. Don't say—

"I've got some nice kitten heels I bought in the L. K. Bennett sale last Christmas." There was a heavy silence. "What? They're my best ones."

Anouk sighed and went to the jumble of shoes in the middle of the floor. She picked up a strappy gold Louboutin with a four-inch heel. "Try that. We're the same size."

"Oh, you have got to be joking. I don't wear anything higher than a welly-boot all year round. You can't seriously expect me to get down the staircase in those. I'd have to slide down the banisters."

"If that's what it takes," Anouk shrugged.

Cassie sighed and slipped them on, instantly rocketing up to six feet. She had to admit they were stunning with the dress, and they certainly felt more comfortable than they looked. But then she hadn't tried moving yet. Which reminded her . . .

"I hope you've all remembered there's reeling later on. You'll need sensible shoes."

"There's no such thing," Anouk and Kelly declared in unison.

"Sweetie, the only thing I intend to be reeling from tonight is the drink," Suzy said, wriggling into her dress and making them all—even Cassie—dissolve into laughter.

14

*　　*　　*

Forty-five minutes later, the four women descended the winding staircase arm in arm like a daisy chain. Even Cassie couldn't remain oblivious to the stares that met her. None of her friends—Gil's friends—had ever seen her look like this before. She felt incredible. Anouk had plaited her muddy-blond hair in Grecian style across the front, leaving the rest to fall in heavy ripples down her back, and Suzy had made up her huge round blue eyes with gold and bronze shadows and put a matte stain on her wide, ever-smiling mouth.

Her friends had stood back and admired her like a work of art they had produced. She bore no resemblance to the woman who'd been digging in thirty raspberry bushes in the garden in floral dungarees and one of her husband's moth-eaten lambswool sweaters at two o'clock that afternoon. She knew she looked good, but what worked at a fashion show in Paris or at a cocktail party in Manhattan wasn't what cut it with the Scottish shooting set. Gil was ten years older than she was, and all his friends older still. Did she look . . . *appropriate*? She scanned the room anxiously, hoping to find Wiz's eyes before Gil's.

Cassie couldn't see either of them, but there was no doubt that everyone else thought the dress was a hit. As they reached the ground floor, a cloud of guests and perfume enveloped her and she quickly became separated from the girls.

"Hello . . . How lovely to see you . . . Oh, you are kind . . . Hello . . . Are you well? . . . So pleased you could make it . . . Oh, do you think so? . . . You look radiant too . . . I know, divine weather, isn't it? . . . Hello . . . Thank you for coming . . ."

But there's only so much revolution one party can take, and as a glass was placed in her hand by a man who'd matched his sporran to his beard, the conversation returned to the dull but familiar territory of the abomination of the wind farms on the Earl of Luss's neighboring estate.

Discreetly, she let her eyes graze the room. A string quartet was playing in the minstrels' gallery, the men were dressed in trousers or kilts, some with sashes and flamboyant horse-hair sporrans that fell to their hemlines. The women were equally grand in full-length gowns with heirloom jewels. They looked stately and impressive, but as her eyes flickered between them and her modish urban friends in cascading coral silk-plissé ruffles (Anouk), intricate ethnic gold beading (Suzy), and laser-cut jet satin (Kelly), it occurred to her that the grandes dames looked exactly the same as they always did at these events.

Just like the house, she thought. They were hemmed in, curtailed, by tradition. The hall looked imposing as usual— even a bunch of daisies in a teapot would be imbued with gravitas in these baronial surroundings—but it looked the same as it probably had at every party that had been thrown here in the last two hundred years. The antler-framed chande-liers flickered with as-yet-unseen candlelight, thick swags of ivy were draped around the austere family portraits, slightly fraying, faded ceremonial flags hung from brass holsters in the walls, and the enormous stone fireplace had been filled with a profusion of garden flowers and thistles—it was too warm for a fire tonight. Only the bright red balloons tied to the banisters at every other tread and shouting "We Are 10" showed that it was Cassie who was the mistress of the house, not her scary mother-in-law, nor indeed any of the women who glared grimly down from the walls.

Across the room, she could see that the girls—who were sticking together like barnacles—had nabbed Wiz first. More formally known as Lady Louisa Arbuthnott, Wiz was the prized daughter of the most senior judge in the country, Lord Valentine, and as well as being Cassie's best friend was one of the best-connected women in Edinburgh. She did events like these in her sleep. Wind farms, poor grouse stocks, declining peat bogs in the central belt—she could extrapolate and amuse on every topic. Nothing fazed her. No one bored her. Everyone adored her.

Dressed in an elegant olive-colored silk column dress with black pearls at her throat, her reddish-auburn hair wound up into a chignon, she was the only other woman here who could rival the outsiders for style. She was as much at home in the city as in the country, and as a senior partner at Edinburgh's leading divorce firm, McMaster & Mathieson, she retained a personal shopper at Harvey Nicks who made a point of reserving the key pieces from the designer collections for her.

Her head was thrown back in laughter at something Kelly had said and they were all smiling, but Cassie was fluent in the group's microscopic body language and her stomach lurched—Anouk had her eyes fractionally narrowed, Suzy was smiling slightly too brightly, Kelly's chin was dipped a bit too low. Although the girls had never mentioned it, there was an unspoken tension—jealousy, she supposed—surrounding her friendship with Wiz.

Cassie knew they all did their best to keep her in the loop. They spoke regularly on the phone and sent e-mails; they had even persuaded her to leave status updates on Facebook, but after a fortnight's rotation of *Cassie Fraser is—drinking a cup of tea/sitting at the computer/bored*, they had begged her to stop. The simple fact that she'd never seen sausage pants and thought gladiator sandals were last worn by the Romans highlighted just how far outside their orbit she was circuiting. They might be old friends, but their lives were very different now, and the truth was it was Wiz who now knew her best.

When Cassie's beloved father had died four years ago, it had been Wiz who'd booked the tickets for her to go back to Hong Kong for a couple of months to be with her mother. And it worked both ways. When Wiz's husband, Sholto, had walked out on her when she was five months pregnant with their son Rory, it was Cassie who had attended all the ante-natal classes with her, held her hand during the birth, and become a besotted godmother.

For nearly ten years, the two separate strands of friend-ship had worked in perfect harmony because they had never overlapped. Tonight was a first for all of them.

Making a vague excuse about circulating, she tried to make her way over to the girls, but the demands of cour-tesy in response to the attention engendered by her dazzling dress meant it was like wading through mud. By the time she grabbed Suzy's arm, Wiz had gone.

"Where is she?" she asked, disappointed. She desperately wanted her opinion on the dress. Gil was still cloistered in a group out of eyeshot somewhere.

"She had to take a phone call. Someone called Martha?"

Cassie nodded. "That's her nanny."

"Right. Well, she's in the study."

"Thanks. I'll come straight back," she said, smoothing her palms anxiously on her thighs.

She wound her way through the crowd, trying to keep her eyes down. "Sorry, phone call . . . excuse me . . . I'll be straight back . . ."

The door to the study was ajar, but she could hear Wiz's

18

soothing voice as she said goodnight to Rory. "I love you, darling," she heard. "Be good for Martha, okay . . ."

Cassie smiled and stopped just short of the doorway, not wanting to intrude. Rory was three now and had just started at nursery, but he already had a social diary that outranked Cassie's, and she had joked on more than one occasion that it would be easier to schedule a meeting with the Pope than a playdate with Rory. If he wasn't at kindergarten he was at baby-gym, yoga, French classes, or toddler football, or otherwise napping. Cassie knew from the newspapers that "over-scheduling" was a modern parent's malaise, but there never seemed to be any mention of the other modern dilemma—the earnest godparent worrying about her place on the sidelines of the child's life.

She leaned against the door jamb, tracing the navy and bottle-green tartan wallpaper with her fingers.

"And remember to brush your teeth. Martha told me you had ice cream for dessert . . ."

Cassie looked back toward the hall and watched as the waiters walked around with trays of drinks and the guests took them graciously. No one would do anything as improper as get drunk tonight.

"Okay, Daddy's here to say night-night . . ."

What?

Cassie stood up straight, the sound of blood rushing to her ears. Sholto was *here*?

She shook her head. Wiz had had no contact with him since he'd left—nearly four years ago now. And there was no way Gil would have invited him. He knew as well as she did what a betrayal—not to mention humiliation—it had been for Wiz when he'd walked out.

"How's my little man been today?"

The pounding in her ears got louder and she felt her heart begin to pump more quickly.

"The castle? . . . Good boy . . . Well now, do as Mummy says and brush your teeth . . . I'll be home in two sleeps, okay? . . . I miss you, Ror. Sleep tight . . . ," said the voice, that oh-so-distinctive voice that she had first fallen in love with.

NEW YORK

Chapter One

Cassie watched as the city rose up toward her, leaping out of the ground in huge sculpted shards of steel and glass, the famous rivers meandering like copper snakes around them. She tried to understand what the fuss was all about, but it was difficult from ten thousand feet up. It was one of those cities that everyone said you simply *had* to visit at least once in your life, but she'd never had the faintest interest in coming here. Not that she could publicly say so—it would be like admitting that she didn't really want Mandela as her ideal dinner guest or that *Pretty Woman* was her all-time favorite film.

But now here she was—first decision made. The last place she'd wanted to come had been her first. It was as far outside her comfort zone as she could imagine, everything she'd never wanted—loud, bright, glaring, and blaring. A great honking, seething mass of urban humanity that would guarantee to distract her, at the very least, from the ruins of her own life.

The plane circled the Statue of Liberty—tall and proud and as green as a peppermint—twice, as though making a heavy-handed point to her: *See? Liberty. Freedom. Independence. It's all good here.* But she wasn't fooled. There was nothing great about freedom as far as she could see—it was just a piece of PR spin on the word *isolation* or *loneliness*.

She shook her head and finished the rest of her drink. She knew she was drunk and depressed. Both would pass, one faster than the other. She wondered whether Gil was either of these things right now, whether her immediate flight off the estate and out of the country had brought sudden clarity to his actions and made him realize what a mistake he had made.

But even as she thought it, she knew that probably the only thing he felt right now was relief. In so many ways—socially, historically, Scottishly—he and Wiz were a much better fit, and now he was free to give up the charade of weekly commuting and just be with his second family.

She paused.

Were they the second family—or the first? Was she just the appendage? After all, they had had a child together. They had a blood tie. She just had a gold ring and a legal document. Then again, she'd been married to him *first* . . . She tried to debate the dilemma rationally, but six back-to-back gin and tonics made it difficult. Aha! Wait! Her legal document had also been sworn before God. She had *God* on her side . . . And the girls.

She sank back against the headrest and closed her eyes. God *and* the girls. Who could argue with that? Certainly Gil couldn't. Hadn't.

In the frigid aftermath of her discovery, Gil and Wiz had just watched as Suzy, Kelly, and Anouk had sprung into action—whisking her upstairs, pulling her dress over her head, and packing a bag for her, finding her passport, pushing her feet into the muck boots by the door, bundling her into the car, even doing up her seat belt for her as she sat shell-shocked, too fractured to pull herself together and fight back, just waiting to be spirited away to her next life. Wherever that might be. Down there, perhaps? She peered out of the window again.

Or would it be London? Or Paris? She shut her eyes and tried to imagine herself as the girls had predicted for her in the car—slick, metropolized, heels clicking as she sashayed down a busy shopping avenue, men turning to stare. She couldn't see it herself. For the past ten years, the only things that had turned to stare when she passed were the chickens. But as they had bumped away from the estate, a plan had slowly and painfully come together. The girls had argued fiercely around her silent, teary form as to who knew what was best. London was nearest and most approachable, Suzy had argued, for a girl who'd never lived in a city before. Kelly had countered that what Cassie needed was a complete break from everything she knew, a baptism of fire to get her going with her new life, and that New York was just the city for her culture shock. Anouk believed that she was better suited to Paris's quieter sophistication, and she was already fluent in the language.

They had argued all the way to the airport, no one able to edge ahead of anyone else because, in truth, nobody, not even Cassie, knew what kind of life she really ought to be living, much less where. In the end they'd hit on a compromise. Just as their mothers had implored them to as toddlers, they were going to share.

Share Cassie. She was to spend four months in each city, living with them in turn. She would stay at their apartments—Anouk and Suzy had guest bedrooms; Kelly had a trundle bed—not only because the shortest rental period would be for six months, which was too long, but also because she wouldn't be able to afford anything. Cassie had no money of her own, just a joint credit card that Gil could cut off at any time, and although she had inherited a modest trust after her father's death, the girls were unanimous, in this at least, that she shouldn't touch it until she knew where she was going to settle. It was going to be months before the divorce settlement came through, but here again the girls could help. Both Kelly and Suzy ran their own businesses and could feasibly bring her in on a temporary basis. Anouk was self-employed as well, although her business was too niche to employ anyone without specialist training, but she promised to work on some of her contacts and get something lined up for Cassie when she arrived in the new year.

So that was the plan—a city with a friend in it, a bed to sleep on, and a temporary job. The girls would rebuild her from scratch, and each friend would get her turn to exercise her own influence. Cassie had agreed to give herself up to them completely, and had promised she wouldn't protest or refuse any of their ideas for her. After the year's end, she would know which was the real Cassie and how she was going to live; her life would be up to her again, but she would be a *new* Cassie by then—confident, sexy, worldly, and full of purpose.

It was getting started that was going to be the hard part, and she'd had to plead for a day's grace between lives. The girls hadn't wanted to leave her alone for a minute, but Cassie had insisted that she needed a few hours to herself before this new chapter in her life began, and they had reluctantly booked her into a drab airport hotel room with a hard bed and a well-stocked minibar. Kelly had flown out that night, Anouk and Suzy had caught a train back to London together, and by midnight on the tenth anniversary of her wedding,

Cassie was alone and sobbing where no one could see. And when the tears were still falling on the plane twelve hours later, she simply comforted herself that anonymity brings with it the shamelessness of being able to cry very loudly in public.

She looked out through wet eyes at the famous skyscrapers closing around her, the big sky folding down into smaller parcels of blue as the plane prepared to land. She might as well be landing on the moon as in New York City, and she felt a cold chill of panic surf through her as reality bit.

Cassie had left her husband and her home, her past and her future. Her life was in Kelly's beautifully manicured hands now. She could only hope her friend had more of an idea of what to do with it than she had.

The cab pulled away with a squeal, absorbed within seconds into the yellow stream traveling south down Lexington Avenue. Cassie looked down at the crumpled piece of paper in her hand, which she had been clutching more closely than her passport. The pen had rubbed into her palms and she absentmindedly wiped her puffy eyes with grubby hands. *Apt. 16, 119 East 63rd St. between Lex and Park, 10022.* It meant nothing to her. She could navigate her way over sixty-five thousand acres of grouse moor, but the Manhattan grid? Not a chance.

She looked around at the cross streets and saw a sign saying East 63rd Street to her left. The buildings, all light stone and mid-height, were grimy to her eye, but Kelly had told her proudly that this—the Upper East Side—was Manhattan's most prestigious district. Who was she to disagree? She'd spent the past ten years in a bog.

Ahead of her, awnings in bottle green, claret, and navy

were stretched taut like limbs toward the street, and door-men in caps and gray braided uniforms loitered upright near the revolving doors, occasionally stepping to the curb to help elderly residents out of cabs and limos. She noticed that min-iature dogs were carried around here like bags, no doubt to keep them from interfering with the eyes-dead-ahead pedes-trian traffic that wove and swerved down the pavements in a perfectly synchronized dance.

The buildings were all of rather stately bearing. She was pleased to see that Kelly's had a new bright red awning— that would be easy to remember at least. The doorman— silver-haired and slim, probably in his fifties—greeted her as if he'd been waiting for her specifically, although she hadn't missed the quick up-and-down he'd given her as she'd ap-proached the building. She knew she looked a bedraggled mess. Her muck boots still had peat on them, and her an-cient pink and gray Woolworths jacket, which had always seemed so cheery in the Scottish rain, now seemed garish and gauche.

Taking her bags, the doorman held the doors open for her and she walked into a smart lobby with wood-paneled walls and a limestone floor. Everything was gleaming and polished, clean and new—all the things she wasn't. The door-man handed her an envelope Kelly had left at the desk for her. There was a key inside and a note.

"Be sure to let me know if there's anything I can do to as-sist you, ma'am," he said, smiling at her as he pressed the floor number for her in the elevator. "Ask for Bill."

"Thanks," Cassie managed, hiccuping inelegantly and no doubt confirming his impression of her as down-at-heel.

The highly polished doors eased shut on his polite smile and she unfolded the note:

Welcome to New York! Make yourself at home.
I'll be back by seven. K xx

Great, she thought, folding up the note and putting it in her jeans pocket as the doors opened onto a small landing. It was six-thirty now. Hopefully she would have just enough time for a shower and freshen-up—cheer-up, sober-up—before Kelly got back.

Finding number 16, she opened the door—and gasped. The building was so imposing and grand downstairs. But up here? Her understairs cupboard at home was bigger than the entire flat! She walked into the hallway, which was tiny and square and demarcated only by a token mat that read I AM NOT A DOORMAT.

"You don't say, Kelly," she mumbled to herself.

To the right was a bathroom, very metropolitan, with white brick tiles, a plastic shower curtain, and glass shelves groaning beneath the weight of toiletries. Adjacent to it was a bedroom. She peered in. There was just enough room to walk around the white leather button-pocketed princess bed, which was covered with a mink-colored waffle throw and so many plumped-up cushions they practically reached the footboard. A small gray and white gingham bedroom chair was covered with clothes, mainly black, and an entire wall was given over to shelving exclusively for shoes. Her mouth dropped as she took in the rows upon rows of them. It was like Gil's gun room!

Back down the hall, the sitting room was similar in size to the bedroom, with just enough room for a sofa and two armchairs—no TV, she noticed—and the in-out kitchenette was squeezed between the sleeping and living areas of the apartment like a room divider.

Cassie stood looking at the pathetic kitchen. She had bigger towels. It was pristine, that was about the best thing she could say about it: two black gloss wall units and a single floor unit, all without a smudged fingerprint anywhere. There wasn't a grain of sugar or puff of flour or even a single crumb beneath the toaster because . . . she looked along the yard-long worktop—there *was* no toaster.

Okay, she knew Kelly wasn't big on wheat. It figured she wouldn't have a toaster. But the thought of forgoing her customary marmalade on toast first thing in the morning was enough to trigger a panic attack.

In fact, it alerted her stomach to the past twenty-four-hour liquid diet and, rummaging in her handbag, she unwrapped the chocolate muffin she'd bought on the flight. As she munched nervously, her eyes began to tune in to another absence as well. Where was the kettle? She opened a wall cupboard—and found a towering pile of jeans. She opened the other one, already sensing that it would be too much to hope for cups, and, as she thought, found a jumble of bras and knickers inside.

She looked down suspiciously at the oven, one hand on her hip. It was doll-sized, with only a single ring on the stove top. It didn't seem likely that she was going to find the kettle in there.

She heard a key in the lock just as she opened the oven door to discover stacks of color-coded cashmere sweaters.

". . . Obviously," she said wryly, turning around to greet Kelly and motioning toward her discovery. "Although, if you're trying to get rid of moths, I hear it's best to put them in the freezer."

Kelly dumped her bags on the floor and gave her a bear hug. "You made it! You actually made it!"

Cassie nodded, somewhat amazed herself. "I guess I did."

"So what do you think, huh? Like it?" Kelly asked, taking the half-eaten muffin from Cassie's hand. "No carbs."

Cassie watched as the muffin was dumped in the trash bin without further comment. "Uh . . . it's so . . . cosy."

"I know what you're thinking," Kelly called behind her as she marched toward the bedroom, wiping crumbs off her hands. She sat on the bed and took off her shoes, placing them tenderly on the shoe wall. "Small. Not what you're used to." Cassie heard the sounds of zips and buckles clattering to the floor.

"Well, no, it's certainly not . . . what I'm used to," Cassie admitted. "But it's . . . charming."

"You *say* charming, but poky is what you mean," Kelly said, grinning as she came back out into the hall in a wheat-colored cashmere all-in-one jumpsuit.

"Oh my God!" Cassie cried. "You look like one of Jennifer Lopez's babies!"

Kelly elbowed her, but she was giggling. "You'll be begging for one of these once winter starts to bite! Just you wait."

"Oh yes, me in a babygro! I can see it." Cassie giggled even harder. "And I can see the face Gil would make if he saw me in it even more."

Kelly considered the prospect for a moment and then she began to laugh even harder, setting Cassie off until both women were doubled over and leaning against the wall for support. Their ability to give each other the giggles had been legendary at school—earning them both numerous detentions—but Kelly stopped when she realized that Cassie was no longer crying with laughter but just crying. She put an arm round her and they slid down the wall together, Cassie resting her head on Kelly's shoulder as she stroked her hair, just like they had always done when they were younger.

They sat like that for a long time.

"Oh dear, that's not the start I was hoping for," Cassie sniffed finally. "I was expecting to hold out for at least *half* an hour before the wailing hysterics took over."

"Well, it's going to be like that for a while," Kelly said quietly. "It's all got to come out somehow. How were you on the plane?"

"Oh, utterly mortifying—louder than most of the toddlers. You'd have left by parachute."

"Don't doubt it," Kelly nodded, beginning to get up. "Come on, let's run you a bath. You need to unwind. I'll pop out and get dinner while you soak."

"Oh no, I'm fine. I'll come with you."

"Plus you stink," Kelly said, walking into the bathroom and opening the taps. "There. I've poured my favorite Jo Malone in for you." She pulled on a pair of knitted Uggs and a sleeveless Puffa jacket. "Put your pajamas on after. I'll be back in a little while."

The door clicked softly and Cassie climbed into the bath, letting the water fill up around her. She realized she hadn't showered or washed at the airport hotel. After drinking her way through the minibar, she'd collapsed fully clothed onto the bed and, on being woken by her prebooked wake-up call, had simply stood up, grabbed her bag, and staggered out the door to the departures terminal. She wiped an eyelid and a smudge of bronze shadow came off on her finger. God, she was still wearing the party—literally wearing the makeup, the body cream, the shock and horror of that night . . .

Taking a deep breath, she slid below the surface of the perfumed bubbles, desperate for their cleansing, transformative effect. It meant she was being submerged in someone else's scent—perfumed, sophisticated, unfamiliar—but that was okay. That was what she wanted. So long as she could be anything but herself.

When Kelly got back, Cassie was wearing a pair of green checked flannel pajamas—an ancient pair of Gil's, her warmest pair for cozying up in front of the fire on those long evenings alone when he'd been working in Edinburgh during the week. A chilled bottle of Sauvignon Blanc, which she'd picked up at Duty Free, was sitting on the table in front of her, with two colored water glasses beside it.

"You don't have any wineglasses," Cassie said as Kelly eyed the tumblers suspiciously.

"That's because I don't drink wine," Kelly said, picking up the bottle and reading the label as if it were dry-cleaning instructions. "Although I'm going to have to make an exception tonight. This is an expensive bottle and it is your first night in Manhattan."

"Why don't you drink wine?"

"Cass, the calories! That bottle adds up to the same as dinner," she said, holding up two steaming white paper bags that were slightly soggy at the bottom. "We might as well eat twice!" She smiled forgivingly. "But it doesn't matter too much. We'll be running it off in the morning."

"We will?"

"Yup. Every morning. Central Park, seven A.M."

"*Seven!* Kell, I'm not even breathing at that time of night."

Kelly chuckled as she pulled the foil off the bottle. "You always were a sleepyhead. Do you remember that time you slept through the alarm and you had to sit your math exam in your nightie?"

Cassie rolled her eyes. It was true. She'd never been a morning person.

Kelly walked over to the bookcase on the far wall and took a couple of plates from on top. Cassie noticed for the first time that there were a few bowls and a glass full of cutlery there too. So that was where they were hiding. The kitchen cabinets were clearly an extended dressing room, completely devoid of culinary purpose.

"What are we having?" Cassie asked, pouring them each a glass and handing one to Kelly, who was kneeling on the floor (no table or dining chairs either) and pulling tiny cardboard boxes out of the bags.

"Japanese. You've had it before, right?" Kelly asked, glancing up at her.

"Not especially. Chopsticks become lethal weapons in my hands."

"They become hair accessories in Anouk's," Kelly replied. "Did you ever see those antique jade ones she bought at Christie's?" She sighed. "Stunning."

"Let's face it, she doesn't know any other way to be," Cassie said, looking down at her squashed thighs encased in the flannel pajamas. Not a look Anouk would understand—or want to. Anouk oozed chic the way other people ooze blood. Privately, Cassie wondered what it was going to be like staying with her in Paris. It had been a long time since school, when they'd lived in each other's pockets, arms permanently linked, heads thrown back in laughter as they roared at private jokes. She wondered whether Anouk would be able to tolerate her still-persisting need for sleep and food and bedsocks. Out of all of the girls, Anouk's life seemed the most alien, most foreign, most removed from Cassie's.

Kelly, on the other hand, for her all hyperactivity and

brusque manner, was a kitten beneath it all, with a big heart that she endeavored to keep hidden—protected—from all but her most trusted friends. For Cassie hadn't been the only one to marry early. Not two years after Cassie's marriage, Kelly had fallen hard for an insurance broker she'd met on holiday in Saint Lucia, and they'd married four weeks later, only for him to do a disappearing act with her bank savings when the IRS came calling for $2 million in back taxes. She never saw him again, and his lies—on top of his disappearance— had had a devastating effect on Kelly. He'd been the first man she'd ever loved and she'd given herself to him completely; and although she had long since moved on and had plenty of romances, none had ever endured beyond six months. Something in her had changed—the trust, the childish belief in One True Love, had gone. She changed her men with her handbags, often going on two, even three dates a night. In fact, she told Cassie now, as she opened the boxes, she was having cocktails with one guy later, at eleven, when Cassie would be tucked up in bed, sleeping off the jet lag and hang-over.

The very notion of meeting a near-stranger for drinks in the middle of the night was as alien to Cassie as the unidenti-fiable parcels of seaweed wraps and raw fish that were pass-ing for dinner in Kelly's hands. But she knew she had to try to embrace it. This was what it was to be a New Yorker. She had to get with the program.

Chapter Two

Twelve hours and sixteen minutes later, she was already lagging behind, wishing she were in Paris instead. They were running round the Jacqueline Kennedy Onassis Reservoir, and all Cassie could think about was getting back into her warm, soft trundle bed and lying in the recovery position. The training watch, which was attached to the heart-rate band beneath her bra, was bleeping and flashing red numbers at her, practically screaming at her to stop—something Kelly's trainer, Raoul, was clearly never going to do.

She did, and watched dismally as they began to pull away—again.

"Guys! Guys!" she panted, bending forward so that her head was practically on her knees. "You go ahead!" she gasped, waving them on.

Kelly rounded back, jogging on the spot, a vision of perpetual energy in her silver and blue running kit. "Don't be ridiculous, we'll wait," she smiled, looking over at Raoul, who apparently whipped all the top catwalk models into shape and was looking distinctly underwhelmed by Cassie's geriatric attempts.

"Kell, you've been running for a quarter of an hour now and your body isn't even aware it's *moving* yet!" Cassie wheezed, tottering over to the nearest park bench. She began greedily drinking her water like a bottle-fed calf. "You're doing the marathon in two months, for heaven's sake. You're hardly going to keep to your training schedule if you have to keep waiting for me to catch up. Honestly, I'm fine. You go on."

Kelly looked unconvinced. "But how will you get back?"

"I won't. I won't move from here. You can collect me on your way back." She sighed feebly. "I might just have recovered by then."

"I'm not sure."

"Please . . . just go?" Cassie pleaded, using her arms to lift her legs onto the bench and then turning so that she could lie flat. "I'll be fine . . . Oh God, that feels good!"

"*Tch!* First morning in Manhattan and you're already sleeping on a bench in Central Park."

"Just keeping it real," Cassie said, closing her eyes and dropping an arm languidly across her face. The sun was bright already in the cloudless sky, although the September air was cool and some of the leaves had just started to turn, the incipient yellow tint spreading through the tree canopies like a fever.

"Well, I'll be back for you. Don't move from here," Kelly said, her voice beginning to fade as she jogged back to Raoul.

"Wouldn't dream of it," Cassie mumbled, mainly to herself. Her heart was still galloping like a Grand National winner, and she could already feel the telltale heaviness in her muscles. Tomorrow was going to suck.

All around her, she could hear New York waking up. The drone of traffic on the periphery of the park was becoming as constant as waves, and stalls selling bagels, hot dogs, and pretzels were setting up. The smell of frying onions drifted over and Cassie sniffed like a Bisto Kid, feeling her own hunger begin to awaken, though it would do her no good to get an appetite going—Kelly had decreed she should go without carbs while she was here and cut back on red meat. For someone who'd never dieted in her life and was used to eating what she liked whenever she was hungry (which admittedly wasn't usually between meals), the very idea of restriction and prescription tasted bitter.

The Japanese food had been delicious last night—Kelly had laughingly found some cutlery for her when Cassie had ably demonstrated her tae kwan do skills with the chopsticks—but that was because it was freshly made with high-quality ingredients. She'd have said the same of spaghetti *aglio e olio,* or roast beef with Yorkshire pudding and hot horseradish sauce. Just buy quality, cook simply, eat in moderation. That had always been her mantra.

Then again, she thought, as her body wheezed and ached after the few paltry minutes of exercise, it wasn't as if she were a paragon of physical beauty. Sure, she was slim, but she had no muscles, and the ones she did have were soft and untoned. She'd nearly fallen over when Kelly had padded around the apartment in her underwear, showing a stomach that was so defined Cassie would have been able to do brass rubbings on it. Absently, Cassie prodded her own tummy. It yielded without resistance. It wasn't fat, just spongy. Neglected. Unloved. Unworked.

With a burst of resolve, she swung her legs around off the bench—and straight into a runner (he was going way too fast to be called a jogger). It was like sticking a spike into a spinning wheel—there was an almighty clatter as he flew through the air, landing badly on a trash receptacle before slumping to the ground.

"Oh my God!!" Cassie cried, running over to him. The man was lying facedown, his chest pushed away from the ground slightly in a half push-up as he tried to catch his breath. There was an arrow of sweat between his shoulder blades and his dark blond hair was damp. She could see his knees were bleeding.

Cassie crouched down. "Oh-my-God-I'm-so-sorry," she gabbled. "I didn't see you coming."

"No shit, Sherlock," he muttered, rolling himself over into a sitting position and pulling up his shirt. Cassie rocked back on her heels at the sudden sight of this stranger's torso—so tanned and muscled compared with Gil's anemic, hairless chest, like chicken flesh, and every bit as soft as her own. Her eyes followed the wriggle of hair that stretched from his waistband up to his chest, and saw there a faint purple bruise—in the shape of a New York City trash can—imprinting itself and gathering color like a teenage blush.

"That's my fault," she gulped, pointing at it.

"Yes, it is," the man said, dropping his shirt and looking at her for the first time with cold eyes. "What the hell were you think—*Cassie!*"

Cassie stepped back in surprise. "Henry!"

"I don't believe it!" he bellowed, his grumpiness forgotten. "What are you doing here? Apart from taking out passing strangers."

Cassie laughed and helped him stand up. "Oh, you know . . ." she began, then suddenly faltered. It was the first time anyone had asked her that since the party. The first time anyone who knew her and Gil had asked her that . . . and she wasn't prepared for it. To all the other eight million strangers in New York, she'd be able to say she had just moved here, that she was starting a new job, living with a friend. But

Henry knew her. He knew Gil. He'd been there when she'd met him. He'd *kissed* her the night she'd met him . . .

"I . . . I . . ." She looked up at him helplessly, completely unable to shake off the paralysis that wouldn't let her say the words.

Henry stared at her, concern mounting. She could see him reading her panic. "Is Gil here?"

Cassie shook her head, and she didn't need to say anything else. As the tears started to fall, he enveloped her in his arms so that New York receded and she was back in a place of safety, back in her past—a past that preceded Gil. "I'm so sorry," she heard him say, the words rumbling and deep in her ear, which was pressed against his chest.

"Sorry, sorry," she sniffed finally. "It's all very fresh still." She pulled back to look up at him properly. The last time she'd seen him—Suzy's little brother—he'd been eighteen with a bad haircut and at the end of some vicious growth spurts that had seen him grow twelve inches in two years. Knocking six foot four, he wasn't so little now. There had been little indication back then of the imposing man standing before her— athletic, with a shaggy haircut that stopped just above his lashes, and bright blue eyes so inquisitive and keen. She had always got the impression that he saw much more than other people. If he'd been a superhero, his power would have been X-ray vision. Hers would have been invisibility.

"Have you seen Kelly?" he asked.

"Yes. In fact, I'm staying with her for the next few months, just till I . . . you know, get back on my feet."

"Sure . . . She's a good friend."

"I'm so lucky to have her. I don't know what I'd do . . ." Her voice cracked and she stopped, biting her lip hard. She had to get a grip. "I'm sorry . . . exercise unhinges me."

He laughed.

"So what are you doing here? Do you live in Manhattan now?" she asked. Better to be the one asking the questions.

"No. No. The city's not my thing."

"I remember," she said, smiling, feeling safe as her thoughts were cast back to her past again. Her abiding memory of him was of shinnying up and down trees. "Trees."

He nodded. "And ice."

"Ice?"

"And jungles."

"*Jungles?*"

"And mountains."

"Mountains?"

"And the bottom of the sea on occasion too."

"Jesus! Exactly what is it that you *do*, Henry?"

"Well, there's not technically a job title for it, but I'm basically a freelance explorer. I guess you could say I'm a botanical bounty hunter."

"A what?!" She'd been expecting banker or accountant or something.

"I go looking for rare specimens in the most inaccessible places in the world—so the Amazon, the Arctic ice cap, up in the Andes . . . that kind of thing." He shrugged.

Cassie stared at him. "*Why?*"

"Sometimes for rich collectors, but pioneering research mainly. All kinds of industries hire me—beauty, oil, car manufacturing. A lot of scientists believe that there are remedies in plants and flowers, not just for health benefits, but for other things as well."

"But cars?"

"Sure. They're looking for ways to run cars without tapping into the existing fuel supplies, so they're investigating whether algae could be developed as a biofuel, for example. And now, with the Arctic ice cap melting, it's not just shipping routes that are opening up. We're discovering previously unknown plants that have been protected by the snow and ice and that were once inaccessible to man."

"How do you even become a . . . a . . . one of those?"

He gave a small shrug. "I've got a B.S. in biology and marine biology, and a master's in zoology."

"That's a lot of ologies. And so you've—what? Basically been all over the world? The very top, very bottom, and all around?"

"Pretty much. Saw more of Borneo than I wanted to when I discovered a new species of giant slipper orchid and got chased through the jungle by Abu Sayyaf bandits."

"Oh my God!" she cried, appalled. "Were you okay?"

He held his arms out and looked down at himself. "As you can see, a happy ending."

"I bet you haven't been to the North Pole, though," she teased.

"Sure. I've been there three times and the South Pole once. I was on the expedition where they discovered the lost world in the Dry Valleys. Fourteen *million* years old. Can you believe it?" He shook his head in amazement.

"Not really. Your poor mother!"

Henry chuckled, baffled by her response. His *mother* wasn't what most women thought of when he told them he battled the harshest conditions on earth as a living. The alpha-hunter image tended to have a devastating effect on women. "My mother?"

Cassie slapped a hand across her heart in pity. "She must never sleep for worrying that you're going to be mauled by polar bears or shot by pirates—"

"Or be used as a skittle by speeding penguins," he quipped.

"Don't joke! It all sounds *so* dangerous," she chided.

"So's crossing the street in this city," he said.

"It's not the same thing. There must be peril at every turn—disease, hypothermia, even just getting lost . . ."

"We navigate by GPS. It's all done by satellite now."

"Well, what if the satellite, I don't know, stops working?"

"Like it runs out of batteries?" He laughed. "You worry too much, Cass. But thanks for the optimism. Maybe you could be the mascot on our next expedition!"

"You're going away again?"

"Next year. That's why I'm here, actually. Trying to drum up sponsorship. I've been invited to join an arctic biodiversity assessment for two months next spring."

She shook her head, aghast. "Why has Suzy never mentioned any of this to me?"

"Why would she? I don't suppose I feature much in your conversations," he said, laughing lightly. "Although I'm sure they're all the poorer for it."

Cassie shook her head, trying to absorb the scope of his world. His horizons, his adventures, his memories were literally global.

"Wow. And to think I thought it was a big deal coming *here*."

"Your first time?" he asked.

"My first time *anywhere*. I haven't even crossed the border into England since Gil and I got . . . married."

There was an awkward silence as Cassie attempted to sustain the impression of someone who was *absolutely fine*.

Henry rescued them both. "Well then, seeing as this is your first time here, I hope you've drawn up your list," he said, changing tack.

"List?" she repeated blankly.

"Yes. You know, the one you have to draw up every time you go somewhere new, of all the things you're going to do, places you're going to see. A bit like the Things to Do Before You Die list, but less ambitious. You don't need to bungee jump off Trump Towers, for example."

Cassie giggled. "So you mean like having tea at the Waldorf—that kind of thing?"

"Precisely. Something that gives *you* the New York experience." He folded his arms, waiting to hear about her planned cultural adventure.

"Hmmmmm." Cassie pursed her lips and thought. And thought. And thought. And slowly began to panic. "Ummmmm . . . Hmmm . . . Yes, tricky."

And it was. She wasn't here as a tourist or an executive. She was a refugee. On the run. She was here because her friend had taken her in, and of all the options open to her, it had been as far away from Gil and Wiz as she had been able to get. Drawing up a list and getting the lowdown on the Big Apple wasn't flashing up on her radar yet. Hell, she'd been here less than a day.

"Okay, I get the picture," Henry chuckled. "Tell you what, I'll write it for you. I'm an expert at these things, even if I do say so myself. I draw one up for every place I go."

"You do?" Of course he did, she instantly chided herself. As one of the last true explorers of the world, he probably managed to turn even a weekend city break into a great odyssey.

"Sure."

The sound of springy feet slapping the pavement like Riverdancers made her turn. Kelly and Raoul were back from their "light" run.

"Hey!" Kelly beamed, spotting Henry, then his bleeding knees. "Ooh. What happened? Some nutter?"

"Yeah," Henry laughed.

Cassie rolled her eyes. "Ha-ha."

Kelly looked between the two of them. It was clear that Cassie had been crying again. She walked over and linked arms casually with her, giving her a little squeeze.

"How long are you here for?" Kelly asked him.

"Just a couple of days. I'm in with Breitling next week. Thanks so much for putting a word in for me, by the way."

Kelly shrugged. "Hey, what're big sisters for, right, Cass?" Technically, he was Suzy's little brother—only by eighteen months, although that was like the distance between the earth and the moon when they were children—but as they'd all grown up like sisters, they all regarded Henry as their own little brother.

"Breitling's one of my clients," Kelly explained to Cassie. "I suggested they talk to Henry, given that National Geographic have given the go-ahead on the documentary now. It's a good branding exercise for them—after all, extreme conditions are their USP. And with the boy looking like that"—she reached up and patted his cheeks like a doting mother—"what's not to love? I'll see if I can muscle in on the meeting too," she said, winking at him.

Cassie smiled, nodding. Wow. Television as well. His star was rising—she could see it, almost like a vapor trail. It was hard to remember him as the little brother they'd forced to be their baby when they played Mummies and Daddies, and whom they'd performed mock surgeries on when they played Doctors. And—oh God, she remembered now—they'd all paid him fifty pence to let them practice kissing on him (not Suzy, of course—the thought grossed her out), which, given his rigid terror, meant they graduated on to boys their own age with all the technique of having snogged windows.

Poor man. It was a wonder he seemed so normal.

"Well, we must get together before you go," Kelly said, lunging into some elastic stretches. "Tomorrow night?"

"Sounds good."

"I'll put our names on the door at the usual, shall I?"

"Great." He smiled at Cassie. "You'll like it," he reassured her.

"Okay," she said, smiling back.

"Is Lacey with you?" Kelly asked.

"Yes, she is."

"Great. Then it'll be the four of us."

He nodded. "Yes."

"Who's Lacey?" Cassie asked, looking between Henry and Kelly.

"Henry's fiancée."

"Oh!" She looked back at him. "Congratulations, Henry."

"Thanks."

"When's the wedding?"

"Next summer. After I get back."

"Great. Great. That's great," she nodded.

"Well, I'd better go. I'm in a rush—as you probably saw from the comfort of the bench," he chuckled.

She went to smack him on the arm, but he dodged out of the way, laughing, already out of reach.

Chapter Three

"Why won't you tell me where we're going?"

"Because it's classified. Today's itinerary is on a strictly need-to-know basis."

"But I do need to know."

"No you don't," Kelly said, striding ahead with her arm out. A cab screeched to a halt beside her. "Get in," she commanded.

Cassie sighed and slid along the seat.

"Two twenty-two Broome, between Lafayette and Broadway," she said to the driver. "And don't take Park. They're still digging up around East Fourteenth and traffic's a bitch."

Cassie cupped her chin in her hand and looked out through the foggy window that looked like it had been cleaned with milk. Eww. She moved her face a little farther away and made a mental note to put a pack of antibacterial wipes in her bag—her new bag. She reached down to her lap and stroked the green ostrich skin and the large hooped bamboo handles of the bag Kelly had given her after dinner last night. She had "negotiated" it for her from her new client, Maddy Foxton, and Cassie's insistence upon paying had died away instantly when Kelly had told her what it cost.

"So, how did your date go last night?" she asked, turning to Kelly, who was frantically checking texts. As soon as they'd left the apartment, she was back in Manhattan mode and the Kelly of yesteryear would now be held on ice till they were alone again. Apparently, Fashion Week was in a couple of weeks' time and this was one of the twin peaks of the New York social calendar. Everything was needed *now!* and *yesterday!* and Kelly had been glued to the phone the second they'd got back from their run, barking orders and taking them in turn. But even with emergency demands bearing down on her from all sides, the appointments she'd made for Cassie's "Manhattan makeover" were still mandatory. Supposedly the need for it was *that* urgent.

Until landing here, Cassie had thought she looked all right. Not amazing. Not like a model or actress or socialite with long legs and twiglet arms. But she was slim, with "lovely" breasts, Gil had always said (although clearly he'd said a lot of things that were lies), elegant hands, and thick "autumn" blond hair that fell down the middle of her back in ropelike twists. But as she looked out of the window at the ultrablonded, tweezered, blow-dried women getting into limos and cabs, she knew she just looked plain, disheveled . . . a mess.

"*Tch,* not well, I left after ten minutes."

"Ten minutes! But Kelly, that's so rude. He must have been so offended."

Kelly stopped texting and looked at her. Cassie could see the pity in her eyes. "Sweetie, if there's one thing you're going to have to learn out here, it's that you can't go around worrying about what other people think."

"But . . . But . . . doesn't that just make you . . ." She hesitated. "Obnoxious?"

Kelly raised a threaded eyebrow. "It makes you *efficient,*

Cassie. Nobody's got time to waste chatting inanely to someone they clearly have nothing in common with." She shrugged. "He knew the score. I imagine he was grateful not to squander the rest of his night too. We're all busy."

Cassie shook her head and looked back out of the window. Miles of plate-glass windows stretched ahead of her, all immaculately polished, with artfully positioned mannequins behind them toting jewel-colored dresses or preppy trench coats and slacks, or glittering watches or feathered hats, or plush furs, or . . . the reflections farther along became too dazzling to see through, and she watched instead the reflected workmen holding up the traffic ahead.

"It was nice bumping into Henry earlier," Kelly murmured in a softer tone.

"Yes, it was such a surprise. It's been so long since we last saw each other. Over ten years, I think."

"He must look pretty different from when you last saw him, huh?"

Cassie smiled. "He certainly does. He's going to draw me up a list of things to do out here. I can't wait to see what he's going to put on it," she said, shrugging her shoulders excitedly. "I got the impression he knows this place pretty well."

"Yeah. He's pretty . . ."—Kelly searched for the word— "worldly. A lot of the companies that sponsor his sort of gig are based out here." Kelly was texting again. "I see him from time to time."

"I like the idea of a list. It'll be good, I think—you know, give me a focus."

"Oh, don't you worry about that," Kelly said, patting her leg. "Bebe Washington will give you focus when you step through the door tomorrow. Trust me! There's nothing like 'two weeks till showtime' to show you what focus looks like."

A look of terror washed over Cassie's face as she wondered for the millionth time what she was letting herself in for. It was one thing Kelly putting her up out here—but giving her a job too? Hell, not even giving her one, *making one up*. Cassie didn't have a scratch of experience in any industry. She'd been married since the age of twenty—had dropped out of her sociology degree at Bristol in the process—and all she'd done since then was manage the estate and the shooting season. Which wasn't to say it didn't have its organizational demands, but it didn't carry over well on a CV. Kelly knew as well as Cassie did that no one would give her a second look. They were both of them going to have to wing it.

But Cassie was worried. Kelly's company, Hartford Communications, was one of the most prestigious fashion PR firms in Manhattan. She had Bebe Washington (womens-wear), Maddy Foxton (accessories), Breitling (watches), Paloma Morriss (shoes), and Dilly (jewelery) on her books. She ran a tight ship, never doubling up on the categories, so that each account benefited from her sole attention on its brand in its market. And it worked. She had been known to move fledgling or struggling brands into profitability within six months, and revive ailing brands by placing them with the right "personalities" and starting underground word-of-mouth campaigns that got everyone salivating. As a result, she could charge whatever fees she liked. She had become a one-stop shop for each market, and she was the envy of every other fashion PR firm on the East Coast as they struggled to juggle and place their competing accounts. Rumor had been rife in the industry that when the accessories slot came up (the predecessor, Tilbury, having been bought and amalgamated into the Richemont stable, thereby reluctantly bringing its PR in-house), there had been no fewer than thirty-six pitches, and that Kelly had interviewed them all individually. Maddy Foxton had been an outsider for the position, but her hand-dyed leathers in jewel colors and traditional artisans' techniques had impressed Kelly. With her "patronage," Maddy Foxton was now on the cusp of becoming a sensation.

All of which was great for Kelly, but none of which soothed Cassie's nerves.

"Here, you're going to need one of these, by the way," Kelly said, opening a small enamel pillbox and handing her two white tablets.

Cassie gasped. "Kelly!!"

Kelly dropped her shoulders and shook her head. "They're ibuprofen tablets, Cassie! Painkillers. Just here, driver," she commanded, tipping the tablets into Cassie's hand.

"And why would I need *those*? I'm not having a tattoo or anything like that, Kell. I don't care if they're 'in.'"

"'In?'" Kelly echoed, wrinkling her nose and teasing her. "Did you really just say that?"

Kelly paid the driver, held the door open for Cassie, and, linking her arm in Cassie's, led her toward an industrial-looking building. "We've already had this conversation—remember? Need-to-know only," Kelly said, patting her arm soothingly. "Look, I'm one of your oldest friends in the world, Cass. Everything I'm doing is in your best interests." She pushed the door open with her bottom as her BlackBerry *beep*ed again. "Just trust me."

"Where are we?"

"The only place that justifies traveling south of Fifty-Seventh," Kelly said, draping herself over a granite reception desk like a lounge singer. "Hey, Trudie. Bas ready for us?"

"Oh yeah," the receptionist nodded. "He cleared his morning for you."

Cassie felt the panic mount. What the hell was going to happen to her here?

"Come this way," Trudie smiled. She handed Cassie a black wraparound cover-up and led her across a polished walnut floor. Everywhere Cassie looked, she could see women with foils, towels, dryers on their heads. So far, so conventional.

Then she saw him. The man Kelly had run over to and was hugging like a long-lost friend.

"Cassie, this is Sebastien. Bas," Kelly said, taking a deep breath. "This is Cassie." The way she said it suggested that her "unveiling" of Cassie was a momentous event.

"Hi," Cassie said quietly. She was appalled. Rail-thin, six foot three and covered in acne scars, all she could think of as she looked at him was deep-fried Ryvita. She'd never seen someone so overly tanned. The man had clearly sailed past mahogany without stopping.

But that wasn't the worst of it. The way he was looking at her, it was as if *she* was the one who needed saving.

He narrowed his eyes. "Hmmmm. Sit down," he said imperiously.

She slid into the chair and he swung her around to face him. Carefully, he pinched a strand of hair disdainfully between two fingers. It was true she hadn't washed it since the party, and what with jet lag, an international flight, heartbreak, and a near heart attack on the run this morning (Kelly had used up all the hot water in the shower, so it wasn't as if she'd been able to wash it even then), she knew her hair wasn't looking its best. Cassie watched Bas and Kelly scrutinize her hair intently, and her mouth began to dry up. It all seemed terribly serious and suddenly very important that he should be able to help.

"When was this last colored?" he asked, peering closely at the strands. "It must have been *years*," he murmured.

"Actually, I've never colored my hair," she said. It had always been a point of pride for her to have remained naturally blond for so long, though her mother kept telling her that would change when she had children.

Bas dropped the hair in fright, his eyes roaming her face and taking in the airplane clothes, unwaxed eyebrows, unmanicured nails . . . if he only knew what was under her jeans.

"You're not from here, are you?" he said sympathetically.

Cassie shook her head. Wasn't it obvious? Little green men from Mars would do a better job of blending in than she would, it seemed.

Kelly checked her watch. "Are we good? You can do something?"

Bas paused dramatically and then nodded. "Yes. I can do something," he said with intensity, as though he were going to perform lifesaving surgery.

"You're a king! I'll come back in two." She kissed Cassie on the cheek and squeezed her shoulders reassuringly.

"Make it three!" he called after her.

Cassie shrank a little deeper into the chair as Kelly skittered out, straight back into a cab.

"Soooooo," he exhaled. "What kind of blond were you thinking of?

"Just the usual, I guess," she shrugged.

He looked at her. "What does that mean?"

"You know, kind of yellowish?"

"Kind of *yellowish*?" he echoed, shaking his head. "Oh boy, this is worse than I . . ." He blew out his cheeks and started at the beginning. "My standard colors are butter, baby, champagne, flax, vanilla, platinum, canary diamond, honey, clotted cream. I *never* do ash. And that's just for base block. If you say chardonnay, I'll ask oaked? If you say honey, I'll ask New Zealand, Clover, or Manuka? *Capiche*?"

There was a long silence as Cassie tried to visualize the different tones. She dropped her face into her hands.

"Oh God. And I asked for yellow." She cringed. She peered at him through her fingers. "I'm your worst nightmare, aren't I?"

He stared at her, assessing her intently.

"Actually," he said, brightening up and spinning her chair back to face the mirror. "You're my dream come true. It's women like you who allow me to show everyone exactly what I can do." He picked up her hair in his hands and this time let it fall like water through his fingers. "And I know exactly what to do with you!"

Four hours later, she was lying on her back—knees out, feet together—like a woman having a Pap smear. "Except this is so much worse. Much, much worse," she thought as she struggled to keep the little scrap of tissue paper in place.

Kelly was in the next cubicle. Not room, cubicle. It had been like walking into a World War Two field hospital when they'd got to the top of the stairs and rounded the corner. Line upon line of six-foot cloth screens separated one client from the next, sparing them the indignity of watching each other being plucked and waxed, but not sparing them the sound. Some women weren't entirely successful at stifling the small yelp that burst out when the hot wax was ripped off—unlike Kelly, who was no doubt still texting—and Cassie was getting more tense by the second.

"So what did she say when you told her you just kept applying over the old coats?" Kelly asked from the other side of the screen.

"She nearly threw up," Cassie mumbled. "I felt like I'd just told her I eat babies or something."

Kelly burst out laughing, interrupting the sound of ripping and yelping coming from the rest of the room.

"Then, when she got the color off, she said my nails looked like rhino horn."

Kelly laughed even harder. "Well, if you're not going to use base coat . . . ," she managed, before descending into another fit of the giggles. "Anyway, they look great now. She does the best French polish in the city. That's why she's so in demand."

"Yeah, well, don't be surprised if she suddenly moves to L.A. on the grounds of ill-health, that's all I'm saying."

The woman who'd ordered her to strip came back into the cubicle. "Okay, let's see what we've got here," she murmured, whipping away the strategically placed scrap of tissue paper and leaving Cassie with even less dignity than the pedicurist had. "Hmmm, I'll need to trim," she said, turning for the scissors.

Trim? She'd already lost half the hair on her head today. She must have lost two pounds already.

"Here, have a look at this while I get you prepped." *Prepped?* Oh God. She actually was going to go into the operating theater—on painkillers!

The woman handed Cassie a laminated card printed with various different shapes. Cassie squinted at it. What was it—a sight test? Plane safety card? Tattoos? Shape recognition for toddlers? She turned it over. It was blank on the other side. "You mean you want me to choose one?"

"Uh-huh," the woman muttered as she clipped away.

Cassie studied the card furiously, trying to distract herself from the fact that this stranger—this nameless Brazilian woman—now knew her more intimately than any other person on earth, former husband included. He'd never been particularly up for going down there.

Hearts, oblongs, rhomboids, stripes, stars, and leaves swam before her eyes. Was that a dollar sign? For the second time today, she was faced with making a decision about something she'd never before considered in her life but that now required an instant opinion from her.

She sighed. What did it really matter anyway? No one was going to see it, and as decisions went—well, it was hardly up there with leaving her husband and country, was it? And wasn't everything she was doing today part of showing that she was learning to live with the consequences of her departure—showing that she was surviving, moving on, growing up, evolving?

"Heart," she smiled bravely as the woman put the scissors away and reached for the warm wax. She had a pretty good idea that she was going to walk out of here looking even more stunned than when she'd walked in.

"You *never* told me that was what they'd do!" Cassie hissed as they got out of the cab and Bill rushed to open the doors for them.

"Well, of course not," Kelly soothed. "No one would ever go if they knew. It's like having kids or something. If you knew how bad it was beforehand . . . *tch*, it would be the end of the human race in fifty years." She paid the driver. "But it feels nice, doesn't it? Clean? Thanks, Bill."

"No, it doesn't," Cassie grumbled. "Thanks, Bill." She was

still feeling violated. She thought she might be in shock. She felt like she did the morning after she'd lost her virginity to Gil—that everybody must know! "It makes me feel damp. I used three times more toilet paper when I went to the bathroom. At the very least it's bad for the environment."

They stepped into the elevator, and the aroma of Thai vegetables wafting from their bags instantly filled the tiny space. Kelly looked at her, shaking her head. "I have *never* heard that argument before. And absolutely everyone I know has Brazilians."

"They can't do," Cassie protested. The idea that there was an entire "movement" of women out here, that this was the norm men were presented with, was beyond belief.

Kelly shrugged as they got to her floor and the doors opened. "Well, I think it's all been worth it. You look divine. I can hardly believe you're the same person who collapsed on a park bench this morning and mugged Henry Sallyford."

"I did not mug him."

"Are you going to try those clothes on when we get in?" Kelly asked, opening her door. "I can't wait to see that ruby dress again."

"It doesn't fit."

"Only a little bit. And remember, it is a sample size. It's officially teeny. But a few more days of running and you'll be in it, no problems."

"It would look a whole lot better on you."

"Well, we can share it," Kelly said, a brief look of relief crossing her face as she took off her heeled boots and padded up the hallway to put on her babygro.

Chapter Four

"Who the hell ordered this?" resounded the voice again. Cassie felt herself flinch and freeze. "I can't work with this! I ordered Duchesse lace, not guipure. I can't possibly trim the fucking dress with that! I might as well use fricking carpet!"

Cassie slid her eyes—the only things she dared move— over to Kelly, who was staring solemnly at the open box of offending lace. From the look on her face, it appeared that this was a catastrophe.

There had already been a few this morning. First off, the makeup artist who was supposed to be coming in today to run through his "test look" for the upcoming show had been stranded after Krakatoa erupted while he was in Indonesia for a magazine shoot, and not only did "his people" not know when he'd be able to get back, but despite Cassie having gone through the three-page-long list Kelly had hurriedly given her, every other makeup artist of international rank was now booked. Twenty minutes later, the supermodel who was supposed to be closing the show and walking out with Bebe for her lap of honor reneged on her booking "option" because some photographer called Mario Testino was in town and he wanted her for his new project. Bebe had actually screamed when Cassie had relayed that message. And although the shoes had all arrived, after a three-week delay while the factory in Naples shut down for the summer, sadly only those for the left feet had been sent. And now, well, now the dresses were going to have to be trimmed with carpet.

Cassie chewed on her lip furiously while she waited for the next set of orders to be shouted out. It was her first day in her new job. When Kelly had introduced her to Bebe—tall, broad-boned, with a crêpey bosom, deep, rasping voice, and the nearest Cassie had ever seen to a man in drag—she had called Cassie her new senior account executive. Cassie had gulped at the insinuation of experience her title carried and waited with dread for the barrage of questions about her fictional CV, but Bebe had merely looked her up and down and nodded her head approvingly. Her makeover, she realized, had been her interview—now she blended correctly into the Manhattan fashionscape. She had quickly cottoned on that although she knew nothing about PR and even less about fashion, all her job required her to do was keep Bebe happy. And right now, Bebe wasn't happy.

"You know," Kelly said slowly, picking up a wheel of thick black lace, "I quite like it. It's got that . . . fifties Sicilian thing going on."

"Sicilian?" Bebe howled. "Sicilian? How can I possibly work Sicilian into my theme, Kelly? You of all people should know this entire collection is based on a turn-of-the-century Dagestani teenage bride who escapes over the Caucasus Mountains into Europe and ends up as the toast of Paris. Every item of clothing tells her story. I mean, just look at the embroidery. I practically had to genetically engineer people with small enough hands to work at that scale. Fricking labor laws! Why they couldn't just let me get in some kids . . . ," she muttered under her breath. She planted her hands on her hips and shook her head. "No. I simply cannot detour through Sicily. There are only twelve days to go and I haven't the time to go that far south."

"Bee, call on line one for you," said an assistant in an impressively unwavering voice.

"Tell them to call back," Bebe snapped.

"It's Fiona. She wants a quote for the teaser to the show."

Bebe crossed the room in a flash. "Fee . . . ," she purred huskily, taking the phone into her office.

"Who's Fiona?" Cassie whispered as Kelly quickly brown-taped the box. It was important to know who could turn Bebe's mood around so quickly.

"Fiona Millar," Kelly said distractedly. "Fashion critic. Real heavyweight. Her words determine whether the buyers buy."

Cassie nodded, memorizing the name.

"Which reminds me, don't let me forget to give you a list and photos of all the front row. You need to know who's who. It's vital to the success of the show."

"Why?"

"Because they all hate each other," Kelly said, as though it were obvious. "If there's a feud going on, they have to be seated at least three chairs away from each other, and they can't sit there waiting for more than ten minutes. It's too volatile if one's getting more paparazzi attention than the other. But if one goes, they all go, and that's *death*," she said, drawing a hand over her throat.

"Gosh," Cassie mumbled, amazed that feelings ran so high at a mere fashion show. Her tummy rumbled loudly and she smacked a hand over it. "Whooops," she said, smiling sheepishly. "I'm starved. Is it nearly lunchtime yet? We could go and get a sandwich, maybe?"

Kelly looked at her as she tossed the box of lace toward a junior, instructed her to send it back, and picked up her bag. "Tell Bee I'll be back later," she said to the black-clad serf. "I've told you, Cass, no carbs, and little and often. There's no time for *lunch*. Where's the box of seeds I gave you? Surely you haven't finished them already?"

Cassie shook her head and decided to keep quiet about the fact that she'd finished them while Kelly was still in the bathroom getting ready.

"Good. Now come on. We've got to get across town to Maddy Foxton. She's doing the accessories for the Oscar show—"

"Oooh, I didn't know the Oscars were on," Cassie interrupted excitedly. "Will we get to go?"

"No," Kelly said, her heels click-clacking down the stairs. "Because they happen in L.A. and not till after Christmas. I'm talking about Oscar de la Renta—one of the most venerable names in New York fashion."

Cassie had never heard of him. "Oh."

"So we've got to get some shots of those and a press release ready before they go over to Oscar's . . ." They burst out of the building and started stalking down Seventh Avenue. Well, Kelly stalked. Cassie kind of clattered after her, trying to get to grips with speed-walking in heels.

"Then we're expected at the *Harper's* offices to discuss their Christmas offer. I've got a meeting with Paloma Morriss at four—she's previewing her new heel shape. We'd better show our faces back with Bebe after that, make sure she's not threatening to jump—or push! After that, we're pretty free. I've booked us both a kick-boxing session for six. Just wait till you see what it can do to your thighs."

"Oh good," Cassie panted, the sounds of her wheezing and

the midtown traffic drowning out her disgruntled tummy. She briefly wondered whether Kelly had learned how to do circular breathing, being able to walk and talk that fast at the same time.

"And then we can go home?" She was practically hallucinating about sofas.

"Yeah, I thought you might need a rest." Kelly smiled as she looked at her. "So I've got La Cornue delivering dinner at eight, and then when you've recharged, we're hooking up with Henry and hitting Mischka later on."

"What's Mischka?"

"Hot new club off Madison. You'll love it."

"This place is the nuts!" Kelly shouted to no one in particular as she expertly wove her way through the crowd from the bar, holding their drinks aloft. Cassie had been trying to keep up, but seemed to be permanently three people adrift and had had to stand with her arms pinned to her sides in the middle of a group of telecom salesgirls from Brooklyn on a hen party. Not that moving freely was much of an option. She was shoehorned into a black dress with bondage straps criss-crossing her hips, and, being bought from a sample sale, it was still far too small.

"Come over here," Kelly laughed, handing her a tall, suspiciously pink drink.

"What is it?"

"Delicious!" Kelly said, winking. "Cheers!"

They had been dancing for over an hour already—Cassie swaying like a potted palm to minimize foot movement in her vertiginous spike boots—and she had a raging thirst. She emptied the top third of the drink in a single gulp, surveying the frenzy around her with apprehensive eyes. She'd never been around so many white teeth and sharp shoulders in her life. Back home she had socialized among plus fours, gentle tweeds, and melodic burrs that soothed like birdsong. Here, people kept talking about "collateralized debt obligations" and "leverage ratios." What did it all mean?

"They won't bite, you know," Kelly said, leaning toward Cassie as she apologetically moved herself left, then right, then left again to get out of other people's way. Kelly took her by the elbow and made her stand on one spot.

"Let them go around you," she said kindly. "They're the ones moving."

Cassie nodded uncertainly. There must be well over three hundred people in here, all wearing the same intense expressions as they scanned the crowd for friends and yet-to-be-met lovers.

"So what do you think?" Kelly asked, bopping her head to the beat and sipping her drink delicately.

"I was just wondering whether they've got a coherent fire-evacuation policy."

Kelly rolled her eyes. "I mean, what do you think about the *music*? The *people*? The *scene*?"

"Well . . . it kind of reminds me of the discos we had at school. But with alcohol instead of punch." She peered at her drink suspiciously again. It was too sweet, too drinkable, and her head was beginning to spin.

"That's because tonight is nineties night. Retro! I thought you might like some familiar tunes. Break you in gently. I thought it might be a bit much to plunge you straight into dance music. Can you see Henry yet?"

Cassie shook her head, feeling the telltale tickle in her throat again as another flurry of coughs erupted upward. Dry ice was a new phenomenon to her and not a particularly good one, setting off the mild asthma that had only ever really bothered her in school lacrosse matches.

"Hey," said a voice behind them, and Cassie felt a large warm hand slap her lightly between her shoulder blades. "You okay there?"

A man with blue eyes that drooped slightly at the edges was smiling at her, both confident and concerned at the same time. He was wearing a charcoal suit with a clubby dove-gray and vanilla striped silk tie, and a chunky, very expensive-looking watch was peeking out from beneath his cuffs.

Cassie, red-faced and spluttering, tried to nod in the affirmative and the three of them stood there for a few moments until the coughing passed.

"Better?" he asked, rubbing her back gently. Kelly stepped in closer to Cassie, as though she needed physical protection from the male of the species. He dropped his hand.

"So I was wondering," he said, addressing himself to Cassie." I've been watching you two since you got here and you haven't let a single guy buy you a drink, dance with you, or even talk to you for more than a minute."

Cassie grinned idiotically. He was very handsome, with a muscular physique and the kind of confidence that only money or good looks can engender. From the looks of his watch, he had both.

"And what? You're here to break that record?" Kelly asked, irked to be so blatantly ignored.

The man looked at her briefly, still smiling, then turned back to Cassie. "I was just wondering why. You're clearly two very beautiful women. So what's the problem?"

"The problem," Kelly said, one hand on her hip and her head waggling a little, "is that Prince Charming hasn't made his entrance yet tonight. But do us a favor and let us know if you see him, will ya?" she finished, oozing sarcasm, and took Cassie by the elbow, moving as though to lead her away.

Cassie shrugged apologetically and the man pulled a face as if to say "Ouch!"

"But wait . . . ," he said, clearly determined not to join the ranks of other suitors who hadn't broken a minute. "How can I alert you to his arrival if I don't know how to get hold of you?" He shrugged haplessly. "You know how serendipitous Fate can be."

Kelly raised a freshly threaded eyebrow. "Wow. Long word."

"Perhaps I could take your card?" he said to Cassie.

"I don't have one," Cassie stuttered. "I'm . . . I'm new," she said, as if Manhattan were a school and she'd just entered the fourth grade.

"Well then maybe your lovely friend could help me out," he said, looking back at Kelly again.

They stared at each other stubbornly, Kelly refusing to be lovely, the stranger refusing to be frozen out. He was very good-looking, but she wasn't going to reinforce his dazzling impression of himself.

"Here, why don't I go first: you take my card," he said, pulling a pristine business card from his jacket pocket and handing it to her. Kelly pocketed it without looking at it.

The man smiled at her blatant insolence. "So now you know my name's Brett," he said pointedly, shoving one hand in a trouser pocket. "What's yours?" Again, his focus was on Cassie.

"Cassie. And this is my best friend Kelly," she said, smiling with her head to one side.

"Cassie and Kelly," he said, nodding his head as though he

agreed with them. "I can't help noticing Kelly's very protective of you, Cassie."

"You'd better believe it, *Brett*," Kelly said, snaking her arm through Cassie's. "You only get to her through me, understand?"

The man beamed. "Well then I guess I'd better take your card, Kelly."

He held out a hand.

"If it's the only way to get rid of you," Kelly said, sighing wearily and fishing one out of her bag.

He read the details. "Well, Kelly Hartford, now I know how to get hold of you—both of you—I'll keep my eyes peeled. For Prince Charming, I mean." He slipped the card into his pocket. "Have a nice night." And he stepped back into the crowd.

Cassie watched him go and clocked all the other girls' eyes following him as he moved past them. "D'you think he'll call?" she asked.

"Probably," Kelly muttered, refusing to watch. "But we won't hear from him."

"What do you mean?"

"I gave him an old card. All the numbers have changed. He'll get the message soon enough." She shrugged. "Anyway, you need to be a bit more discerning," she reproved. "You were giving him eyes the whole time, encouraging him."

"I was not."

"Yes you were."

Cassie's shoulders sagged. She felt drunk, and now confused. "Well, I mean, he was pretty cute. And . . . isn't that what I'm supposed to be doing? Meeting other men and flirting?"

"Flirting? Honey, you were way out of your depth with

him. If I hadn't been here, he'd have had you in a cab by now and halfway back to his place. No. No. No. It's way too soon for any of that. You're still in shock, whether you realize it or not. For now it's enough just to be back out in the world again, expanding your horizons. All the other stuff can happen later when you're back on your feet. Maybe when you get to Paris."

"*Paris?*"

"Sure. Anouk says she knows someone who could give you your confidence back. You know, woo you, not just seduce you."

Cassie looked at her, appalled that her recovery was being micromanaged to this degree.

"What? Don't look at me like that! You wanted us to help you. That means protecting you, as much as directing you. Just let us do our jobs, okay?" Kelly said, putting a hand on her arm. "Come on, let's dance again."

Cassie shook her head. "Honestly, I can't. I'm not used to balancing my body weight on the balls of my feet. I'm in agony."

"But this is the best song!" Kelly protested.

"That's fine. You go. I'll sit down and watch from here. I'll protect our drinks," Cassie said firmly, putting her hands around the two pink-filled glasses.

"Well, don't go anywhere," Kelly warned, swaying off toward a group of acquaintances in the center of the dance floor.

Cassie watched her from the sidelines, feeling envious at how easily Kelly integrated herself into the group, dancing sexily, a ready smile on her face. Cassie felt like the proverbial wallflower by comparison. She still danced as if it were the nineties and got drunk on sugary drinks that only looked right with umbrellas stuck in them. Even worse, the Brooklyn hen party had spotted that her bar table—with only Cassie sitting at it—was available, and the hens were beginning to surround her and talk over her in the clear hope of forcing her to move.

"Hi."

She turned and saw that Henry was standing behind her. He leaned over to kiss her hello. He was wearing a navy shirt and jeans, and the lights kept bouncing off his hair, making it appear more golden than it had the other morning. She wondered whether his knees still hurt.

"Hi! Where's Tracey?" she asked, looking around him.

"Lacey," he corrected.

"Sorry, Lacey."

"She's on her way. She'll be here any minute."

"Great. I can't wait to meet her. Have you got a drink?"

His eyes fell to the pink glasses in her hands and Henry held up his beer protectively.

"I almost walked right past you," he shouted. "I can't believe the change in you." He indicated her hair, which was now butter-blond and spaghetti-straight. "What did they do? Iron it?"

"Perm!"

"Seriously?"

Cassie chuckled, leaning in to him to talk over the music as he sat down beside her. "Not like the one Suzy had when she was thirteen! It's a Brazilian one. This type takes the curls out rather than putting them in. It means I won't have to blow-dry my hair for the next three months—which is just as well. I didn't like to tell them I've only ever used a roller-brush to pill Gil's sweaters . . ." She stumbled at the mention of Gil's name and quickly tried to hide it with a smile.

Henry was watching her intently, as if it was difficult for him to absorb the transformation from the previous morning. Aside from the perm, her hair had been cut to half its previous length into soft, framing layers around her face, which was now immaculately made up, with vivid red lipstick on her generous mouth.

"You just look so . . . different."

"Yeah, well, apparently I was a *severe* case."

"Of what?"

"I'm not entirely sure," she said, grimacing. "But it was bad. From the looks on all their faces, it was baaaad."

"Why?" he asked, baffled. "What was wrong with the old you?"

Cassie tipped her head to the side and smiled gratefully, her eyes tearing up slightly at the unconsciously kind gesture.

"Oh, Henry, you are so lovely," she said. "Bless you for thinking I was okay the way I was before."

"But you were," he protested.

"Well, you're the only one who thought so," she said, smiling.

He smiled back, his expression soft and indulgent—almost nostalgic—as an amused smile flickered on his lips. His face bore the first traces of five o'clock shadow.

"So what else have you had done?" he asked, taking a swig of his drink.

"Not much that I can show you," she said, causing him to raise a quizzical eyebrow. "But I'll show you this," she continued, lifting the hem of her dress to reveal an inch of bald thigh. "What's that about? What could possibly be considered offensive about thigh hair?" she asked, palms up in wonder.

"It's not men who consider it offensive. It's all you girls setting these daft rules."

"Then Kelly took me shopping to some sample sales. But none of it really fits," she said, tugging her dress down a bit. "I could do with a girdle!"

He laughed. "I haven't heard the word *girdle* for a while. I thought girls were always in those Spanx pants now?"

"Is that what they're called? I don't remember what we bought. It was easier just to let her choose and get on with it. She knows what goes with what. She can give me lessons later."

Henry smiled. "Well, at least she's done now. You can rest in peace, knowing you've let her play."

Cassie spluttered on her drink. "You must be kidding! This is just stage one. I've got to keep this up now. I'm already booked in to have my nails redone on Friday, I've got to have my roots redone every three weeks—it's the only way you can be this blond, you see," she said earnestly. "Plus I'm seeing a dermatologist the day after tomorrow for a 'procedure.'"

Henry frowned. "What procedure?"

"Botox," Cassie mouthed.

"Oh—now, that's ridiculous!" he exclaimed. "You can't freeze your face. You'll look like a robot!"

"Better that, I'm told, than looking over thirty. Anyway, this chap Kelly's taking me to apparently keeps you very 'mobile' and natural-looking. Kelly's been seeing him for years and I have to say I'd never noticed she'd had any work done."

"*Tch*, they all say that, Cass." He shook his head crossly. "Honestly, that's too much. Why exactly are you letting Kelly do this to you, anyway? I don't understand why you're being her guinea pig. It's as if you've turned into that plastic-head thing you and Suzy always played with."

"What? You mean her Girls' World?" Cassie said, clapping her hands together with delight at the sudden memory.

"Yeah, that thing. It's not good, Cass."

Cassie stopped smiling suddenly, and a white, but soon-to-be-whiter, tooth bit into her red lip. "No," she said quietly. "But sadly necessary."

Henry stared at her for a long moment, suddenly catching the drift of the ominous undercurrent to all this experimentation. "Cass, what happened with Gil?"

"He's in Edinburgh." She took a deep breath. "With my best friend." His eyes widened and she took an even bigger breath. "And their son."

"Their *what*?"

Cassie nodded her head slowly, almost as though trying to convince herself. "I only found out on Saturday night."

Henry stared at her. Today was Tuesday. In the space of three days, her ten-year marriage had crumbled, she'd left the only home she'd ever known as an adult, flown halfway across the world, been completely transformed, and waded straight into Manhattan's exclusive, high-octane social scene.

Cassie watched him put his glass down and study it for a few moments. He seemed to be trying to keep from breaking it. "The arrogant, supercilious, beaky little shit!" he murmured.

Cassie looked away. She knew Henry had never liked him. He'd said right from the start that Cassie would be swallowed whole by him and his superior family. He had said that Gil would never see her as anything more than a pretty figurehead to sit at the end of the table, preside over the kitchens, and eventually pop out an heir and a spare. But Cassie wouldn't be told. She'd fallen hook, line, and sinker, and in the blink of an eye, the deal had been done.

"God, I'm sorry, Cass," he said finally.

"Mmmmm. Me too." Her hands were trembling and she was trying very hard not to cry. He studied her face and Cassie felt as if he were unveiling all her deepest insecurities.

"So that's what all this is, then? A new start, a new you?"

"Exactly," she said, looking up and nodding vigorously.

"And do you think it'll work, all this?" He waved a hand at her transformed persona.

"It has to."

He nodded encouragingly. "Well, Kelly's a good friend. Although she's not, shall we say . . . fluffy, her heart's in the right place. God knows she's gone out of her way to make connections and introductions for me."

"She's a true friend. They all are. Suzy. Anouk."

"Have they had any say in this?"

"They will do."

"What do you mean?"

"I'm going to be staying with them all in turn. They're all convinced they know what's going to make me happy again, so . . . I'm letting them show me. They've got it all planned. For the next year I'm in their hands." She shrugged. "I may as well be. I've got nothing better to do. And you never know— it *might* work."

"It might," he agreed, though there was a note of skepticism in his voice. A few more beats passed. "So how long are you here for?"

"Four months in each city. So here till New Year's. Then I'm off to Paris to stay with Anouk. After that, London for the summer with Suzy."

"A grand tour."

"Yes, a grand tour," she echoed, trying the words on for size. "I like that," she said, smiling faintly. "Although possibly without commissioning any paintings."

He wrinkled his nose, playing along. "PR doesn't tend to pay *that* well."

"And being educated in matters of Louboutin rather than Leonardo."

"Naturally."

"I'm more fluent in French than I am in dressing myself."

He gave her the once-over. "You seem fluent to me."

Cassie giggled and leaned back. Her grand tour. Yes, it had a good ring to it. It made all this sound like an adventure—planned and wanted—not some desperate escape on a standby ticket.

"Have you ever wondered what you'd be like if you lived in, I don't know—Venice!" she said, her eyes bright with the fantasy. "Just imagine—going to dinner by launch, reading the papers on a balcony at breakfast, hearing the bells of I don't know how many thousands of churches, all out of time with one another." She clasped her hands together. "I might be a brunette there. With a bob. And I'd wear flat ballet shoes like Audrey Hepburn. And I'd eat prosciutto with figs for lunch and live in a really grand old building with vast, airy salons with gilded interconnecting doors." She closed her eyes at the notion. "I would be living a completely different life. I'd be a completely different person."

"Would you, though?"

She opened her eyes and found Henry staring at her.

"I travel the world all the time," he said. "I change locations like other people change underpants. But I'm always the same person."

"So you're saying you're completely rigid? You're never affected by the places you visit?"

"They affect me, of course. But they don't change me. I know who I am."

There was a tense pause. "And I don't, is that what you're saying?"

Hot color crept up her neck. His expression softened and he leaned forward on the table. "I think you feel like the old Cassie failed—that she's not good enough somehow and you need to make a new one. But all this change you're putting yourself through isn't going to change who you are. It's just the shell, surface stuff."

"No. It's more than that. I'm going to be learning about new things, having experiences I never thought I'd get to have when I was alone in that big house. I'm going to meet a whole raft of people who've led entirely different lives from mine, and who can tell me about new things. It's not just about a haircut and having my nails done. I'm going to change from the inside out."

Henry shook his head. "I don't think it works like that," he said sadly. "I don't think you can just cast off your personality like you have your marriage."

Cassie looked down at the table, trying to hide her face beneath a curtain of hair. Oh God, he'd made her cry.

"Look, I'm not trying to make you feel worse," he said quietly, leaning in to her, his hand on her arm. "I'm just worried about you."

"Well don't be," she sniffed. "I've got the girls looking out for me."

"That's kind of what I'm worried about."

Cassie looked at him, shocked. "They are the best friends anyone could ever hope to have."

"Yes, but that doesn't mean that their way of getting you through this is necessarily right for you."

"Well they all seem to be doing a much better job of living

their lives than I've been able to manage with mine. It makes perfect sense to follow their examples."

"So you're going to spend your time in New York drinking, dancing, and dressing up?"

"In between working and getting fit, yes! What's wrong with that?"

Henry shrugged. "Well, I just hope you can cope with it, that's all. I mean, look at you. You've just morphed into every Manhattan bachelor's dream woman. Every guy with eyes in his head is going to be hitting on you and you're going to have to learn how to deal with it."

She shook her head dismissively. "That's not really a concern. I couldn't be further from wanting to date right now. And much less here. Kelly went on a date—practically at *midnight*—and then dumped the poor guy within ten minutes!"

"But that's my point. That's how it is out here. And you're not going to be able to hide, not looking like that."

Cassie looked down at her engineered cocktail dress. "I hardly think I'm going to suddenly turn into a man-magnet who needs to beat men off with a stick," she quipped.

Henry stared at her. "You think? Because I could point out, right now, six different guys who've been looking like they want to shoot me for standing here talking to you." Cassie's mouth dropped open, but before she could say anything he went on, "And if today was the first time you've had a wax or worn lipstick . . ." He shook his head. "God help you when it comes to men. If you're not careful, you'll be pregnant or engaged within the month. Maybe both."

Cassie grew hot with anger at his patronizing tone. So much for the pliable little brother she and Suzy and Kelly and Anouk had tortured for years. He was acting more like her father right now.

"You're cross with me," he said.

"Yes, I am," she said huffily, her cheeks pinking up. "I thought you were my friend. Instead you're just . . . *attacking* me for trying to move on with my life. I wasn't the one who threw away my marriage, you know."

"I just know the real Cassie, that's all. I don't want to see you get lost in this city. This place is more of a jungle than any I've ever been to."

Cassie stared at him hotly, trying to find a way to regain her ground. "Well, I think you're wrong. I don't think you do know the real me. You were a teenager when we saw each other last. What makes you such an authority on who I am?" She drew herself up taller. "And you know what? I don't think I am going to get lost here. I think this city suits me. I think that the person I was *before* was the wrong Cassie. And now I'm just putting everything right."

He stared at her for a long while before finally shrugging and looking away. "You're probably right. What do I know? It was all a long time ago."

As he said this, a slim hand suddenly slid around his waist and into the button placket of his shirt, tweaking his chest hair slightly. A beautiful face appeared, resting on his shoulder— like the sun rising above the horizon—and the girl gave a dazzling smile. Her light brown hair had been lifted with sunny streaks around her face, highlighting her hazel eyes, and she eclipsed everyone there. Cassie felt her heart dive to the floor.

"You must be Lacey," she said, taking a deep breath and managing to smile back.

*   *   *

Three hours later, Cassie had the hiccups. "Well, you've just single-handedly proved Henry wrong," she said, as Kelly looped her arm through hers and walked her slowly along Park Avenue.

"Henry? What's he been saying?"

"*Tch!*" Cassie tutted drunkenly. "He was *so* annoying. When did he get so bossy? He's absolutely convinced you and Anouk and Suzy are going to get me engaged or pregnant within the month." She hiccuped and stopped suddenly. "No, let me rephrase that. He doesn't think *you're* going to get me pregnant," she said, doubling over with laughter.

Kelly giggled along. She was half-cut, unlike Cassie, who, unaccustomed to nineteen-hour days and take-your-eyebrows-off cocktails on an empty stomach, was completely slaughtered.

"He thinks your *plan* is going to get me pregnant," she slurred, straightening up again. "Because I'm a man-magnet now, did you know that?" She giggled again, swishing her hair around her shoulders.

Kelly nodded. "That was patently clear tonight. I must have intercepted—what? Eleven business cards?"

Cassie squeezed her arm fondly. "See, that's what he underestimated. The protection of old friends. You were better than any bouncer tonight."

"It's too early for you to date yet," Kelly said, patting her arm.

"It *is* too early for me to date yet," Cassie agreed happily. She sighed and rested her head on Kelly's shoulder. Her feet had broken through the pain barrier and were now numb, and the alcohol had done a great job of numbing the rest of her pain. Already her life in Scotland seemed to belong to another person. She couldn't imagine how she'd ever lain alone in that horrid four-poster (she'd never liked it; it was too ornate, and having been built four hundred years ago, also too short) counting down the days until Gil returned home for the weekend. Edinburgh was only sixty-eight miles away, but it was too far to commute to during the week, and although he was always home by six on a Friday, it was usually with a rowdy shooting party in tow.

Look at me now, though, she thought, taking in the scene around her. It could have been two in the afternoon, there were so many people around still—some eating in burger joints, others talking in groups outside clubs, the restaurants still full, the streets still jammed. And the lights, so many lights. It was as though the sun were giving Manhattan island a special extra-late bedtime, like an indulgent mother on the holidays.

"I think I'm going to like it here," she mumbled.

"Hmm? What was that?" Kelly asked, putting her phone back into her bag. She'd been quickly checking her texts. No doubt Bebe was working through the night.

"I said I like it here. I mean, I don't know exactly where I am right now," she said, looking around blankly at the wall of glass skyscrapers. "Or what I'm officially supposed to do during my days as a senior account executive"—she enunciated her title in a particularly posh voice—"and I don't think I've ever been so scared of anyone as I am of Bebe, and I've certainly never been so tired in all my life. But I am still just so happy not to be back *there*, sitting down like an adult and discussing things rationally." She shook her head vehemently, and her hair swung half a beat behind her. "He'd have found a way to make it be my fault, you know."

"I know," Kelly said, squeezing her arm. "Which is why we need to get you a divorce lawyer."

"I know."

"Suzy says she knows a good one—one of her former grooms. We can't have the bastard cheating you out of what's rightfully yours. He's cheated you enough already."

"There's not going to be much coming to me, I can tell you that now. I signed a prenup. Everything's tied up in trusts," Cassie said wearily as they reached the red awning.

"Thanks, Bailey," Kelly said as the night porter opened the doors for them and called the elevator.

"Thanks, Bailey," Cassie echoed drunkenly.

They stepped inside and the doors closed. Cassie felt vaguely unhappy about the way the elevator seemed to be rocketing up the elevator shaft.

The doors opened and Kelly let them into her apartment.

"I'd offer to make you a coffee, but . . ."

"You don't have a kettle," Cassie intoned, sitting down on the sofa to unzip her boots. The sensation of her bones spreading out in her feet was so good it was almost painful.

Kelly did the same, closing her eyes for a moment as her stockinged feet made full contact with the floor for the first time in nineteen hours. "Men—if they only knew what women have to go through . . ."

Cassie got up and wove her way over to the bathroom, using the walls—because the floor seemed to be swaying—for support.

"You okay?" Kelly asked, as Cassie paused for a moment at the doorway before lurching in and slamming the door shut with her foot.

The sounds coming from behind the door suggested not.

Chapter Five

Kelly was at Bebe's—having already taken a spinning class, held an updates meeting with her staff, and hosted a press brunch for the Maddy Foxton–Oscar de la Renta partnership—when Cassie finally made it in. Five minutes before noon.

She looked as bad as she'd sounded last night.

"Did you even try to get a brush through your hair?" Kelly whispered, grabbing her by the elbow and steering her to the bathroom before Bebe saw her.

"I don't . . . I don't . . . I don't think this Argentinian perm thingy has read its job description," she moaned feebly as Kelly grabbed a brush from her bag. "I mean, I did try to get it flat and untangly but—*ow!*—*that* kept happening. *Ow!*"

"Stop complaining," Kelly said brusquely. "You'll be saying more than *ow* if Bebe catches sight of you looking like this. Have you eaten?"

Cassie shook her head.

"Right. I'll get an egg-white omelete sent up."

At the thought of it Cassie instantly slapped a hand across her mouth and shook her head vigorously.

"No?" Getting some blusher and brushes out of her bag,

Kelly quickly dusted over Cassie's pallid complexion. "Hold out your finger."

Cassie obeyed. Kelly squeezed a small stream of sparkling colored goo on it. Cassie looked at her. "Don't say I have to *eat* that?"

Kelly rolled her eyes. "Oh, for God's sake, Cassie. It's Juicy Tubes. You put it on your lips." She put her hands on her hips, exasperated. "Jeez-us."

"There's no need to shout," Cassie said, one eyebrow raised.

"I'm not sh—" Kelly stopped and took a deep breath. "Okay, let me see you." Kelly appraised her. "Well, you look half-alive, at least. Though God only knows what you're wearing." She took in the outfit, arms crossed. "That is wrong on *so* many levels."

Cassie looked down at her black pleated leather midiskirt, Fair Isle sweater, and red Converse sneakers. Her feet had gone into spasm just thinking about sliding into a pair of heels. "I wasn't joking when I said I couldn't remember what went with what," she said petulantly. Suddenly she gasped in horror. "Is it okay that I'm wearing a bra? Didn't you say it's too straight?"

"That was for the V-neck." Kelly bit her lip. Toddlers could dress themselves better. There was a frustrated silence. "Okay, look—I told Bee you were leading the brunch at the Hudson this morning, so just lie low, okay? Don't bring attention to yourself. I'll give you some paperwork to get on with."

Cassie tipped her head to the side gratefully. "You're such a good friend," she said emotionally as Kelly steered her back toward the studio. "Honestly, I don't know what I'd do if I didn't have you to put me up, make up a job for m—"

"Yeah, yeah, yeah," Kelly muttered, rolling her eyes. "Keep it for the Christmas card."

Bebe was back in the room and back in full strop as the girls reappeared.

"Kelly, there you are," she boomed. "Tell me what you think. Don't you agree that the sequins are just *wrong* on this dress," she demanded rhetorically as she held a barely there model by the shoulders and swung the poor girl around to face them. Her red tartan dress—asymmetric and ragged— was embellished with black "tattoo" embroidery and a heavy spattering of gold paillettes. "I mean, she's at a traditional Orthodox wedding. She's supposed to look like she's been showered with coins. Instead—look at her! She looks like she's the love child of Aladdin Sane and Bonnie Prince Charlie."

Cassie's head ached at the nebulous metaphor. It was a journey too far for her mind today. She wished to goodness she'd stayed asleep—fully clothed—on the sofa and hadn't bothered trying to be brave. But she hadn't wanted to let Kelly down. It was only her second day on the job.

Kelly's mobile rang. She held up a finger. "I've got to take this, Bee. I've got a call in with W. I'll just be a moment," she said, turning away.

Bebe stared at her, then at Cassie, as if she wasn't sure she was the girl she'd seen yesterday. "What's that you're working?" she asked, eyes narrowed.

Cassie looked down at her hands to see what they were doing. She felt *that* bad, she couldn't be entirely sure that she had full control over her body. She looked back up, confused. "I'm sorry—what's what I'm working?"

"Your look. What is it? Slutty librarian?"

Cassie's eyes widened. "Uh . . . uh . . . I . . . don't really have a *title* for it," she said slowly. "I just thought it looked . . . nice?"

Kelly came back from her phone call, the smile sliding off her face as she saw Cassie in the full glare of Bebe's attention.

"Nice?" Bebe repeated, looking over at Kelly. "And you get her to write press releases?" Bebe hauled the model around to face Kelly, tipping her head disdainfully back toward Cassie. "Olivia Palermo she ain't," she drawled. "Now, what's your opinion on this?"

"Cassie, I've left some urgent paperwork on your desk," Kelly said briskly, sending Cassie running for cover before turning her attention to the trembling model. "And I think you're right about the sequins, Bee. Too harem. They're the wrong gold, don't you think?"

Wrong gold? Cassie wondered. Was there such a thing?

"That's the problem. They're too brassy. They should be lighter. I've got a contact in Tribeca. They owe me—I'll make a call. Oh, and that was *Bazaar*. They want to call in the leopard print . . ."

"Jaguar print," Bebe corrected sternly, as though the difference between the prints was as big as the difference between spots and stripes.

"Yes, you're right, sorry—the *jaguar* print—for a cover try with Scarlett . . ."

Chapter Six

Cassie nodded slowly, a gleam of encouragement in her eyes as the girl came toward her. A week in and she was beginning to get the hang of this now. It wasn't personal. It was just about the story, the mood, the *journey* Bebe was taking them on through her clothes.

Bebe leaned toward her slightly, a question mark implicit in the gesture.

"Well," Cassie said slowly, "she's got great hair, and her shoulders and hips are so narrow, she'd definitely look like a teenage bride."

"Hmmmm." Bebe scrutinized the model critically. She was startlingly pretty and had probably sailed through life thus far, fawned over since birth, the most popular girl at school and the living incarnation of every male's fantasies. But in this huge, echoing, whitewashed studio, she was merely the sum of her parts, and easy pickings to a seasoned fashion veteran like Bebe Washington.

"Pretty enough, but she walks like a cow," Bebe drawled, making no effort to lower her voice. "And look at her ankles," she said as the girl came to a stop before them and struck her pose position, sinking into her back leg, hands on hips. "I've seen more contour in an RSJ."

Cassie saw the girl staring at the back wall, her eyes shining with unshed tears. "Oh, Bebe, you do have *such* a funny sense of humor," she said, desperately trying to laugh the comment off but unable to drum up a convincing on-the-spot laugh. Bebe turned sharply and stared at her strangely schizophrenic PR who was on-trend one day, off the planet the next.

"She's got lovely ankles," Cassie insisted, but she already knew Bebe's mind was made up. The designer was still in a monumental sulk about having been blown off by her star booking—"Fucking airheads, acting like they're the talent!"—and as a result, Cassie wasn't really there as a second opinion, but rather as a conduit, allowing Bebe to humiliate the models by pronouncing her thoughts to Cassie.

"No. She'll kill the clothes. She's only good for shampoo ads," Bebe said loudly before turning to the girl and addressing her directly, as though this were a kindness. "You shouldn't be doing runway," Bebe said slowly. "But you're pretty enough." The girl's face fell. *Pretty* in high fashion was the equivalent to GSOH in the civilian-looks scale. "Next."

The steamrollered model slunk sadly away as the next sacrificial victim came forth, picking up her feet in an exaggerated fashion while rolling her hips and swaying her arms languidly from side to side.

Cassie felt Bebe lean in toward her again. "Hmmmmmm?"

Her BlackBerry—which Kelly had given her—buzzed in her bag. "Oh, excuse me a moment, Bebe," she said quietly, catching the look of panic that came into the model's eyes as she saw Cassie's moderating influence distracted from her performance. "Yes?"

"Cass, it's me," Kelly said breathily.

"Are you running?"

"I was," she panted. "I'm just . . . leaning . . . against the wall . . . for a second . . ."

Cassie waited while she got her breath back.

"Phew! That was good—twelve stories in seven minutes. A PB."

"A what?"

"Personal best, dummy."

Cassie rolled her eyes. As well as kickboxing lessons every other evening, and the seven o'clock training runs each morning, Kelly was also a devoted tower-runner, even in heels. Cassie had been let off a few runs—on compassionate grounds—but she was "due" out again tomorrow.

"Anyway, look, the reason I called—I've left the file for the Breitling presentation at the office. Can you go back there and bring it over for me?"

"But I'm with Bebe. We're in the middle of the casting session for the show."

"We both know Bebe doesn't actually need you there. Just tell her there's an emergency at the office and you have to go. Take a cab and get a receipt. The address is on the folder. We're on the twelfth floor."

And she hung up.

Fifteen minutes later, Cassie was standing in the lobby, impatiently pushing the UP button. She had no intention of racing up the stairs, even if she did have to wait seven minutes for the elevators to come back down from the heavens.

The doors opened, and after the stream of occupants had spilled out she stepped in.

"Cassie! Hold the doors!" called a voice as they began to close. She quickly turned back to the panel, looking blindly for the DOORS OPEN button, but there was no need. Henry suddenly leaped sideways through the half-closed opening, falling heavily against the mirrored wall at the back. Cassie pushed herself to the side wall in fright—not that her face registered it. The Botox doctor Kelly had taken her to the day before hadn't been quite as light of touch as she'd hoped, and every time she went to the bathroom, she spent ten minutes practicing lifting her eyebrows in the mirror, like a sumo wrestler heaving a foot off the floor.

"Hi," he smiled, and then stopped at the sight of her expression. He straightened up and looked away from her as the elevator started moving up the shaft.

They stood in silence for a few moments.

"Are you in on this meeting too, then?" he asked.

"No. I'm just the delivery girl," she said, holding up the file.

"Ah." He slid his eyes over toward her, watching the way her lips silently read the changing numbers on the display.

"Look, Cass . . . I'm sorry if I overstepped the mark the other night," he said, staring straight at her. "I crossed the line saying those things to you. I confused knowing you since birth with knowing you now. You have every right to . . . rebuild your life however you see fit."

"Thanks, Henry," she said, smiling weakly. "I appreciate that. I couldn't bear to think of you feeling so . . . disappointed in me."

"You could never disappoint me, Cass," he said hurriedly.

A moment passed and they watched the numbers zoom up on the LED display.

"Oh. I got you this!" he said, holding up an envelope. "By way of apology. I was going to give it to Kelly at the meeting. I didn't expect to see you again before I go."

"When are you off?"

"Tonight."

"Oh." They'd only just become reacquainted, and the other night hadn't been an unmitigated success. It made her feel sad to think he was going again so soon. She needed all the friends she could get at the moment.

She took the envelope. The contents rattled loosely, like rice.

"What is it? Confetti for your wedding?" she joked, before suddenly blushing as she realized she might not be invited. Old friends didn't mean close friends. "Lacey seems lovely, by the way."

"Yes. She is."

"Absolutely gorgeous."

"Yes. She's very pretty."

The doors pinged open and Kelly practically fell in. "There you are!" she said, rushing forward and taking the file from her arms. "Oh, Henry!" she said, catching sight of Henry stepping out after her. "You're here too. Great. We've been waiting for you. Everyone's ready to start."

"Well then, I guess this is it," Henry said, turning back to Cassie. He took a deep breath and smiled at her. For all the forty-two-inch chest and bear-paw hands, he looked at that moment just like the little brother she remembered.

"Good luck with the expedition," she said. "When will you be back?"

He shrugged. "Depends on the weather and acts of God. But hopefully by June." He held her lightly by the shoulders as he kissed her good-bye. "Well, see you around."

She looked up at him and gave a small smile. He was going to the end of the world and she might not see him for another ten years. "Yes, see you, Henry." They stared at each other for a moment. "And be sure to ring your mum."

He chuckled as the elevator doors trilled open and she

stepped back in. She stood at the back of the elevator, holding her green handbag over her tummy, her poker-straight, baby-blonded hair fluttering softly under the air-con. And then the doors slid shut and he was gone.

Cassie checked her watch. It was nudging five. Strictly speaking she ought to go back to Bebe at the studio, but she couldn't face being party to any more character assassinations today. She felt the sadness that she was trying so hard to keep under wraps pushing up like a malevolent jack-in-the-box, and she wasn't convinced that even the shock of Bebe's cruelty or the mania that passed as a typical working day here would be enough to divert her attention.

It was because she was tired, she knew. She and Kelly had gone out every night for the week and a half she'd been here—very often after eleven, when Kelly was done with her work functions and just when Cassie's body was curling itself into sleep—and tonight she really didn't want to "check in" and have Kelly organize her evening for her. She didn't want to eat raw fish or superbeans. She wanted to eat a burger and drink a goddamn cup of tea. Her constitution demanded it in the way Kelly's needed adrenaline or Anouk's needed satin bras. She wanted to curl up on the sofa and read a book. If her feet weren't so sore, she'd maybe have taken a detour and gone for a walk in Central Park on the way back. It might have helped clear her head. Ever since the Botox injections, she'd had a dull headache she just couldn't shift, and vats of cocktails and scarcely any sleep weren't helping. But the four-inch-heeled boots Kelly had put out for her before leaving that morning—she had actually numbered her outfits for her after Cassie's disastrous freelance effort—left no room for negotiation. They were called "limo shoes" for a reason.

Having darted into Dean & DeLuca to buy dinner, she decided to treat herself and caught a cab home. She let herself into the apartment and immediately filled a small saucepan with water and put it on to boil. Pulling a box of tea bags slyly out of her shopping bag—not PG Tips, but better than nothing—she found a cup at the back of Kelly's underwear cupboard, although traces of soil in the bottom of it suggested it had last been used as a flowerpot.

As the water started to bubble, Cassie changed out of her dress and pulled on a pair of NYC gray joggers and a matching navy hoodie that she'd bought at a tourist shop down the block. She craved this time of the day before Kelly got back and gave her the evening itinerary. And tonight, since Kelly was expecting to meet her at Raoul's at six, she was going to get a bonus hour of peace and quiet and rest.

She already knew that she was going to spend most of it crying. The first call from her divorce lawyer had come through earlier that afternoon and she could feel the tears—swallowed down in front of Bebe—pumping from her heart and moving through her body like a secondary blood supply. It seemed to be the only way to mobilize the pain, to expel it like carbon monoxide or some other toxin contraindicated for survival. She just hoped, scared though she was by the fierceness and frequency of the tears, that if she let them come, it would wring out of her heart that heavy, rotting, sodden feeling, like a towel that had missed the spin cycle. "Better out than in," her mother had always said, and she supposed she was right—but not at any old time. Not randomly. After the first few days of uncontrollable tears, she had tried extra hard to let them out only when Kelly wasn't around, not because she didn't trust or couldn't confide in her friend, but because she knew Kelly was scrutinizing her every move. Was she off her food? Lethargic? Pining? She'd overheard Kelly several times on the phone to Suzy and Anouk, reporting back on her "progress": ". . . pretty good day today, although she was crying in the shower for fifteen minutes this morning. Thought I couldn't hear, of course . . ."

She didn't want to let anyone down—they were all so worried about her, trying so hard to make it okay for her, that she felt she ought to keep her tears private and self-contained. But she was always astonished, when the tears did fall, at how very hot they were, as if they'd been simmering for hours; as though she were at boiling point inside, burning up with rage.

She made her tea and sent a text to Kelly: *"Got headache. See you at home after. Cx"*

A reply came back almost immediately. *"Don't believe you. Hot date?"*

"Ha ha," she typed back, before sighing and throwing her BlackBerry on the cushions. She sank down into the sofa just as her mobile suddenly rang, making her jump. Kelly had changed her ringtone for her from *Four Seasons: Spring* to a demented frog chorus, and it still took her a moment or two to realize that it was her phone ringing and not an apocalyptic invasion of toads.

"Hello?"

"Chérie! C'est moi!"

"Nooks," she said, trying to brighten her voice.

There was a pause. "'Ow are you?"

"Me? Oh, I'm fine—working hard, meeting loads of new people, wearing lipstick every day. You wouldn't recognize me." She exhaled deeply. "I'm great."

There was a long pause as Cassie put a hand to her temple. She could feel the tears swelling behind her skin.

"Okay, now let's try that again. 'Ow are you?"

Cassie gave a sigh that said everything. "Truthfully? Well, I want . . . I want to be able to sleep through the night. And when I am awake, not to have a heart rate that's constantly in high revs. I feel like a car doing a hundred and forty miles an hour in first gear." She stared at the backs of her hands and was shocked to see that the skin looked thin and gray. "I want to be able to breathe without feeling like someone's kneeling on my chest. I want to be able to think about the past decade of my life without feeling winded." She steadied her voice, aiming for truth without emotion. "Honestly and truly, Nooks, if a doctor offered to put me in a medicated sleep for the next six months, I'd gladly take it. Or a cryogenic coma, maybe. They could deep-freeze me for a year." She tried to laugh, to shake off her gloom, but it didn't work.

"Oh, *chérie*," Anouk whispered. "It is early days. So early still. Nobody expects you to move forward without looking back. It is all to be expected, this."

"I guess," Cassie said, letting a hot, fat tear slide silently down her cheek.

"I know it is a cliché to say so, but it is true that time makes it better. It will hurt for a very long time, but then one day you will realize that . . . maybe you did not think about him today, or you forgot it was his birthday, or . . ."

"Or I won't read his horoscope, or stop off at Saks to smell his aftershave, or ring up to hear his voice on the answer phone . . ." Her voice cracked as the sobs broke though. So much for keeping everything under wraps.

"Sorry, sorry. Sorry, Nooks," she said finally. "You've caught me at a low ebb. End of the day and all that." She wiped her eyes with the back of her hand. "God, how boring for you to have to listen to this."

"Cass, you are my friend. If I cannot help you in this, then what use am I? Apart from dishing out anticellulite remedies and good shoes, I mean."

Cassie's face cracked into a smile.

"The day will come—it is coming—when you will meet someone who eclipses him. Someone better. Someone who will cherish you like you should be cherished. It is the very least you deserve."

"Yeah," Cassie mumbled. Anouk must be confusing *cherishable* with *perishable*—after all, she was fast approaching her sell-by date. She was going to be thirty-one this year, and she was not just alone, but broken too. It would take her years to recover from this and put herself back together. Meanwhile, what did they say the chances were of a thirty-plus single woman meeting someone in Manhattan? She was more likely to be hit by a meteorite, wasn't she? No. Her eclipsing man wasn't on his way. He had a good ten years of bachelordom and casual sex left before he needed to start making his way to her.

Fondly they said their good-byes. Anouk seemed to sense that solitude was Cassie's best companion tonight. Somewhere close by, a clock ticked, and outside the sooty window, the Manhattan skyline began to light up, room by room. She lay down on her side, the tears still coming, but less violently as her despair gave way to an exhausted, defeated calm. She stared at the multicolored swirls of the Paul Smith rug, her eyes like a child's pencil in an activity book, following the red line, then the black, then the yellow in a rhythmic meditation. She was navigating the turquoise loop at the bottom left of the rug when the envelope in her bag caught her eye.

Her energy rising slightly, she opened it carefully. If Henry's sense of humor hadn't moved on in the past fifteen years, she could expect his toenail clippings to drop out. She peered in. Inside there was a cream paper tag that read, in loping brown ink:

Energy in adversity

Huh? A self-help motto. How un-Henry.
She turned it over.

Plant in potting soil, 2 inches deep.
Store in sunny, light spot.

The door slammed. "I'm back!" Kelly hollered as though the apartment were spread over four thousand square feet, not four hundred, and with no regard for Cassie's headache. She kicked her shoes off immediately, sending one slingback rocketing down the hallway to narrowly miss deadheading the one token plant in the apartment. "What's that?"

Cassie tipped the envelope on its side and poured some of the contents into her hand. "Seeds," she said, baffled.

"Seeds? What the hell are you going to do with those in Manhattan?" Kelly said and laughed.

Cassie carried on staring at the gift. "What indeed."

"Now look," Kelly said, swirling the short straw in her drink and shouting above the music. (As usual, she'd won the argument about going out. *It's important to keep busy, Cass,* she'd chided the second she'd clocked Cassie's swollen eyes and soggy sweatshirt. *You can't afford to mope.*) "There's this guy. He's called for you seven times in the past five days. Even *I'm* getting embarrassed and we both know I've got the hide of a walrus."

"But not the complexion, happily," Cassie joked.

"He's driving me mad. He says he won't give up. We have to do something."

"Call the police?"

Kelly smiled. "He's not like *that*," she reassured. "He's very funny, actually. And polite. And amazingly easy to talk to . . ."

Cassie raised an eyebrow. "Maybe *you* should see him."

"He's not calling to see *me*."

Cassie took another gulp of her drink. She'd given up asking what Kelly was ordering for her each night. They all tasted the same after three, and, much as her head throbbed in the morning, she was so grateful for the numbing that came after four that she'd have drunk cod liver oil if she'd had to.

"More's the pity," Kelly muttered under her breath.

Cassie looked up. "You *do* like him!"

"I do not."

"Yes you do."

"No. I've simply got to know him a little bit through intercepting all your calls and having to explain what a lying, conniving little shit your husband was."

Cassie shifted position at the mention of Gil and rejigged her waistband, which was cutting into her tummy. She looked down at the skinny black jeans Kelly had forced her into and the black ankle boots that wound around her ankles with pirate straps. Two weeks ago she had been in Laura Ashley velvet and Hunter wellies. Now she looked like a rock princess. She guessed it was progress of sorts.

"I don't suppose it's occurred to you that perhaps he isn't ringing to get to me at all," Cassie said after a minute, when she was convinced she could trust her voice. "I mean, if you two are speaking that much, maybe he's ringing because he knows he'll get *you*."

The idea clearly hadn't crossed Kelly's mind. "You think?" Her eyes immediately sparkled at the prospect and Cassie was surprised to see that well-hidden vulnerability flash through her friend.

"Sure. Even *I* know most guys don't like being repeatedly turned down. Why don't you suggest drinks with him?"

"Oh no. I'd never ask a man out," Kelly said quickly.

"But why not? I thought that's what everybody did nowadays?"

"Nowadays? What are you? Eighty?"

"I may as well be in dating terms. I'm going to be like a pensioner on the Internet the first time I go on a date." Cassie leaned in, elbows on the table. "Okay, how about this? Next time he rings, suggest you meet up so that you can vet him for me."

Kelly's eyes widened with delight. "I like it! Subterfuge dating. And that way, if I hate him in the flesh, I don't have to go through the rigmarole of blocking his calls. Oh, but are you sure? I don't want to step on your toes."

"*My* toes?" Cassie echoed, placing her hands over Kelly's. "Kell, the kindest thing you could do to my toes is put them in some slippers. Then we'll call it even."

Chapter Seven

Cassie tapped the headset again. "Testing," she said quietly, feeling a bit like a Madonna wannabe.

"Speak up!" the voice snapped down the earpiece. "There are going to be nine hundred people in here in thirty minutes, and I can hardly hear you now."

"Sorry," she apologized, clearing her throat. "Testing?" she called a bit louder.

She heard the voice groan at the other end. "Fine, fine," it said. "Go check on how everything's going backstage."

"Righto," Cassie replied. "Over."

The voice groaned again. "You're not a fucking pilot."

Cassie turned toward the catwalk, making her way delicately. Everything was black—the carpet, the walls, the chairs, the runway even, until they turned the backdrop lights on. "I could make a great career as a cat burglar," she thought to herself. She was barely able to see her own sore-but-toning-up-fast thighs in the skintight black trousers. With diagonal shin stitching and button cuffs, they were from the current autumn-winter collection, as was the black cobweb mohair sweater sliding off one shoulder, and she'd paired them with the black bondage ankle boots, which of all the torture devices she strapped to her feet each day were the least painful and, therefore, her favorites. Still, she couldn't walk the walk in them yet, and her ankle turned as she tripped on an electrical cable that hadn't been taped to the floor.

"*Ow!*" she cried, falling across the seats and sending the programs on them flying.

"What the fuck was that?" the voice demanded in her ear.

"Sorry, I tripped on something," Cassie mumbled.

"Just get backstage. We don't have time for this."

Standing up, she hurriedly put the programs back on the chairs, then made her way to the heavy black curtain by the side of the stage and ducked under.

The other side, by contrast, was all light. Stark lightbulbs and heat lamps were positioned alongside the rows of mirrors as the hair and makeup teams transformed the grungy, sulky, seen-it-all models into rosy-cheeked, heavy-browed Eastern European virgins.

She could see Bebe in a far corner, holding her head by the temples as a particularly long-legged model tried in vain to squeeze her feet into some shoes.

"She's the prettiest ugly sister I've ever seen," Kelly muttered, coming up to her.

"Tell me about it," Cassie sighed. She'd never seen or heard anything like this before. Everything was bedlam. Hairdryers were blowing, music was chopping and changing as the DJ tested for sound feedback, dressers were pushing along hanging rails like the trolley attendants at supermarkets, and models, who looked like they'd all been put on the rack and s-t-r-e-t-c-h-e-d, ran about in nothing but flesh-colored thongs and rollers, waving their hands daintily as they let their nails dry or screech-greeted one of their other best friends across the room. On every counter stood pots and trays of powder, cream, mousse, sponges, brushes, mirrors, mobiles, mini champagne bottles, and over on the walls, polaroids of the "looks" flapped like scales. By the stage exit, someone had written in furious black type: PUT THE FUGEE INTO REFUGEE—FRIGHTENED BUT FUNKY. WORK IT!

"Seriously?" Cassie asked, exasperated. "That's so exploitative. I mean, how can anyone trivialize refugee status by saying it's '*funky*'?"

"Remember, this is just a drama where the clothes are the narrative," Kelly replied loftily.

Cassie turned and looked at her. "You don't actually believe that."

"'Course not," Kelly said under her breath. "But beneath all that shit there are actually some killer shirts and pants and a season-defining blazer that the retailers are going to go nuts for, and I'll bet you my apartment that the emerald evening dress ends up at the Oscars. Those pieces are what pay my fees, but it's more than our jobs are worth to say that," she continued in a low voice, keeping her attention on the flurries of chaos in the room. "Bebe wants creative acclaim. She's fed up with being seen only as the working woman's basics pit stop. She wants to be hot. That's why she's called me in to reposition her, so we're the last people who can call her on it. Oh, shit! I've gotta go. Selena's going into the bathroom again. She is *not* ODing on my watch. Go see if Bas is nearly done. They're doing the final run-through in five."

"Bas? *My* Bas?" Cassie asked happily, looking around until she found him brushing out a girl's hair at the far end of the mirrors. Given that she was seeing him every third day for blowouts (in spite of the Brazilian perm, Kelly still felt this was mandatory) and every third week for color touch-ups to her roots, they were growing close, fast. He was a devil with gossip. The fact that Cassie didn't know who any of the players were made it okay for both of them, and although she loved the way he made her look, she loved the way he made her feel even more. The first time he'd shampooed her hair, he'd given her an Indian head massage that had promptly and inexplicably made her burst into tears. Only when he swore not to tell Kelly about her crying did she confide in him about everything that had happened with Gil and Wiz, and ever since then he'd taken her under his wing, insisting that she get double shampoos and an extra sprinkle of chocolate flakes on her cappuccino, and when she fell asleep during her second Indian head massage, he simply covered her with a towel to keep her warm and waited until she woke up.

Though she'd known him less than a month, and on paper their lives had nothing in common, there was a trust between them, and their appointments had started to spill over into drinks afterward as he joined her and Kelly on their nights out and dared them into dance-offs.

"Bas!" Cassie beamed.

"Teabag," he replied, jumping up to kiss her. Teabag had become his nickname for her, due to his amusement at her almost obsessive search for a decent cup of tea in Manhattan. "Holding the fort for the men in black?" he asked, one eyebrow raised at her CIA-style headset.

"The women in black, maybe," she laughed. The only colored clothes in the room were swinging from hangers.

"The girls look great," she gushed, looking at the intricate coils of plaits he'd wound for ethnic effect into their hair.

"Well, Bebe wanted *naïf*," he said, moving her head to the side and examining her hair. "You know, you'd look great with this style."

"You just can't help yourself, can you?"

"Uh-uh. Sit down and I'll give you a quick finish. I'm done

for the next five minutes at least. They're into wardrobe and the final walk now."

"God no, I can't, Bas. I'm working." She lowered her voice. "Well, supposed to be. Although between you and me, I don't have a clue what I'm supposed to be doing back here."

"Join the club, sweetie. I'm sure they'll let you know if they need you," he said, taking off her headset. "We all know these girls can shout."

Cassie relaxed and let him mist her hair. As he picked up his hair-dryer and began quickly styling it, she watched the models dress in the mirrors. The transformation was incredible. They were able to shrug into the intricate creations, all overlaid with mesh and sequins, in moments, while the dressers fastened the shoes to their feet simultaneously. Their overly long limbs that had seemed so slouchy and adolescent when unclothed became elegant and sculptural now, and the girls seemed to move differently too. The lights for the runway—orange, pink, and red, for a Caucasian sunset, apparently—clicked on and the atmosphere changed.

She looked back in the mirror, and was amazed to see what Bas had done. He had given her the same style as the models. Well, almost.

"Oh my God!" she exclaimed. "That's so *cool*! I've never been cool in my life!" she remarked, genuinely astonished as she looked at herself from every angle in the mirror. She looked five years younger, and like she lived in a loft in SoHo with a band.

"I love it!" She looked up at him and a flash of doubt crossed her face. "But I can't keep it, Bas. Everyone'll think I'm trying to be like them," she said, nodding her head toward the disappearing models who were filing onstage for the final dress rehearsal.

"Nonsense. You look better than those bags of bones any day," he said. "Although you're getting so skinny!" he admonished, squeezing her thigh. Three weeks of heartbreak, early-morning runs, and sushi for dinner had begun to take their toll, and her new sample-size wardrobe slid on easily now. "Anyway, I've given you the style that was *supposed* to go out till Madame threw a last-minute hissy fit . . ."

A sharp crackle of interference brought the headset suddenly to life.

"Cassie! Get to front-of-house now. We're opening the doors in four." It was Hannah, Bebe's PA.

Cassie looked back at her reflection and sighed. It was too late now. She didn't have time to worry about what people were going to think.

"Dinner after?" Bas asked as he began rearranging his brushes, ready for the hasty touch-ups as the models came back.

"Great," she beamed, loping toward the stage. "I'll tell Kell."

She lifted the curtain and was suddenly dazzled by a fury of white flashing lights rushing at her. She raised her hands to her face instinctively and crouched low. Five feet above her, the models were stalking through the glarelike mist, the director shouting instructions—"More knee, Freya!" and "Feel her flight!"

"Cassie! Where the fuck are you?" the voice in her ear shouted. It was Hannah again. She was more frightening than the designer herself.

"Coming," she said, turning away from the overstuffed block of photographers standing at the end of the runway, their professional hierarchy marked out by the yellow gaffer-taped Xs on the floor. Many of the ones at the back were standing on their sturdy camera cases to lift their lenses above the heads of the guys in front, and there was a riot of badinage and innuendo every time one of the models got to the end of the runway and practiced her turn.

She skipped up the aisle toward the back, grateful for the enveloping blackness. The limelight wasn't for her. She instinctively preferred the shadows. Always had. Even as a child, she'd been the one who played the debonair owl when Suzy, Anouk, and Kelly took it in turns to be a swooning Princess Aurora, and when they'd got older and gone to formal balls for real, she was usually in the cloakroom helping someone pin up a torn hem or rushing around trying to locate a pencil sharpener for their kohl. She liked to be the support act.

Which was probably why everyone had been so stunned when she turned round and got married first. There had been an unspoken assumption that out of the four of them, Cassie would probably be the last to find her man. Suzy was so forthright that men couldn't ignore her, Anouk so sultry men didn't want to, and Kelly had a worldly edge that even at fourteen boys found irresistible. But Cassie? She was too . . . not meek . . . too modest. She didn't shine or put herself out there. It wasn't that she wasn't every bit as attractive as the others, but it was easy to overlook her in such a dazzling group.

"Where do you want me?" she asked into the darkness, looking down on the action. The standing-room-only people had been allowed in and were beginning to grab the backs of the back-row chairs, guarding their spaces as jealously as any editors in the front row. The pecking order was distinct.

"Keep an eye on the standers," Hannah muttered. "They'll do anything to get a seat."

"I'd do anything for a tuna sandwich," Cassie thought to herself, fed up with Kelly's tidbit diet. So much for little and often; little and rarely, more like. She was losing weight. It was impossible not to, with the adrenaline of nineteen-hour days and a smashed heart. But unlike Kelly, who looked on enviously as Cassie started shrinking before her eyes, she had no desire to get thinner. It wasn't currency to her, just an outward manifestation of misery.

"Where's Aspen?" Hannah hissed in her ear as the room filled up. "Can anyone see her? She's supposed to be doing the front row."

Cassie scanned the room. Aspen was the queen of Kelly's team—rail-thin, chic, rich as Croesus, and with stellar contacts. In fact, she was the one who had talked most of the Park Avenue princesses into attending today. She and Kelly had known each other since kindergarten as their mothers had moved in the same circles, but whereas Kelly had gone to school in Europe, Aspen had been a pupil at the prestigious Nightingale-Bamford School in Manhattan, and therefore had much closer connections with the society set here.

"Cassie? Can you see her? I've got word Olivia Delingpole's car's pulled up."

Who? Cassie began looking more urgently. Where was Aspen?

Another voice came through on the headset—Zara, the junior account executive. "She's backstage with Bebe and Kelly. There's a crisis. Selena's broken the zip on the finale dress and they can't get her out of it without unpicking the seams. Aspen and Kelly are having to rejig the entire running order."

"Fuck! But she's the meet-and-greet girl." There was a pause. "Okay, look—fuck it! You'll have to get down there, Cassie. Go get Olivia."

Cassie froze.

"Now! Move it!"

Quickly she skipped down the steps. "Um, so just tell me, quickly . . . who is Olivia Delingpole? I mean, how will I recognize her?"

She could tell by the silence that followed that it was the wrong question to have asked.

"You don't know who Olivia Delingpole is? Editor in chief of *Bazaar*?"

Cassie got down to the front and found herself back in the glare of the lights. The models were backstage again and the runway was empty. Occasional pops from the photographers' lights flashed as they tested their exposures. She looked up toward the lighting booth at the back of the room, where she knew Hannah was standing, watching her. She couldn't see in, but she knew Hannah could see her. She shook her head apologetically, biting her lip.

She saw an important-looking woman in top-to-toe camel holding a red bag. She headed toward her.

"Not her, you fool!" Hannah shouted, following her trajectory. "She's just the accessories editor at *Red Carpet*. The woman in the Tory Burch coat—she's walking straight toward you."

Tory Burch coat? How was that helpful? Did it have a third arm? There was a gaggle of women heading straight toward her, all wearing coats.

"A bit more, please," Cassie said nervously. "Hair color?"

"Blond."

She scanned the group. There were only two brunettes. Oh God, Kelly, where are you?

They were upon her. Her headset gave her away as the go-to person for the show. They stood waiting, silently. The thought that she didn't have a clue who they were clearly wasn't crossing their minds.

Cassie tipped her head to the side and smiled. "Hello, ladies," she said, grinning nervously. "We're so pleased you could come to the show." They carried on staring. "Do you, uh, have any tickets?"

Hannah instantly started shrieking in her ear. "What the fuck are you doing? Of course they do. They're not at the fucking movies! Their names are on the seats. Just lead them there. Just lead them!"

Cassie lifted the earpiece away from her ear a little. Much more of that and she'd have a perforated eardrum.

"Let me show you to your seats," she smiled, walking along the front row and then standing back slightly so that they could find their names on the chairs.

They sashayed over, then stopped. "No. This is wrong," one of them said, pointing to the seats. She was wearing a navy trench with tortoiseshell buttons and huge round matching sunglasses.

Cassie looked at the cards. Oh God—when she'd fallen, had she put them back in the right order? She tried to think, but Hannah was heavy-breathing down the line at her. "Are they sitting? Cassie, I can't see you. I've got a TV camera blocking my line of sight. Where are you? I need you ready. I've got the *Glamour* girls coming through."

Oh help. More strangers wanting the VIP treatment. She looked back at the seats. Jesus—what the heck did it matter if someone was a space over from the seating plan? They were sitting, weren't they?

"No, this is correct," Cassie said hurriedly in her most authoritative voice. "Bebe oversaw the seating plan herself.

We're just so tight for space in here." She shrugged apologetically.

The woman's nostrils flared slightly and Cassie wondered whether she was going to be shouted down on this. But after a disdainful stare and a contemptuous sniff, the woman sat down and the others followed suit, their group punctuated by empty seats. They all instantly began busying themselves with their iPhones. Cassie noticed that the woman in the navy coat had taken the Delingpole chair. So that was Olivia Delingpole. So that was a Tory Burch coat.

She turned to find the *Glamour* girls holding out their tickets, smiling rather more than the other set, and she quickly took them to their seats. Hmm, not so tough after all.

The room was packed now. The show was running forty-five minutes behind the official schedule, which was normal, she was told. The eight tiered rows were completely filled apart from a few keep-you-waiting spaces in the front. The photographers had finished setting up and were jostling restlessly, crammed like sardines into their demarcated rectangle at the foot of the runway. On the opposite side from the fashion editors, where the buyers sat, a huddle of paparazzi were crouched low in front of the celebrities Aspen had sweet-talked into coming—Gwyneth Paltrow, Liv Tyler, Natalie Portman, Sarah Jessica Parker, Heidi Klum—and television reporters were asking them questions as the cameramen sat on the side of the runway.

"Get them off the stage," Hannah barked. "I want everyone in their seats. What's that? You're kidding me? *Yes!!!*" Cassie could practically hear her punching the air. "Right, I'm being told Alexa's car has just pulled up. We're gonna be good to go in two minutes."

Who? Cassie skittered round to the other side of the cat-walk, shooing the cameramen and reporters away surpris-ingly easily. Her headset and all-black look radiated authority.

"She's coming in now," Hannah commentated. "Cassie, I can't see you. Too many fucking photographers. Give me the cue when she's seated."

"Could you tell me something by which I can identify her," Cassie asked quickly, too panicky now to prevaricate about revealing her ignorance. There were still lots of people moving about, mainly "standers" bagging the last few un-taken seats as the lights went down.

There was a furious silence. "You have *got* to be kidding me! How can you not know what Alexa Bourton looks like? She's the new fucking editor of *Vogue*. You have heard of *Vogue*, I take it?" she snarled sarcastically. "Where the hell have you been living?"

"Scottish Borders," Cassie replied, trembling, as a woman came into sight radiating the kind of couture-as-casualwear chic that no amount of all-black and high heels would ever endow her with. "It's okay, I see her," she said, taking the initiative and walking to meet her, smiling brightly.

"Right, lights down, cue music," Hannah ordered. "I want the first girl out ten seconds after she's seated. Let's not keep her waiting, people! This is the first time we've had a *Vogue* presence in seven seasons."

"Hello," Cassie beamed. "We're so thrilled you could make it to the show. Would you like to follow me and I'll take you to your seat. The show's about to begin."

The woman followed. She did indeed look like she was at the top of the fashion tree. Her hazelnut hair tumbled ex-pensively onto a giraffe-print coat, and she was carrying an enormous squashy burnt-orange bag. Cassie took her to the last remaining seat in the front row—hell, the last remaining seat in the house now.

The music, which had been an unidentifiable blend of ambient dance music, ratcheted up in volume and segued, curiously, into pan pipes, which were then overlaid with a thumping rock tempo for the girls to walk to.

Cassie moved out of the way, her pulse racing, grateful that the show was under way and she could relax at last. She sat discreetly on the front step in the aisle.

The first girl came out, her cheeks flushed and eyes bright (due to her activities in the bathroom backstage, not to the mountain air). A polite scatter of applause skipped through the audience as the model began to stomp her way down the catwalk. It had been amazing to Cassie to discover during the castings how many girls just couldn't walk—not only because of the ridiculous heels, but actually losing all opposite-arm-to-leg coordination.

The girl got to the end and sank into her back hip, just as the second girl came out and began her march. All the celebrities were watching, appraising their bodies and nodding appreciatively through narrowed eyes at the clothes. The editors were sketching, the photographers whistling and calling as the second model's jacket shifted, revealing a bare, pert breast beneath.

Cassie started tapping her feet. This was the funkiest thing she'd ever been to—just like she'd always thought a concert might be, but more exclusive, and with better-looking people. Although she didn't belong in this world, knew less about it than she did about quantum physics, she felt its draw. No wonder Kelly thrived upon it, no wonder she loved her career and put it first. It was about being part of something. This was the "Zeitgeist" that Kelly was always banging on about.

A man to her right leaned toward her. He looked concerned.

"I think you might have a problem," he said, jerking his head toward a woman who was standing in the shadows of the aisle opposite.

Cassie looked back at him. "I do?" He was crazily good-looking with a fresh tan, two-day-old stubble, and hazel eyes.

"Yeah."

Cassie carried on staring at him blankly.

"You must know who that is," he said finally.

Cassie shook her head but looked back at the woman, feeling a cold shiver beginning to gather in her shoulders.

"Alexa Bourton?"

Cassie's face crumpled. "But I thought I . . . I mean, I put her . . . she's over there," she protested, looking over at the woman she'd seated, who had taken off her giraffe-print coat and was now sitting with a laptop on her knees.

The man looked at her pityingly. "That's Jazzy Lucas. Otherwise known as fashgurl."

Cassie didn't respond.

"She's a blogger." From the tone of his voice, that was a dirty word.

Oh. My. God. Cassie looked from Alexa back to Jazzy, then back to this man. "I'm screwed," she said, her eyes filling with tears.

There was a silence between them as the music blared all around, cameras flashing out of tempo. "Right, you look new to this. I'll help you out," the man said finally, a weary tone in his voice. "Get her over here quickly. She can have my seat."

"Seriously?"

"Go!"

Cassie darted over to the other side of the catwalk, getting in the way of the photographers in the process and igniting a tirade of abuse.

Miss? Mrs.? "Ms. Bourton," she gasped, wiping her eyes hastily. "How wonderful that you made it."

The woman raised an eyebrow questioningly. Made it? The show had already started by the time she'd got through the standing-room scrum, and she'd been standing here for two minutes now. It was also perfectly clear that someone was in her seat. Not only was there not a space for her anywhere across the entire front row, but her cache of senior editors was broken up by both Olivia Delingpole, her fiercest rival, and a *blogger*, sitting between them.

"Would you follow me, please?" Cassie half-pleaded, aware of the eyes beginning to swivel around to watch them. *Oh, please don't look, please don't look,* she thought desperately. That would be the death knell—Alexa's humiliation going public.

Alexa stared disdainfully at Cassie for a long time, hostility radiating from her like a force field. Then she said, in a voice so low that Cassie couldn't hear but could only lip-read: "I don't think so."

With the slightest tip of her chin, her clique of editors on the far side of the runway stood up, leaving great gaping gaps in the front row as they conspicuously filed out, making no attempt to hide as they walked side by side with the models coming down the catwalk.

No one could miss it now—*Vogue* was walking out, and absolutely everyone stared as the editors trooped past her, their high-heeled Manolo boots stabbing the carpet in a muted staccato rhythm. The photographers turned their cameras as one onto the drama unfolding offstage now. Bebe's creations were being ignored. A flock of cameramen swooped out of the room, chasing after Alexa and the Voguettes, desperate for an interview.

"But . . . but . . . please . . . ," Cassie cried, as the *Harper's Bazaar* crowd followed suit. They couldn't be seen to stay at a show *Vogue* had stormed out of.

"What's going on? What the fuck's happening down there?" Hannah cried down the microphone. "Where's everybody going? Is there a fire alarm? Is there something going on that I don't know about?!"

Desperately Cassie swung round, looking for the stranger who'd tried to help. But his seat—along with many of the others—was empty.

Chapter Eight

"Oh, poor you," Suzy soothed, noisily slurping her tea at the other end of the line.

"No, not poor *me*, Suze. Poor Kelly. I've completely dropped her in it. I mean, I've made her an absolute laughingstock. She must be the only fashion PR in New York with an employee who doesn't know who Alexa Bourton is. I mean, I thought . . . you know . . . um, what's-her-name . . ."

"Anna Wintour?" Suzy suggested helpfully.

"Yes. I thought she was the editor. Even *I* knew what she looked like."

"She left two years ago, Cass," Suzy said sympathetically.

Cassie groaned.

"But look, Alexa Bourton's a fashion insider, Cass. She's well respected, but she doesn't have the same stature. Most people on the street don't know who she is yet."

"But I'm *not* a person on the street anymore. At least I'm not supposed to be. I'm a PR at Hartford Communications. No one else would have made this mistake."

There was a sound of heavy munching.

"What're you eating? Don't tell me it's one of those cupcakes?"

"Mmmm . . . ," Suzy mumbled. "But all in . . . the name of . . . research, you understand."

"Of course," Cassie concurred; even her empty tummy was too dejected to rumble. There was a comfortable silence as Suzy ate cake and Cassie ruminated on what the press had dubbed "The PR Supremo's PR Disaster."

"Oh God," she wailed, putting her head in her hands. "This is all such a mess. I mean, what am I doing out here, Suze? I'm completely out of my depth. Kelly's spent nine years building up this company and I'm going to pull it down within a month."

"You're being way too hard on yourself."

"No I'm not. She's already been fired from the Bebe account because of this. And that's not even the worst of it—the *Vogue* girls and all the other magazines at Condé Nast are refusing to call in any products from our other clients. They've blacklisted us. They've already reneged on an At Home piece with Maddy Foxton to launch her new collection with Oscar, and he's terminated their alliance for next season."

"Oscar?"

"De la Renta," Cassie mumbled.

"Hmmm, well it doesn't sound like you're *that* naïve," Suzy said, impressed.

"Honestly, Suze, I'm not exaggerating. I've screwed up massively. It's only a matter of days before the other clients drop us too—it's like a game of dominoes. I've made Kelly look a joke."

"Has she fired you?"

"No. I keep telling her that I'll go and do some temping somewhere else, but she won't hear of it. In fact, she's actually insisting it's *her* fault for forgetting to give me the list beforehand so that I could study up on who everyone is. Can you believe that?"

"Loyal to a fault, that one."

"Mmmm. I think she thinks it'll tip me over the edge if I lose my job as well as my life."

"You haven't lost your life, Cass," Suzy protested, sounding aghast at the bleakness of her comment.

"Well, I have. I've lost my life *as I knew it*. I'm having to start from scratch and reinvent myself." She stared out of the window, watching the lights come on in the building opposite. "And I'm doing a shit job of it, frankly. I have to read from a notepad Kelly leaves out for me so I know how to put my outfits together in the morning. I only eat what she says, when she says. I basically pay a man to beat me up every other day, I'm bollocks at my made-up job and everyone there hates me, and I'm spending whatever money I do earn on maintaining a new look that's so alien to me, I don't even recognize my own reflection in shop windows."

There was a short pause. "D'you want me to come over?"

Cassie shook her head down the phone. "You're in London! You're thousands of miles away. You can't just hop on a plane."

"Sure I can. I could be with you by breakfast."

Cassie sighed, touched by her friend's generosity. Suzy, bossy though she was with Anouk and Kelly, had always been gentle with her.

"Thanks for the offer. But I don't think Archie would be too pleased about that. Anyway, I'll be okay. Particularly after I've had a hot bath and a ten-hour sleep tonight."

"Oooh, get you, spa girl."

"Yeah, well, Kelly's dragged me out literally every night

since I got here. Sometimes we go to four parties in one evening! Four! I used to think I was going some if I did four a month! I don't know how she does it. She's like a Duracell bunny."

"So how come you're off the hook tonight?"

"Kelly's got a hot date. Some guy called Brett who pretended to hit on me to get to her. He saw she was being my bouncer and . . . well, it's a long story, but I think she's dead keen on him. They've spoken loads on the phone. She was going to cancel with all this going on, but I persuaded her to see him. Despite the brave face, she could do with some cheering up."

"Well, keep me posted on how it goes."

"Yeah," Cassie sighed. "So what about you? You up to anything tonight?"

"Not really. Henry's back, so we're all having dinner tonight."

"Oh, that's nice."

"I'm not so sure. *He's* cooking."

Cassie chuckled. Henry's fish-finger sandwiches had been the stuff of legend in their teenage years.

"He said he saw you guys in New York."

"Did he?" Cassie wondered what else he'd mentioned—the fact that he thought she was a complete fraud and nut job? "Yes. It was nice to see him. It's years since we last caught up."

"Yeah. He said you looked really different—'hot' was the word he used, I think!"

"Really?" He'd been so disapproving when they'd met.

"He said he gave you a present to remember him by."

"Well, it wasn't so much to remember *him*. It was more of a 'keep your pecker up' gift. He wrote . . . what was it again?" she said, walking over to the small brown seed tray by the window and turning over the brown tag. "Oh yes—'energy in adversity,' my motto for living in Manhattan."

She heard a small snort. "How very motivational!" Suzy said wryly, moving on to another cupcake. "So what was it?"

"A packet of seeds."

"*Seeds?*" Suzy screeched. "God, it's a *wonder* he's got a girl-friend! What are you going to do with seeds in Manhattan?"

"That's just what Kelly said."

"What kind of seeds are they? Probably something from Mum's garden, I expect."

Cassie considered. Hattie Sallyford, Suzy and Henry's mother, was an eminent retired landscape designer, and her gardens at their country house in Gloucestershire were opened to the public every year after the Chelsea Flower Show, drawing huge and international crowds.

"I don't think so. I think it was a spur-of-the-moment thing. Anyway . . . ," she said, bending down to the tray on the windowsill to inspect the sappy shoots beginning to thrust through, "I don't think they're flower seeds. I think they're . . . *grass.*"

"Grass?"

"I know. A slightly off-the-wall choice. I expect he thinks I'm missing the countryside at Lammermuir, and my own little patch of grass will stop me being so homesick."

"That's kind of sweet."

"Yeah."

"He can be surprising sometimes, my brother. I always think of him as so gung-ho, going off on dangerous expedi-tions to unearth triffids and stuff. And then he goes and does something thoughtful like that."

"Well, tell him they're coming along nicely. I'm very good at watering them every day. It makes me feel very . . . zen."

"Righto. Oh, that sounds like Archie. I'd better go. Now look—ring me if there's anything, okay? Day or night—anytime. I'm not just saying it. I'm right here."

"I know you are. Thanks, Suze."

"And don't let this incident get you down. I mean, how bad can it be? It's only a fashion show. She'll get over it. They all will. They'll move on to something else next week. You just need to concentrate on keeping going. You're doing great. We're all very proud of you."

"Bye, Suze. Kiss Arch and Henry hello for me."

"Sure thing. Laters!"

The line clicked off and Cassie replaced the phone in the handset, a smile on her face as her fingertips softly brushed the green, green grass of home.

Chapter Nine

Cassie stood at the stop on Eighty-sixth Street, jigging her leg anxiously. The line was already thirty-strong and Bas was still nowhere in sight. He'd promised he wouldn't be late; she'd never caught the jitney before, but from what she'd heard, it was a bit like the first day of the Harrods sale and she wanted some support—and a bony set of elbows.

It wasn't as if she'd *had* to travel by bus. Kelly had taken a limo down to Southampton earlier that morning with Zara, and they'd naturally offered her a ride. But since the *Vogue* debacle three weeks earlier, Cassie had been lying low. Half of Kelly's accounts had now defected—and as a result, Kelly had had to let three people go. Cassie knew very well that absolutely everybody blamed and hated her for it. They fell silent when she walked into the room, deliberately didn't inform her of meetings, and her products kept mysteriously vanishing from the fashion cupboard.

Kelly, of course, was stubbornly trying to remain supportive and upbeat, but as her clients shook their heads and left, and Hartford Communications began to look disaster square in the face, the underlying tension between them was growing like bacteria. In fact, things probably would have come to a head by now had Kelly's fledgling relationship with Brett not been going from strength to strength. They were seeing each other "almost exclusively," which was apparently just a half-step before engagement out here, and she was rarely in anymore, leaving Cassie with plenty of time in the evenings to rest, recover, water her grass, and weep. On the nights they did come back, Cassie made her own excuses and caught a cab to Bas's Midtown apartment, where they drank copious amounts of red wine, played with her hair, and tried to understand men.

Cassie pulled her parka closer and shivered, just as she saw the legendary bottle-green coach bearing itself proudly through the traffic uptown. She looked around anxiously as the crowd suddenly converged and swelled around the bus stop. There was no way she'd get on, and it was two hours till the next bus. Grabbing her phone from her pocket, she tried Bas's number again. It rang.

"It's okay, it's okay, I'm here, darling," she heard his voice drawl—not down the line but behind her.

She turned and threw her arms around his neck in relief.

"Hey," he said, surprised. "You didn't think I'd leave you to do this on your own, did you?" He smiled, took her by the wrist, deftly pulled her around the crowd, and walked ten yards farther along the street. The jitney came to a stop smack-bang in front of them, as the rest of the crowd awkwardly disbanded and regrouped at their heels.

"How did you know?"

"There's a pothole by the curb that smacks the top of the coach into the post if they roll into it," he informed her. Cassie looked down. Sure enough, there was a manhole cover set too low in the road.

"You've always got the inside track," she smiled as the doors hissed open and they hopped on first.

"This is my favorite seat," he said, walking toward the back. "We're close enough to the coffee machine, the restroom, got our own TV screen—plus you get the best views on this side."

"How did I ever manage without you?" Cassie sighed, shrugging off her parka and rolling it up.

The coach filled quickly, making another three city stops before they were through the tunnel and past the airport. She felt a bubble of bile leap to her throat as she remembered landing there just hours after her life was forced into a U-turn. It had been the last day of summer and the city had still boasted the deep blue skies of wishes fulfilled. No longer. It was the middle of October now and autumn was in full stride, with the low sun bouncing off every mirrored-glass surface and bathing the streets in a peachy tint that belied the icy, streaking wind. She'd been here for six weeks, and apart from the fact that she was still managing to breathe in and breathe out, she didn't have much to show for it. She had one new friend, yes, but an old one was in danger of slipping away, and as much as she adored Bas, she didn't want to trade Kelly in for him.

She sighed heavily as Bas came back with their coffees.

"You're brooding," he reproved.

"I'm the most hated person in Manhattan. I'm allowed to brood."

"You are *not* the most hated. That accolade definitely belongs to Petra Richley—you know she's snapped up Alex von Furstenberg?" He paused. "Besides, at least everyone knows your name now. There's a lot to be said for that over here."

"Oh yeah, so they know to chuck my CV straight into the trash when it lands on their desks."

"It was just bad luck. It wasn't your fault that Gucci has

reduced its ad spend in the glossies to court the bloggers." He leaned in conspiratorially. "And when I say bloggers, I specifically mean fashgurl. Did you hear she holidayed with both Dolce and Gabbana *and* Valentino on their yachts in Europe this summer?" He shook his head in admiration. "That's strictly A-list territory. Most of those editors have spent fifteen years enduring ritual humiliation to work their way up to those privileges. It's like fagging for the fashion industry. But fashgurl? She's been around for three seasons, and look! She's already stealing Alexa Bourton's seat at the shows." He whistled softly. "Times are a-changin." It was just a classic case of putting the wrong people in the wrong place at the wrong time. Drink your coffee."

Cassie took a slurp and stared out of the window. It was the first time she'd stepped off the island since arriving, and she felt her spirits gradually lift as concrete steadily gave way to grass, and tower blocks to trees. The buildings that they did pass were no longer thrusting and dynamic monoliths, but suburban houses in pretty pastels and old-fashioned county stores selling ride-on mowers and grass seed; normal-sized mongrels replaced the mini toy dogs, children on bikes replaced the size-zero shoppers, and scarcely any of the cars parked had blacked-out windows or V12 engines.

"This is us," Bas said two hours later, gathering his bags. They disembarked, and Cassie looked around her as Bas tried to locate the car Kelly had sent for them.

"So this is Southampton," she said to herself, looking up and down Main Street and taking in the art galleries, the branch of Saks, the quaint boutiques selling tapestried cushions and monogrammed slippers. The streets were wide and tree-lined, with wooden benches dotted up and down the sidewalks inviting you to sit and idle and watch.

Though she'd never heard of the Hamptons in her previous life, she'd heard of little else since living in New York, and absolutely everyone she met regaled her with stories of their summers in Sag Harbor or Amagansett, East Hampton or Southampton. Supposedly they all had a distinct identity and reputation, and which one you spent your childhood summers in said as much about you as your hair, shoes, and watch—the markers of status in Manhattan. As far as Cassie could tell, holidaying in Southampton meant you were even more exceptionally loaded than if you holidayed in the others. Kelly had mentioned that George Soros had a place here, and Bas had entertained her during their two-hour journey with the nefarious activities of the members of the golf club, where the membership fee alone was six hundred thousand dollars.

Their car pulled up, a sleek gunmetal-gray Lincoln, and after they'd stowed their bags in the trunk and Bas had nipped off for another round of coffees to go, the driver took them to the house where the shoot was taking place. Kelly's own summer place, where she and Cassie would be staying, was over in Sagaponack. It was a two-bedroom condo she shared with a friend, but they were prepping at the Southampton house today, and wouldn't get back there till late. Bas, the makeup teams, the model, and the photographer, meanwhile, were all staying at a guest house in the center of Southampton Village.

It didn't take long to get there. The roads were quiet, the throng of summer visitors had long since departed for the mainland, and the Hamptons International Film Festival, which drew out the summer season a little longer, had finished the weekend before.

The car turned through some electronic gates and swept up a long, gently curving drive. The house was covered in beautifully aged cedar shingles that had weathered to a discreet silver-fox hue, and there were chunky off-white wooden casement windows and a wide, half-glazed front door. A covered verandah crept around the left-hand side of the first floor, but it was the two white-trimmed pointy gables—one central, the other positioned over the right-hand wing of the house—that most enchanted her, fluttering out at the ends like curled lashes.

"Look at that," she whispered. It was like something Martha Stewart had fashioned from a Hans Christian Andersen fairy tale.

"Looking's about all we can afford to do," Bas sighed, patting her knee as the car came to a stop. "That baby would set you back fourteen million dollars. In *this* market."

Cassie raised her eyebrows as the driver opened their doors and they stepped out. Kelly came skipping down the steps to greet them, her welcome almost imperceptibly warmer for Bas than for Cassie.

"You're just in time. Luke was just asking how you've interpreted the brief." She leaned in closer to the lanky hairdresser. "Remember, nothing too freaky, Bas. Selena's got hair like a fricking kelpie, so don't count on it working with you."

"Darling, the only time I do freaky is Halloween." He gasped and took Cassie's arm excitedly. "You haven't done Halloween States-style, have you?"

Cassie shook her head, no idea what he was on about.

"You shall be my sacrificial virgin," he beamed, grabbing her hand.

They walked into the house together. It had a large square hall with rooms going off to each side and a cherrywood staircase ascending across the back. To their left, in the sitting room, a skinny leg, visible from the knee down, was swinging over the arm of a sofa in time to the tinny acoustics of an iPod. Bas went up and squeezed it, making the owner jump and give a screech so high you'd think only dogs could hear it.

"Bas, baby! I was hoping it would be you."

Bas reached down and pulled back up by the wrist a languid beauty with dark-as-sloe eyes and waist-length raven hair. She sat on the arm of the sofa appraising Cassie, who, lacking the eagle-eyed scrutiny of Kelly lately, had put together an outfit that looked like it was having an identity crisis of its own.

"Hi, I'm Cassie," she said with a friendly smile. "You must be Selena. I've heard so much about you." The Prada, Louis Vuitton, and Burberry contracts, namely.

"Mmm. And you must be Cassie," Selena smiled cruelly. "I've heard so much about *you*."

"Now, now, Selena," Bas said, cutting straight in. "If you bitch to my friend Cassie here, I'll make your plaits too tight," he said, stroking her distinctly unkelpie-like hair.

Selena gave him a sweet smile, but retreated, sliding backward off the arm onto the sofa again.

Great. Another flying start. Cassie looked over at Kelly nervously, but Kelly was looking straight ahead, a determinedly impervious smile stuck to her face. "Drink, anyone?" she asked, turning on her heel and heading toward the kitchen. Bas and Cassie shot each other a look before following after her.

Kelly was grabbing a bottle of wine from the fridge.

"Who else are we waiting for?" Cassie asked, fingering the glasses anxiously.

"Only Molly. Luke's already here. He's outside taking a look around the grounds. The weather's supposed to be bright tomorrow, and he's trying to find somewhere that isn't covered with yellow leaves."

"Oh, why's that?" Cassie asked, before being kicked in the ankle by Bas. "Ow! What?"

Bas rolled his eyes.

"Because this campaign is for the spring-summer season, Cassie," Kelly said wearily. "It won't do to have autumn leaves everywhere in a March issue." She didn't mention that the planned shoot in Antigua had had to be scrapped after only six orders came in for the collection after the show.

"Yes, of course," Cassie replied quickly, stung by the boredom in her friend's voice. She just wasn't picking up quickly enough on the fast-forward nature of the fashion calendar. Trade fabric shows a year in advance, catwalk shows six months, magazine issues three to four months . . . When she'd tried to impress Kelly by conspicuously studying up on the trends in the October issue of *Vogue*, Kelly had snatched it off her, telling her not to bother. Those trends were for civilians now, and therefore *over* in fashion terms.

"When's Molly getting here?" Bas asked as Kelly poured five glasses. He had worked with Molly Kentish at many of the shows this season, and they were old friends.

"On the next jitney. She was waiting for some product to arrive before she left."

"And dare I ask . . . ?"

"No," Kelly said abruptly. "Bebe's not coming. It was Luke's condition for doing the job. He's going to e-mail her the edit tomorrow night."

Cassie frowned, still baffled as to what was going on with this job. Bebe had fired Hartford Communications on the day of the show, yet one call from the photographer and they were rehired, albeit only for the ad campaign. "Closure," Kelly had said soberly when she'd taken the call. "We worked on that collection together. I'm second only to Bebe herself when it comes to sharing her vision for the line."

It still didn't make sense, though. Why wouldn't the photographer let the designer attend her own ad campaign? But she kept her puzzlement to herself. She'd only put her foot in it with Kelly again.

A door banged behind them and Cassie turned to see a man wiping his feet on the mat, a camera slung from a strap over his shoulder. His shag of light brown hair was wavy and brushed his collar, and his cheeks were flushed from the dusky chill that was beginning to settle outside. He seemed familiar somehow. The door opened again and a skinny redhead followed him in. She was carrying a light-bouncer under one arm and a tripod under the other.

"Here you go, Lou," she said, handing him another camera dangling from her wrist. He took it and turned the camera on, holding it up as he scrolled back through the memory card. Cassie gasped, a hand flying to her mouth.

It couldn't be!

Lou looked up and saw her horrified expression. He smiled.

"Well, well," he said, walking toward her. "I believe we've met before."

Chapter Ten

"Why didn't you tell me you knew Luke Laidlaw?" Kelly hissed as they pretended to refill the wine glasses.

"I wouldn't say I 'knew' him, Kell. I only met him once. He was the one who saw that Alexa was . . . you know . . . *standing*." She saw Kelly flinch. She might as well have said "falling from a great height"—the calamity was the same. "He tried to help, that was all."

"Do you have any idea who he is?"

"A photographer?"

"The photographer *du jour*, Cass. He's key in Alexa Bourton's revamp of *Vogue*—the new typeface, layout. He's under contract to do a lead fashion story and cover-try for every issue." Kelly lowered her hiss to a whisper. "And rumor says he's sleeping with her. No wonder he was so keen not to see her slighted." She looked at Cassie pointedly. "Which is why I'm concerned about you being here."

"What do you mean?"

Kelly shrugged. "Plainly put, you dissed his girlfriend. He might refuse to work with you."

Cassie put her hands up immediately. "I don't want to cause any more trouble, Kell. I'll go. Straightaway."

There was a click.

"Go where?" said a voice from the doorway.

They both turned, startled. Luke was walking back into the kitchen. He was wearing faded jeans and a pale gray sweatshirt, and he still had his camera in his hand. He hadn't put it down since he'd come into the house. He came and stood by them, examining the picture he'd just taken.

"I was just saying to Cassie that, unfortunately, she's got to go back to the office . . ."

Luke frowned as he zoomed in on it.

"A few things have come up that I need her to take care of for me."

There was a short pause as he fiddled with buttons.

"Can't you go?" he asked after a moment, putting the camera down and looking at Kelly.

"Me?" Kelly asked, surprised. "Well, I hardly think so," she said, laughing harshly. "I mean, in Bebe's absence, it's clear that I'm the most senior representative of her vision. I worked with her closely on this collection. I see through her eyes."

Cassie could have sworn she saw Luke's left eyebrow twitch slightly. He passed them each a refilled glass.

"Oh no, not for me, thanks," Cassie said, putting the glass back on the worktop. "I'm going to head off. Get out of the way."

"Nonsense," Luke said, holding the glass back up to her. "You must stay. I insist."

His intonation on the last word suggested that indeed he did. He was pulling rank. Cassie looked over at Kelly, who was staring at him quizzically.

After a moment Kelly shrugged lightly. "Well, if Luke feels that . . . the shoot will benefit from your presence, Cass, then you must stay." She forced a smile. "Those other matters can wait till next week." She walked briskly out of the room, leaving Cassie standing awkwardly with Luke.

She felt a blush begin to creep up her neck as they stood in a silence that Luke felt no compulsion to fill.

"I know this probably isn't the time, but . . . there might not be another opportunity to say this, and it's important that I do say this—"

"There's going to be plenty of opportunity for us to talk," he corrected.

"Well, yes, of course . . . but it's going to be a busy few days, and just in case, I wanted to say thank you—you know, for trying to help me at the show."

He stared at her but said nothing. Which made her even more nervous. She'd dissed his girlfriend!

"So thank you. It was very kind."

He nodded. "I felt sorry for you," he said finally.

Most people do, she thought to herself.

"This can be a hard industry. Easily cruel. And I could see it was a genuine mistake on your part." His face cracked into a small smile. "If the lot of us weren't so power-crazed and status-obsessed, it would have been almost funny."

There was nothing funny about Kelly losing three-quarters of her revenue or three people losing their jobs, she reflected. She took a sip of her drink distractedly. It was warm and smoky-tasting.

"So, have you got any ideas about what you're going to do tomorrow?" she asked.

"We'll hit the beach to begin with. The wind's going to be westerly, so it'll be a bit warmer and I want some shots of her in the water."

Cassie spluttered on her drink. "But it's the middle of October! You can't have her lying down in the Atlantic. She'll freeze."

"It's her job," Luke said cheerfully. "Besides, you can make sure there are plenty of blankets and towels and tubs of hot water for her to soak her feet in."

Cassie shivered at the thought of it and wondered whether Selena knew how her day was going to read. Tomorrow hadn't started yet, but Cassie already sensed that, like every day recently, it was going to be cold and long and not without event.

Chapter Eleven

Cassie and Kelly were pounding the beach together, running along the tide line where the sand was still damp and hard. Cassie thought her heart might explode at any moment, but she kept up. She could feel Kelly pulling away from her day by day, and running—although unnatural to her—felt like one of the only ways to show her "I'm here . . . I'm with you . . . I'll stay with you like you've stayed with me . . . we'll stand shoulder-to-shoulder . . . this is what friends do . . . we'll get through this . . ."

But Kelly seemed oblivious to the message, and now she easily moved up a gear so that she was one, two, three strides ahead, and within a minute she had entirely broken away.

"I'll see you back at the house," she called over her shoulder. "I want to finish on a sprint."

Cassie kept her legs moving, but her energy sapped away, completely deflated by Kelly's abrupt dismissal. She felt a stitch coming on from the strain of trying to keep up, and by the time she got back, Kelly was in the shower, a half-drunk espresso on the kitchen counter.

It took two tries before Cassie got her outfit right. The all-black outfits that passed as a uniform in Manhattan were *de trop* out here in the Hamptons. In the end she pulled on her spare running kit—thin gray leggings from American Apparel and an oversized red hoody. Kelly was wearing four-hundred-dollar jeans and a caramel-colored cashmere cable-knit sweater. "Let's go," she said.

Kelly had organized the rendezvous the night before. They left the car in the beach parking lot—they didn't need a permit out of season. Everyone was already there, including Molly, the makeup artist, who'd stayed back in New York till she'd taken delivery of the perfect blush for Selena's coloring. Busty and short at five foot two, Molly was Bas's physical opposite, and Cassie felt a stab of jealousy watching them joke around as she approached over the dunes. "Teabag!" Bas cried as he caught sight of her. "Come and meet Molly. One of my oldest *chums*." He tried to pronounce it with an English accent, and both Cassie and Molly rolled their eyes. She had a plump, open face that Cassie liked straightaway.

"Hi," she smiled.

"All right?" Molly asked in a broad London accent that was more Albert Square than Bas's Belgrave Square. Her light brown hair was cut short with a fringe that stopped halfway down her forehead and she was wearing a purple fleece beneath her denim dungarees. Even Cassie's eye had tuned sufficiently to see that Molly was no fashion bunny, but her skin—Cassie tried to stop herself from peering—was amazing: porcelain pale and as smooth as glass.

Luke and his assistant, Bonnie, were down by the water's edge. Luke was firing off rapid shots as Bonnie stood in self-conscious, deliberately unmodely poses for him so he could check the light and composition on his playback. Selena was playing Angry Birds on her iTouch, sitting in the canvas bell tent that had been pitched at the foot of the dunes to keep the wind from messing up Bas's and Molly's efforts.

Kelly blew a whistle—the only way to be heard over the sea and wind—and Luke and Bonnie turned. Giving a quick wave, they made their way back up to the team.

"Right," Kelly said as they all warmed their fingers around enamel teacups. "We're going to shoot the Caspian Sea segment here. You said you wanted Selena appearing over the tops of the dunes, Luke, yes?"

Luke nodded. "The water's too gray to get in today."

"Thank Christ for that," Selena quipped, lighting a cigarette.

"So Molly and Bas, we want the same looks as the show, please, although lighter on the eye color for this, Molly. Bebe wants more focus on the brow."

"And I think I'll drop the plaits down to here on Selena," Bas said, gesturing to the midpoint of the model's head. "She's got ears like wings," he said, patting her shoulder and bending down sympathetically. "I love you to death, sweetie, but God knows you do!"

Cassie bit her lip to keep from laughing. She realized Luke was staring at her and rearranged her expression quickly, but to her astonishment, he just smiled.

"Actually, can you do her hair the way you did Cassie's at the show?" Luke asked, looking back to Bas.

Everyone immediately stared at Cassie, whose hair was now scraped back in a limp, off-center ponytail to keep it from blowing in her eyes. It was difficult at this particular moment to see her as a source of inspiration.

Selena glowered. "She wasn't *in* the show—as I'm sure we all remember."

"I remember," Luke replied, giving nothing away about

how he'd been the first to spot the "situation." "But Bas had done a variation on the theme for her that I preferred. That okay with you, Bas?"

Bas arched an eyebrow and preened. "Of course," he said slowly. "If that's what you want."

"It is."

"Riiiight," Kelly said, looking slowly from Luke to Cassie to Bas and back to Cassie again. "Well then, if everyone's happy with the brief, let's get this show on the road. Cass, can you help me steam the clothes?"

They trudged up the beach back to the parking lot, where the clothes were hanging from rails in the back of a rental van.

Kelly expertly started up the steamer. "Can you get the clothes out of those bags, Cass? I need the peacock mohair dress first."

Cassie stepped into the van and handed her the dress.

"So," Kelly muttered as she started brushing the dress in long, sweeping strokes. "Why did Bas do your hair at the show? You were supposed to be working."

"I was. Remember, you asked me to check on him? He'd just finished the last model, and"—she crouched down so that she was kneeling—"he'd done it before I'd even noticed. He's always playing with our hair—you know what he's like. We're like his dolls."

Kelly turned the dress around.

"And why is Luke so keen to replicate you?"

"Well, he's not replicating *me*, Kell. He obviously just prefers the style Bas did for me. I don't know why. I don't know the man. He's the one with the vision."

"He's the one with the reputation, Cass."

Cassie stopped unzipping the hanging bags. "What do you mean?"

"Isn't it obvious? He's hitting on you—or he's going to. Why else would he *insist* that you stay? Why else does he want Selena to look like you? Hell, why else did he insist that Bebe reinstate us for this campaign? Because, let's face it, she couldn't get a ten-year-old with a disposable camera to take a snapshot for her after what happened at the show. So why did he—the hottest photographer in New York City and supposedly Alexa Bourton's lover—suddenly ring her up and offer to shoot for her, *completely free of charge*?"

Cassie shook her head, unable to reply.

"Have you heard what his nickname is?"

"No."

"Coody."

"Coody?"

"As in could-he-get-laid-more." Kelly raised an eyebrow. "It's meant rhetorically."

Cassie gasped, horrified. "That's appalling."

Kelly shrugged. "He's a good-looking straight man in a predominantly female and gay industry. You can't blame him for taking the opportunities he gets given. Just be aware that he's *rampantly* heterosexual. That's all I'm saying."

She picked up the dress and walked back down the beach, leaving Cassie crouched in the back of the van getting pins and needles.

It wasn't going well. They'd been shooting for four hours already and there wasn't a decent shot—not quite Luke's words—in any of the hundreds of images he'd taken.

"For Chrissakes," he cried, raking his hand through his hair and wheeling away from the blue-tinged model. It was two in the afternoon now, and although there wasn't a cloud in the sky, it was barely above freezing. Everyone was shivering, huddled around the firepit that Kelly and Cassie had hurriedly brought over from their terrace—everyone except Selena, Luke, and Bonnie, who were still shooting. Bonnie could have kept warm, but she stuck by Luke's side as if she'd been Velcroed to him.

"What the hell's wrong with you, Selena?" he shouted into the wind. "Put some feeling into your arms. You're supposed to be savoring your freedom! I want . . . Julie Andrews coming over that freaking mountain. You look like you're scaring crows."

Selena shook her arms out and tried again, but there was no disguising the sinews in them as she braced her exposed flesh against the cold, and you could see the whites of her eyes from halfway up the beach.

"Jesus! Forget it!" Luke shouted. "There's no point even wasting the battery on this!"

He stomped angrily up the beach. They all looked at each other nervously as he approached. It was clear no one was going to mention the umpteen bathroom trips Selena had made between styling changes.

"This isn't working!" he grumbled. "No wonder Bebe wanted her to play a virgin. I wouldn't sleep with her either, looking like that."

"Well now, that's saying something," Bas murmured to Cassie, and a nervous giggle escaped her.

Luke looked up, but this time he didn't smile.

Selena stumbled into the tent, crying from the rawness of the wind chill and Luke's harsh words. Kelly immediately wrapped her in a duvet that she'd grabbed from the little house. Luke carried on staring at Cassie.

"I . . . I . . . I'm sorry, Lou," Selena chattered. She looked almost ill as the glow of the fire threw orange light onto her ghostly skin. "I'll be f-f-f-fine in a minute. I just need to w-w-warm up for a bit."

Luke seemed not to have heard. But then he looked back at her and his expression changed. "What? I—no. No, *I'm* sorry, Selena. I've been too hard on you. It's bitter out there. It's not fair for you to stand in those temperatures in just a scrap."

Selena smiled, as grateful for his kindness as a kitten pulled from a bag in the river.

He rubbed his hands along her arms. "God, you are frozen. You're going to get sick. You need to get back to the house straightaway. Jump into a bath. Here, Bonnie will drive you back to the house." He threw his Jeep keys over to Bonnie, who looked exceedingly put out at the prospect of being the model's driver.

"Thanks, Lou," Selena breathed, getting up and kissing him on the cheek, close to his ear.

The two girls left the tent and everyone else turned around to start packing up. "Well that's that, then," Bas muttered.

"Not so fast," Luke said, clearing the memory card on the camera. "We're not done for the day yet."

"But you've just sent Selena home," Molly said, gesturing to the retreating figure. "We've got no model."

Luke looked up. "Yes we have," he said steadily, staring straight at Cassie. "I want *her*."

"No! I won't do it!"

"You have to!"

"I don't! I am in charge of my life. I am master of my own destiny. *I* am!" Cassie thumped her chest for emphasis.

"He wants you!"

"Yes! And why? You've already warned me off him. Told me what a rogue he is."

Kelly sighed and shifted position in the van. Cassie was huddled up against the side of it, her knees drawn up to her chest defensively.

"I don't know why," she shrugged. "Maybe *this* is why. Maybe this is what he had in mind all along. He likes your look! Photographers are like that. They like to have a muse, someone who inspires them. Maybe I was wrong about him meaning, you know . . . funny business."

"I am *not* a model, Kell!"

"I know that—but maybe that's what he likes about you. You're natural-looking, wholesome. Remember how this entire collection is based around the story of a Dagestani teenage bride on the run? Youth, innocence . . ." Cassie marveled at how her friend managed to utter that sentence with total earnestness. "Maybe Selena's just too much of a face for what he wants in these pictures."

"I don't even understand what that means," Cassie muttered, bending her face into her knees. "Anyway, if a professional like Selena can't hack those temperatures in hardly any clothes, how the devil does he think I'm going to manage?"

"What's so 'professional' about standing on a sand dune in a pretty dress? You think that's something she learned at university? It's instinct, Cass. Grit. Grim determination to get the picture. Anyway, he wants to shoot back at the house instead. Get the sunset from the attic."

"There won't be a picture to 'get' with me."

"If Luke Laidlaw says there will be, there will be. Come on," Kelly cajoled. "At the very least, it'll be a story to tell your grandkids one day! The day you modeled for Luke Laidlaw! He's one of the legends, Cass."

"I am not a model. I am a private, plain, boring individual who would like it to remain that way, thanks."

Kelly sighed wearily. "Look, Cass, Luke has to all intents and purposes fired Selena. He's wiped every shot he took of her this morning."

"Well that was a bloody stupid, rash thing to do," Cassie cried hotly.

"If you don't do this, the shoot will collapse and things will get even worse for Bebe. Luke Laidlaw shooting her ad campaign might be the only thing now that can save her business."

Cassie sniffed. She was having trouble visualizing Bebe Washington as a tragic figure. Besides, the entire situation was ridiculous. How on earth had it come to this? "Bebe will go nuts—the PR who destroyed her breakthrough show becomes the model in her ad campaign? I don't think so. I would *not* want to be in the room—no, the city!—when she heard that."

There was a short pause.

"Then do it for me," she heard her friend say in a smaller voice.

Cassie looked up, surprised by the timidity. Kelly was looking at her beseechingly.

The old friends stared at each other in silence, words redundant. It didn't need to be said that this could be Cassie's opportunity to undo the awful harm she'd done to Kelly's business and reputation, to repay the constant kindness and favors Kelly had extended to her since she'd left Gil.

Cassie sighed. There was simply no argument against that. She should just be grateful it wasn't a *Playboy* shoot going on out there.

"Okay," she said finally, pulling herself up and sliding her bottom along the floor of the van. "For you. I'll do it for you."

They opened the doors and the bleached glare of sunlight rushed in at them.

"She'll do it," Kelly smiled, nodding at Luke, Bas, and Molly, who were leaning against the beach regulations sign.

"Yay!" Molly said cheerfully, wholly convinced that this was a dreadful idea.

"That's my Teabag," Bas said, hugging her by the shoulders. "I'll make you look doubly gorgeous, darling."

"That's great news," Luke said. "We'll head back to the house now, and once you've worked your magic, the rest of you can take the day off—fully paid, of course."

"But—" Kelly frowned. "You'll need them for touch-ups, surely? They can't just disappear."

"Sure you can," he said, including her in the dismissal. "It won't take long. Besides, Cassie's never done this before. She'll be a lot more relaxed if there aren't loads of people standing round staring at her."

"Three's hardly loads," Bas countered, looking worried.

Luke looked at him. "Like I said, she's not a professional, Bas." He turned back to Cassie, and she saw a smile in his eyes. "I want a closed set."

Chapter Twelve

"*Usher in the new spring mood with Maddy Foxton's sublime—*"

"No, scratch *sublime*," Kelly muttered. "Too gushy. Change it to . . . *delicious*. Let's get tactile with it."

"*Usher in the new spring mood with Maddy Foxton's delicious new collection—*"

"*Capsule* collection. It sounds more exclusive. It screams waiting list."

". . . *delicious new capsule collection of day-to-night clutch bags.*"

"No, hate it. Change that."

"All of it?"

"The *day-to-night clutch bag* bit. Too done. I only change my bag from day to night if I'm going to the Met Institute. Women expect their bags to be versatile."

"Okay." Cassie blew out through her cheeks. "What if we go in on the craftsmanship angle instead? I mean, logistically I still can't work out how they weave a plaited bag from one piece of leather."

"Okay. It's what allows them to charge three grand a pop," Kelly said. "And get the quality of the leather in as well. Ring Maddy's studio to get the specific details. I can't remember what she sources exactly—the placentas of woodland fauns or baby unicorns or something."

The phone on her desk rang and Kelly's eyes brightened as she saw the number. "It's Brett. Let me see that before it goes out."

"Sure."

Cassie walked out of the office, closing Kelly's door quietly. Hannah looked up. As one of the only four employees left—from an original tally of sixteen—there was no hiding from Hannah and her death stares. Aside from the original three Kelly had had to let go, the other employees, Aspen included, had jumped ship when it became clear that *Vogue*'s displeasure was going to last for more than a week, and only a few die-hard loyalists had stuck around.

Certainly getting Luke to shoot the Bebe Washington campaign had bolstered Kelly's reputation somewhat, but with the images and new collection not out till February, the man on the street—or rather woman in the shops—remembered only the fiasco, and Hartford Communications was left treading water in the interim.

Cassie shook her head to bring herself back to the present and stared across the half-empty office from her desk. At least she was settling in to the PR world better. With fewer chefs in the kitchen, she was beginning to forge links with the journalists, most of whom were delighted to accept her invitations to lunch, if only to get the inside track on what had *really* happened with Alexa Bourton. Needless to say, she hadn't found the courage to call the *Vogue* office, even though she'd written a contrite but eloquent letter of apology to Alexa the very day of the debacle.

She understood now the mechanisms of the industry—who did what and when—and she'd become so used to her "dressing by numbers" outfits that she was able to put her clothes on in the morning without first checking the labels.

She looked the part. She was beginning to act the part. Could she write the part? Ironically, she had bigger responsibilities now that there were fewer people to share them with.

She looked down at her press release. If she could just nail this and get people—the right people—lusting after the collection, she could make another difference for Kelly. First Bebe. Now Maddy. She just had to do it one pigeon-step at a time.

"This is mental," Cassie giggled as a werewolf held open the elevator doors for her. "Thanks, Bas."

"Pleasure's all mine, m'lady," he growled wolfishly.

"You can't call me a lady when I'm dressed as a toad!" she said, as he pressed the floor button.

"You should have come as a werewolf too. You always look lean and hungry these days."

Cassie shook her head. "You don't know the half of it. I'm hoping Anouk will put me on a steak tartare diet when I get to P—"

"Don't say it!" Bas commanded dramatically. "The P-word. I don't want to hear it." He turned his face to the wall.

"Oh, Bas. You know we'll always be friends," she said, hugging him to her. "And who knows, I might decide to settle here after my Grand Tour. Anyway, won't you go out for the shows?" she asked. "I can see you then. There's the couture in January and the autumn-winter collections at the end of Feb."

Bas clutched his hands to his heart and looked down at her proudly. "Oh my duckling," he said. "You are ready to fly."

The doors opened just as Cassie whacked him in the stomach. The party was spilling over into the hall, and a cacophony of witches, vampires, pumpkins, black cats, and zombies

was mooching about, leaning on walls and dancing in door-
ways.

"Okay. So Halloween's a big deal here, then," she said, taking in the collective effort. Men who wouldn't deviate from a
two-button to three-button suit by day were in full makeup
and character dress. It was certainly a far cry from her Halloween the year before: Gil had been away and she'd invited the
local primary school to throw a party in the Great Hall. She'd
spent days beforehand carving out giant pumpkins to sit next
to the massive front doors, and had dangled big black spiders
from the chandeliers and tacked black gauze to the windows.
The children had loved it and had spontaneously shouted out,
"Three cheers for Mrs. Fraser," before they'd left.

"You'd better believe it. Come on. Let's get some drinks."

They pushed through the doorway—quite some feat since
she was wearing a bulbous and warty solid-foam body-
suit that was wider than the door—and headed toward the
kitchen.

"You stay here," Bas commanded. "I'll get the drinks. Once
we get you in there we might never get you back out again."

Cassie turned and stared out of the enormous floor-
to-ceiling, wall-to-wall glass window. The views from up
here—so, so much higher than Kelly's apartment—were
staggering. If she looked north, she could see the lights of
Harlem, and south, the very tip of the Statue of Liberty. In
front, between the towers, she caught glimpses of the East
River, inky black and viscous-looking in the night.

Now this *is New York living,* she thought to herself.

"Hey! Thought I recognized that backside."

She turned around. Kelly was standing in front of her
wearing a red PVC corset, red fishnet stockings, tiny red silk
panties, and flashing horns on her head.

"Oh! My! God!" Cassie shrieked. "What would your mother say if she knew you were out like that?"

Kelly laughed. "What? You think they didn't do this?"

"No!"

"Don't you remember that time they all did Halloween together?"

"No!" The thought of her parents in any type of dress except black tie, was . . . well, unthinkable.

Kelly raised her eyebrows. "Your mother went as the Bride of Frankenstein."

"She did not!"

"And your father was . . . well, you can guess."

"Frankenstein? Daddy?!"

Kelly held her arms wide. "The very same!"

"You know, there's a lot of rubber and PVC and leather going on," Cassie said suspiciously. "You're sure we're not just at some fetish party?"

Bas came back with their drinks. "Oooh, you look saucy! I take it Brett approves of that sexpot outfit?"

"Oh yes. He's already approved me," Kelly said. She winked. "Twice!"

They laughed, just as Brett—dressed as Dracula—came to join them. "What's so funny?"

"Nothing," Bas said. "We were just giving Kelly our approval rating."

Brett leaned over and gnawed affectionately—and vampirically—on Kelly's neck.

Cassie smiled to see her friend look so happy. In love, even. Brett had played his cards cleverly, right from the very beginning. It was just as Cassie had suspected. He'd noticed how Kelly had been defending her at Mischka that night, so he'd decided to get to her by pretending to get to Cassie—that way, Kelly forced herself between them and straight into his arms. Cassie thought it very romantic.

"You look gorgeous too, Cassie," Brett said with a grin when he'd lifted his head.

"Thanks, Brett!" Cassie laughed. "I'm covered in warts, have green makeup on my face, and an arse the size of New Jersey. I feel like a million dollars!"

"Well your legs look great. At least we can see those," he said, before looking back at Kelly. "Am I allowed to say that?"

"Of course. But only to Cassie," she admonished, smiling as he patted her scantily clad bottom.

"Of course."

They drifted off, locked at the lips, leaving Cassie and Bas to steadily empty a jug of "virgin's blood" and try to people-spot, although it was difficult with all the wigs, warts, and appendages in place.

"It's like a really, really ugly masked ball," Cassie said, trying to identify a bat in the corner.

"The problem with this outfit, of course," Bas grumbled after a while, "is that it makes bathroom trips long-winded." He sighed. "I may be awhile."

"Don't mind me," Cassie smiled, feeling sufficiently drunk to be left happily on her own.

She had just perched herself on the back of a sofa and was drinking in the power skyline when a slinky black cat, dressed in a skintight black leather jumpsuit, furry mittens and ears, with a feline mask over her eyes, "meowed" suddenly at Cassie as she passed, swiping a not-so-playful paw at her face.

Cassie jumped, startled, as the cat laughed. She didn't need to raise her mask to know it was Selena. Her body graced every billboard. It was one of the most recognizable in Manhattan and set off to staggering effect tonight.

Cassie went cold as the model looked her up and down and laughed. Of all the times to be dressed as a toad.

"So it is you. I did wonder," she purred, shaking her head at Cassie's vanity-free costume. "Well, I can see why he chose you," Selena said sarcastically, leaning in to her. Her breath smelled of whisky and cigarettes, and her pupils were dilated. "I can't *wait* to see the pictures."

"You were . . . sick," Cassie faltered. "I was just trying to help."

Selena lit a cigarette between cupped hands. "Oh really? And how exactly does you pushing me off the job constitute helping?" she sneered, blowing smoke in Cassie's face. "Bebe *needed* me in that campaign. She cried down the phone to me, begging me to do the job. She kept saying it was going to be the end for her, that I was the only one who could pull her out of this. I only did it because Lou was on board. And now *Bazaar* has just crowned me the Girl of the Year. Meanwhile, she's left with some mug shots of the girl who undermined her business in the first place. I don't really call that helping, do you?" Her eyes narrowed thoughtfully as she blew careless smoke rings. "In fact, aren't toads traditionally an omen of bad luck?"

A figure in a bedsheet with holes cut out for eyes and plastic chains rattling round its middle came over, making unconvincing ghostly noises.

"Whoooooo," he called, sounding more like an owl than a ghost, as he held his arms wide and swooped toward Selena. He straightened up suddenly and looked at Cassie. From the way his eyes were crinkling behind the cutouts, she could tell he was smiling. "Hi, I'm Lou."

Cassie gulped. "I'm . . . Toad," she managed, retracting her head further into the foam balaclava. Oh, please don't let him recognize me, please don't let him rec—

"Great costume . . . and great legs!" he said, winking at her before he swooped away after Selena, who had begun to sway off, swinging her tail hypnotically in one hand and moving sinuously to the music.

Cassie turned away, grateful for the narrow escape, and saw Bas chatting with a bat in the corner. She ran over—not inconspicuously in her toad costume. "Bas," she whispered, kissing him on the cheek. "I'm off. I'm sorry."

"What? But why?" She saw the conflict cross his face. Close up, the bat he was talking to was very good-looking.

"It's fine, you stay. But I have to go. Luke Laidlaw's here and I refuse to be in the same room as him." And she turned and fled.

She never, ever wanted to see that man again.

Chapter Thirteen

Cassie waved her yellow flag frantically as she saw them clip round the corner. It was almost impossible to spot them among the thousands of other runners, but a man running in a trash can kept clanging into them and it was Kelly's scowl she spotted first. They'd done eighteen miles and been running for two hours already, but she and Raoul had barely broken a sweat, save for an appealing rivulet that was trickling idly down the central groove of Kelly's stomach. Her ponytail—back-combed and tonged by Bas as a good-luck token before she'd set off—swished prettily from side to side, and Cassie felt a rush of love for her proud, ambitious, kind, and phenomenally fit friend.

Not that she was doing so badly herself. She was at least able to get around the reservoir every other morning now—it was still less than two miles, but hey! she'd come from a standing start—and she had to admit Kelly had been right about the kickboxing lessons, not just about what it would do for her thighs (she'd always quite liked her legs), but also what it would do for her arms, shoulders, and waist.

She was five back from the front of the crowd, and there were that many rows again behind her, but in her now customary stacked boots, she stood an inch above most other people, and she could see Kelly looking for her—they'd pre-arranged the spot—finally catching sight of the flag she was flapping about like a demented canary.

She elbowed Raoul and they both raised a hand in salute as they passed.

"Only eight more to go, Kell!" Cassie hollered. "You can do it!"

"Hey!! That's my new jacket!" Kelly shouted back, clock-ing the sumptuous cinched Burberry leather jacket that had only arrived from London the day before. It was sold out everywhere in New York, and Suzy had only managed to get her hands on one by pulling some strings with their market-ing director, whose wedding she'd organized.

Cassie put her thumb to her nose and waggled her fingers teasingly, knowing she was safe—for the time being at least. Kelly laughingly shook her fist as she was swept along in the bobbing current.

Cassie watched the backs of their heads for as long as she could, and then waved her flag and clapped for another cou-ple of minutes as scores of other runners, all with their own supporters, stories, and motivations, passed by. But what had been a vital, personal event just moments before now morphed into an anonymous heaving crowd that kept stand-ing on her toes and trying to push her back.

She let herself be squeezed out, people rushing to fill the gap like water, until eventually she was out and walk-ing slowly along the sidewalk, past the windows of all the closed-up shops. She felt the melancholy that was only ever one step behind her begin to quicken its pace, trying to catch up and hitch a ride on her shoulder. The day before, in contradiction to her divorce lawyer's advice, she had chosen *not* to contest the prenup, and Gil was in her every waking thought.

She took the path of least resistance and walked with the traffic, unaware of the admiring glances checking her out. She didn't see the effect on men of her legs encased in skinny indigo jeans, or the way her hair wafted silkily beneath the woolly hat, or the way other women coveted the on-trend "stolen" jacket. From her point of view, it had just been the warmest thing she'd been able to find, as the New York winter was really beginning to show its teeth—strong northerly winds had been prevailing for over a fortnight already. Pulling her hat further down over her ears, she stepped into a Starbucks to get a coffee and try to thaw her hands.

"Hi, I'll have a skinny, almond-milk, decaf double macchiato to go, please."

"That'll be four bucks."

She handed over five and shivered as the grinding of coffee beans competed with the hiss of foam being frothed.

"There's your change. You can collect it over there," the barista said. "Next!"

"Thanks," Cassie said, unzipping one of the jacket pockets and dropping the coins inside. She was surprised to feel something already in there, and pulled out a small folded envelope. She was even more surprised to find her name written on it, and underneath, in parentheses "(Sorry, this was supposed to go in with the seeds)".

Frowning, she opened it. A piece of paper with faint lines and torn tabs at the top, which had clearly been ripped from a notebook, was covered in penciled doodles and a collapsed scrawl:

- *Visit Ground Zero*
- *Host a dinner party at Kelly's apartment*
- *Read "A Christmas Carol" at the Public Library;*
  ask for Robin
- *Run the perimeter of Central Park*
- *Get to Paris, no matter what.*
                        Henry x

This was her list? She'd been expecting him to tell her to take tea at the Plaza and shop at Bloomingdale's. "Skinny decaf double macchiato!" a voice bellowed for the third time.

"Huh? Oh, that's me," Cassie said, tuning back in and jogging over. She picked the cup up gingerly and walked over to the condiments bar. She began to reread the note, intrigued by the out-of-left-field suggestions, as she idly stirred her coffee. Host a dinner party? In Kelly's kitchen? What was he—crazy?

Run around Central Park. Hmmm. Well, it wasn't beyond the realms of possibility. She wasn't doing badly, as it happened.

Read a book at the library—ho-hum. Visit Ground Zero. She looked up and out of the window, at the throngs shuffling past, all heading in the same direction—to Tavern on the Green in the park, where the marathon was ending. If the island were a ship, it would surely capsize today as all the city went to congregate in that one spot. Ground Zero, though . . . The race started downtown, on Staten Island, but crossed over to the other side of the East River. It would be deserted there today.

Folding the list and zipping it back up in her pocket, she strode out and caught the first bus going downtown. She swung into a seat and watched as the bus crossed the invisible boundaries, transporting her out of the deluxe Upper East Side and into Midtown, crossing to the West Side at Broadway and traveling south into chichi Chelsea, down to the West Village, boho SoHo, Tribeca, and finally into the financial center.

Henry was right. She had to see this. Her experiences here were so narrow, so confined to the glossy world of fashion and magazines and blowout brunches with Bas, that she'd seen scarcely anything else of the city. And when all this was over and she was settled . . . *somewhere* . . . how could she claim to have experienced New York if she hadn't seen and felt for herself its most vivid scar?

She got off at Broadway and walked along Liberty Street toward the viewing platform. Ground Zero.

So this was it, where history had happened. But as she approached, it wasn't the ground that caught her eye. It constantly struck her as a great irony that New Yorkers—patrons of the greatest skyline in the world—walked through their city with their eyes down, or, at best, raised to shoulder level. The buildings that so characterized them—branded them, even—weren't designed for looking up at; they were designed for looking down *from*. It was all about the view, scaling the great heights.

But here, at the bottom tip of the island, everyone walked with their eyes up as the sky blossomed like a flower, blooming through the new sixteen-acre gap amid the remaining towers that tried to scrape it. It was an irresistible pull to the eyes away from what was left on the ground to what once had been.

Still, she knew she had to look down eventually. To a certain extent, she already knew what she was going to see. She had seen pictures of the moonscape left in the wake of the attacks—the craters and dust and rubble—but there was no evidence of that now. What she saw instead—what her ears had already been telling her, even as she stared at the sky— was that it was now a building site. There were men in yellow vests and hard hats, megaphones and JCBs. Russet-steel girders and electric blue cranes were creeping along the city floor, stretching out and colonizing the space already, until soon the only place left to go would be back up again, alongside the other buildings.

Everywhere people around her were taking photographs. An Asian couple asked her to take their picture as they huddled together, holding hands in the wind and smiling brightly. It took her four attempts before she managed to hit the right button at the right time and not catch them blinking.

"You're better in front of the camera than behind it," a voice said behind her.

Cassie looked around. Luke Laidlaw was leaning against the wall, his camera, as ever, in his hand.

"What are you doing here?" Cassie asked accusingly.

"I live four blocks from here. I come here every day."

The Caribbean tan suggested otherwise, and Cassie scowled at him.

"I was due to have breakfast in Windows the day of the attacks," he said, offering an explanation even though she hadn't asked for one. "I was running late, and . . ." He sighed heavily. "Well, I've made it something of a personal project to document the rebuilding. I come here every day and take pictures of the onlookers, the workmen, the site. I always stand on the same spot for that—the one you're standing on," he said, smiling.

Cassie didn't take the cue to move, but she saw his eyes were glittering. "You seem amused."

"You look so different from last time we saw each other, that's all."

There was a heavy silence. "I don't want to talk about that," Cassie said, her cheeks beginning to flame at the memory of what he'd said to her in Southampton, the things she'd done. She began to walk away.

"But why not? You looked so cute. I'm just sorry I didn't recognize you."

Cassie stopped dead. *"Cute?"*

"At the Halloween party. I didn't mean to be rude. I just didn't recognize you. Selena told me afterward, but you'd gone."

She gave a peremptory laugh. "Rudeness is the least of your worries when it comes to what I think about you." She started walking away again.

"Oh? What does that mean?" he asked, hurrying along after her.

"You'd better take your shot, Luke. You wouldn't want to miss a day."

"I've already taken it, actually. Broke one of my cardinal rules and took a step back so that I could get you in it."

Cassie shook her head but carried on walking.

"So tell me—what is it you think I am, if not rude?" he persisted.

"You mean, not *just* rude."

"Okay, not just rude."

"I think you're sleazy."

"Sleazy?"

"Yes."

"What makes you say that?"

Cassie shot him an evil look. "You know why. Those things you said to me."

"What? That you're beautiful?"

She shook her head. "I'm not talking about it."

He walked alongside her, matching her stride. "Well, I'm not going till you do. I don't see what was so terrible. I had a great time."

"Oh, I bet you did! Telling me to imagine I was having *sex*. I mean—what the hell? Who do you think you are, going around talking to women like that?"

"Every photographer says that," he shrugged. "It's the professionals' equivalent of 'say cheese.' It brings something into the girl's eyes when there's a little flirtation. It just gives a bit of edge."

He pulled her by the elbow so that she swung back to face him. He looked down at her, the flecks of his stubble glinting like metal shavings in the sun. "But it obviously put *you* on edge. I'm sorry."

Cassie crossed her arms. "You knew I'd be more nervous trapped in there on my own with you."

"You weren't trapped. It's not like I locked the door and pocketed the key. And I knew you'd be more flustered with everyone staring at you."

"And then plying me with champagne."

"One glass. To make you relax. Was that such a crime? I'd seen less uptight cardboard."

"*Tch*, you think you're sooo witty!" Cassie cried, throwing her hands up in the air, circling away from him on her heel.

"Come on, let's have lunch and make up."

"What!"

"Let's eat. I want to take you out."

"I want to take you out too . . . with an AK-47."

Luke burst out laughing. "You're so funny." He leaned in a little closer. "Look, I can help, you know."

"Help what?"

"Put things right for you. I know things still aren't going well for Kelly. You need someone with a little influence. I've got contacts—a call here, a dinner there." He straightened up. "Come on. It's only lunch."

"That's only blackmail."

"It's only lunch. And then I'll show you the pictures."

He took her to a "great little burger joint" three blocks away. He had suggested Japanese at first, but one look at Cassie's face had been enough to tell him the girl needed something bloody—and not just his head on a plate. Now she was sitting in his apartment, on a black suede sofa, watching as he unzipped various leather portfolios, looking for the one that contained images of her.

She looked around apprehensively as he chatted away. Why had she agreed to come? She didn't give a damn about what the photos looked like.

"I knew the second I saw you at the show that you had the look. I just couldn't believe no one else saw it." He turned around and smiled. "This campaign is going to be a sensation."

"That's not how Selena sees it. She thinks it's all a joke."

"Selena," he said, pausing a moment. "She's a beautiful girl."

"Mmm, you do tend to become one of the most famous models in the world for that reason."

He sat on his heels and shook his head. "But she's using

far too much. She wasn't right for this job. Bebe wanted innocence. Purity. No one too knowing. I mean, didn't she say the entire collection was based around a—"

"Dagestani teenage bride on the run—I know! My God, if I have to say that sentence *one* more time in my life . . ."

Luke laughed, resuming his search through the files. "Bebe wanted her because she's the money shot—that's natural. There's a security that comes from using the big girls. You can't blame her. But right now, with everything hanging in the balance . . ."

His voice faded out. It didn't need to be said that everything hung in the balance because of her.

He found what he was looking for and stood up. "All I'm saying," he said, indicating for her to join him at a light-box table across the room, "is that *this* is when she needs to push the boundaries. This industry runs on a sheep mentality—one person leads, everyone else follows—and the only way to bring them back is with something new. You might have messed up for her, but you've put it right with this, trust me." He patted the portfolio.

"I did it for Kelly, not Bebe," Cassie said curtly. "And certainly not for you."

He stared at her, locking her eyes with his, and she immediately regretted being so combative. His full attention disconcerted her. He was still a fiendishly attractive man, even if she did hate him.

He didn't bite back, but began scanning her face as though mathematically breaking it down into equations. No one had ever looked at her like that—really *looked* at her.

He unzipped the case and pulled out the prints. "I've been working on these a lot in the darkroom. I went back to film with you. The light up there that afternoon was so hazy and diffuse. I didn't want it to sharpen up or flatten. I just loved the way it warmed your skin . . ."

He fanned them out on the table.

Cassie stared down at herself. The sunlight blazed back at her, scorching her, warming her, lifting her out of the day's blue November light into a sun-drenched summer's evening.

"I can't believe they were only taken last month," she murmured, forgetting to be hostile.

"I know. Who'd believe it, right? I've been picking up the yellow and orange notes. I wanted it to feel really . . . ripe. To catch that moment when a girl blossoms into a woman. You've still got that, somehow."

Cassie picked through the prints slowly, gazing at the red silk dress with the twisted strap falling off her shoulder, her hair seemingly swept over by a lover's hand, the setting sun their only witness in the darkening room.

"I can't believe it's me," she whispered.

"I can." His voice was low. He brought his hand up to her hair, twisting it off her shoulder to echo the picture, and she felt his finger run down the groove at the nape of her neck. "Look at your eyes—you can see the hesitancy, the caution, like you want to let go but can't. That's what I saw in you. It's what Selena's lost." He placed a finger on her cheek and turned her to face him. "I'm not the bad guy, Cassie. I just know the right girl when I see her."

The way he was speaking to her so intimately was just like it had been that day when she'd stood embarrassed and awkward, wondering what to do or how to pose—when he'd started to follow her around the room like a lover, giving slow chase as he trapped her in corners and straddled her on the floor, the camera stripping her back, revealing her to him as his eyes never left her, and he had made her feel beautiful, desirable—all the things Gil had taken away from her. He had kept telling her how much he wanted to touch her as he leaned over her—into her—for the shot, and she had begun to want it too, but his hand had only smoothed her hair or fiddled with a strap or lifted her chin just a fraction. It was a game to him, but he had turned her on. And when, in that one moment, he had seen it through the lens and had dropped the camera down . . . she had fled.

His desire had scared her then and it scared her now. He was too much for her. Too good-looking, too experienced. She was used to men talking to her about poor pheasant drives and peat burning, not the curve of her cheekbone or the flecks in her eyes.

But she couldn't look away from him. Where would she run to this time?

She was staying, and they both knew it.

Cassie felt his finger hook around the belt loop of her jeans and he pulled her closer to him so that their bodies were just inches apart. She held her breath, too terrified to move, as his hands slid down her arms and locked around her wrists. Slowly, he pulled them wide, pushing her back so that she was lying beneath him and against the light box—but he didn't kiss her. Letting go of her wrist, he ran one hand flat down her body—firm, sure—between her breasts, down her stomach, and before she had time to react, to protest, he unbuttoned her jeans, sliding his fingers inside them, inside her.

Cassie cried out at his slow, silky touch. She had never been touched like this before—expertly, unselfishly—and she saw the lust in his own eyes grow as she writhed on his hand, his fingers quickly finding the spot that made her gasp with pleasure, rendering her helpless to his stroke. She was completely at his mercy as he began to move his fingers more quickly, more firmly, pushing his hand against her, forcing her to his rhythm, until he took her over the limits of her own threshold and she arched against him, lost and found all at once, pulsing, crying, won.

Chapter Fourteen

There was a long, loud gasp. "Noooooo!"

Cassie giggled. "I'm afraid so!"

"Turn around. I want to see the back."

Another gasp.

"Stand up! Let me see what you're wearing."

Cassie stood up. She was in her new favorite outfit—chocolate velvet MiH jeans, knee-high shearling-lined boots, and a chocolate-and-camel-striped slouchy boyfriend sweater.

"You're so thin!!" Suzy said accusingly, as though she'd been betrayed.

"Yuh, what can I tell you? Little and often—what a joke. I'm like the Hungry Caterpillar these days, foraging for food where I can. I've become a secret opportunist eater. If it's sitting on a desk, it's mine."

She sat back down and smiled shyly at the screen. Suzy was staring back, utterly gobsmacked.

"I can't believe the change. You look like an entirely different person. I swear to God I'd have walked right past you in the street—well, I might have stopped to give you a good slap. No one should look that good. You're like a bloody poster girl for divorce, Cassie! Archie will go into a flat spin if he sees you looking like that. He'll think you're giving me ideas!"

She heard Archie offstage, calling through the flat. "What's that? My ears are burning."

His head popped around the doorway and he looked at the screen from behind Suzy, who was huddled up on the sofa, a tub of popcorn by her knees. "Who're you talking to? Hey! Is that . . . Cass?" His familiar, jovial face came into focus—the ruddy cheeks and curly red hair as comforting to her as a childhood bear. "Bloody hell! Get a load of you!"

Cassie giggled, but not curled over with one hand covering her mouth like she always used to. She had her legs double crossed, one foot snaking behind the other leg, and the opposite arm sliding down it like a bow on strings. Suzy sat up, squinted, and leaned in closer to the screen. "There's something else, though," she murmured. "What else have you had done?"

Cassie looked down at herself—shiny, painted, shaped nails, cuticles pushed firmly back; swingy, glossy hair, perfectly blow-dried; designer wardrobe bought at cost at sample sales. "I think that's probably it, isn't it?"

"No. There's something else. It's . . ."

"My makeup?"

Suzy shook her head.

"It's something about . . . your energy or something. You're moving differently. When you turned just now, it wasn't how you usually move . . . There was a bit of a . . . wiggle in your hips," she said, trying to work it out. "Holy cow! You've got a man!!"

Cassie blushed bright red and went straight back to her schoolgirl self. "Suzy!" she cried, mortified to have her shout it out in front of Archie.

Suzy clapped excitedly, delighted with herself for having discovered the secret without being told. She grabbed a huge handful of popcorn. "Tell me *everything!*"

"Absolutely not," Cassie said, her eyes flicking over to Archie, who looked just as fascinated as Suze.

"Oh, bloody hell—bog off, Arch!" Suzy said, whacking her husband on the shoulder to shoo him away. "She's never going to dish the dirt with you hanging around like some old pervert. Go and stack the dishwasher. God forbid you or Henry should ever help around here."

Archie leaned in as close to the screen as he could, planting a big smacker on it. "I'm pleased for you, girl. You have some fun," he beamed. "Don't worry, I won't eavesdrop—I'll hear all about it from Suze later."

Cassie burst out laughing as Suzy hit him over the head with a cushion and a brief pillow fight ensued, which Suzy, of course, won.

"Right," Suzy gasped finally, a feather in her hair, as Archie trotted out of the room. "Where were we? Oh yes!" She leaned forward till she was practically going to topple off the sofa. "So—are you bonking yet?"

Cassie covered her eyes with her hands, peering at Suzy through her fingers. Suzy's hand—full of popcorn—was poised in midair. Clearly, this moment was too big to munch through.

"Yes," she whispered, her eyes star-bright. "Last night."

Suzy dropped the popcorn. "Oh. My. God!"

They stared at each other over the Atlantic. They both knew what a big deal it was for her. Gil was the only man she'd ever been with.

Suzy started munching double-time. "Was it good?"

"*Mind*-blowing. Every time."

Suzy gasped. "How many times?"

Cassie giggled. "Four."

"I hate you!" Suzy cried, throwing a piece of popcorn at the screen. "Where were you?"

"At his."

"Did you stay the night?"

"Yes."

"And how was it this morning?"

Cassie sighed. "Lovely. He went out and got me breakfast, and today's issue of *WWD*."

"*Women's Wear Daily!*" Suzy almost choked on her popcorn. "Oh well, then that's definitely love!" she quipped.

Cassie stuck her tongue out at her.

"When are you seeing him again?"

"Wednesday. He's flying to Costa Rica this afternoon."

"Costa Rica? What is he—a coffee salesman?"

"He's a fashion photographer," Cassie admonished, giggling.

That brought Suzy up short. "Oooooh, Cass," she said, sucking on her teeth. "Photographers are . . ." She shook her head.

"What?"

"Well, they . . . you know, they're . . ."

"What?"

"Well, they're surrounded by beautiful women in hardly any clothes most of the time. They don't make the most reliable boyfriends."

"That's such a cliché," Cassie said, pooh-poohing her. "Anyway, it's not like I'm looking to marry the guy or anything. It's only a bit of fun."

"I just don't want you to get hurt, that's all."

"Well, I think we're all a bit too late on that score, Suze."
She sighed heavily and tried to smile, but Suzy carried on
saying nothing, not even eating, which was even more dis-
concerting. "Look, Gil hurt me more badly than I've ever
been hurt in my life, okay? That's the bad news. The good
news is that no one *could* hurt me again as much as he did, so
I reckon this is a win-win situation for me now."

Suzy smiled—somewhat sadly—through the screen. "I
guess that's one way of looking at it."

"Don't worry about me! I'm a big girl!" she said, as Archie sauntered back into the room. He had stripped down
and was wearing just a pair of pink and green mini-gingham
checked boxers. "Bloody hell!" Cassie whispered. "When did
Archie start hitting the gym?"

Suzy turned around. "Oi! Arch! I told y— Oh, Henry!
It's you."

"Who'd you think it was? The postman?" His voice
sounded faint at the back of the room. He was rummaging
in the bookshelf. "Here, have you gone off with my Kings of
Leon CD?"

"What? No! Listen, clear out. I'm trying to have a conversation here."

"Huh? Who're you talking to?" Cassie heard his voice
coming closer as his body came into crystal-clear definition.

"I'm Skyping. Can't you go hog the bathroom or something?"

"Well, I can't be rude, can I? . . . Who's that?" Henry leaned
over the back of the sofa, his eyes twinkling. "Cass!"

Cassie smiled shyly, feeling rather foolish to be "beamed"
to him through a computer screen.

"Hi, Henry." She held up a feeble hand.

"You were right," Suzy said, looking up at him. "Hot!"

Henry smiled without taking his eyes off her. "Yeah," he nodded.

"She's got a new man," Suzy said slyly.

"Suze! You're supposed to be discreet!" Cassie tutted, rolling her eyes and blushing again.

"What?" Henry frowned, looking shocked. "Well, who is he? Is he . . ."

"Credentials checked?" Cassie teased. "God, you're all so overprotective! Don't worry, I don't intend to get pregnant or engaged."

"Has anyone else met this bloke yet? Does Kelly know him?"

"Yes, she knows him. It's all fine."

"But . . ."

"Honestly, it's *fine,*" Cassie insisted, laughing. "And I'm very happy. Isn't that the main thing?"

Henry stared at her and she wondered whether he was even aware that he was talking to her in just his underpants. His skin had a deep golden tan.

"Your bruise has gone, I see," she said, nodding toward his chest.

"Oh . . . yes. Just the broken rib to heal now and getting over my phobia of running in open spaces and I'll be fine."

Cassie chortled. "Are you going out somewhere?"

"Just to the pub with some friends."

"Will Lacey be there?" Suzy asked, happily munching again.

"Yes. Along with others." He looked back at Cassie. "How about you? You seeing your new fella tonight then?"

"He's in Costa Rica till Wednesday," Suzy replied for her.

"Costa Rica! What's he do? Sell coffee?" Henry quipped.

"Already done that one," Suzy crowed, with a satisfied grin. "He's a *photographer*." The tone of her voice suggested it was a controversial career choice. More so than Arctic exploring, for example.

Cassie held up a stern finger. "Just don't."

He sighed and stared at her, seemingly feeling no need to fill the silence with chatter.

"Well," he said finally. "I'd better go. It's eight o' clock over here."

"I'm aware of that," Cassie grinned.

"They'll all be waiting for me."

"Sure."

"It's good to see you."

"And you."

Cassie noticed Suzy's head moving back and forth between them like a tennis match.

"See you soon."

"Yeah."

He straightened up and began to walk away.

"Blimey! And they say women can talk!" Suzy said, collapsing back into the cushions.

"Oh! I forgot to ask—" Henry said, bounding back into view.

"Oh, for pity's sake, man!" Suzy cried. "What's wrong with you?"

"Did Kelly give you my list? I put it in the pocket of that jacket."

"Yes, thanks. I found it," Cassie laughed. "You've got a good sense of humor. A dinner party in Kelly's kitchen, huh?"

"You've got to do it."

"Yeah, yeah."

"Yeah, yeah yourself. And the Central Park run—you realize it means you've got to do it in one go, right? Not over the course of a week."

He laughed and strode off, leaving Cassie shaking her head at the screen.

"Brothers," she muttered. "I'm glad I don't have one!"

Chapter Fifteen

Cassie blinked sleepily, unperturbed by the clicking sound that was now her alarm clock. It had become something of a ritual in the past few weeks. Every morning, Luke took a picture of her in the few moments before and during waking, and even though she was always convinced she'd been snoring or was dribbling, his images proved otherwise—her cheeks were maiden-pink with sleep, her hair tousled, lips parted like she was blowing a kiss. It had been odd at first—intrusive, even. But he liked shooting her in black-and-white, printing them up in the softest tones of gray, without any artificial light, just the sun slanting in, bouncing down from the opposite tower blocks like a periscope. She'd grown used to it.

"Rise and shine, Beauty," he whispered, planting a small kiss on the end of her nose.

Cassie groaned and rolled onto her back, her arms thrown above her head. Luke knelt above her, still clicking away.

"Stop, enough already," she mumbled, hiding her face with an arm.

"Never. Never enough," he smiled, looking at her through the lens. She moved her arm away and looked back at him.

"I'm supposed to be your lover, not your new project," she

said, pronouncing *lover* ironically. She couldn't bring herself to say it in earnestness, and Kelly had fully briefed her that she wasn't allowed to say *girlfriend*. You only became that when you stopped dating other people and became "exclusive," like her and Brett, but that was a conversation she and Luke hadn't had—and weren't likely to either, if Kelly had been right about his reputation.

She had no intention of sleeping with anyone else while she was with Luke, although Kelly still insisted on dragging her out for token clubbing at Mischka every now and then, even though neither of their hearts was in it and they only stayed for one drink. But she had decided to assume that Luke was still seeing other people anyway—that way she couldn't be disappointed when she did eventually find him with another woman. After all, it was obvious that was how it would end between them. Until then, she was taking a what-she-didn't-know-couldn't-hurt-her approach, because this wasn't about love. She wasn't looking for another husband. She was just looking to feel better, and sex with Luke was making her feel better than she'd ever felt in her life. It made her wonder what she and Gil had been doing all those years, fumbling awkwardly, whispering politely in the dark.

Out of all the girls, Anouk had been the only one who was delighted by the news. "I always say that the best way to get over one man is to get beneath another," she'd trilled in all seriousness. Suzy and Kelly had been a lot more reticent, especially when Kelly had discovered exactly *which* fashion photographer it was she was involved with—she'd thought any chance of seduction between them had evaporated when Cassie had stormed out of the attic room, red-faced and flustered, two hours after she'd entered it. But whatever had made Cassie leave him then, she clearly couldn't walk away from him now. She just kept telling them all that she was involved with him with her eyes wide open, and reiterated to Kelly his assurances that the relationship with Alexa had finished a good month before they got together.

"You're both," said Luke, leaning forward and kissing her softly on the mouth. "I can't survive you being one without the other. I can't get enough of you."

Cassie bit his lower lip gently. "Well, you're going to have to," she said with a smile, moving as though to get out of bed. "I'm meeting Bas for brunch."

"What? But I thought we had the day together. I've only just got back. I haven't seen you for four days," he protested, grabbing her by the wrists.

"And whose fault is that?"

"Bonnie's," he grumbled.

"Yours, actually. You shouldn't be so good."

He stared at her for a moment, watching the way her pupils dilated as he kept her pinned to the bed. "Actually, I'm very, very bad," he said, before diving under the duvet and proving his point.

An hour later, her hair was still unbrushed and her cheeks still flushed, albeit not from sleep anymore.

"You're late," Bas moaned as she skipped toward the wooden bench he was sitting on outside the café. "And even across the street I could see *why*." He stood up. "Look at you. You might as well have a sign on your head saying JUST GOT LAID."

"You make me sound like a free-range egg," Cassie said, squeezing his arm and planting a smacker on his cheek. "Besides, you can't possibly tell that just by looking at me."

"You've got bed hair and stubble rash all over you." They opened the door and nabbed their usual favorite table—"and I think I'm probably on the money when I say *all* over you—am I not?"

Cassie grinned back. She blushed less these days. Being with Luke the past few weeks had helped her shed many inhibitions, and along with them her customary flushes.

"I couldn't possibly comment," she said, pretending to read the menu, even though they both knew she was holding it upside down—and knew it off by heart. "I ought to have the egg-white omelet," she mused.

"Yes, you ought. I'll play Mother in Miss Kelly's absence."

"Mmmm. But you see, what I *really* fancy is a bacon sandwich," she said, peering over the top of the menu. "Will you rat on me?"

Bas held her gaze for a moment before sighing dramatically and looking away. "I can get an alibi for where I am this morning."

Cassie chuckled and they placed their orders with the waitress.

She looked around as she shrugged off her Puffa—Kelly had long since stolen back the leather jacket and was safeguarding it by keeping it on at all times. This little café, Tea and Sympathy, had become "their place" when they met up, just she and Bas. It had been set up by an Englishwoman who'd despaired of ever being able to get a "proper" cup of tea in a city powered on coffee. Cassie loved it because it meant she got to indulge her PG Tips habit, and satisfy (on the sly) her cravings for Heinz baked beans, proper Cumberland sausages smothered in HP sauce, and her beloved crispy bacon. She didn't come here with anyone else—certainly not Kelly, not Luke—and Bas, after much suspicion and interrogation about the exact provenance of what he was eating, had slowly acquired a taste for black pudding, for which she loved him.

"So you're still happy, huh?" Bas asked.

"Still happy."

"Huh." He nodded. "It's sickening." Poor Bas was in deep pining for a foreign Ph.D. chemistry student called Stefano who was engaged to a timid brunette—and Tom Ford, of course.

Cassie covered his hand affectionately with hers. "I was thinking."

"Easy . . ."

"We should throw a dinner party."

"Say what?"

"We should," she said, laughing. "You and me."

"Why?"

"Because it would be a lovely and loving thing to do. It shows our friends how much we care. And I do have to keep doing things that reassure Kelly I'm actually her friend and not her nemesis."

"Things still not great?"

She shrugged. "Limping along. Luke's doing what he can to turn the tide, but it's going to take time." She looked up and paused as the waitress set down a giant china teapot. "Anyway, isn't Thanksgiving coming up? Isn't that quite a big deal over here?"

"Quite a big . . ." Bas looked around the café. "Honey, you are lucky this place is filled with limeys. You'd be lynched for saying that anywhere else. It's like burning the Stars and Stripes."

Cassie rolled her eyes at his dramatics. "So what do you think?"

"I think it's a dreadful idea. Why do you think we always eat out or order in? No New Yorker can cook."

"But I'm an excellent cook. It's my favorite thing. I did it all the time back in Scotland."

"Well, you cook, then. What shall I do? Style their hair on the way in?"

Cassie laughed. "You can choose the wines. That always used to be Gil's job. He used to disappear down to the cellars and come back with some dusty bottle and cobwebs in his hair. I don't have a clue."

Bas speared some black pudding onto his fork. No matter how much he ate, he always remained spike-thin. "And who's on your guest list?"

"Well, we'll keep it small: you, me, Kelly, Brett—and Luke if he wants to come. He might be away."

"Ooh, look at you playing it so cool."

"Not playing it any way, Bas." She slurped her tea. "It's just the way it is."

"Okay, lady," he said, sighing heavily. "You get your way. You can hold it at my place."

There was a tiny pause. "Actually," Cassie said, biting her lip, "we kind of have to hold it at Kelly's."

"Kelly's? What are you—insane? You know she keeps her knickers in the kitchen, right?"

"It's an order."

"An order?"

"Well, maybe not an *order*. But it's on the list. It has to be at Kelly's."

Bas peered at her, instantly alert. "List? What list? I've not heard of any list."

"The one Henry wrote up for me."

"Henry?" Bas asked, palms outstretched. "And who—pray

tell—is he? And why am I only hearing about him now?"
He gasped suddenly and leaned forward. "Is he the reason
you're playing it so cool with Coody?"

"Don't call him that!" Cassie said, annoyed. She poured
more tea.

"Sorry," he soothed. "But who's *Henry*?"

"Henry's no one, an old family friend. He's just Suzy's little brother. He's an explorer, you know."

Bas shook his head. "No. I didn't know. I didn't know
there was any such thing these days."

"Me neither. But there you go." She blew gentle ripples on
the surface of her tea. "Anyway, he always draws up a list
of things to do every time he goes somewhere new, to try to
get the essence of the place, you know?"

Bas nodded, taking in her earnest expression.

"So he did one for me, and it says I've got to throw a dinner party—from Kelly's kitchen."

"*Tch.* He's obviously never stood in it." Bas shook his head.
"What else did this list say?"

"Ummm, go to the public library . . . run round Central
Park . . ." She and Bas pulled faces at each other. "I know. Visit
Ground Zero—which I've done. That's where it all kicked off
for me and Luke," she said, a dreamy smile coming over her
face as she remembered the way he'd chased after her that
morning, clicking away as she'd run nude across the apartment to the bathroom.

"That's it?"

"Pretty much," Cassie shrugged. "The last one just said I
had to get to Paris no matter what."

Bas threw his hands up in the air in disgust. "Hate him! I
totally hate him!"

"You'd love him. If you ever met him, you'd *love* him,"

Cassie insisted from behind her tea cup. "He looks phenomenal in his boxers!"

Bas's jaw dropped. "And how do *you* know that?"

"It's not like that, Bas. I just told you—he's Suzy's little brother. He's practically *my* little brother. No!"

Bas looked at her from beneath raised eyebrows. "You're the one who brought up the sight of him in his boxers."

"*Tch.*"

"There's no point in getting all huffy on me." He drank his own tea. "Anyway, you do realize Thanksgiving is all about the turkey? I hope you're good with turkey?"

"Actually, I was thinking of going one better than that," Cassie said, arching one eyebrow. "I figure if I'm going to actually do this, then I might as well go the whole banana. I'm going to do Thanksgiving *my* way."

Chapter Sixteen

"Tell me you're kidding," Bas gasped, looking pale for once as he scanned the deflated birds laid out in descending order on the tiny, yard-long worktop. The turkey's left leg and wing were dangling precariously over the side.

Cassie shook her head, hands on hips.

"And where are we supposed to work, given that the birds are completely filling up the kitchen?"

"Well, we'll have a whole lot more room in a minute," Cassie said, opening the small fridge she'd bought and that was sitting out in the hall area. "And look, I've already made the stuffing. Smell that." She held a bowl up to Bas's face, but he recoiled as if he were expecting her to hit him with it.

"Isn't it gorgeous? Minced pork, goose fat, herbs, mace, chopped apple, and cranberry. Mmmmm."

Bas looked skeptical. He couldn't stop looking at the birds. "And you're seriously telling me you're going to be able to get all those birds into each other, like babushka dolls?"

"Mm-hmm." Her sleeves were rolled up to her elbows, her hair pinned up in rollers. It was three in the afternoon, and Kelly, Brett, and Luke had been told that Bill wouldn't be granting them entry before eight o'clock. "I've already deboned them, look." She stepped on the pedal of the garbage can and Bas looked down, bracing himself.

"Ewww!" he said, jumping back. "It's like archaeological dig meets slasher movie."

"You can't be feeble about it," Cassie said, walking over to the smallest bird and beginning to fill it with the stuffing so that it regained its shape again. "This is where I need your help."

"I thought you said I was just doing the wine."

"Yes, I might have lied about that," Cassie said, reaching for the pheasant. "Now, come and hold this in position for me while I stitch."

Bas moved toward her slowly. "You have checked no one's vegetarian, right?"

Cassie gave him a sidelong grin as the doorbell rang.

"Who's that?" Bas asked. "Not loverboy, I hope. You said there would be no conjugal visits today."

"It's Cupid." She looked up, mischief all over her face. "You'd better get that, Bas. Things have stepped up somewhat since we spoke last."

"What does that mean?" he asked warily.

"Answer the door and I'll tell you."

Luke arrived bang on the hour, a half case of Château Margaux in his arms that was even more expensive than the camera swinging from his shoulder. He was wearing a black sports jacket and gray cable-knit rollneck that Cassie vowed to pinch next time she stayed over.

"I've missed you," he murmured in her ear, his hands shimmying up her body as Bas deplored the colored tumblers—which looked like they'd been pinched from a kindergarten—that he was going to have to decant the Margaux into.

Bas had done a fine job of decorating the rest of the apartment as Cassie got on with preparing the vegetables and dessert. An absolutely enormous display of pink roses, vanilla chrysanthemums, and night-scented stocks was positioned on the coffee table, and he had lit tiny Moorish tealights along the shelves so that the room flickered with milky light. Nat King Cole crooned softly from the iPod docking station, Cassie's baby lawn had been moved to center stage away from the cold windows (her nod to the dinner's countryside theme), and Bas had even polished the silver frames that housed Kelly's favorite photographs—Kelly on Southampton beach aged eighteen months, with her father planting a bucket on her head; her parents on their wedding day in Nantucket; her little twin sisters blowing out the candles on their sixth birthday cake; Suzy and Archie running out of church together in tails and taffeta, hands held, confetti flying; and, of course, the picture they all had a copy of—Kelly, Cassie, Suzy, and Anouk lying on a bed together in striped pajamas with braced teeth and plump cheeks, crying with laughter at the camera—their first night at boarding school together. It had been one of the few things Cassie had had the presence of mind to pack as she left Gil.

Kelly and Brett rocked up just as they were moving on to the second bottle, Kelly looking a vision in a black silk blouse and heavily embroidered matador trousers. Cassie was wearing boots and a plum-colored dress with a turtleneck, long sleeves, and a cutaway back that Luke just couldn't keep his hand from, tracing secret messages like "Let's go to bed" with his fingers.

"I can't believe you're actually cooking in my kitchen," Kelly said, coming to join her after a while. "It's like I've entered a parallel universe." She peered inside the oven, somewhat amused to find the light on inside and the Thanksgiving feast just about ready. "Where did you put my sweaters?"

"In your room."

"It'll be awhile before I can put them back in here, I guess. How long do turkey smells linger, do you think?"

"Long enough to permeate cashmere. Besides, it's not just turkey in there. There's goose, chicken, pheasant, and pigeon as well. You *don't* want to smell of pigeon."

Kelly stared at her, astonished. "You've got all that going on in my little oven?" She bent over again and stared in at the browning birds. "Will it cope?"

"Will I, you mean? Honestly, when I get my hands on Henry . . ." She took another glug of the wine. "He's got a perverse sense of humor. I had to soak the potatoes in the bath, the carrots in the sink, and the parsnips in the . . . you know."

There was a horrified silence.

"Not the . . . !" Kelly gasped.

"No!" Cassie chuckled. "They went in with the carrots—just—but I was seriously eyeing up the fish tank, I tell you. There was nowhere else to go."

"Well, you didn't have to make it quite so hard on yourself, doing a *five-bird* roast. I mean, what's wrong with a pasta bake?"

Cassie rolled her eyes. "Even students would look down on that, Kell. Besides, this was my speciality back—" She stopped herself from saying "home." "Back in Scotland. I rustled these babies up every week in the shooting season. I had to. Cook couldn't be trusted. On one shoot we cut into it and found a miniature bottle of Gordon's in the woodcock." She paused for a moment, treasuring the memory of Gil's face.

"Can I do anything to"—Kelly looked around the destroyed kitchen, immaculate in her black shirt and trousers—"help?"

Cassie wrinkled her nose at the polite but insincere offer. "Just ask Bas to take the flowers off the table now. I'm going to serve up. We're going to be kneeling, I'm afraid—that an option in those trousers?"

"Kneeling at a dinner party? Henry didn't have that in mind."

"Knowing Henry, he probably did."

Everyone whooped with delight as Cassie carried the bird to the coffee table, her arms trembling slightly with the strain. It weighed nigh on thirty pounds, and with all the trimmings as well, it was all she could do not to thump it down like a weight.

Luke jumped up to help her, positioning it safely in the middle of the table and taking the opportunity to "kiss the chef," which elicited more whoops of delight.

"Who's carving?" he asked, fork and knife in his hands as Cassie brought through the hot plates.

"I will," Brett said, sharpening the knife against the fork with a flourish, the blades flashing. He was casually dressed in navy chinos, a blue Oxford shirt, and orange Ralph Lauren V-neck, and Cassie noticed how Kelly's eyes followed him everywhere. When they sat, it was with legs touching. When they talked, it was with eyes locked. When they laughed, it was together. Her friend was a goner.

Within minutes, the plates were heaped with food and the scented candles completely overwhelmed by the aroma of gravy and peppery red wine. Brett stood up to say grace, and as Cassie closed her eyes, his voice faded away and she was back in the dining room at Lammermuir, the dusty deer staring down from the walls, huge bunches of heather picked from the moors arranged at the windows, an aromatic peat fire in the ancient fireplace throwing out ferocious heat and making the cut crystal twinkle in its glow. And Gil, his mellifluous voice soft against the harsh laughter and boorish shouts of the shoot dinner as he told an elegant joke—or maybe a filthy one, just told elegantly . . .

"You okay?" She felt a warm hand on her back.

She opened her eyes. Everyone was looking at her. Luke was scanning her face.

"Sorry—what?"

Kelly glanced at Bas, concerned. "Brett just raised a toast to you and Bas for putting this together. It's absolutely wonderful, Cass—thank you."

Everyone raised their glasses. "Hear, hear."

"Although," Kelly said, looking from her plate to everyone else's, "why have I got the smallest bird? Is it the woodcock?"

"Pigeon."

"Why have I got the entire pigeon and everyone else has got the medley?"

Brett winked at her. "Because it's got the tenderest flesh. Carver's prerogative. Why else do you think I offered?"

Kelly tipped her head to the side, touched, and everyone tucked in. Nat King Cole had segued into Ella Fitzgerald, and were it not for the fact that they were eating their roast sitting cross-legged on sofa cushions on the floor, they could have been anywhere but the center of Manhattan. The room glittered like a jewel with the tealights, and the conversation bubbled and hummed along with the clatter of cutlery and bursts of laughter.

"Oh!" Kelly said after a while. "I thought this was boned."

"What's wrong? Hit gold?" Bas asked, drinking his wine. His lips had stained to the color of port, and in the gathering dark, his eyes beamed out against his tan. He looked drunk but happy, and for once didn't look like he was thinking about Stefano.

"Wouldn't that be nice," Kelly said, trying to extract the bone with her fork. "That would solve a few problems."

"Maybe it's the wishbone," Luke said, looking at Cassie. "She could make a wish, right?"

Cassie frowned. "Does a pigeon have a wishbone? Do you know, I'm not sure." A small light suddenly shone in her eye, making her wince. She moved away as the light bounced around the table, darting from one person to the next, like Tinkerbell on day-release from the bell jar.

The gasp that followed drew all eyes to Kelly. A diamond solitaire was dangling on the prongs of her fork, and Brett, thanks to the shortcomings of the apartment's dining facilities, was already, conveniently, on his knees.

"I know it's only been a couple of months," he began.

"Ten weeks last Thursday . . ." Kelly murmured. "But I'm not . . . , you know, counting."

Brett shook his head at her. "Well, it's been the longest ten weeks of my life, wondering how long I had to hold out before enough time had passed for me to acceptably do this. But I just can't wait another day, Kelly. I knew the moment I saw you shielding Cassie like some . . . bodyguard. I just knew you were the one."

His voice wobbled, and he coughed to try and regain some composure. Then he took the ring off the fork, quickly dunking it in his water glass. "Thank God it's platinum," he murmured. "God knows what temperatures it got up to in the middle of five birds." Everyone chuckled, as he polished it with his napkin.

He looked at Kelly again and everyone else was forgotten.

"Kelly Emma Hartford . . . will you make me the happiest man alive and agree to be my wife?"

There was a deafening silence—Bas had grabbed the remote as soon as she'd started fishing for the wishbone—as Kelly beamed back at him, the answer never in doubt.

"There's only one thing to say to that," Kelly whispered, a smile on her lips and a tremor in her voice. "What's taken you so long?"

"Is that a yes?" he croaked.

Kelly wrapped her arms around him. "Just try and stop me."

Cassie and Bas yelled with joy, jumping around the apartment, arms around each other as the two lovers kissed until they came up for air and were mobbed as well. And in the background, Luke's camera whirred and click-click-clicked, capturing the happiest Thanksgiving day ever for posterity.

"You realize those will be the best engagement photos of all time," Cassie slurred happily, her arm locked through his. They were walking back to his apartment downtown—a formidable walk, but Cassie was craving some fresh air after a day spent cooped up in the kitchenette.

"I know," Luke smiled. "I'll give them the set as an engagement present."

"The girls will go nuts. Nooks because it'll mean a fabulous new dress; Suzy will just be panicking because it's so soon."

"Yeah, but she hasn't seen them together. She'd be fine if she did. They're clearly meant for each other."

Cassie nudged him in the ribs. "Who knew *you* were such a romantic," she teased. "Don't tell me you believe in destiny."

Luke looked down at her. "Of course I do. Doesn't everybody?"

Cassie stared at the yellow taxicabs moving stop-start down Park Avenue. It was two in the morning but as busy as if it had been twelve hours earlier, truly earning the name of the city that never slept. The only people in bed were the under-tens. Everyone was in party spirit.

"No," she shrugged. "I don't."

Luke stopped walking. "You don't believe that there's someone out there who's destined to be with you—and you alone?"

Cassie shook her head. "Nope." She sighed, trying to smile. "Not anymore."

"So what do you believe in, then?"

"I don't believe in anything—fate, destiny, serendipity. Call it what you will. It's all just sentimentality for justifying the choices we make and choose to live with."

"I never had you down as cynical."

"I'm not saying I don't believe in love. I just don't believe that there's only one person we're supposed to live our lives with. I mean, I think we can love various people in our lives— it just comes down to timing and circumstance when you decide to finally quit the search and say, 'Okay, I'll stop with you. You can be The One for me.'"

"Wow," Luke said softly after a moment, stroking her cheek with his hand. "I bet you didn't think that three months ago."

Cassie looked away. She hated seeing the pity in his eyes. "Well of course not. You don't stay in a marriage for ten years if you don't fully believe that your life belongs with that person." She gave a derisive laugh. "Although obviously Gil managed it." She breathed out slowly.

After a moment she looked back up at him, her poise recovered. "But look at me now. I'm living in New York, working in the *fashion* industry, for God's sake, enjoying a delicious affair with a renowned and highly disreputable photographer. I didn't see *that* coming three months ago either." She stood on tiptoe and kissed him. "I am living proof that there's no such thing as destiny."

Luke, drawn though he was by her kiss, pulled away.

"And what if this—your life out here, with me—*this* is your destiny? What if you made a mistake marrying Gil? Maybe I've been waiting all these years for his secret to come out so that you would be propelled over here and into *my* arms. What about looking at it that way, huh?"

Cassie laughed. "It's a nice thought," she said, giggling. "But I don't think so. You can hardly wait for the bath to run." She tickled him and he laughed with her.

"I'll tell you one thing I definitely can't wait for," he said suddenly, shooting out his arm to hail a passing cab. "I can't wait to get you back to bed." And he grabbed her hand, pulling her into a run, determined not to lose another second.

Chapter Seventeen

The doorbell buzzed insistently. Both Cassie and Luke wriggled further beneath the duvet rather than face the insolent morning that was trying to wake them so early, like a toddler wanting a 5:00 A.M. breakfast.

It buzzed again.

"Urgh, what time is it?" Cassie moaned, her slender arm reaching out from under the goosedown and patting the bedside table for the clock. They'd been up—down, all around—till four, and, having both booked the day as a holiday, had no plans to stir before noon. She was vaguely aware of using Luke's torso as her pillow.

Eight-forty-two A.M.

"Tell me this is a dream. A really, really bad dream . . ." His voice faded back into sleep.

The buzzer again.

"Oh, for God's sake!" she muttered, sitting up crossly and throwing the duvet back so that they were both uncovered.

Luke shielded his face from the sudden brightness of the overcast November morning, but made no other attempts to move. "Ignore it. They'll go."

Again.

"That's it!" she said through gritted teeth, focusing enough to see the door and make her way over to it.

"Who the *fuck* is it?" she shouted angrily. Working for Bebe had taught her a few choice words.

"You *swear* now?" came back the startled voice.

There was a stunned pause on both ends of the speaker system.

"Suzy?"

"Not just . . . ," purred another voice.

"Nooks!"

"So are you gonna buzz us up or what? Because I could kill for a coffee and it's bloody freezing out here."

Cassie pushed the entry button in a daze. Luke was sitting up in bed, his hair one entire matted mess, woken at last by Cassie's flabbergasted tone.

"It's the girls! They're here!" she said in a panic, looking at the state of the two of them. Both nude, hungover, and reeking of sex. Quickly she sprinted across the floor and pulled on the first clothes she came to—his blue boxers and the gray cashmere sweater she'd so coveted the night before. Suzy was right. It was a cold morning. She was just pulling on his socks when the heavy steel door swung open and she found herself staring at her two supposed-to-be-far-flung best friends.

"What are you doing here?" she screeched, skittering over to them, slipping on the floor slightly.

"You buzzed us in, remember?" Suzy smiled, hugging her hard. Anouk, in a gray rabbit-fur jacket, was especially cuddly.

"I mean, what are you doing in New York?" she said, laughing.

"Sweetie, do you not know what today is?"

"A write-off? It was Thanksgiving last night."

"Precisely. And today is Black Friday, the biggest shopping day of the year," Anouk said, pulling off her fawn leather gloves.

"We're on official Christmas business," Suzy beamed. "That's what I told Archie, anyway!"

Cassie stared at them both in shocked delight, still scarcely able to believe that she was awake after so little sleep, much less chatting in person with Suze and Nooks.

"I just can't believe it!" she kept repeating.

"And are you going to introduce us?" Anouk asked, motioning toward the equally dazed, naked man sitting up in bed, watching the reunion.

"Oh God, yes, this is Luke, my boyfriend." She clapped a hand over her mouth. "Sorry, honey," she said quickly. "I mean he's my—"

"I'm her boyfriend." Luke smiled.

"I'm Suzy," Suzy said, waving from afar. "I'd shake your hand, but you're . . . naked. Husband probably wouldn't approve of that."

"Probably not."

"I don't care if you don't," Anouk said, walking forward and offering her teeny hand. "Anouk Montparneil."

"Luke Laidlaw." He looked at Cassie. "I don't suppose you could pass me a bathrobe?" he asked, grinning boyishly. "I'm feeling rather . . . vulnerable."

Cassie threw him the navy waffle robe from the bathroom door.

"I'll go take a shower, let you girls get reacquainted," he said, happy to escape.

The girls watched him in silence as he disappeared into the bathroom.

"Oh my God, he's gorgeous!" Suzy stage-whispered, eyes wide, as the door shut.

"Very sexy," Anouk drawled. "Your taste in men has improved immeasurably. As has the way you dress," she said approvingly, looking at Cassie's borrowed getup. "I like it."

Cassie looked down sheepishly. "Yuh, well, we were—you know, sleeping."

Suzy chuckled and started walking around the huge open-plan loft. Steel beams ran across the ceilings, the stripped wood floors were dusty and unvarnished, exposed brick walls were hung with galleries of black-and-white prints—some Luke's, others by Herb Ritts, Bruce Weber, Man Ray, and Annie Leibovitz. The kitchen was just a stainless steel preparation counter and a jumble of plain white cups and crockery stacked on industrial shelves. A very expensive Italian coffee machine took pride of place on the polished concrete worktop.

"Ah, just what I was looking for," Suzy said, walking up to it and looking at it from all directions. She looked back at Cassie. "Any idea how to work this thing?"

Cassie smiled. "Sure. You too, Nooks?"

"*Bien sûr.*"

Cassie made them all coffee—it had taken a week of living in the loft almost full-time before she'd mastered the damn thing—and they collapsed on the black suede sofa, the arm of which Anouk instantly began stroking like a pet.

"So how did you find me here?"

"Kelly gave us Luke's address when we told her of our plans. She said you were here almost all the time now."

Cassie smiled shyly. "Yeah, things are going well, so . . ." She felt rather embarrassed to be so evidently happy, so soon after everything that had happened with Gil.

"We're all really pleased for you," Anouk said, guessing her state of mind. "It is *absolument* the best thing for you right now. Some fun. Some flattery to rebuild your confidence."

Cassie nodded. Fun. That was all it was.

Then she remembered what had happened last night. "Uh . . . when did you speak to Kelly last?"

Anouk and Suzy looked at each other. "Two days ago? Something like that."

Cassie nodded. "And is she . . . going to join us today?"

"Yup. Brunch at Sant Ambroeus at eleven. You know where that is?"

"Sure, coffee shop on Madison." Good. She wouldn't have to keep the secret for long.

"Look at you—knowing your way around Manhattan and living in a trendy loft with a sexy photographer," Suzy said. "Dare I say it, you could pass for an urban animal."

"Who, me?" Cassie laughed. "Nah. I'll always be a square, the nerdy one."

Anouk shook her head. "Not from where I'm sitting." She lowered her eyelids. "Paris is going to *love* you, *chérie*."

"Shhh," Cassie said, looking behind her to make sure the bathroom door was still shut. "You're not allowed to mention Paris in front of the boys. They get upset."

"*Boys?*"

"Bas too. It's the big unmentionable."

They nodded in unison, both wondering how she was going to move on to their cities when she was so clearly setting up a new life in this one.

"Well, come along. Let's get going. We can't sit around here all morning," Anouk said briskly, clapping her hands. "There's shopping to be done."

"Will Luke be okay about us kidnapping you?" Suzy asked as she shrugged her coat back on.

Cassie looked toward the shut bathroom door. Tendrils of steam were escaping beneath it.

"Oh, he'll be fine. I'll leave him a note," she said, getting up and hunting for her discarded dress on the floor. "He's a big boy."

Ten minutes later, the cab stopped outside the telltale red awning.

"Hang on a second," Cassie protested as the cab stopped. "You said we were meeting Kelly at Sant Ambroeus. What are we doing at the apartment?"

"Well, we are going to be having brunch with Kell there, but there's something we all have to do first," Suzy replied.

Anouk raised an eyebrow. "When she says *we*, what she means is *you*."

"Huh?"

"Come on. Upstairs," Suzy commanded. "All will be revealed in a moment."

Chapter Eighteen

"You're telling me you've flown all the way from London and Paris to watch me do this?"

"Hell, yeah." Suzy laughed, looking down at Cassie from her camera phone. "I have to record you doing this. I promised."

"This is not funny."

"It really is," Anouk said as one of the horses nudged Cassie, just about knocking her over. Her balance hadn't fully recovered yet.

"Do you have any idea how hungover I am?" she said, eyeing the horse warily. "We got through half a case last night."

"Yeah, but there were five of you, lightweight," Suzy riposted.

"Well, Brett doesn't count. He's teetotal." Cassie sighed and watched Fifth Avenue disappear out of sight. She was going to have to run that, then over the top, back down the other side, and along the bottom. Six-point-three miles in total. She wasn't ready. She wasn't anywhere near ready. She'd been shirking her training for the past few weeks, her sessions between the sheets with Luke providing more than enough exercise.

"Anyway, Henry never said anything about there being a

time limit on when I had to do this, just so long as it was be-fore I left." She turned to face them all, hands planted crossly on her hips. "And who said I *had* to do everything on the list, anyway? They were just supposed to be suggestions, ideas, you know? Not a flipping diktat."

"The sooner you start, the sooner we can all get some brunch," Kelly called, keeping her hands firmly hidden below the blanket and not just because of the cold. She'd greeted them at the apartment with her coat and gloves already on. Her news could wait a little longer.

"*Tch*, bloody bossy, the bloody lot of you," Cassie moaned, breaking into a prolonged stumble that gradually became recognizable as a jog.

The girls cheered from the comfort of the horse-drawn car-riage as Cassie ran ahead, her ponytail bouncing from side to side, her legs stronger than she'd given them credit for.

Kelly gave a commentary along the way. "... See the Plaza over there? That's where Brett took me for our first date ... And here's where the marathon ended, it was like being homecoming queen. I managed to run a PB of three hours eleven ... That street cart there sells the best burgers in Manhattan ... and over by that trash can, that's where Cassie mugged Henry ..."

"I did not mug Henry," Cassie called back. "I can hear you, you know!"

Kelly winked at them. "She totally mugged him."

The coffee shop was heaving by the time they got over there. Most of the stores had been open since six that morning—a few had even opened their doors at midnight—and the crowds made the marathon's supporters look straggly by comparison. All the windows had been dressed for this offi-

cial start to the festive season, and—overnight—heavily gar-
landed Christmas trees had appeared inside every doorway,
and tinsel and baubles across every ceiling.

Cassie had run a good time—one hour four—and after a
hot shower and quick change back home was eagerly antici-
pating the coffee and Danishes that she would flagrantly eat
in front of Kelly. After all, those gloves couldn't stay on forever. As soon as they came off, she'd get the pastries in. No
one would be paying any attention to her by then.

Sure enough, Kelly had only got one glove off when
Suzy caught the glint. As someone who spent all her days
around brides, she had an automatic scanning ability with
rings—usually because they gave her a good indication of the
wedding budget—and this was no exception.

She gave a gasp, holding Kelly's hand up for closer scrutiny a split second before crushing Kelly in an exuberant hug.
"I knew it! I knew he was the one for you."

"He's the one for me too with that ring," Anouk said drily
before blowing Kelly a delicate kiss across the table. "How
could you bear not to say anything before now?" she scolded.
"We've been together for nearly two hours."

"Well, I've been ready to burst, I have to say," Kelly said,
smiling. "But it was important to get Cassie's *challenge*"—she
pronounced it in French—"out of the way first. And don't
think I haven't noticed you ODing on carbs over there, Cass."

Cass stopped chewing. "I've got the munchies," she protested, her mouth as full as a hamster's.

"So, how did he propose?" Suzy asked, desperate for all
the details. One of the things she loved most about her job
was hearing the engagement stories—the things people did
for love. Archie had been particularly inventive, having arranged for *"Will you marry me, Suzy?"* to be written in shells

at the bottom of the Indian Ocean before they went on a scuba dive together. It had nearly ended in tragedy, of course, when he couldn't find the exact spot, and they'd used up almost all their air circling over the same thirty-yard patch—forcing Suzy into an underwater tantrum—but it had come right in the end. It always did.

Kelly relayed how Brett had asked for Cassie's advice on the ring, and she'd come up with the idea of hiding it inside the five-bird roast, while Anouk, who had fished a loupe out of her bag, inspected the ring with a professional eye.

"Mmmmm. He has good taste, your boy," she said when Kelly had stopped telling and Suzy had stopped cooing, both with tears in their eyes and their hands over their hearts. Cassie was still eating. "Cushion cut, four point . . . three carats, I would say; D color, no?"

Kelly sighed in amazement. "I will never know how you can tell all that just by looking at it," she said, staring at her hand again, like Cinderella waiting for the clock to strike twelve and everything to return to how it had been before.

"It's my job," said Anouk. "And I have some diamonds back in Paris that would make beautiful earrings to go with it. I shall let him know when I meet him, no?"

"Lose no time," Kelly beamed.

"And when shall we meet him?" Suzy asked. "We've already met Cassie's man. And by the way, you never said he was *all that*, Kell. No wonder she couldn't keep away from him." She patted Cassie's hand.

"You'll meet him tonight. He's working today, but I've made reservations for us all to go to dinner at Landseer's and then on to Mischka. Bas too. You've got to meet everyone."

"I can't wait. Honestly, you all sound like a proper little family out here," Suzy said. She turned to look at Cassie with something almost approaching concern. "It's going to be difficult for you to leave, isn't it?"

"Oh, well . . . I mean, I haven't really . . . well, I'm trying not to think about it too much," she blustered, taken by surprise. It was true, it was going to be hard. She was putting down roots—something she hadn't expected to happen here—and every time she tried to imagine saying good-bye to Kelly and Bas and Luke, her brain just froze and wouldn't go there. She could no sooner imagine starting up all over again in Paris than she could being on an expedition to the North Pole.

"But look around you—you have a career here," Anouk said.

"A very shaky one," Cassie snorted, shooting an anxious glance at Kelly.

"And a new relationship. Plus Kelly and Bas are here." Anouk shrugged. "It is a lot to give up again."

"You sound like you don't want me to come and stay with you," Cassie protested, laughing feebly.

"Not at all," Anouk replied. "If I have my way, you'll settle in Paris for good. But you seem happy here. I just wonder how many times you can rebuild your life from scratch?"

There was a long silence as Cassie took in her words. Anouk was right—the ingredients for a full life were falling in place, and her happiness with Luke was beginning to spill out of the neat little box she'd created for "them" in her life.

"Well, me staying here isn't on Henry's list, for one thing," she said, reverting to jokiness. "It says I have to get to Paris no matter what."

"That thing? That's just a fatuous list of dares. God almighty, don't listen to Henry!" Suzy cried, almost falling off the chair. "Honestly, why would you put any store by what he says?"

"Excuse me! You've just flown across the Atlantic to referee me doing something on that list. You're the ones putting store by it. And anyway, Henry's seen a lot of the world." She shrugged. "I trust his judgment."

"His ju—!" Suzy spluttered on her coffee. "Sweetie, you have *clearly* forgotten what he did to our clothes that time we went for the midnight swim in my parents' lake when they threw their twentieth wedding anniversary party. That boy's not to be trusted, ever."

Anouk, Kelly, and Cassie burst into sudden laughter at the memory—tiptoeing past the terrace, teeth chattering, modesty protected only by the cushion pads on the steamer chairs.

"God, you're absolutely right," Cassie giggled, slapping her forehead in despair. "I don't know what I was thinking."

"He's the devil in disguise," Anouk drawled.

They all tinkled with laughter at the shared memory.

"How is he, anyway?"

Suzy took a bite of her peach Danish. "Well, hmmm . . . things haven't been so great for him, since you ask. He's been a bit stressed recently."

Kelly frowned. "Anything to do with the expedition? Can I help at all?" She seemed to have forgotten that she was no longer running the Breitling account.

"Oh no, I'm sure he's fine, just a bit too much going on, you know. I think it's just a combination of the trip *and* the wedding. He's got to get everything sorted before he leaves in April, and we all know organization's not his strong point."

"I take it you're sorting the wedding for them?" Kelly asked.

"Supposedly. But Lacey seems to want to do most of it.

Henry's organizing the honeymoon and Anouk's doing the rings."

"Are you?" Cassie asked.

"Of course. I'm using pink gold," she said. "Twenty-two carats. Gorgeously pure."

"Wow, so he's really keeping it all in 'the family,' then," Cassie muttered. With Kelly behind the financing for his trip, she wondered how she could contribute in some way, but, as ever, she seemed to have nothing to offer.

Chapter Nineteen

Winter had the city in its grip, and Christmas Eve sailed in on storm clouds. The blazing, fluttering magnificence of fall—which tinted the city in every hue of gold, amber, caramel, and ochre—had blown away with the north winds, and all that was left was naked structure and fleshless bones. The trees were stripped back to hardy bark, the littering leaves that danced down the avenues were at their most friable, the sky was an ominous dove-gray and swollen with unspilled snow.

Cassie and Luke jogged up the vast, wide steps to the library holding hands, darting past the famous lions and through the thick wide marble pillars, eager to find refuge again from the ice in the air.

"Why *do* we have to do this?" Luke asked as they swept in and the humming warmth of the library enveloped them like a blanket.

Cassie smiled and put a hand on his arm. "Because it's on the list."

"I don't get what's so important about this list."

"It's an adventure, showing me how to get under the covers of the city. You know, feel its pulse. And anyway, it's thanks to that list that you and I are together. You should show it more gratitude," she said, kissing him into submission.

"Fine." He rubbed his hands together. "At least it's warm in here."

"Thank God." She fished around in her pocket and took out the list, which was now as close to collapse as the leaves on the ground. "Right. It says I've got to ask for Robin and read *A Christmas Carol*." She looked at him and pulled a face. "I don't think he means the whole thing."

"I hope not! I've got to finish my Christmas shopping. Couldn't you have done this another day?" Luke asked, walking forward and staring up at the lofty gilt-decorated ceiling.

"Absolutely not! My father always read it to me on Christmas Eve. It's tradition."

Cassie looked around at the imposing landmark. The library was fast approaching its centenary, and she could practically feel the weight of history contained within it. The air in here felt different somehow, thicker, and sound seemed to travel differently—amplifying the shuffle of pages being turned, the vibration of murmured conversations, the muffled *thwump!* of books hitting tables.

"Come on, let's ask at one of the desks." She started walking, still staring up at the ceiling. It had frescoes that made you think you were looking through to the sky. "My God, this place is so huge." The Reading Room looked as long as a city block, with rows upon rows of tables running down it. "We could spend the day in here."

"Not likely," Luke said, coming up and patting her bottom.

They walked over to one of the wooden arches that swooped down to the librarians' desks. A bald man in his midforties was standing there, working at a screen.

"Hi," Cassie smiled. "I'm looking for Robin." She hoped that would be enough information. Henry hadn't supplied his surname.

The librarian stared at her, mildly surprised by the request. "And you are . . . ?"

"Uh, well, my name's Cassie, but he doesn't know me."

"Robin is the chief archivist of Rare Books, ma'am. He's very busy. Perhaps I can help you?"

"Well . . . it says specifically to ask for Robin," she hesitated. "My list, you see."

She held it up feebly, aware that it looked more like a shopping list than a ticket to the heart of New York. "Maybe if you tell him Henry Sallyford sent me. They must know each other." She shrugged hopefully.

The man hesitated a second, his breathing impatient, then picked up a phone. "Robin, it's Doug. I've got a lady here asking to see you. Says she was sent by . . ." He cupped the receiver and raised an enquiring eyebrow.

"Henry Sallyford," Cassie whispered.

"A Henry Sallyford. Uh-huh . . . uh-huh . . . Okay."

He replaced the receiver and looked back up, his eyes sweeping the length of her curiously. "He's coming up."

"Oh, right, thanks," Cassie said gratefully, shoving her hands into her pockets and turning away from his scrutiny.

They stood waiting for a few minutes, watching as people came and went, alternately bracing themselves for, and shaking off, the cold.

"Hi, Cassie."

She turned around. A tall, lanky man, thirtyish, was smiling down at her, his hair in a long bob. "I'm Robin."

"Hi. Nice to meet you." She shook his hand. "This is my friend Luke."

She saw Luke throw a glance at her. Except for that one time when she'd slipped up in front of the girls, she absolutely refused to call him her boyfriend.

"Thanks so much for coming to meet us," she smiled, suddenly feeling a bit embarrassed to be interrupting someone's work day for a *list*. "Uh, so this is probably going to sound completely mad, but my friend Henry Sallyford told me to come here and ask for you . . ."

"Sure. He told me you'd be coming."

"He did?"

"He did," he smiled. "Follow me."

They walked back to the desk where she'd spoken to the librarian, and Robin began writing something on a slip of paper. "Thanks, Doug," he said, handing it to his colleague.

Doug glanced at the slip and then tilted his head as though double-checking the request.

"If you wouldn't mind . . .", Robin added. He led them to a door and punched in a code, opening it onto a staircase. "I hope you're wearing suitable shoes," he said, glancing at her boots. Thankfully, she'd switched into Uggs now that the pavements were getting icy. "It's a bit of a walk."

"Oh, trust me, my fitness has improved no end since I've been here—thanks to Henry," she chuckled.

"He's had you on goose chases all over the city, has he?" Robin asked, leading them down one flight of stairs after another.

"You could say that."

They walked farther and farther down before arriving in an enormous room.

"My God, where are we?" Cassie gasped.

"We're in the storage extension, under Bryant Park now."

"I can't believe I haven't got my camera," Luke muttered

as they walked past row upon row upon row of dark, narrow alleys all lined with books. "I mean, when do I ever come out without it?"

"I'm afraid it wouldn't have been possible anyway," Robin said. "The stacks are closed to the public, and many of the books here have to be stored in special conditions. Light from camera exposures can degrade them quite badly."

"How many books are there?" Cassie wondered aloud. It was so different down here, cramped beneath the building, compared with the vaulted, expansive space of the majestic Reading Room. Trolleys stacked with books stood motionless in some of the aisles, and a poster of the library rules, dating back to 1921, was still taped to one of the walls.

"In total? About five million."

"Wow. Don't say they all have to be dusted?" she joked.

"Well, it's not in my job description."

They carried on walking. There were literally miles of shelving stacked around them, and every row looked the same as all the others. She wondered how he could find his way around them all so effortlessly.

"So how do you know Henry, Robin?" she asked, letting her fingers trail lightly over the spines of some of the books. Luke was a few steps behind.

"Oh, we've overlapped many times. He finds and we collect, so we often bump into each other," he said. "Many of his private clients are also our benefactors, and I often see him at Christie's."

He came to a stop by a nondescript stack. "Right, it should be . . . yes . . . there it is."

They walked toward a small desk positioned halfway down one of the rows. A shaded lamp was already switched on and a maroon leather-bound book was placed on it. Several pairs of white cotton gloves were on the table.

"Here, you'll need to wear these," Robin said, handing them each a pair.

"Why?" Cassie asked as she pulled on hers.

"This is a first-edition copy of the book. It's one hundred and sixty-seven years old. Charles Dickens himself used to read from this at public readings."

"He didn't!" Cassie gasped, staring down at the antique pages.

"He did. This is an extremely rare privilege. Only a very few people have had access to this book."

"And Henry's one of them?" Cassie sounded incredulous.

"Well, like I say—he's an old friend. And he helped us purchase some of Charles Darwin's unpublished field notes from the Galapagos. I'm more than happy to extend him this favor."

"Crikey," Cassie whispered.

"Here, take a seat," Robin said, motioning to the chair.

She sat down carefully. "Oh, I *love* that smell," she said, inhaling the musty old scent from the book. "I love nothing more than going into antiquarian bookshops and just smelling the pages."

"Yes. I know what you mean."

"Modern books just don't smell the same, do they?" she asked. "It must be the paper quality or printing process, or something."

"Both. But it's also what we call VOCs—volatile organic compounds. It's actually the smell of the paper degrading."

"Oh no," she said, looking down at the old book.

"Don't worry. This book's kept in perfectly controlled conditions." He smiled. "You can read some of it if you like."

"I can?"

"Sure. Just tell me when to turn the pages for you."

She looked back down, but she didn't need to read it to know what it said.

"Marley was dead to begin with. There was no doubt whatever about that," she intoned, her eyes closed, her father's voice resonating in her head. He had always read her a chapter a night up to Christmas Eve when she returned to Hong Kong from school, and she could still hear where he made his stresses. It *was* Christmas to her. "Best first line of a book in my opinion," she said, looking over at Luke. "Have you ever read it?"

He shook his head and she looked back down, disappointed. She read the first chapter, resisting the urge to race through it, even though she sensed that she was keeping him waiting.

But soon enough, she was done.

"Thank you so much, Robin," she said finally, sitting back. "I can't tell you what a thrill it's been to see this. To think that Dickens himself read *this* book." She placed her gloved hands lightly on the pages, as though communing with the words. "Just wait till I tell my mother."

She looked up at Luke, who was leaning against a pillar. "Can you believe we're one of the handful of people in the entire city who've had access to this?"

Luke nodded tersely. "It sure is a heck of a list," he said reluctantly.

She stood up. "It sure is." She extended a hand to Robin. "Thanks so much for your time, Robin. I'm sure you've got a lot more to be getting on with besides chaperoning a Brit abroad."

He shook his head, laughing. "Not at all. It's always intriguing to get caught up in Henry's adventures." He smiled, shaking her hand, then Luke's. "And before I forget, he told me to give you this."

He handed over a small square white envelope. Inside was a charity Christmas card with a robin on the front. She opened it and read the message.

"Oh my," she murmured, looking up at Luke.

"What now?" he asked, dread hanging off his words like cobwebs.

She handed it over to him.

> *That was your Christmas Past.*
> *For Christmas Present, go to Tiffany's on Fifth.*
> *The ultimate New York experience.*
> *Love, Henry x*

"Do you think he's got me a present?" she asked excitedly.

"No," Luke said flatly.

She deflated like a burst tire. "Oh. But why not?"

"You said he was just a friend."

"He is."

"I don't buy my friends presents from Tiffany's, Cass," he said pointedly.

"You don't buy your girlfriends presents from Tiffany's either," she teased. "But you can rectify it while we're there, if you like." She laughed, pulling his arm into hers.

"I'm not happy with this," he said in a low voice. Jealousy bounced off him like sparks.

"He's just an old friend, *and* he's engaged," she reassured him for the umpteenth time as she checked her watch. "You should see his fiancée. In fact, you've probably photographed her." And she shook Robin's hand again and bounded back through the stacks, hell-bent on getting to Fifth Avenue before the store closed for Christmas.

There was only half an hour till closing time once they got there, but it was as busy as if it were the first day of the sales. Every counter was crammed, mainly with men in heavy cashmere overcoats and pensive expressions making costly last-minute purchases in the hope that the "wow factor" of the distinctive blue box would compensate for any lack of originality on their part.

"What now?" Luke asked, stopping just inside the doors. He had settled into a belligerent sulk, thoroughly put out that he and his girlfriend were making their first pilgrimage here under another man's instructions—even if he was only a *friend*.

"I'm not sure," Cassie said reverently, taking in the scene. Everything was exactly as she'd seen it in films—the cherry-wood cabinets and glass counters gleaming under the lights, a mammoth Christmas tree at the back of the store with boxes artfully scattered all around. It did utterly epitomize the megawatt glamour of New York society. "I guess we . . . mingle. Become part of it all."

Luke shot her a puzzled look, but she just shrugged. As a native, he didn't see it the way she did. It was just a store, about to close for the holidays. But to her—for whom Christmas shopping had meant new Arans from the farmer's wife—it was the embodiment of all her city fantasies. Behind her, a choir from Harlem was singing carols beneath the massive Baccarat crystal UNICEF snowflake. In front, staff were circulating, offering flutes of champagne and chocolate truffles to customers as they browsed. Cassie felt as steeped in traditional Christmas cheer as a pear in port.

Luke shrugged and wandered off, preferring to shop on his own, and Cassie made a point of not watching him. She'd only been joking about his buying her a gift here—after all, he must surely have bought her present by now. But then, if he was anything like the dozens of men here, leaving it till the last minute . . .

She began walking slowly around the store, peering into the cabinets she could get close to. An assistant offered her a glass of champagne while she browsed, and she accepted as happily as if she'd been among friends. She admired highly polished silver bone cuffs by Elsa Peretti, jewel-bright cabochon rings by Paloma Picasso, diamonds sold by the yard, gold mesh collars that draped like velvet, and of course the famous engagement rings that glittered like the royal jewels in the center of the store.

Steadily, as the clock ticked toward closing time, the crowds began to thin out, and Cassie looked around for Luke. She saw him examining a ribbon-patterned cheese plate, which she hoped to goodness he was buying for his mother.

She accepted another glass of champagne and ambled slowly toward the giant Christmas tree to wait for him and listen to the carols. The choir really was excellent. She was determined to vacuum up every last atom of Christmas in New York.

She looked up at the tree, just about the only thing in the store she hadn't scrutinized. It was tall and plush with needles, with empty boxes of every size piled around the foot, adorned with sumptuous white satin bows that blossomed atop the lids. It was like stepping into a fantasy, and she wished she were wearing a cocktail dress and chignon, rather than jeans and a—

She blinked and looked more closely, blinking again for good measure. But her eyes weren't deceiving her—for there, beneath the tree, in beautiful trademarked blue, was an enormous box with a card dangling from the ribbon, and on it her name.

She bent over and stared at it more closely. It couldn't be! And yet it was. Her name.

Cassie Fraser.

She looked around furtively—probably sending security into overdrive—and went to pick it up.

Instantly, a man was at her side. He didn't say anything or make a scene—his hands were behind his back, his chin up, eyes ahead—but it was clear she wasn't going anywhere with that package.

"It is not permitted to touch the display, madam," he said quietly.

"I'm so sorry," Cassie said apologetically, her voice almost a whisper. "But it just took me by surprise." She pointed to the label. "You see, that's my name. That's *me!*"

The man didn't look at it. He just kept his eyes on the shop floor. "You're Cassie Fraser?"

"I am!" she confirmed in a hurried whisper, feeling like a spy.

"Are you able to produce some identification to corroborate that, madam?"

"Yes, of course," she replied, rummaging in her bag for her wallet. She pulled out her credit cards and driver's license. "See?"

The man finally looked at her. His eyes flicked down toward the name on the cards and a smile crept onto his face. "We thought you weren't going to make it in time," he said. "We've had someone on watch for you all day."

"You have?" Cassie was amazed. Tiffany's had been waiting for *her*?

"Oh yes. The gentleman was insistent that you must not pass unnoticed. You gave us all quite a scare. I was not looking forward to having to call him and tell him you'd slipped through our fingers." He gave a sigh of relief and beamed at her. "Let me put that in a bag for you."

He picked up the box and led her over toward the counter in the middle of the store. A massive chandelier bathed her in its glow as she watched him pull out another extravagant length of ribbon and begin double-wrapping the box with flamboyant flourishes so that it shimmered silkily within its satin trusses. He slid it into the biggest bag they must surely produce and handed it to Cassie.

"Thank you for spending Christmas at Tiffany's," he said, smiling.

Cassie gasped, scarcely able to believe that he was actually going to give her the bag, just as Luke walked over, a more modest-sized bag in his hand. His eyes popped at the sight of Cassie's parcel.

"Don't tell me he got you *that*!" he exclaimed jealously.

"It was under the tree!" she trilled, as though that made it doubly exciting, and not just the fact that it was absolutely huge and from Tiffany's.

"You said he was engaged!" he protested, furious. "It doesn't look like his mind's on his fiancée this Christmas."

"Oh Luke, you have nothing to worry about," she beamed, squeezing his arm excitedly. "You haven't seen his fiancée. *I'd* marry her." She turned to the sales assistant. "Thank you *so* much for all your help."

"A pleasure, madam," he said, amused by her excitement. "And Merry Christmas."

"Merry Christmas to you." Cassie beamed happily. The man smiled as he watched her go, the bag swinging in her hand, boyfriend sulking by her side.

She couldn't wait till the next day to open it. Not a chance. The moment they got back to the loft and she placed it excitedly beneath the tree, she started pacing around it like a mental patient. It was so big! But so light! And so blue! Who could resist the blue? What could it be?

"You know, we always opened one present on Christmas Eve when I was growing up," she lied, sidling over to Luke as he mixed them each a martini.

"That's a Scandinavian tradition," he replied, eyes narrowed to slits, even though he was just as curious as she was to discover what was inside the giant box.

"Is it?" she blinked, all wide-eyed innocence.

"Yes."

"Well, we've always admired . . . Scandinavia."

"Really?" he drawled. "All the way from Hong Kong?"

"Oh, yeeessss. We just . . . love Ikea! And Daddy always drove Volvos!" she sputtered, delighted with her logic.

"So open mine then," he said.

Her face fell as he called her bluff.

"Oh fine! Fine! Open it then! You're only going to drive us both mad if you don't."

Cassie clapped her hands together excitedly and gave a little shriek, running over to get it from the tree.

They sat together on the sofa as she gently tugged at the ribbons. They fell away easily and she lifted the lid off the box. She peered in.

Luke watched her face, keeping his impassive.

"So? What is it? A baby hippo? A forklift truck?"

"It's . . ." She reached her arms in . . . "another box," she whispered, lifting out a smaller—but still pretty big—box.

Luke's eyebrows shot up in surprise—or perhaps relief, Cassie thought. Again, Cassie pulled at the ribbons, her small white teeth biting down on her lower lip as she lifted the lid again.

More silence.

"And?" Luke asked. He looked as if he wanted to rip the damn boxes open himself.

She looked up at him. "Another box."

A small smile of satisfaction began to spread across Luke's face as box after box revealed an ever smaller box within. "Maybe he's just giving you boxes for Christmas," he quipped.

Finally Cassie lifted out what must be the last small box. It sat in the palm of her hand, and both knew this was it. The boxes—and there must have been twelve of them—couldn't shrink in size any further.

Cassie opened it slowly and a sudden spasm of fear crossed Luke's face. The box was ring-sized.

"Oh!" Cassie gasped. "It's a necklace!"

Relief flooded Luke's face and he gave a generous beaming smile at the news. "Let me see."

She turned the box toward him. A silver padlock, like the kind you saw on young girls' charm bracelets, was strung upon a delicate chain. "Oh," he said, nodding vaguely. "Nice."

"It's gorgeous," she said, lifting it out. "Here, will you fasten it for me?"

She lifted her hair and he clasped the necklace around her

neck. The padlock felt weighty upon the chain, and she went to hold it in her hand, but it fell.

"Oh!" she exclaimed, shifting position to see where it had fallen. She found it and tried reattaching it to the chain, but although the arm closed, it wouldn't lock into position. She took it off again and studied the mechanism. There was a keyhole, like a real padlock. "Is there a key in the box?" she asked.

Luke checked. "No. Why?"

"Huh. I just can't get this to lock properly. It looks like there should be a key with it."

Luke checked again but there was no key. "Nothing doing," he shrugged, taking the padlock from her and studying it himself.

"*Tch*, that's a shame," she sighed. "I guess I'll have to go back in after Christmas and exchange it for another one."

"I'm not sure you'll be able to," Luke said after a minute. "There's some kind of personalized message on the back."

"There is?" Cassie gasped, clambering forward. "What does it say?"

Luke squinted. "It doesn't make sense." He looked up at her. "Does 'Maiden's Blush' mean anything to you?"

"Maiden's Blush?" she echoed. "No! I have *no* idea what that means."

"It sounds medieval," he said.

Cassie pondered the words—was it a book title? A song from their past perhaps? But it rang no bells. She just couldn't think what he was alluding to.

Next to her, Luke began to shake with laughter.

"What? What's so funny?" she demanded, mildly irritated. She felt disappointment rising up in her, that after all the treasure-hunt clues and the excitement of the boxes-within-boxes, the trail had led to a faulty padlock and a cryptic message.

"Well, it's just occurred to me that maybe . . .", he cried, as his amusement took a proper hold . . . "All this talk about maidens and padlocks! I hope to God he's not going to follow this up with a chastity belt!"

Chapter Twenty

"So what did you get?" Cassie asked. Luke's pajamas were hanging loosely off her shoulders and she had her hands around a mug of wake-me-gently-I'm-not-a-morning-person tea. This was the problem with Skype. You had to be dressed for it.

"Well, Arch was *very* naughty." Suzy beamed. "I told him not to spend too much money on me," she said loudly, before leaning in to the screen and whispering: "You were right—the Post-its worked a treat!"

She was dressed in a new cream Temperley dress with gold embroidery and butterfly sleeves. It was half past two in the afternoon in London and the telly was on mute behind her as they waited for the Queen's Speech. In the background, Cassie kept getting flashes of the Sallyford Christmas—Lacey wafting through the room looking delectable in a pink chiffon tea-dress, Hattie arranging the flowers on the dining table, Henry clattering around with bottles, a purple paper crown skew-whiff on his head, and Archie intermittently popping his head around the doorway, red-faced and brandishing carving weapons.

"How about you?"

"Well, Kelly and I did our presents practically at dawn

this morning—she's spending the day with Brett's folks so they can go through the wedding plans together—and would you believe it? We ended up giving each other the *same* Louis Vuitton scarf!"

"No!"

"Oh yeah."

"You've become clones," Suzy teased.

"Well, wasn't that the point?" Cassie quipped. "I guess it means I qualify as a fully-fledged Manhattanite now."

"Never thought I'd see the day," Suzy said, shaking her head. "Just you wait till I get you in London. We'll soon have you out of black and into prints!"

"And eating carbs, I hope."

"Defo! Hang on—what?" she asked, turning around to someone behind her. "Oh, right." She turned back, a grimace on her face. "Archie's having a fit in the kitchen. Something about the turkey fighting back. I'm gonna have to go."

"Sure. Well, Happy Christmas to you—and the family!" Cassie said the last bit a little louder, hoping to attract Henry's attention, but he had gone out of the room. She desperately wanted to thank him for the necklace—even if it was faulty, it was still a remarkably generous present—but she felt awkward, for some reason, doing it in front of Lacey.

Hattie coo-eed from across the room. "Bye, Cassie darling! Come and see me when you're back in Old Blighty! And well done you for not taking any nonsense from that errant husband of yours. Such a silly tosser cheating on a precious girl like you."

"Mother!" Suzy hissed. "It's hardly the time . . . Anyway, she's got a boyfriend! She's very happy." She turned back, rolling her eyes apologetically. "Sorry."

Cassie shook her head. "No worries." The doorbell buzzed.

"I think that's Luke arriving now. I'll catch you before I leave for . . . you know." Bas and Luke weren't the only ones struggling to say the P-word now.

She opened the door for him, snaking her arms around his neck as his hands locked casually around her waist and he kissed her deeply. She'd left him shortly after the present opening, having promised to spend the evening with Kelly.

"Merry Christmas, Cass," he said, his voice hoarse as he looked at her, still mussed up from sleeping. "I wish I'd caught a picture of you waking this morning," he sighed, skimming his hand over her hair.

"Well, it wasn't a pretty sight, I can assure you. Kelly and I drank far too much mulled wine."

"It's the most beautiful sight," he countered, kissing her again. "How's Suzy?"

"Oh, reveling in her cunningness."

"Reveling in what?" he grinned

Cassie giggled, slapping him. "Filthy boy."

He began unbuttoning her—his—pajama top, which slid easily off her shoulder.

"Oi! This is supposed to be a family broadcast, you know!"

Cassie jumped, startled. What?

"Over here!"

She looked down at the laptop. Skype was still running.

"Oh my God!" she said, clutching her top and running over. "I thought I'd disconnected."

Henry shrugged. "Clearly not."

"No."

A silence stretched out over the width of the choppy Atlantic, as she struggled to cover herself up.

"I . . . I wanted to speak to you anyway," she said, managing a smile. "To thank you for this." She fingered the padlock that she had managed to secure to the chain by looping it through the safety chain. She hoped he wouldn't notice. It wasn't his fault that it was faulty. "I absolutely love it. But it's far, far too generous, Henry. You *really* shouldn't have."

"Henry?" Luke said coming up behind her. "This is him, then?" he asked rudely, peering at the screen.

Cassie winced. She'd felt awkward at the prospect of thanking him in front of Lacey. It hadn't crossed her mind that it would be worse in front of Luke.

The two men squared up online, displaying jutting jaws, narrowed eyes, and manly nods.

"Luke Laidlaw, Cassie's boyfriend." He said the word with a certain defiance. "Pleased to meet you."

"Henry Sallyford," Henry muttered with as much dignity as he could while wearing a purple paper crown.

"We're having a ball with your list, aren't we, Cass?" Luke said, placing a proprietorial hand on Cassie's shoulder. She nodded, though what she really wanted to do was kick him in the shins. He was behaving like a jerk. "Yeah . . . went to the library yesterday, then on to Tiffany's. Got my mother's present sorted too, so thanks for that."

"Great," Henry said, and Cassie could tell from his face how furious he was to have his list—itself a gift with all the experiences and treasures it gave her—bandied about like some YouTube link.

The stilted three-way conversation lapsed into crackling silence again.

"Well, better go. Lunch is on the table . . . Happy Christmas and all that jazz," Henry said finally.

"Yeah, you too, Henry. Give my best to Lacey."

He looked at her, and nodded briefly. Then the screen turned to snow.

"Well, that went well," Luke said, straightening up and walking away. "Good to put a face to the list at last."

"Yes," Cassie murmured, feeling upset by the conversation. Henry had clearly gone to a lot of trouble setting up her New York Christmas surprises, and her thanks in return had been clumsy and graceless. She wished the past five minutes had never happened.

She wandered into the bedroom, buttoning up her pajama top. Luke was in there, two black boxes—one little, one large—next to him on the bed. "Don't say those are for me," she gasped, wondering whether yesterday's trip had prompted some kind of psychotic box envy.

"Well, they're not for Kelly. Come on. Open them." He threw himself back on the bed, his ankles crossed, arms behind his head, a satisfied smile on his handsome face.

She clapped her hands, her discomfort forgotten, and ran across the room to pull off the lids. Inside the smallest was a pair of black leather gloves, lined in cashmere and trimmed with rabbit fur.

"The fur's a by-product," he said quickly, checking her reaction. "I wasn't sure of your take on that."

She stroked them gently. "Luke, I have skinned and stewed more rabbits than you would care to know," she quipped, sliding them over her hands.

"Really?" He gazed at her as she held her hands up like a Beaton model. "Your other life sounds . . . so different from all this," he said. He sat up and leaned in toward her, like a child trying to get his mother's attention. "Do you think we would have liked each other if we'd met in those surroundings instead?"

Cassie grimaced. "Probably not. You'd have thought I was a terrible square."

He laughed at her old-fashioned choice of words—a clue
that she had indeed once been a terrible square. "And what
would you have thought about me? That I was sleazy?"

She pulled a glove off and threw it at him. "Give it a rest,
will you! God, you'll never let me hear the end of it. One
lousy comment and I have to pay for it for . . ."

"For the rest of all time? Yes!" he said, springing up and
cupping her face in his hands. They kissed, and for a few moments forgot about the boxes between them.

"Come on, then," he said, pulling away reluctantly. "You'd
better open this before I decide we skip Christmas lunch altogether."

Cassie raised an eyebrow. "Bas would have something to
say about that. He'd come over brandishing red-hot straightening irons."

"Ouch."

She slid the lid off the big box, her eyes as bright as an
eight-year-old's. She gasped as her hands flew up to her
mouth. "It's the one I was admiring the other week," she
whispered, lifting out a navy blue Moncler padded coat. It
had been in the window of Barneys.

"Here, try it on," he said, slipping it on over her pajamas.
He pushed her hair back behind her ears and pulled up the
hood. A thick swathe of fur encircled her face, Eskimo-style.

"Oooh, I'll sleep in it too—on the nights when I'm not with
you," she said, snuggling into the crook of his arm.

"There shouldn't be any of those," he murmured, resting
his chin on the top of her head.

She looked up and kissed him again. "It's too much. You're
spoiling me."

"Nonsense," he said, pressing the tip of her nose gently.
"You're in New York. You've got to keep warm."

"Yes, but . . ."

"No buts . . . you're always shivering in that parka. And it's not going to get any easier over the next few weeks. Wait till February hits. That's when the fun really starts." He kissed her gently. "Now get dressed. I'll ring Bas and let him know we're just leaving. You can wear it on the way over there."

He stroked her chin and winked, padding off toward the living room, pulling his mobile from his back pocket.

Cassie watched him, rooted to the spot.

February?

She pressed her nose to the glass and looked down the twelve stories to the ground below. Everything had changed overnight and she was as captivated as a child.

"Honestly, anyone would think you'd never seen snow before," Kelly said, shrugging on her coat. She and Brett were seeing in the new year at the Waldorf Astoria, where there was a black-tie ball.

Cassie turned to look at her friend—her roommate for one more day. She was privately devastated that they were spending this last night apart. It was the end of their adventure; they ought to be together. In fairness, Kelly had tried to persuade her and Luke to come too. And Cassie would have done. It would have been fun to have had one last hurrah all together, spending all night awake with her friends in the city that never sleeps.

But Luke had been adamant that he wanted to spend it with her alone. He didn't want to "share" her with a bunch of strangers, he'd said. And anyway, he hated wearing a "penguin suit."

She cast an admiring eye over Kelly's dress. It was the same one Cassie had worn on her last night in Scotland, but in different colors—black silk with nude lace inserts. And she was wearing it differently too—knowing, provocative, seductive. Not embarrassed and thinking she was out in her nightie.

"You look stunning," Cassie smiled, shaking her head through teary eyes. "Brett's going to be so proud walking in with you."

Kelly looked at her sitting huddled by the window, her hand absentmindedly brushing over the top of her lawn. It had become something of a soothing habit.

"There's still time, you know," Kelly said, sitting down next to her. "I know the head of events over there. I could get your name put on the—"

Cassie shook her head. "No, it won't make any difference. Luke's insistent we spend it together."

Kelly opened her mouth as if to say something . . . then changed her mind and bit her lip.

"He's nuts about you. That's the problem," Kelly said, patting her knee. "Who'd have thought it? You come to New York having no idea *at all* about the fashion industry—who's Oscar de La Renta, Kelly? Who's the editor of *Vogue*? . . ." Cassie blanched and Kelly squeezed her knee . . . "And yet you end up taming its prodigal son. I didn't know you had it in you," she said fondly. "Look, I'll be back first thing, okay? We'll have breakfast together at Sant Ambroeus—for old times' sake."

"Sure," Cassie said, taking a deep, brave breath.

The buzzer rang. "That'll be Brett. I'm meeting him in the lobby," Kelly said, getting up.

"I'll walk down with you," said Cassie, pulling her new coat from the back of the sofa.

"Are you going to be all right on your own? I'd offer to take you to Luke's in our cab, but we're going in the opposite direction," Kelly said apologetically.

"Don't worry. I'm going to walk. I love walking in the snow."

Kelly grimaced. "Have you got any suitable boots? You don't want to wear your leather ones in the snow. They'll get trashed."

"Ah-ha!" Cassie said, pulling out her welly-green muck boots from the hall cupboard and staring down at them wistfully. How ironic, she thought—that they'd remained unworn since her first day here, only to be worn again on her last.

They traveled down in the elevator together, waving cheerily to Bill, who was about to clock off.

Brett looked dashing in his penguin suit and Cassie felt a well of resentment rise up in her as she waved them off. She knew that right now, this very instant, across the pond, the Hogmanay reel that she and Gil had held every year would be in full flight. The bells would have sounded an hour ago, the first-footers would have turned up with their lumps of coal, and kilts would be flying, sashes slipping, men whirling, and women twirling as they danced in the new year.

She wanted to be doing something that could compete on that scale too—laughter and noise, music and drinks, finery and flirting. She didn't want to spend it sitting in an empty loft with fairy lights in an artful heap on the floor and Blondie on the iPod. This New Year's Eve had to be memorable, iconic. It had to show Gil she was okay without him—even if he'd never know it.

She set off and trudged through the snow alone. It was still pristine, and as clean and fluffy as freshly washed feathers, but she knew that by daybreak it would be tainted, melting into a gray slush as revelers and snowplows and multitudes of cabs did their worst. She was almost pleased that she wouldn't be here to watch the city sink back into its grayness.

Almost.

She walked along, past partygoers and couples all en route to somewhere vibrant and alive. She felt their energy and good cheer as they smiled and wished her a happy new year as they passed. If they only knew what this one had been like, she thought, smiling back.

She tried to buck up, to be flattered that Luke wanted her all to himself. Kelly had been right. Who would have thought it? In spite of his reputation and her determination not to get attached, things had turned serious between them. He wasn't making it easy for her to leave, and she already knew they weren't going to sleep at all tonight.

She turned into his street, past the redbrick buildings that characterized this part of the city. All around, the sounds of parties in high-up apartments bounced off the walls, echoing and mixing until the city seemed almost to vibrate with celebration.

She pressed the entry buzzer and waited for the street door to click open.

"Hi, babe," he said through the intercom.

She climbed the stairs and rapped on the door.

"Hey," he said, opening it and sweeping her into his arms there and then in the lobby.

"You're . . . you're in black tie!" she said, wriggling back to get a better look at him.

He shrugged and smiled at her. "What can I tell you? I wanted to make tonight special for you."

"But you said you hate wearing penguin suits," she said, the irritation spilling out in her voice as she looked down at her padded coat, skinny jeans, and muck boots. "Look at me! You could have warned me," she moaned, shrugging off her coat and stamping her feet on the floor to dislodge the snow. Swinging the door open, she walked into the loft. "If I'd known, I'd have—"

"*SURPRISE!!*" came a cheer from the far side of the room. In front of her, Kelly and Brett and Bas, Stefano and his fiancée, Ilya, Raoul, Bonnie, Molly, and a scattering of Luke's friends cheered loudly. They were all wearing sparkly cone hats on their heads and holding glasses of champagne in their hands. Balloons bounced across the floor, stirring up dust, and streamers hung dreamily from the black-and-white galleries. Someone started up the music.

"I can't believe it," she said in utter amazement, turning back to him, her hands up at her mouth. "You threw me a leaving party?"

"Not exactly," he smiled, fishing in his jacket pocket and bringing out a key.

He was biting his lip, but his eyes betrayed his excitement. He took a deep breath. "I want you to have this. I want you to move in with me, Cassie." He linked his arms around her waist, pulling her in to him. "I want you to . . ."

But she'd already caught sight of a huge banner hanging above the door. It said just one thing.

"STAY!"

PARIS

Chapter Twenty-One

The driver let her out on the corner, clearly without giving any indication to the cars behind, whose drivers honked their horns and shook furious fists at her—as if it were her fault—as they swerved on the cobbles, their tires squealing, while the driver unloaded her bags from the trunk. She had arrived here with vastly more luggage than what she'd arrived in New York with. Had she been stopped at customs on the way through, they'd have assumed she worked in the undertaking trade, such was the quantity of black clothing inside the suitcases.

Anouk was sitting watching from a table next to the window, her signature tortoiseshell shades on, even though it was New Year's Day and the sky was boasting all the brightness of a duvet. A tiny espresso was sitting in front of her, and she was holding a cigarette between her fingers.

Cassie clattered over, having to make several trips to get her bags through the narrow gaps between the tables.

"*Chérie.*" Anouk beamed, getting up at last to proffer three kisses. "*Bienvenue à Paris!*"

She put a gentle hand on Cassie's shoulder, tipping her head slightly to the side as if in sympathy. "I must be honest, I did not think you would come. Even yesterday, all day, I was waiting for the call when you would say you were staying after all."

"He threw a Stay party."

"A *what*?"

Cassie bit her lip hard and nodded. "Talked Kelly and Bas into it too. Told them I'd be *bound* to stay if he asked me to live with him."

"I see," Anouk said quietly, taking in Cassie's gray pallor and swollen eyes. "Come. Sit," she said, turning and catching the waiter's eye—which was easy enough since he hadn't stopped staring at her since she'd arrived—for more coffees.

Cassie crumpled into the chair, vaguely tuning in to the different frequency in the café. In New York, when she and Kelly had hung out at Sant Ambroeus, it was to a backdrop of steamed milk, soprano laughter, and Marc Jacobs's Daisy. Here, the coffee was as dark as treacle, Shalimar hung in the air like the chandeliers, and the conversational pitch was at tenor level.

She resisted the urge to rest her head in her hands, even though, being the first of January, she could probably pass herself off as weary reveler rather than lovelorn émigrée.

"Tell me what happened."

Cassie sighed, wishing she didn't have to. All she had done all night was talk. Talk, talk, discuss, extrapolate, and argue. And all to no avail.

"He just doesn't understand," she shrugged. "He thinks this . . . 'plan,' coming to stay with you all . . . is nonsense. 'It's not how the real world works,' he said."

Anouk considered for a moment. "I suppose that's understandable. He's underestimated what you've been through. I don't mean just in the past four months, but in the past ten years." She lit a cigarette and inhaled deeply. "He doesn't understand that when you married Gil, you were barely an adult. You'd seen nothing of the world. He, meanwhile, crosses it three times a month for work."

The waiter arrived with their coffees, but Anouk ignored him.

"You were living in a big house, on your own most of the time, in the middle of nowhere. And then you found yourself thrown back out into the world, with no warning, no planning. You didn't see it coming. You were on a plane to New York within hours of finding out. You mustn't blame him for not being able to imagine all that. I can scarcely believe it myself—and I was there."

"Me neither," Cassie mumbled, managing a wry smile.

"As far as he's concerned, he just fell in love with a beautiful new divorcée."

Cassie blanched at the word. And anyway, it wasn't true; they weren't divorced yet. Not even close, in fact. Even though she had done the "right thing" in honoring the prenup, they were clashing over the cause being cited in the papers. She wanted it to go through on his "unreasonable behavior" but Gil wanted "irreconcilable differences," and they were both digging their heels in over it. Owning up to what he'd done to their marriage was the very least he owed her.

"You were new to the city, new to the fashion industry, new to being single . . . Everything about you was fresh, unpretentious, innocent. That must have been exciting to him—you must have been totally unlike the other girls there. But you *have* had your heart broken," she reminded Cassie. "Badly. And while on paper you're free to fall in love again, in the real world, it's going to take a lot longer than a season in New York to put you back together."

Cassie nodded gratefully. Her earlier concerns about

staying with Anouk had been overtaken in recent weeks by concerns about their vastly different attitudes toward men. Anouk was secretive to the point of paranoia about her boyfriends. No one ever met them. She just had her fun, then moved on, it seemed, so Cassie had been more than a little worried that Anouk would brush Luke off as of no consequence, just a rebound relationship, a plaything to have kept her amused in the evenings and at weekends, when in reality he had been so much more than that—she wasn't capable of using someone in such a cavalier way.

"I tried explaining all that to him—that I'm still trying to find out who I am. Do you know what he said?"

Anouk waited.

"He said I sounded like I'd been living in Los Angeles. Me!" She shook her head. "I mean, when has my life ever been about navel-gazing? I'm the least self-informed person I know." She looked straight at Anouk, whose luxuriant hair tumbled casually about her shoulders. She was wearing a navy trench belted at the waist and a dusty-pink dotted Hermès scarf at her neck. "You've never doubted who you are, have you?"

Anouk twitched her mouth side to side, not even able to pretend for camaraderie's sake. "*Non*. Never."

Cassie sighed. "I wanted him to come out here and visit. I'd bought him a ticket."

"Did he take it?"

"He wouldn't. I ended up giving it to Bas. You know, I told him that these other trips—here, London—weren't forever. Just a few more months, and then if we were still . . . strong, happy, whatever, then I'd go back to New York at the end of the summer. Like you said, there were lots of reasons for me to stay there. Not just him." She shook her head, lacing her fingers together. "But he doesn't believe in long-distance relationships."

Anouk gave a little sigh. "Well, I don't think I do either, *chérie*, if I'm honest."

"No?"

"*Non*. Always been a disaster."

Cassie looked up at her. "Do you think I did the right thing, coming here?"

"Yes." Anouk placed a warm hand on her wrist.

"So does Bas, even though he didn't want me to go either. He really didn't. But Luke . . . he's so angry with me. He's taken my coming here as a rejection of *him*. All I know is that . . . I have this feeling that I'm not quite there yet, wherever 'there' is. I've got this instinct that I must keep going."

"Well you were right to follow it, and I for one am glad you're here. If you are supposed to be with him, it will happen," Anouk smiled. "Love always finds a way."

"Don't tell me you believe in destiny too?"

"Of course. Doesn't everybody?"

Cassie sighed and picked up the tiny cup, its handle so small she had to pinch it. "It rather seems they do. Yet again I think I might be the odd one out."

The apartment was half a block away. They wheeled two bags each along the pavement, coming to a stop after a minute outside a pair of solid black arched double-height gates. Anouk unlocked them with a huge old key and they stepped into a courtyard. It was paved with gray cobbles worn to a rounded shine, and a fountain encircled by a dwarf wall sat in the middle. The apartments facing this side of the courtyard were flat-faced, boasting tall, narrow windows with silk curtains lavishly draped behind the glass, and topiaried trees were spaced equally, Versailles-style, along the wrought-iron balconies that were as finely rendered as filigree.

They walked into the building facing them at the back. It felt chilly and austere in the hallway, with no pictures or warm paneling on the walls, just a huge gilt mirror above a marble-topped console and a salmon-pink damask Louis Quinze chaise longue.

Anouk started climbing the sweeping stone staircase. "No elevators here, I'm afraid," she said. "Although it doesn't matter so much when there are only three *étages*. How many were there in Kelly's building?"

"Well, she was on the twelfth floor, but there were sixteen in total. And her building's considered pretty low."

"*Mon Dieu.* Elevators must be a basic human right there."

"They are," Cassie smiled. "Although Kelly's a committed tower-runner."

"What's that?" Anouk asked breathlessly, clearly unused to carrying anything bigger than a Birkin up the steps.

"Nutters running up the stairs of skyscrapers and tower blocks."

"*Non!* What—for fun? Or for exercise?"

"In Kelly's case, both. She even does it in heels."

"I am even more amazed you are here, then. I do not know how you survived," she said, shaking her head and dropping the bags outside a door on the top floor. "*Alors*, we are here."

As with Kelly's apartment, what went on in the communal areas had no bearing on her friends' living quarters. In New York, the difference had been scale, but here it was taste. It was like walking into a spread for *Elle Decor*. The walls were lilac with overscaled modern art canvases hanging on them, and the parquet floors were hidden beneath enormous, vibrant rugs. A forest-green Roche Bobois corner sofa ran the entire length of two walls and a purple fiberglass molded table sat in the middle, with stacks of art books piled high. In one corner, a glass-topped Ligne Roset table and eight chairs sat in front of the windows overlooking the river where tourists sailed by snapping pictures of her neighbors, Notre Dame and Sainte-Chapelle.

Cassie wandered through in silence as Anouk unbuttoned her coat. The kitchen was long and narrow, galley-style, with a window and Juliet balcony at the far end, and the units were matte gray, with no handles but push-release doors, and white Corian worktops. With something approaching euphoria, she clocked the kettle.

The apartment had two bedrooms—that was a relief to note too. Kelly's trundle bed had quickly lost its nostalgic "sleepovers" appeal, and once they'd started dating Brett and Luke . . . well, it meant one of them always had to stay out.

"Anouk, this place is amazing!" she exclaimed, turning back and joining her friend at the windows. Paris was still sleeping off its hangover, even though it was nearly 2:00 P.M. The streets on the other side of the river, the Left Bank, were quiet, with just the occasional scooter zipping past, stray lovers walking hand in hand over the bridges, and limp tourists flopping back in their seats on the city tour buses. "*Tch*, you smoke too much, Nooks," she tutted, spying another cigarette in her hand.

Anouk shrugged. "It helps me think."

"What do you need to think about?" Cassie asked, slipping off her jacket to reveal the black "I heart NY" T-shirt Bas had given her for Christmas, her black Bebe biker trousers, and buckled ankle boots.

Anouk turned to look at her. "You," she smiled.

Cassie was surprised. "Me? Why?"

"How to make you happy here. The job to give you, the people to make you laugh."

"I hope that's not code for 'set you up with,'" Cassie warned.

"No. Not if you don't want," Anouk smiled, giving a little shrug. "Although I do know—"

"Nooks!"

"Fine." She looked Cassie up and down. "You've really lost a lot of weight."

"I know," Cassie sighed. "Hopefully you'll be doing something about that? Tarte Tatin for breakfast, *chocolat chaud* before bed . . ."

Anouk giggled at the preposterousness of the suggestions. "Don't count on it. Although you will be going straight back to wine. All those pink cocktails . . ." She gave a little shudder.

"Well, that's a relief," Cassie said. "I never did acquire a taste for them."

She went and stretched out on one of the sofas. The jet lag was catching up with her. "This is okay, isn't it?" she asked, worrying that she was making the place look untidy.

"Sure." Anouk came and joined her, concertinaing herself into tiny folds on the adjoining sofa. "Suzy has asked for us to Skype her tonight. She's worried about you. I think she couldn't quite believe that you were going to make it either. And Kelly texted me four times to check whether you had arrived yet. Ayayay." She waved a little hand dismissively. There was silence. "Cassie?"

She bent forward, trying to see her friend's face through the sheet of butter-blond hair.

"*Non-non non,*" she said, jumping up and rubbing Cassie on the shoulder. "You must not sleep yet."

"Why not?" Cassie moaned, her voice already thick with slumber.

"Up. Come on. Up! I have just the thing. It will cure you of jet lag and give you a kick-start to Paris life. Come. The hammam is what you need. Come."

It didn't take long to get there. The cab stopped in the deuxième arrondissement, in an anonymous courtyard with a few Vespas parked badly on one side and some giant box-hedge balls in large lead planters flanking a black door. There was no sign or plaque to indicate what they'd come to—or for.

Anouk rapped twice softly on the door, and after a few moments a dark-haired, olive-skinned woman—Moroccan possibly?—opened it. She smiled in recognition of Anouk and stepped back for them to enter.

Inside, everything was a soothing off-white color, with dark wooden arched doors and matching architraves, and the temperature was set at a coddling warmth. Cassie un-zipped her jacket, feeling suddenly like a rough-tough biker chick dressed all in black and buckles in this mellow room. Anouk was wearing dark teal wide-cut trousers and a pale pink shirt, with a chunky rope of amethysts around her neck.

"Wow, if I were asked to design a womb, it would proba-bly look a lot like this," Cassie whispered as the woman led them through to a changing area where she gave them each a locker, a pair of flip-flops, some disposable knickers, a robe, and a towel.

Cassie held the paper knickers up after the woman had left the room. "Tell me that's just a joke," she said nervously.

Anouk smiled and shook her head, stripping down quickly to a lemon-yellow bra embroidered with tiny black polka dots and a matching thong. Cassie looked on anxiously. Last time Anouk had seen her in her underwear, she'd nearly had a stroke—what Kelly referred to as "knickergate"—and for all the leaps forward she'd made in New York with her outer wardrobe, to be honest, nothing much had changed on the underpinnings front.

She quickly peered inside her T-shirt to see what she'd pulled on before leaving for the airport. Hmmm. Gray jersey Gap bra and pink and red striped Calvin Klein hipsters she'd bought at a sale. She blew out through her cheeks as she pulled her shirt over her head. It could be worse.

Or maybe not.

"*Mon Dieu*, she has taught you nothing!" Anouk said, wrapping the robe around herself crossly.

"Who? Kelly?" Cassie asked, hopping about on one foot as she tried to get the knickers on without Anouk catching sight of the "extreme waxing" situation. She had a gut feeling the Brazilian wax would cause yet more consternation.

"Yes. What was she thinking? I mean—why are you wearing lipstick when you haven't even got your lingerie sorted?"

Cassie smooshed her mouth to the side, trying to work out the connection between lipstick and lingerie. "You've lost me."

Anouk sighed. "It's all about priorities, Cassie. Why on earth would you want a man to kiss you on the mouth if you can't then take him to bed?"

There was a baffled pause. "I don't understand. Why couldn't I then take him to bed?" Cassie asked, bewildered.

"Wearing that? Those panties and that bra? Surely you wouldn't want a man to see you like that." It wasn't a question.

Cassie bit her lip, abashed. Luke had liked it—he'd called it "sporty."

The woman came back through again, and ushered them

into a lounge where mint tea and almonds were served up on wenge tables. Anouk smiled as they sat opposite each other on the white chairs taking dainty sips. All around them, little niches were carved out of the walls at random heights and intervals, and were filled with flickering votives and baskets of sandalwood.

"Luckily, I know the best place to go for getting you sorted. Rosa Beaulieu. She's a client of mine." She thought for a moment. "She's pretty expensive, but I have a necklace that she always admires when I see her. I could see if she would barter a week's set of lingerie for it?"

"Great," Cassie said feebly, feeling slightly beaten up by the dressing-down in the dressing room.

"Hey, don't be cross with me, Cass," Anouk said quietly. "I cannot help it if I get frustrated sometimes. I just want to help you make the most of yourself, that is all."

"I know. I'm just tired."

"Of course you are. And that is why we are here. We have four hours of relaxation ahead of us."

"Four hours?" Cassie thought of what Kelly could achieve in four hours, and yet she was going to spend it in paper knickers . . .

"Four hours. It cannot be rushed," Anouk said, stretching her arms above her head. "That's what I was trying to explain to you just now—you cannot paper over the cracks with brash makeup or trendy clothes. Over here, *chérie*, beauty starts from the inside."

Chapter Twenty-Two

Cassie looked down at her coffee, wondering whether her spoon would actually stand up on its own in the thick, strong liquid. "This makes me miss my grass," she said, craving a light cup of the chamomile tea that had become her waking ritual. It had been during the girls' shopping weekend in November, when Suzy had tripped and planted her hand in the middle of the grass—promptly releasing the telltale scent—that they had finally discovered that she was growing a chamomile lawn and not just your common garden variety.

"You make it sound like a pet," Anouk quipped. She was reading *Le Monde*. It looked like it had been ironed.

"It almost was, I guess. I had to look after it—make sure it was getting enough sun but not too much, move it away from the window during frosts, water it—"

"Walk it, groom it, give it vitamin supplements, tell it you loved it . . . ," Anouk teased.

"You're just jealous because you don't know what it is to have a lawn of one's own."

Anouk chuckled, deeply amused. Their spirits were restored again since they'd both slept well. In fact, Cassie couldn't remember ever having slept better. She wasn't sure exactly what had done it—the eucalyptus-infused steam room, the all-over exfoliation lying on a heated granite table (surprisingly comfortable), the nourishing hair mask, the antiaging honey facial, or perhaps the full body-wrap made from brewer's yeast. Either way, she'd practically levitated above the bed last night, and no trace of jet lag remained this morning.

Cassie took a sip of her espresso and felt the hit immediately. "You know, I never drank coffee before eleven in New York."

Anouk, wearing a thin taupe cashmere robe, raised her eyebrows but didn't look up. "*Vraiment?* How did you get going for the day, then?"

"A run, usually."

Anouk grimaced. "How brutal."

"Yeah," Cassie said, stirring the coffee. "What do you do for exercise over here?"

Anouk shrugged. "I walk. Cycle sometimes."

"I can't imagine you on a bike, Nooks. What is it— mountain or racer? No! Don't tell me, you've got a BMX."

Anouk looked up, turning the paper over. "Actually, it's a chopper," she said with a straight face, making Cassie keel over with laughter.

"Aaah, that's a powerful image!" she sighed, wiping her eyes, when she'd eventually recovered. She tore open her croissant with her fingers and covered it with butter and jam, scarcely able to believe carbs were back on the menu, although she noticed Anouk hadn't had one. She did hope she was going to be able to eat normally here. She'd lost six pounds living in New York and she didn't want to lose any more.

She wondered what else would change with her location. It had been so strange waking up in her new room this morning, the sounds of the neighbors' voices bouncing around the courtyard in a language she hadn't used for so long—although a gap year as a chalet girl at Anouk's parents' place in Méribel meant she was pretty much fluent. It would take a while to get her ear back in, though.

She took another bite of croissant and looked out of the window. It was Monday and the rumble of cars on the bridges suggested the city was emerging from its holiday cocoon.

"So, what's the plan for today?"

"Well," Anouk said, folding the paper and putting it down on the table. "We are having lunch with my dear friend Florence later, but I am afraid I shall have to go to the studio this afternoon. I have an important client coming over to pick up some pieces that I've done for her holiday in St. Barts, and she's flying out tonight so I cannot put it off. But first we shall have some fun."

"Fun?" Cassie put down the croissant. "That's not a word you use."

"*Non?*" Anouk gave a casual shrug.

Cassie looked at her suspiciously. "Define *fun*."

There was a pause. Anouk quickly looked back at the paper. "Hair with Jean at ten, endermologie at eleven-thirty."

"Ender*what*?" Cassie considered for a moment. "Isn't that the study of insects?"

Anouk chuckled again.

"And what's wrong with my hair?"

"Nothing, nothing," Anouk said, her eyes flicking over it as if she'd just seen it move. "I've just asked him for a few tweaks, that is all—to help you become a Parisienne. That is what you want, *sûrement*? You don't want to look like a *tourist*." She said the word with the same disdain Luke had reserved for *blogger*.

"Well, no . . . ," Cassie said, her hand flying up to the glossy mane that Bas had lovingly blown-out for her on her last day in Manhattan.

"So don't worry, *chérie*. There is nothing to be concerned about. Everything will be terribly subtle. Paris is nothing, Cassie, if not subtle."

"This is *not* my definition of subtle, Nooks!" Cassie hissed, trying to catch sight of herself in parked-car windows. "I mean, at least my poor mother would have had a chance of recognizing me before. But this?"

Anouk stared at her, appraising the new look. "It suits you," she said finally. "That blond was far too harsh. And look, you've got dark eyebrows and lashes. You can take it," she nodded.

"But I liked my hair the way it was."

"Kelly had turned you into an American girl. You would have been a constant kidnap threat." She winked at Cassie, just as the lights turned green and the pedestrians flooded across the road. "These colors—what did he use in the end?" she asked, striding out.

"Caramel and chestnut," Cassie said sullenly. "No. No. It was *hazel*nut." Like that made a difference. It was still dark brown. She couldn't stop stroking her hair. It was an inverted bob now—saved from Charleston pastiche only by the way it broke into twists at the front—and her neck felt cold.

"Yes, well, those colors typify *absolument* the difference between New York and Paris. There it is about fashion. Here, it is about style. Subtlety, elegance, chic." She tugged Cassie's arm. "Quick, this way. We are late."

She turned a sharp left down the rue Saint-Jacques and along a street where the average age dropped sharply to twenty-one.

"The Sorbonne is just over there." Anouk smiled, clocking Cassie's even more frantic hair-soothing as cliques of girls in tight jeans and ethnic scarves sloped by.

"You still haven't explained what this enderthingy is," Cassie said, trying to keep up.

"It's probably best if I don't," Anouk said, stopping suddenly at a glass door and pressing the entry buzzer.

"What on earth does that mean?" Cassie cried in alarm.

"Listen. Would I ever steer you wrong?" Anouk asked, stepping in and leaving Cassie with no choice but to follow her.

Ten minutes later, the answer was a clear yes. Cassie was wearing a white sheer bodystocking that rolled from her neck down to her wrists and ankles, and a woman in a white coat, who looked like she should be giving her either a facial or ECT, was brandishing a machine with rollers on it.

"So just run me through that again," Cassie said, hands on hips, momentarily forgetting that she looked like a blanched sausage. "You want to put that thing up and down my body and it will roller up my fat bits—"

"And break down the fatty deposits, yes," the woman sighed.

Cassie looked at Anouk, who was sitting on the bed, swinging her legs. "But you were telling me only yesterday how skinny I was."

"And you are. But this is *fantastique* for getting rid of *peau d'orange.*"

"But I don't have cellulite . . . do I?" She twisted around to get a better look at her bottom. Again, she was wearing paper knickers.

"And also it's great for making sure it never starts." Anouk shrugged happily. "I swear by it. But never tell Suzy or Kelly, okay? There are some secrets that cannot leave Paris."

"But she's basically going to be *vacuuming* me," Cassie said imploringly.

"Cassie, trust me," Anouk said, tapping her watch and reminding her they had lunch plans. "Inside out, remember? Beauty is the foundation for happiness and self-esteem. In Paris, this is just what women do."

New York felt a long ways away. She felt separated from it not just by the thirty-five hundred miles between the two cities, but by time too. New York was about the moment, the Zeitgeist, the cutting edge. Here—Cassie looked around the formal restaurant with its sky-frescoed cupola and seventeenth-century tapestries on the walls—all homage to the riches of the past. Classical statues that looked like they'd been pinched from the Louvre were spot-lit in the corners, the marble floors were as polished as mirrors, and giant ten-foot urns were spilling over with lavish floral displays as rich in scent as in color. This hotel, one of the city's landmarks, could have looked like this two, even three hundred years ago; the only difference would be the hair, clothes, and shoes of the people populating it—pompadour wigs and buckled shoes instead of the Chanel quilted pumps and helmet blow-dries that were out in force today.

Cassie offered up a silent prayer of thanks for having had the good sense to put on her all-camel Michael Kors outfit— skinny polo and wool A-line skirt with shearling-lined boots. This morning, absolutely everyone in the room was wearing navy, gray, or chocolate brown. There was no black to be seen anywhere. Having said that, when she'd pulled the clothes on, she'd still been a long-haired butter-blonde. Now she was a bobbed brunette, and the "match your clothes to your hair" look that had seemed so chic earlier now just look washed out, which was more than could be said for her thighs, which were still red and tingling from the endermologie session.

"So, it is your first time in Paris?" Florence asked, her English as flawless as her face. She was the marketing director for Dior, and Cassie had been able to tell just by looking at her that she was a fashion thoroughbred. Her dark hair was a shimmy of cocoa lowlights, her cheekbones were as sharp as if they'd been filed, and several of Anouk's signature oversized cocktail rings clunked on her elegant hands.

"Yes, I can scarcely believe it myself," Cassie smiled, slapping herself on the forehead as though it were something she'd just forgotten to get around to. "It seems so gauche, somehow, to have got to this age and not made it here before now."

"Well, you were busy with other things," Anouk said tenderly. "Anyway, Cassie's just spent the past four months living in New York, and she's moving to London in the summer, so she's making up for lost time." She put her hand over Cassie's. "You shall be quite the international jet-setter by then."

"Maybe."

"And what are you going to do with your days here?" Florence asked, delicately spearing an asparagus tip.

"Well, I'm not sure yet. It's all slightly tricky jobwise. My trip's too short for a permanent job, but I've never done temping before. I don't think I'd be qualified enough to go on an agency's books."

"Well, maybe you could spend it trying to talk Anouk into coming on board with us," Florence smiled. "We've been trying to strong-arm her into working exclusively for us for years, but she won't listen. I have recurring nightmares that I'm going to lose her to someone else."

"That won't happen," Anouk replied, sipping her Beaujolais Nouveau. "I like my independence. It suits me to work for myself and come and go as I please."

"Talk some sense into her," Florence said, leaning toward Cassie. "You are old friends, after all. I am sure she would listen to what you have to say."

Cassie shook her head. "I'm afraid I'd be absolutely the last person Anouk would listen to. I'm utterly clueless about all the things she holds dear."

"Oh," Florence said, sitting back, clearly shocked.

There was a prolonged, embarrassed silence. Anouk stared openly at Cassie, who was in turn staring openly at the tablecloth. She hadn't meant it to come out as such a rebuke to the bonds of their friendship.

"Well, I hate to contradict you, Cassie," Anouk said, after a moment, "but you are my very first port of call on lots of matters. For one thing, I would give anything to be able to cook like you. I can still ruin a saucepan just boiling water. You are the only person I would want around me in a crisis. And as for your loyalty and bravery, well . . ." She looked at Florence. "Did you know she scored the winning goal in the lacrosse finals against our most avowed enemies with two broken fingers—and didn't utter a word about it until after the trophies had been handed out!"

Florence's eyes widened, probably more at the incongruous image of Anouk playing lacrosse than at Cassie playing it with broken fingers.

"And none of that even comes close to the pride I feel in seeing how she's carried on with such dignity in the past four months. I know I couldn't do it."

There was another silence, just as stunned, but for different reasons this time. Cassie's eyes were shining with tears.

Anouk took a deep breath and looked at her colleague. "So I would say, Florence, that you need to give my dear friend here a job for the coming season. Because your chances of getting me to sign are going to be very much higher if you can get Cassie on your side."

"I didn't know you felt like that," Cassie said as they walked back over Pont Saint-Louis, the bridge that connected the two islands in the middle of the Seine—the kernels from which Paris itself had grown.

"I didn't know *you* felt like that," Anouk smiled, squeezing her arm.

Cassie shrugged. "I'm sorry if I embarrassed you. It wasn't my intention."

"I know."

"I guess I've just always felt out of step with you, as if I could never catch up. You seemed grown-up even when we were children. I never thought for a minute you got anything back from me."

"Apart from compassion, humor, loyalty, steadfastness . . . apart from that, no, you're right . . . nothing at all."

They stopped in the middle of the bridge and looked downriver. Two swans were gliding on the brown water beneath them.

"They mate for life, you know," Anouk said, lighting a cigarette.

"Lucky things," Cassie murmured.

Anouk blew out a trail of white smoke. It disappeared instantly into the cloudy sky. "Are you missing him?"

"Who—Gil?" Cassie turned around and leaned against the

bridge. A passing gleam of sunlight washed over her like a breath of wind. "Yes. And no. I've got used to being without him, at least. That's where Edinburgh came in useful, I suppose. It wasn't as if we lived in each other's pockets. But"— she inhaled deeply—"it's the little things that catch me out. Little boys just kill me. And there was a man on the plane who was wearing Gil's favorite tie. And on his birthday— well, I was *that* close to ringing, I tell you."

"You haven't spoken to him at all?"

"Uh-uh. What's the point? We couldn't go back even if we wanted to. Everything was built on a lie. Out of ten years of marriage, Rory was there for three of them, and I still don't know when it actually began with Wiz. Was it two years before that? Before we even married?" Her voice faltered and she shut her eyes quickly.

"Well, I'm sure it won't be long before he does to *her* what he did to you."

Cassie shook her head. "No. No, he won't. They're right together. I can see it now."

"*Mon Dieu,*" Anouk said quietly. "You were the perfect wife; now you're the perfect ex-wife." She looked at Cassie. "And Luke? Have you spoken to him yet?"

Cassie shook her head. "That's almost the harder thing. He won't take my calls. I don't understand why he's so all-or-nothing. It's just . . . over."

"Keep trying. He'll come around. Didn't you say he'll be over for the shows?"

"Yes, mid-Feb."

"Well, that's only six weeks away."

Cassie looked at her friend. "It's funny. I'd have thought you'd have said it was undignified chasing after a man like that."

Anouk shrugged. "It's not always so easy to find someone. Sometimes, you have to break out of your comfort zone."

"I bet you've never begged anyone to pick up the phone."

"Maybe not," she shrugged. "But maybe I should have." She stared blankly at a Bateau Mouche chugging past, most of the orange plastic seats flipped up and empty. She finished her cigarette and stamped it out beneath her velvet ballet pumps. "Come. We must head over to the studio. I want to get everything set up before Katrina arrives."

They started walking again.

"So who's Katrina?"

"Katrina Holland. Currently married to Bertie Holland, the CEO at Index Bank. She's one of my best clients."

An image of a willowy blonde with plumped-up lips floated through Cassie's mind, along with an anecdote about her preference for handsome young "walkers." Had Bas known her? He was her usual source of outrageous gossip.

"Where does she live?"

"Manhattan and Geneva mainly, but she's over for the couture shows next week. Dior passed her over to me, what, eight seasons ago? I've been designing collections for her twice yearly ever since. We go through what she orders at the shows and I come up with pieces unique to her."

"How the other half lives, eh?" They passed down the quiet streets of the Ile Saint-Louis, so much more tranquil than Ile de la Cité, where the tourists buzzed; she felt more like she was in a tiny provincial village, not one of the most popular tourist destinations in the world. The island, in years gone by, had been mainly given over to fields for grazing sheep and cows, which was why there were so few houses there, and even now, Anouk had told her, when residents crossed the bridges back to the Left and Right Banks, they said they were "going to Paris."

"It's so peaceful here. You could almost forget you're in a city."

"I know. That's why I love it so." They stopped outside a glossy aubergine-painted door and Anouk fished around in her bag for the key. "Of course, Katrina gets annoyed because there's nowhere to land her helicopter," she smiled, rolling her eyes.

They walked into a tiny hallway with black-and-white marble tiles on the floor and three doors opening off it. A narrow staircase clung precariously to the right-hand wall.

"Up we go again," Anouk said, hoisting her bag over her shoulder. She was wearing a faded red toile-print chiffon blouse with waterfall ruffles peeking through her red tweed jacket—apparently the sleeves had been spiral-cut to make them so skinny—and cropped navy trousers. Cassie caught sight of herself in the reflection of a window on the way up and was surprised—again—by her own reflection. Anouk had been right. The new color did suit her (and, moreover, it suited Paris), but being a brunette was going to take some getting used to. And she was going to have to break it to Bas gently. He'd have a fit.

Anouk unlocked a small door—painted the same glossy aubergine as the front door—and they stepped into a long, narrow room that seemed to have hoarded every light particle that hung over Paris. They were on the top floor, and the roof section here, set back from the dormers of the neighboring buildings, was made of glass. Crittall window frames bound it together so that it looked like a miniaturized version of the famous Musée d'Orsay.

At the far end of the room, next to the window that looked down on the courtyards at the back, was a workbench and a panoply of tools that for the life of her Cassie just couldn't imagine Anouk using. Handling and designing diamonds, sapphires, rose quartz, and coral? Yes. Bosch power tools? No.

Anouk unlocked a safe and brought out several tobacco-colored suede roll-bags filled with goodies. She started laying out pieces on a long box padded with black velvet—a coral lariat, a stack of turquoise cuffs, tiny rubies laced onto a delicate waist chain, a necklace made of huge rough chunks of amber and wound with rope.

There was a knock at the door. "Just in time," said Anouk, raising her eyebrows at Cassie as she passed as if to say "Brace yourself." She opened the door to let the woman enter—the woman Cassie had correctly remembered as Katrina Holland. Anouk greeted her warmly but formally, and a very tall, lean man in a suit followed her in. He was incredibly handsome—almost model-like—with short, nearly black hair, wide cheekbones, and a narrow chin.

"Eduardo Escaliente. *Enchanté, madame,*" he said, kissing her hand lightly, his gaze hovering over Anouk a fraction longer than was polite.

Cassie stood waiting by the table, suddenly wondering if she shouldn't leave. No doubt Katrina Holland would expect this to be a private appointment.

"And who is this?" Katrina asked, staring at her. Eduardo looked over too and Cassie felt herself blush under their combined scrutiny.

"May I introduce Cassie Fraser from the marketing department at Dior. We were just going over a few things for the upcoming shows. Cassie, this is Mrs. Holland and Señor Escaliente."

Cassie shook hands politely.

Katrina kept Cassie's hand in her grasp. She was staring at her intently. "So you work at Dior? Tell me, how are they in the atelier?"

Cassie picked up a flinty note in her voice. "Uh, well, busy," Cassie bluffed. She wasn't starting her new job till tomorrow, so she had nothing to go on but her recollections of the mania surrounding the run-up to Bebe's show. "Will you be going to the show, madame?"

"No. I only do Valentino and Chanel," Katrina sniffed.

"Oh? But I thought Anouk said she was introduced to you—"

"Through Dior, yes," Anouk said, interrupting quickly. "But then, ah . . . there was an unfortunate *coincidence* at the Elysée Palace."

"They had assured me I was the only person to have placed an order for that dress," Katrina said tightly, her nose in the air. "And so I was. But Madame Sarkozy had borrowed the show sample." She pursed her lips. "I haven't bought from them since."

"I'm so sorry to hear that," Cassie said solemnly, taking her cue from the discreet widening of Anouk's eyes (like she'd always done at school when they'd been caught passing notes in class) to close the subject down. "They must regret their mistake very much."

"I'm surprised you don't know," Katrina said. "I would have thought all Dior employees would know who its most valuable former clients were."

"Ah, well, Cassie is new to Paris," Anouk smiled. "She arrived from New York only yesterday."

Katrina looked back at Cassie. "New York? Really?"

"Yes. But if you will excuse me, I'll give you some privacy,"

Cassie said, eager to make her escape. "It's been a pleasure to meet you, Mrs. Holland, Señor Escaliente. *À bientôt*, Anouk."

Anouk took her to the door, passing the keys to her as they kissed good-bye.

Cassie wandered down the stairs and back out into the street. A bicycle was chained up against a drainpipe opposite, a stray dog cocking its leg on the back wheel. She took her phone out of her pocket and tried Luke's number again.

"This number is no longer in service . . . This number is . . ."

She turned it off, getting the message loud and clear.

Chapter Twenty-Three

Dropping her bag into the basket at the front, Cassie looked all around her before setting off. The first time she'd done this she'd nearly been run over by a Fiat 500 with a ninety-two-year-old man at the wheel, but now it was that heavenly time of day—five-thirty in the afternoon—when the city-dwellers were attending to "matters of love" and the streets were quiet. It wasn't as if she had far to go—the flower market was just on the other side of the bridge—and she was enjoying cycling here. The basket would come in handy, for she certainly wouldn't be able to carry all the flowers back *and* see where she was going.

She'd been here for two weeks now, and among the other things she'd learned—that matching your bra and knickers *does* make you feel more together; that red wine reduces heartache (or was that heart disease?); that weekly facials are more important than weekly blow-dries; that running is bad for you, but hammams are not—was that opulent flower arrangements are the absolute cornerstone of civilization. And tonight needed to be very civilized. Tonight was her official "coming out" party when she'd meet Anouk's friends.

Up till now, the two of them had been closeted away, enjoying quiet suppers at Anouk's apartment. Cassie hadn't felt up to socializing and meeting more new people so soon after leaving a dear bunch of others, to say nothing of the effect Luke's new voice-mail message had had on her. It had propelled her straight back to all the feelings of insecurity that had plagued her in the wake of Gil's rejection.

Anouk's defense had been immediate and comprehensive, as she imparted all her most closely guarded beauty secrets to help Cassie rebuild her self-esteem. It turned out that going brunette had only been the start of it, and most of the time Cassie felt like Eliza Doolittle being dragged from urchin flower-seller to society lady as she had to relearn—in direct defiance of Kelly's advice—never to wear lipstick before 8:00 P.M. but always to have colored nails; to choose a statement scarf or necklace over a trophy bag; and to wear colored, matching lingerie rather than T-shirt bras and seamless pants.

And it seemed to be working. As she began to look better, so she began to feel better. Her skin glowed because she wasn't getting up at dawn to run, and although Anouk wouldn't admit outright that carbs were banned, the "pure protein" Dukan diet they were following meant she wasn't permanently hungry anymore, so she didn't care, and her hair shone because it was nourished like a child and wasn't being permanently touched up (sorry, Bas). In fact, the difference in her appearance was so radical that she was too nervous to Skype Kelly or Suzy. She was pretending that Anouk's connection was down and she could only phone instead.

She pedaled over the isles' connecting bridge, wondering what to buy. In the lobby at the LVMH headquarters, she was almost ambushed by the overflowing bowls of peonies in pinks, lilacs, and reds. But they weren't seasonal. No doubt they were shipped in by private jet, and she'd have to make do with some early daffodils.

She glided down the Quai aux Fleurs, on the opposite side of the isle to Notre Dame, until she came to the encampment of flower stalls, all hooded with blue polyethylene covers, where the ground was permanently awash with water from overturned buckets. She turned into the aisles and swung her leg over the saddle, wheeling along with just one foot on the pedal as she scanned the profusion of roses, lilies, tulips, and early narcissi, which all bent forward provocatively, displaying their lush beauty with all the shamelessness of the burlesque dancers at the Pigalle.

A rack of densely bunched lemon-cream roses with long stems caught her eye. She scanned the rest of the stall for something to contrast them with and found an untouched bucket of lilacs nestling between some double-headed tulips. She bought two dozen of the roses and the same again of the lilacs, and rested them in the basket, having to secure the roses—which were so tall they nearly toppled out again— with a carefully positioned baguette between the handlebars.

She pedaled slowly, in no rush to get back, just enjoying being out and about in this new city, absorbing the smells, taking in the noises. The biggest adjustment was getting used to having the sky just above her again. The Manhattan skyscrapers always seemed to push it up and away, but here it was within touching distance, as much a part of the city as the buildings and river that ran through it.

The lights on the Pont d'Arcole turned red and she eased to a stop beside the other bikes at the front, her head full of the seating plan and trying to remember who was "with" whom, so the bus was almost past her before she realized what she was seeing.

She looked on, astonished, as it heaved onto the bridge, that strip of dazzling sunshine along its side, the flash of red silk as shocking now as it had been on that gray November day in Luke's apartment. She looked around and saw some of the other cyclists and pedestrians follow the image with their eyes. None of them noticed that the model herself was standing next to them. Why would they? She was brunette now, an entirely different creature, the new, updated European version. Only her eyes—with their hesitancy, their caution, that sense of wanting to let go but not being able to—gave her away as a girl on the run.

"It's for you," Anouk said, popping her head around the door. Cassie was standing in front of the mirror, anxiously scrutinizing her reflection for the hundredth time. She was wearing narrow black trousers, a tuxedo jacket, and an Isabel Marant bronze sequined vest that scooped at the front and swung at the hem. Her jacket sleeves were pushed up to her elbows, and Anouk had lent her a couple of huge copper bangles.

Anouk dropped her head against the door frame and smiled proudly. "If I had known what a difference a fortnight could make, I'd have snatched you away from Gil years ago. Such a waste." She disappeared again. "Come along," she called.

"Who is it?" Cassie asked, skittering after her, fiddling anxiously with the bangles. One on each wrist? Or both on one arm? She felt ridiculously nervous. "I didn't hear the phone ring."

"That's because it didn't!" said a voice from the console.

Oh no, not again. Cassie looked over at the laptop. Suzy

was beaming out from it—at least she was till her jaw hit the floor.

"You have got to be kidding!"

A long, long silence drew a line between the two of them as Suzy tried to believe her eyes.

"I just can't believe it," she gasped. "You look like an entirely different person. I mean . . . New York was a stretch. All the black and the ultrablond. But it was still you. I can't believe you've crossed over to the other side."

"What do you mean?"

"Going dark. Blond was *you*, Cass. It suited you—your nature."

"You think this doesn't?" Cassie asked, her customary feeling of panic creeping up on her.

"No, it's not that," she sighed. "You look amazing! Totally amazing! It's just everything. The way you're dressed, your makeup. You're even moving differently again. What has she done—put you on wheels? . . . *Nooks!*"

"She's in the kitchen. We're having a dinner party."

"Not sitting on the floor, I take it?" Suzy joked. Then her eyes widened at the accompanying thought. "Ooooh, has Kelly seen you?"

Cassie grimaced. "No. I've been—"

"Hiding? Yeah, and now I know why. I *knew* something was up. I just thought it was because you were pining for Luke."

"*Tch*, not much point doing that," Cassie said, shifting her weight. "He's made his position perfectly clear."

"Sorry, babe."

Cassie shrugged, coming over as much more blasé than she actually felt. "It's not the worst thing that's happened to me recently. I'll get over it."

"You shouldn't have to," Suzy muttered darkly.

"Well, I'm hardly blameless. I was the one who left. I could have chosen to stay."

"And he could have chosen to understand and to wait," Suzy protested. "You could have been back by July."

"July? What—are you trying to get rid of me early? I've not even arrived yet!"

"Yeah, well . . . I'm going to be needing the spare room, see," she said, grinning broadly.

"Huh? Why?"

Suzy said nothing, just kept nodding excitedly until the penny dropped.

"No!"

"Uh-huh!"

"No!!"

"Uh-huh-huh!"

"Ohmigod, Suze!!!" Cassie shrieked, clapping her hands and jumping on the spot. "You're going to be a mum? And Arch—oh, he'll be such a great dad! Ohmigod—do the others know?" She leaned toward the kitchen. "Nooks!"

Anouk came back into the sitting room, a navy apron covering her matte-gold Louis Vuitton prom dress, which was so low-cut, even her tiny bosom managed to tremble. She was wiping her hands on a tea towel.

"What a lot of noise," she scolded as Cassie jumped about. "What's going on?"

"You tell her," Cassie said, looking at Suzy. She started biting her nails. Anouk smacked her hand away.

"Well . . ." Suzy said, deliberating. "I just wanted to know whether Bonpoint was better priced over there than it is here. Because I know Petit Bateau is sold in supermarkets in France, but it's just silly money this side of the Channel, and you know I'd rather Bonpoint, but if it has to be Petit Bateau, then so be it." She'd managed it all in one breath.

There was an amused silence.

"*That's* how you tell me you're having a baby?" Anouk laughed, palms up, walking slowly up to the screen and planting a kiss on it. "By comparing Petit Bateau with Bonpoint?"

"Well, that's going to be your primary function as godmother. Shipping over crates of the stuff."

"Godmother?" Anouk repeated, an uncharacteristic catch in her voice.

"And don't think you're off the hook either, Fraser," Suzy called around her. "Yours is to teach baby to cook Sunday lunch by the time it's eight, or else it's off to boarding school. Got to earn its keep."

"I'll see what I can do." Cassie giggled, her hands clasped together over her mouth, as if in prayer.

"How are you feeling?" Anouk asked, perching on the arm of a chair. "Is the morning sickness okay?"

"Urgh, the pits," Suzy said. "And the munchies are out of control."

Cassie rolled her eyes. When were they *not*? "Is Arch excited?"

"Beside himself. Walking around with the scan photo like it's membership to the Hurlingham."

"*That* proud?"

"Oh, yeah. Wanna see it?" she asked, holding up a grainy black-and-white picture.

"Oh, Suze! The baby's got your nose," Cassie cooed.

Suzy frowned and looked at the picture herself. "What are you talking about it? It's barely got a nose yet. It looks like a coffee bean," she contradicted, but she couldn't stop beaming and her eyes were as bright as buttons. "Anyway, so long as it doesn't have Arch's ears, it'll be a OK."

The sound of voices outside the door made Anouk jump to attention.

"*Merde!* We have to go, Suzy. Guests are arriving."

"Sure thing." Suzy shrugged. "My work here is done anyway. *Bon appétit, mes amies!*"

Cassie's French was good, but not so good that she could keep up with the passionate debate on Sarkozy's pension reforms, and she sat in silence, hands politely off the table, trying to ignore the fact that she was wishing she were anywhere but here.

She looked around instead at the stage they had set—the flowers elegantly arranged in a low centerpiece, the dimpled water glasses dappled in the candlelight, four bottles of Chianti standing empty and aromatic on the table, just a couple of garlic-tossed mushrooms left sitting in the bowl, an entire Stilton dug out from the center with a long-handled silver spoon, and lipstick-ringed cigarettes littering the ashtrays.

On the surface, everything seemed to be going exactly as it should. The room looked the part, she looked the part, but she felt lonely, isolated, and restless. Like a fake, a drifter. Suzy's reaction to her new look had disconcerted her. She might have tried to hide it, but it had been the same as Henry's in New York—a polite smile, unable to hide the concern in their eyes as Cassie changed again into someone else. It exhausted her too—didn't they realize that? How many more times would she change before she finally gave up the search and said, "Okay then. I'll stop here. This is the one. This is the one I'll be?"

She tried to tell herself that at least she was getting different perspectives from all this change. If they were in New York right now, for example, it would be Grey Goose Vodka in the glasses and salted edamame beans on the plates. In Scotland, single malt, roasted venison, and treacle tart.

She thought back to the last dinner party she'd been to— Thanksgiving at Kelly's apartment. She closed her eyes for a moment and pictured everyone sitting cross-legged on the floor in the warm flickering light, her patch of grass in the center of the table, a hidden solitaire; she remembered the light in Kelly's eyes, Brett's tears, how Bas had whirled her off her feet in celebration . . .

The difference was not down to the food or the drink or the decoration, not even the location. It was that she had been among friends.

"Some more wine, perhaps?" the voice next to her enquired.

Jacques, Florence's husband, was smiling at her kindly, a bottle of Châteauneuf-du-Pape in his hands.

"Yes, thank you. Sorry, I was miles away."

"Sarkozy has that effect," he smiled, pouring, and she fidgeted in her seat, trying to get back into the flow.

"So, what do you think of our city?" he asked, rescuing her from the wider conversation as he pushed her glass back toward her.

Cassie reached her hand out, resting her fingers on either side of the stem.

"It's every bit as beautiful as I had heard."

"And you had really never been here before?"

Cassie shrugged apologetically. "My husband and I . . . we didn't really travel much," she said simply. "And he doesn't speak French, so . . ." God forbid that she should have visited Anouk on her own.

He nodded, as though understanding more than she was saying. "I am very sorry to hear about your divorce."

Cassie just nodded. What did you say to that? It sounded like she had suffered a bereavement.

He looked at her, his dark gray eyes intelligent and inquisitive. He had a "strong" nose and huge hands, the backs of which were speckled with dark hair. Everything about him physically was slightly overscaled and coarse, yet there was a gentleness to his manner that compensated for it. He reminded her of Gabriel Byrne, a larger version. "Were you with someone in New York?" he asked.

She could tell from the question that Anouk must have told him about Luke, but she was reluctant to go into it.

"Yes. Yes I was."

"And what happened?"

"He wanted me to stay there and move in with him," she said in as few words as possible. "But when I asked him to wait till the summer, he dumped me."

"*Tch*," Jacques said, shaking his head. "That is the difference, you see? American men do not understand the beauty of space." He moved his hands like a conductor. "If he had done as you asked, you would probably have remained true to him here in Europe, yes?"

"Of course."

"But his pride got in the way and now he has lost you for good. If only he realized that a little space would have sent you straight back to him."

Cassie pondered this. He was right, she supposed. She would never have cheated on Luke while she was here. The problem hadn't been her inability to commit. It had been his inability to wait.

"It is the same with your husband."

"I'm sorry?" Cassie looked at him.

"No doubt, with a little time, you would have forgiven him too and taken him back."

Cassie exhaled forcibly at the remark, as though someone had come up and squeezed her hard around the ribs. "Uh . . . no. Actually, I wouldn't have," she demurred quietly. "Time wasn't an issue in that instance."

Jacques looked at her. "You mean you really wouldn't have been prepared to even *try*?"

Cassie looked away, indignation prickling all over her, and realized that everyone had stopped talking pensions and was now listening in on their conversation instead.

"That's right," Cassie replied in a quiet voice. "I wasn't even prepared to try."

Jacques sat back, clearly astonished, and a small murmur rippled around the table.

"I think what we have to remember," Anouk said diplomatically, "is that things are different over there."

"Over there?" Cassie looked up at her. She knew her friend was trying to build a bridge, but she'd managed instead to belittle Cassie's response into something gauche and parochial, as though the vow "forsaking all others" were nothing more than a playground rhyme.

"Well, here, an *affaire* is . . . it is not a reason for a marriage to break up," Anouk explained.

Cassie felt her stomach lurch at this sudden shifting territory. What was Anouk saying? That she didn't agree with Cassie's actions after all? That she thought Cassie should have stayed?

"And she would probably have a lover herself, the wife," Anouk continued, trying to placate her.

"A lover herself . . . ," Cassie repeated. "You make it sound so whimsical—self-indulgent almost, as if you're deciding to treat yourself to a cashmere dress or the last of the chocolates."

"I wouldn't qui—"

"But it gives absolutely no hint of the scheming duplicity, lies, and betrayal that come with every kiss, does it? Of the dreams and hopes that are trampled upon with each touch?"

She stared straight at Anouk, pink-cheeked, outnumbered, and mortified to be making a scene at the dinner party where she was supposed to be making new friends.

There was a long, awkward silence as the two hostesses clashed invisible swords.

"Well . . . ," Anouk said slowly, stubbing out her cigarette and grinding it into the ashtray. "Would anyone care for coffee and petits fours?"

Cassie sat chastened and silent as everyone nodded enthusiastically and quiet pockets of conversation started up again. Everyone seemed eager to move on and defuse the tension caused by her overreaction so that it didn't linger over the cheese.

"You must be tired from your flight?" said Guillaume, the man to her right. He was slightly built with an aquiline nose and light brown hair that had once been blond, and he was technically her "date" for the night, although he had spent most of the evening in conversation with Anouk. Anouk had mentioned in passing, with her usual breeziness, that French-women don't date, they throw dinner parties, and given that Florence was married to Jacques, Victoire—a textiles designer—was married to Marc, and Anouk was with her boyfriend, Pierre, an IT whiz so handsome that at first glance Cassie had earmarked him for Bas, it meant that Cassie and

Guillaume, for tonight at least, were a couple. "They always say to allow a day for every hour of time change."

"Well, I don't think I can plead that, if I'm honest." Cassie smiled, grateful for the elegant reprieve. "Anouk took me to the hammam on my very first afternoon."

Guillaume nodded, gentle laughter lines pleating around his brown eyes. "Ah, of course, the hammam! It is almost a rite of passage for women here. Sometimes I think they hold secret meetings in those places—like the Masons."

"Well, I've certainly never known anything like it." Cassie didn't like to mention that she'd been a stranger to cleanse-tone-moisturize before landing here.

He laughed quietly. "The pursuit of beauty is like a full-time job for many women." He looked at her, regarding her thoughtfully. "Not for you, though. You are very beautiful."

"Thank you," Cassie said, blushing, knowing better than to push back a compliment from a Frenchman.

He smiled and started telling her about his last trip to the coast and she listened appreciatively. He was attentive, and attractive too, but he wasn't Luke.

And she wasn't looking.

Chapter Twenty-Four

"There's some mail for you today," Anouk said as she shut the gate behind her. She dropped it into the basket as Cassie unlocked the bike from the pay station. She was lucky. There was a Vélib bike rack directly opposite the apartment, which allowed her to cycle to work each morning and have less than a 200-yard walk at the other end. Anouk didn't bother. Her studio was only two streets away. Even in five-inch Louboutins she could walk that.

"*Bonne journée, chérie,*" Anouk said, kissing her lightly on both cheeks. Their disagreement at the dinner the week before had passed without further mention. There was little point in bringing it up—there were some cultural differences that not even a makeover could remedy.

"Are you seeing Pierre this afternoon?"

"Of course." Anouk smiled and flashed a tiny glimpse of cherry-red bra strap threaded through with a blue velvet ribbon. "New! You like it?"

"Of course." Cassie chuckled as she put on her helmet.

"Shall we eat in tonight? It is the fish market today. I thought I would get some halibut?"

"Great." Cassie smiled, seating herself on the saddle and leaning forward on the handlebars. "I'll go to Poilâne and get us some nice sourdough and black olives to go with it." She resisted the urge to punch the air in glee now that carbs were back on the menu, albeit in morsel quantities. "See you later."

She pedaled off, the tips of her bob fanning out like ruffles from underneath her helmet. She swept over the Pont Saint-Louis and toward the Quai de la Corse, where she joined the main body of rush-hour traffic toward the huitième arrondissement.

It was the end of January and Paris was still in hibernation. The lime-tree buds were still tightly wrapped, and the Seine was a belligerent beige that refused to glitter or gleam except in the most dazzling of midwinter sunbursts. But here and there Cassie could see the city was beginning to flirt with the idea of spring: occasional snowdrops clustered around the roots of silver birches, the fountain was free-flowing most mornings, and there was usually dew, not frost, on the windows when she opened the curtains in the morning.

She parked her bike in the usual spot, and with her helmet under one arm and the mail curled into her bag—she had recognized the handwriting on the top envelope immediately—she walked quickly to the office.

"Bonjour, Martine," she said to the receptionist as she strode through and pressed the button for the elevator. It occurred to her—as it did every morning—to climb the stairs to her office, but the thought was gone as quickly as it came. Kelly might not approve, but then what Kelly didn't know couldn't hurt her. She was in Paris mode now.

She was the first in. She had to be. They were busy-busy-busy at the moment, though without the stress and expletives that had accompanied the busy period at Bebe Washington's. The couture show had taken place the week before to rapturous acclaim, and now the atelier was in back-to-back meetings with stellar clients going through their diaries and choosing suits for the carousel of charity lunches, dresses for Club 55, ballgowns . . . Katrina Holland hadn't shown, but Anouk had told Cassie she'd made a splashy entry to the Valentino show, arriving with no less than three walkers, each holding one of her shih tzus.

On Cassie's desk was a file. Kane Westley, the designer, had been *in situ* and spearheading the label's renaissance for fifteen years now, and to celebrate they were producing an enormous limited-edition coffee-table book charting the company's new legacy. The book would be sent only to the top tier of customers, and there was to be a lavish party to celebrate its closed-doors publication in April.

Cassie was charged with doing the picture research for the book from the archives, researching locations for the party, and pulling together the goody bags. For someone who'd been in the city less than a month, it seemed somewhat perverse to be expected to know about party venues for an international crowd that habitually frequented the most exclusive clubs, hotels, and penthouses around the globe. On the other hand, given that Florence had been put on the spot to conjure up a job out of thin air, location-hunting meant Cassie was basically being paid to explore the city.

Of course, Suzy had waded straight in when she'd heard the brief.

"Sweetie, I've done more Paris weddings than I can shake a stick at," she'd cried down the line. "Everyone wants to get married in the Capital of Love. Look, I'll e-mail you a list of locations, but it's for your eyes only, okay? You go check them out and see whether they work for you. A lot of them are private, uninhabited premises I've got on an exclusive arrangement only thanks to shameless stalking and creeping flattery. Don't let me down!"

"This is it," Cassie thought, as she grabbed her mail from the bag and opened the topmost envelope. The chaotic handwriting gave Suzy away as much as her signature taupe stationery embossed with a pale blue cake. Cassie scanned the contents quickly. There were glossy brochures for two lateral apartments—one of which had roof gardens overlooking the Palais Royal—three townhouses, a château on the southern outskirts on the road to Fontainebleau, and a 220-foot yacht with an exclusive mooring near the foot of the Eiffel Tower. There was bound to be something in that lot that would make even the Dior elite feel excited.

She sent an e-mail to Florence, saying she was scouting locations and would be back before lunch. Folding the list, she put it in her bag, then reached for the other letter—a large brown A4 envelope bound twice over with brown packing tape. As she began to open it, the contents rattled.

Déjà vu? She opened it, and an earthy, musty smell wafted out. Yes, seeds.

The card was written with the same brown ink as before, except that there was no motivational motto this time, just care instructions. "Well, what the heck are they, Henry?" she wondered to herself, pulling out a handful and staring at them. They could be sesame seeds sent over on the Eurostar for a midmorning snack, for all she knew.

She was baffled. Why did he keep sending her plants to grow in foreign cities? The message behind the grass she kind of got—green grass of home, a patch of countryside in the urban jungle, and so on—but what were these? And if he wanted her to have flowers, why didn't he just call Interflora?

There was a postcard inside. It was divided into quarters and had pictures of a punk, a red double-decker, Nelson's Column, and the King's Road sign. "Wish you were here," was written in huge red print across the middle.

Smiling, she turned it over. It was a list. Another one.

- *Visit Point Zero*
- *Acquire a Ladurée habit*
- *Call Claude at (33) 40 26 97*
- *Get invited to the Dîner en Blanc*
- *Go to the catacombs*
- *See The Kiss*
- *Get to London, no matter what!*

  Henry xxx

Some of it made sense on first reading. She'd already been to Point Zero. In fact, she passed it several times a day. It wasn't a historical landmark, as it was in New York, but a geographic one: a bronze plaque on the ground in front of Notre Dame Cathedral and the point from which all distances from Paris were measured. Strike one, then.

And sure, *The Kiss*—even she knew she had to see that. But ringing some random stranger and not even knowing *why*? Don't say Henry was trying to set her up too. If Anouk mentioned drinks with Pierre and Guillaume one more time, she thought she might scream. And what was the Dîner en Blanc? Where were the catacombs—was he expecting her to go spelunking in Paris? And as for acquiring a Ladurée habit? What did that mean—take orders and live a life of celibacy? Could she buy one on eBay?

She shook her head and folded the list back into the bag of

seeds, rolling the package down so that it lay flat at the bottom of her bag. There was no time to decipher Henry's codes now. She needed to hit the streets. That party wasn't going to throw itself.

"I can't believe you've done that to her!" Kelly shouted crossly.

"I had to. The condition was terrible," Anouk shot back. "It would have all broken off anyway in another few months. You cannot keep bleaching hair like that and expect—"

"I expected a little support. I was the one to put her back together again, you know. Do you think it was easy? I was the one who sat with her while she cried and got drunk every night for two months . . ."

Cassie looked up. That wasn't how she remembered it. Hadn't Kelly dragged *her* out—kicking and screaming most nights—and made her drink sugary cocktails till her head spun?

"Well, she's not that together. She's still hung up on Luke and she looks completely miserable when she thinks I'm not looking." She looked at Cassie. "You do."

"At least I made her look like a better version of *her*. You've just made her look like you!"

"And what's so wrong with that?"

"Stop it! Both of you," Cassie said, exasperated. She got up and started to pace about, a large glass of burgundy in her hand.

"I can't see you when you go over there," Kelly said.

"Well, that's probably a good thing," Cassie replied. "It'll stop you both shouting for a minute."

Kelly and Anouk stared at her. She sighed wearily—

and not just because she must have walked over ten miles location-hunting today. She was amazed at how little had changed since school. Those two could be separated by an ocean and still manage to have a shouting match. They were too similar, that was the problem.

"Look, Kell. Anouk wasn't trying to undo everything you've done for me," she said quietly, trying to referee.

"No? She's started from scratch. Made you into a completely different person."

"I was giving her options," Anouk interjected. "Things are different here."

"Different how?"

There was a pause. "Gentler."

"Gentler! What does that mean?" Kelly gasped dramatically. "Are you saying I made her look *brassy*? You think New York girls are *brassy*?"

"Enough!" Cassie cried again, this time coming to stand between them so that she was the only one they could see. "Look, Kell—what Anouk has done is *not* a rebuttal of everything you did. I like my hair like this, but who's to say I'll keep it like this? It's just an experiment, that's the point of this year, isn't it? And I still wear my favorite black Bebe trousers and absolutely nothing will stop me carrying my Maddy bag, even though they wanted to give me a Dior one. And— dare I say it—I'm even beginning to miss my runs in the park, *a bit*."

She crouched nearer to the screen. "I miss you. And I loved being in New York, I really did. It brought me back to life with its energy and ambition and . . . and can-do attitude. I mean, look at me—I'm working at Dior, the center of the fashion universe! I couldn't have done that fresh from the grouse moors, now, could I?"

Kelly gave a small, appeased laugh. "You have come a long way, baby," she drawled.

"Thanks to you," Cassie said. She turned and grabbed Anouk off the arm of the chair and gathered her into her side. "Thanks to *all* of you. You're all keeping me going and showing me new directions, and, yes, showing me different versions of me. I don't know which one's right yet, but we're ticking off the options, right? And you know what, Nooks? You're absolutely right about Luke. I am being a misery. He's behaving like a child, and frankly I could do without it right now. If it's got to be all or nothing, then . . ." She took a deep breath. "I guess it's nothing."

She took a big glug of burgundy and smacked her lips together. She looked at the glass lovingly. "Besides, I've decided I'm going to embark on a deep love affair with French cuisine and wine instead. It's much safer."

"Not for your thighs!" Kelly shrieked. "Nooks, tell her!"

Anouk chuckled before looking slyly at Kelly, allies again. "What did I tell you? Poor Guillaume isn't getting a look-in."

"Oh, I hardly think Guillaume is crying himself to sleep each night," Cassie quipped.

"He's asked after you every time I've seen him."

"I'm sure he has," Cassie said, winking at Kelly. "I have a pulse."

"*Tch*, you may know about French beauty and style, *chérie*, but you still know *nothing* about French men," said Anouk.

"Well, you can take it off the syllabus," Cassie said, patting her arm. "The only man I want to know about is Brett and how he's gonna survive the wedding preparations." She looked back at the screen. "Has the haunted look come into his eyes yet?"

"Cunning diversion!" Kelly said, flicking her Vuitton

leopard-print scarf at the screen. "And no, not even close. He's loving it." She wrinkled her nose. "I think he made the wrong decision going into banking, you know."

"Wow, he's a keeper, Kell! Gil had to read the date on our invitations just to know what day to turn up on."

"Yeah, well, it might have been better if he hadn't bothered," Kelly said grimly.

"So it's all nearly sorted then?" Anouk asked quickly, bringing the subject back around again.

"Well, it *was*. But then Suzy's news has thrown a spanner in the works. She's not going to be able to fly after May, so we looked at bringing the date forward from June to the end of May, but then we couldn't get the venue we wanted . . . Then when I mentioned pushing the date *back* to sometime in July, after the baby's born, she threw a total wobbler about wearing a bridesmaid's dress so soon after the birth. She said she'd look like she'd eaten the vicar if she stood at the altar next to you two."

Anouk giggled.

"So what's the answer?"

Kelly shrugged. "Well, we've decided that if Muhammad won't come to the mountain . . ."

A moment passed.

"No!" Cassie gasped. "You're not having it in London?"

"Well, not technically London. Gloucestershire. At West Meadows."

"Suzy's mother's place?" Anouk asked.

"Exactly. It was our home from home while we were at school." She looked at Cassie. "Don't you remember all those half-term holidays there, and weekend getaways?"

Cassie nodded happily. Anouk had been able to hop on the train to get home, but she and Kelly had had long-haul flights to contend with, so they had always stayed with Suzy at West Meadows instead. "I think it makes perfect sense—if Brett's happy with it."

"I think he'd get married on the moon if I wanted it, but either way, he knows how important it is to me for us all to be together."

"Dare I say it, but it sounds like it's all under control, then?" Anouk said encouragingly from her position on the arm of the sofa.

"Well, it *would* be," Kelly said, rolling her eyes, "if we could get her ladyship to decide whether she's going to be a blond or a brunette bridesmaid." She squinted through the screen at Cassie. "You realize you're holding up the entire wedding with your schizophrenia—there are colors to be decided upon and themes to be arrived at. Suzy's going to hit the roof if I don't come back to her with a decision soon." She threw her arms in the air dramatically. "Honestly, with me getting married and her pregnant—we're women on the edge, I tell you. Women. On. The. Edge."

Anouk tucked her legs under her, and cupped her cheek in one hand. The burgundy had brought a pale flush to her cheeks and a languid smile to her lips. A cigarette was perched between the fingers of her left hand.

"God, I'm glad that's over and done with," Cassie sighed, hugging her knees up to her chin and pulling her sweater—a moth-eaten gardening one of Gil's that always hung from the hook in the boot room—down over them. "I guess it means Paris Cassie is now officially 'go.' Kelly's in the loop, so you needn't rein yourself in anymore."

"Trust me, I wasn't," Anouk smiled, her eyes flicking with satisfaction over her protegée.

"Oh? So that's it for the surprises, then? You've shown me everything there is to being a Parisienne?"

"Superficially," Anouk shrugged, taking a deep drag of her cigarette.

Cassie narrowed her eyes. "What does that mean? That I'm still just a tourist?"

"Well, you don't want to hear it, so . . ."

Cassie put her hand up, instantly alert to the "great unmentionable" that their differing attitudes to men had become. "Oh, I see! Right, well, I don't! Enough of the man talk."

Anouk sighed. "It is the big difference. If you want to know what it is like to live here, you have to know how to love here. I can make you brunette, get you a job at Dior, put you in lingerie, and swap your *maquillage* for a skin-care regime, but if you do not understand the French attitude to love, then you are still just somebody who comes here to climb the Eiffel Tower."

Cassie rolled her eyes. "You are so hung up on love."

Anouk let her arm dangle down. "But that's precisely my point," she said, piercing her with an intense stare. "I'm not."

"Well, neither am I. I've sworn off it."

Anouk shook her head. "No. You are trying too hard, trying to outrun it. Trying not to ring Luke, trying not to say Gil's name . . ."

"They're not the same thing. I didn't love Luke—don't love Luke. He just made me happy at a time when I was very unhappy."

"And I could introduce you to some people here who would do the same for you."

"But I don't *want* to bounce from one man to the next, Nooks. That's not who I am. I can't keep letting people in and then watch them walking away from me."

"You're not getting any younger, Cass." Anouk gave a small sigh. "Besides, you're the one who does the walking."

There was a brief silence.

"You make it sound like I leave without a backward glance," Cassie said quietly. "As though I'm not hurt too."

"I *know* you're hurt. That's why I want you to learn how not to be."

"And how do you learn that, exactly? Anaesthetic to the heart?"

"Practice. Experience. Entering into the relationship with no expectation of Happy Ever After. Just a fond good-bye, somewhere down the line."

"That's what it is to be Parisian, huh?"

Anouk smiled.

"Hmmm, I think I prefer Henry's version—and God knows, between becoming a nun and spelunking, that's saying something."

"Becoming a *nun*?" Anouk echoed, arching an eyebrow. "What are you talking about?"

Cassie refilled her glass. "He's sent me another list. Some more flowers seeds too. I've got them growing next to the coriander, by the way, so don't throw them out."

"Henry's sent you a list for Paris? This I have to see. As if an Englishman could give you a better idea of the city than me." She stubbed her cigarette out and held out her hand. "Show it to me."

Cassie sighed. "God, you're all so territorial. Kelly was exactly the same." She got up and fished it out of her bag. "Tell me it makes sense to you, because I feel like I'm reading the cryptic clues in the *Times* crossword."

She handed it over and Anouk scanned it. "Point Zero . . . Ladurée . . . Claude . . ." She looked up. "Who is Claude?"

Cassie shrugged. "Your guess is as good as mine."

"Dîner en . . . Dîner en Blanc! How does he expect you to get onto that?"

Cassie's eyes widened in panic. "Why? What is it? Please tell me it's just a restaurant with a crazy waiting list?"

Anouk tutted. "You should be so lucky! The White Picnic, it is a secret thing—no one knows who are the organizers, and the members are secret. You can only get onto it by invitation."

"Then how will I get invited if I don't know who to ask?"

Anouk shrugged. "The catacombs—oh, great, explore the dark underground tunnels while you're in the City of Light," she said sarcastically. "*The Kiss*—mmm, predictable." She let the list flutter to her lap and looked at Cassie, satisfied. "I much prefer my version of Paris. Get you looking right and introduce you to a sexy man." She smiled and lit another cigarette.

Cassie picked up the list and scanned it again. The Manhattan list had been such fun. This didn't seem quite so . . .

"I wonder who Claude is?" Anouk mused, her eyes slitted in concentration. She regarded Cassie slyly. "Maybe Henry is setting you up on a date with him. He thinks you need some fun too."

Cassie closed her eyes and shook her head. "It's a goddamn conspiracy."

She heard the digital notes of numbers being punched into the phone and opened her eyes in alarm. Anouk immediately handed the phone to her. "You speak to him, or I will."

"Who? Henry?" The long dial tone pulsed slowly in her ear. "Claude."

"Allo?" The voice was abrasive, and his pickup was more of a shout than a greeting. Cassie gulped down her fright.

"*Allo?*"

"Uh . . . Hi! Is that, uh . . . Claude?"

"Who is this?"

"My name's Cassie." She bit her lip in mortification. She couldn't believe Anouk had done this to her. She'd had no intention of ringing some stranger for a blind date. "I'm in Paris. Henry Sallyford asked me . . . to call you."

A long moment passed. "Henri?"

"Yes. Did he . . . did he tell you I would call?" Please, at least say he'd done that.

Another moment stretched out. "Yes, yes, I remember . . . I'm just checking my diary." He sounded hassled. Cassie heard the sound of pages being flicked. "Okay . . . come over Saturday, eleven o'clock. We'll do lunch. You have my address?"

"Uh . . . uh . . ." Cassie reached around wildly for a pen, not because she wanted to have lunch with this man—they hadn't even said 'How are you?' to each other—but she was in the middle of it now, and she didn't want to be rude.

He dictated his address, somewhere in the middle of Saint-Germain-des-Prés.

"Okay, Saturday then," he said. "Don't be late." And he hung up.

Anouk stared at her as—stunned—she put down the receiver.

"So?" Anouk was leaning toward her curiously.

"Well, if *that* was a taster for the French seduction technique, I think it might be easier to learn the rules of disengagement than I thought."

Chapter Twenty-Five

Cassie returned the bike to the nearest Vélib rack and shuf-fled slowly down the street. It was narrow and quiet, with contemporary art galleries, minimalist furniture boutiques, and rococo antiques shops. She was supposed to have been here forty minutes ago, but she'd overslept. Pierre and Guil-laume had taken her and Anouk ("just as a sociable four," Anouk had protested) to a burlesque club in the Marais the night before, and it had been past two in the morning before her head had hit the pillow.

Cycling in the cold and hooking up with a random stranger was absolutely the last thing she felt like, and it was only be-cause Anouk had hidden Henry's list, which had Claude's phone number on it, that she had made it here at all. What she really wanted to do was lie in bed and groan and have someone silently hook her up to a saline drip, run her a hot bath, and finish with a full-body massage. In fact, she'd nearly wept as she heard Anouk book her own slot at the hammam.

She checked the address again and sighed crossly. Where was the goddamn door? She wasn't that hungover, surely. She could still count. All she needed was to find number 13, but the house numbers seemed to jump from 11 to 15.

An elderly man in a navy overcoat and trilby walked past on the opposite pavement, a bagged baguette under one arm and the paper in his other hand. She tried her best to run over.

"*Excusez-moi, monsieur* . . . do you know where I can find this address?"

The man looked at the piece of paper she was holding out—it was the dry-cleaning receipt she had scrawled the address on the other night. He pulled out a pair of spectacles and struggled to read her writing.

"*Oh, la-la. C'est la bas,*" he said finally, pointing to a tiny alley opposite, next to where she'd just been. Cassie hadn't noticed the alley because it was so narrow that a scooter chained to the drainpipe on the adjacent building had obscured the entrance to it.

"Thank you, thank you, sir," she smiled, running back over. She started down the alley. It couldn't have been more than twenty feet long, and there was nothing down it except for a black fire door, which only opened from the inside, and a fire escape above. She turned around, searching for a name or number, anything at all, but there was nothing. She looked back at the fire door. That had to be it.

She was just raising her hand to knock when she heard voices from the other side—lots of them. She stepped back just as the door was flung open and a couple of Japanese girls came out, talking quickly, cameras around their necks. They were followed by a tall, narrow woman with ebony skin and a wicked afro, a middle-aged man with a gray mustache, and finally a dark-haired, black-eyed man the size of a bear.

"Wait there!" he barked to the group as he punched in an alarm code inside the door. They all stopped obediently, though the Japanese girls didn't break stride in their conversation.

"Oh, excuse me, but I'm going in!" Cassie said, lurching forward, not quite able to bring a smile to her eyes.

"Who are you?" he demanded, clearly as grizzly by nature as by looks. He looked her up and down. She was wearing blue jeans and the Moncler jacket Luke had given her for Christmas. She hadn't been able to face wearing it since leaving New York, but winter was showing no signs of pulling up stakes and the wind was especially bitter on the bike.

Cassie prickled at his abrupt manner. "I'm here to see Claude," she said, deliberately not answering his question.

"*I* am Claude," he said, with such pomposity that he could have been saying, "I Claudius."

"Oh." Cassie's eyes widened. That was bad luck. "Well—hi!" she said, giving a wan smile and holding out a hand. "I'm Cassie."

He ignored it. "You're late."

"Yes." She dropped her hand, insulted by the snub and suddenly determined not to apologize. She planted her hands on her hips and turned the tables on him. "I couldn't find the door."

He scowled at her.

"So, what—you're . . . going out now?"

"Well, we weren't going to wait for you any longer," he said, marching off.

Cassie stared after him. "We?"

Again he ignored her, disappearing out of the alley and making off down the street. Cassie threw her hands in the air in bafflement. Oh, great! Now what was she supposed to do? Leave him to go out with his friends? Chase after him?

She stared down the empty alley, catching snatched flashes of people walking past on the bright pavement beyond. She looked at her watch. She supposed she was forty-five minutes late now. And he was Henry's friend. Clearly if Henry rated him, he must have something going for him. He wouldn't have hooked her up with a bad-tempered Frenchman just for the hell of it.

She ran after him. He was a good 200 yards ahead, but in spite of her splitting headache, she caught up with him easily.

"So, are they joining us for lunch too, then?" she asked, jerking her chin toward the group in front, absorbed in their casual bonhomie.

He flicked his eyes toward her irritably, as though surprised to find her still bothering him. "Is that a problem for you?" he asked.

"No. The more the merrier, frankly," she said with forced brightness. "Where are we going?"

"You would know if you'd turned up on time." He accelerated his pace.

Cassie narrowed her eyes as he pulled away. Quite how someone as easygoing as Henry could be friends with someone like this, she didn't know, but she made a mental note to give Henry a Chinese burn next time she saw him. She wondered how quickly she could get out of this.

They marched along the streets in silence, past the cafés that had been filled since breakfast and were now segueing at full capacity into lunch, past the shops selling rustic lace tablecloths and olive-printed oilcloths, past the lovers leaning on scooters, and below the children playing marbles on the balconies, past the tourist shops selling replica football kits and tricolor flags, until they rounded a corner and walked straight into a riot.

At least that's what the market felt like to her poor beleaguered head. Everything was suddenly louder, brighter, more vivid, as shouts, haggles, cries, and laughter jostled for the ear, and colors vied for the eye. She felt the inevitable headache coming on.

The group came to an abrupt stop and Claude turned to face them all, his face as bleak as before. "So we are here," he said vaguely. They were standing outside a tobacconist. Cassie looked around for the restaurant.

Claude reached into a cross-the-body bag he was carrying and handed each of them a small, pale green laminated card. Cassie's eyebrows shot up.

"It's a *shopping* list," she exclaimed, looking up at him.

"Congratulations on cracking my code," Claude muttered sarcastically, and the Japanese girls tittered with laughter.

Cassie blushed, furious. Who the hell laminated their shopping list? And who the hell got their lunch companions to do their shopping for them?

"Okay, so you have one hour to buy everything. I do not mind which stalls you buy from, but resist the temptation to buy from the first stall you go to. Quality and cost can vary greatly. Your eye for fine ingredients will tell me what you are capable of before we even get into the kitchen."

Cassie stared at him, and then at the group, clearly all strangers to one another, and then at the list. It was beginning to dawn on her that she wasn't on a lunch date here. It was a cooking class! The thought immediately excited her.

"What are we cooking?" she asked, feeling her hangover recede.

"Again, you would know if you'd arrived on time," Claude said flatly, quashing her spirits again. He checked his watch. "We shall meet back here at twelve-fifteen P.M."

He might as well have fired a starter's gun. Everyone dispersed instantly and Cassie sighed as they disappeared into the crowds. The road was closed to traffic, and shoppers milled about everywhere, handling, weighing, sampling the produce casually. Part of her wanted to storm off and leave this rude Frenchman to it, but a bigger part of her was intrigued.

It wouldn't hurt to browse. She stepped off the pavement and into the thick of the flow, wandering at a snail's pace that suited her battered body. The stalls were all covered in the same white sail-canvas, and as she passed, she noticed the artful way they'd been set up, almost like Dutch still lifes: glossy eggplants were clustered like grapes on a vine, chilies were threaded and hanging down like coral necklaces, roasted chickens were set out in military rows, aged and moldy cheeses were wrapped in wax paper and twine like little gifts, live lobsters sat black and angry in straw boxes with their pincers taped shut, yellow squash blossoms lay in trays like trugs of narcissi, roma tomatoes were heaped high, scallions piled up shiny and smooth . . .

She stopped at a stall where four trestle tables covered in navy cloth were laid out with deep bowls piled high with olives—black, green, pitted, stuffed. She tried counting how many varieties there were, but there had to be well over thirty—forty, even. She heard the stall owner—a short man with a doughy face that looked as if it had been dusted in flour—speaking Italian to another, younger man who was standing next to him.

The man noticed her staring. *"Oui, madame?"* he smiled, his arms held out, all ready for a sale.

"I just wondered what these were seasoned with?" she asked, pointing to a bowl of olives in the center row.

"Toscana—sun-dried tomatoes, rosemary, garlic," he said, pressing his index finger and thumb together like a verbal drum roll.

"Really?" She clapped her hand over her tummy apprecia-tively. Her hangover had meant she could only face coffee for breakfast, but she was rapidly feeling hungry. She reached for her purse. "I'll take fifty grams, please."

The man spooned them into a plastic lidded tub and she handed over the money. "You are Italian?" she asked as she waited for her change.

"Si. We come from a small village—Diano d'Alba—near Turin. Twice a week."

"You mean you travel to here from *there*?" Cassie asked, astonished.

"For this market, yes. It is the very best in Paris. We are not the only ones. People come from hundreds of miles around to sell and buy here. My father came before me, and now my son." He patted his son hard on the shoulder. The son gave a polite nod. They must have been up since dawn.

Cassie took her change and smiled her good-byes, am-bling through the crowd and glancing at the list properly. She needed some apples, for a start, and she could see an apple stall a hundred yards farther on with just as much diversity of choice as the olive man's. Giant cooking apples—nobbled and misshapen—sat as proudly as miniature plumped-out pippins; some of the varieties looked highly polished, like deep red garnets trying to pass as rubies; others were matte and richly pigmented as if they'd been colored with wax pastels.

"What are you looking for?" the old woman behind the table asked. She was sitting down, a headscarf knotted over her hair.

Cassie shrugged. "I don't know, to be honest," she smiled.

The woman got up and took the green laminated list from

her, nodding to herself. She turned and jerked a brown paper bag off a string.

"You are with Claude Bouchard," she said, walking to the far end of the table and filling the bag with a dark plum-colored variety.

Cassie watched her. "Yes . . . How do you know?"

She flicked her eyes toward the laminated list. "He always starts with the Tarte Tatin. *Classique et délicieux*. It is the Reine des Reinettes you need." She threw one of the apples to Cassie. "Try it."

Cassie hesitated, but the woman was watching her expectantly. She took a small bite.

"Is crunchy, a little bit tart, *non*? But high sugar content so it keeps its texture when it is cooked." She winked at Cassie. "He'll ask you that, so remember it," she said, tapping her temple. "Then you will be his favorite student and that is a very good thing to be. Six euros thirty."

Cassie fished in her purse for the change. "Hmm, I'm not sure I can be bothered."

The old woman frowned. "Claude Bouchard is a Michelin-starred chef," she scolded, pocketing the money without looking at it and patting her stomach proudly as though she were his own mother. "Or he was. Until he stopped." She shook her head and pursed her lips in disapproval.

"Stopped? How do you stop being a Michelin-starred chef?" Cassie shook her head at the incongruous glory—he looked more like a cage-fighter than a chef.

"Three years ago, he locked the doors. Fired everybody. Not walked into a professional kitchen since. Now he just does a class when he needs the money, but . . ." The woman flicked her hands dismissively. She leaned forward and whispered to Cassie. "He has the melancholy." She smiled, so that her wizened face folded in on itself. "But you are lucky. He does not take on many people. He must like you."

Cassie shook her head. "No, no, he definitely doesn't like me. But he likes a friend of mine."

Another customer, farther down the table, began impatiently filling brown bags with apples herself, and the woman rushed off to serve her. Cassie clutched her rustling bag to her chest and stepped back into the street. She'd seen enough episodes of *MasterChef* to know that the hierarchy in a professional kitchen was as rigidly enforced as a royal household's—and she'd turned up three-quarters of an hour late with an attitude and a hangover. It wasn't what you'd call an auspicious start by anyone's standards, much less a Michelin-starred chef's.

She chewed her lip for a moment, wondering whether the situation was salvageable, then took the shopping list out of her pocket and began studying it with intent. She'd better start making up ground.

She was first back at the meeting point, bags bulging and eyes wide. She hoped that Claude would be back before the others—she didn't want to do this with an audience. She scanned the faces in the crowd, looking for the other students, but noticed Claude coming out of a crêperie opposite. It was his hunched body language that caught her attention. He looked up and saw her. She thought she saw disappointment come into his eyes—and she realized that she wasn't the only one who'd been hoping that she would disappear and not come back.

He made his way over reluctantly, checking his watch and rearranging his features into a scowl.

She took a deep breath.

"I just wanted to apologize," she said quickly, as he came to stand next to her. "There's been a misunderstanding—on *my* part. I didn't realize what we were doing here today. When you said we would do lunch, I didn't realize you actually meant we would *do* lunch. I thought you were just a friend of Henry's who was going to show me Paris."

Claude stared at her.

She carried on nervously, as she spotted the others in the group advancing quickly toward them. "He didn't even give me your surname, so I didn't know that you're . . . you know, who you are." She coughed awkwardly. "Anyway, I'm sorry. That was all I wanted to say."

Claude didn't bother to respond. In fact, from his still-hostile body language, she wasn't even convinced he'd heard. They stood in silence as, one by one, the rest of the group joined them, all holding bags stuffed with identical ingredients. Once the Japanese girls arrived, beaming expectantly and carrying twice as many bags as everyone else (the sight of a striped sweater hanging out of one of them suggested they'd been shopping off-plan), Claude clapped his hands briskly and they all filed back toward the apartment in apprehensive silence.

Despite the building's innocuous exterior, his kitchen was bright and elegant inside, with high ceilings, a tiled floor, and a long iroko worktop that ran down the center of the room. Chopping boards and a selection of sharpened Global knives were arranged at set intervals, and Cassie felt her hangover begin to recede as she caught sight of the dark red Lacanche range. This was no mere tourists' cooking club. Everything she looked at—from the copper-bottomed pans to the diamond-sharpened knives—was of the highest possible quality. It was like being in a professional kitchen with customers in the next room, and it put to shame her once-mooted, never-tried amateurish ambition of setting up her own cooking school, catering to the wives of the guns on the shooting drives.

Claude buttoned up his chef's whites as they all emptied their shopping bags at their work stations. He walked around, tutting as he inspected their purchases: crêpes, chanterelles, tarragon, garlic, sugar, butter, flour, pistachios, apples. "Too acidic . . . not ripe enough . . . too small . . ."

He got to Cassie and peered over her shoulder. She found she was holding her breath. She'd found a fantastic stall set slightly behind the others for the chanterelles and cep mushrooms, and she was confident of the stallholder's choice of apples for her. After a minute, which felt like a month, she felt him nod. "Maybe not so bad as I thought," he muttered with the darkness of a death threat.

Cassie broke out into a huge, delighted grin and tried not to squeal. It was the best thing anyone had said to her since she'd arrived in Paris.

Chapter Twenty-Six

"I don't know what you see in him."

"You mean, apart from culinary brilliance?"

"He has all the charm of a table leg."

Cassie smiled as Anouk exhaled delicate puffs of smoke between two perfectly plumped lips. It was fair to say that Claude had been underwhelmed when Anouk—her interest piqued by Cassie's fast-growing obsession—had accompanied her to the kitchen that morning. Claude had not given her so much as a nod, and Anouk, four hours later, was still sulking.

Cassie took another sip of her espresso—she hadn't found anything to replace Tea and Sympathy here, and in the absence of her PG Tips she was becoming a hard-core coffee aficionado—and watched the traffic squeal and jerk around the square. She had just done her third day on the course. It was supposed to have been daily classes for a week, but her day job meant that was impossible, so Claude had completed the course with the rest of the group and was now instructing her one-on-one every Saturday. Henry's favors seemed to stretch very far with people.

Today, they'd done a fig and almond tart sprinkled with pistachios, and Claude had revealed to her his secret of bringing the butter mixture for the pastry to the boil in the oven. She sighed contentedly at the fresh memory, driving Anouk even deeper into her black mood.

Cassie watched her as she took a deep, jittery drag on her cigarette. Her friend seemed nervy and on edge. She had been working late in the studio recently and going straight to bed when she came in, and Cassie noticed for the first time that she had black circles under her eyes—a previously unthinkable sign of self-neglect for someone who took longer to wash her face than it took to change a tire. And now she was interpreting Claude's customary indifference, which he seemed to direct at any living being, as a snub to her desirability. She wasn't usually so fragile.

"Have you and Pierre had a fight?" she asked quietly.

"*Non*," Anouk replied defensively. "What makes you say that?"

"You seem unhappy."

"Not unhappy. Just busy." She shook her head and her hair came to a caressing sweep under her cheekbones. She rubbed her temple lightly with her free hand. "I am having a problem with my diamond supplier, and Katrina . . . She's not used to waiting for anything."

"I can imagine," Cassie replied sympathetically.

"She wants nine pieces shipped out by the end of next week."

"I'm sure."

"It's *completely* unreasonable."

"It is."

She took a final suck on the cigarette before grinding it out in the saucer. "He thinks I can drop everything at the drop of a hat, just like that. Like I don't have other things in my life."

Cassie paused for a moment. "He?"

"What?"

"You said, '*He* thinks I can drop everything' . . ."

Anouk looked at her. "Did I?" She stared back down at the ash in the saucer. "I meant 'she.' I meant Katrina."

Cassie sighed and put a hand over her friend's. "Wanna talk about it?"

"I told you, there's nothing to talk about." She pulled her hand away.

Cassie sat back and watched her. "Okay. If you say so." They fell into silence and Cassie ruminated on how different it was living with Anouk. In New York, Kelly had practically merged them into one person—same job, same clothes, same bedroom, same lives. But Anouk was different—very independent, and she compartmentalized her life. She had found Cassie a job, but with someone else, as she preferred to work alone. And although things were clearly intense between her and Pierre, she only ever met up with him on a rigidly observed timetable. She never saw him after eight in the evening, and aside from that one dinner party, he never came to the flat, much less stayed over.

In lots of ways, as their days crisscrossed over each other, Cassie felt she was closer to Anouk than anyone—her favorite thing was cooking for the two of them in the evenings while Anouk sat on the worktop pouring the wine and the city lights twinkled in through the windows—but there was a definite boundary that seemed impossible to cross. Conversation rarely moved beyond gossip or work, and activity was confined to shared beauty rituals—the hammam, manicures, endermologie or hair appointments. She had been in Paris for six weeks now, and she could scarcely quite believe it, for she had long held up Anouk as the epitome of glamour, but life was beginning to feel quite . . . narrow.

"Well, why don't you get him over tonight, then?" Cassie suggested. Maybe it was time for them to break out of their boxes a bit. "I'd like to get to know him better and I could cook for you both. I'd rather like to test out what I've learned at Claude's, anyway. You could be my guinea pigs."

Anouk looked away. "He's away this week. Not back until tomorrow."

"What about tomorrow night then?"

"He'll be tired from the journey."

"Right." Cassie nodded, getting the message loud and clear. Anouk didn't want the status quo to change. She might be miserable and tense, but everything had to stay just the way it was.

Bas could be seen from a mile off, like a giraffe in a herd of hippos, like a miner in the snow. Cassie rushed forward and flung her arms around him as he dropped his bags to the floor and hugged her back equally hard. She'd missed him more than she'd realized, especially when he immediately began turning her around and appraising "the hair situation." On Cassie's instructions, Kelly had debriefed him before he'd left (putting the blame squarely on Anouk's shoulders), hoping to soften the blow.

"Good cut; condition's better," he said solemnly as travelers rushed past them, desperate to get to the taxi rank. "And it's got high shine. You just cannot get that kind of luster on blond. And it does make you look very classy." He took a step back and regarded her from a distance. "But it's not you."

"Are you saying I'm not classy?" Cassie teased in mock outrage as he picked up his bag and they started walking, arm in arm, toward the airport exit.

"Classiest girl I ever knew," he said, slapping her hand

playfully. "But it's just not my sweet, ditzy, how-do-I-get-dressed-again? girl."

Cassie giggled.

He stared down at her fondly. "You look all European and mature. Like you know how to seduce a man just by the way you untie your scarf."

They walked outside and straight into the cab Cassie had kept running on meter. The taxi sped through the back streets, pulling up at the Crillon, where Bas was staying for the week—the fashion circus had finally rolled into town on the last stage of its New York–London–Milan–Paris tour—and they checked him in. Not into a suite or anything fabulous like that, but still, a deluxe room with a view of the Eiffel Tower.

He had been booked by Valentino, Chanel, Sonia Rykiel, Isabel Marant, Balenciaga, Chloé, and Vanessa Bruno, which meant he could afford to splash out a little, but it also meant he didn't have a single free day. Cassie wondered exactly how much time she'd actually get to spend with him. After all, it wasn't as if he'd be around every evening for dinner. If he wasn't actually at a show—which would invariably be running an hour and forty-five minutes behind schedule—he'd be at the ateliers until the small hours, working through briefs with the designers until they agreed on the looks. She'd be lucky to get him for coffee.

Cassie had just about managed to pin him down to dinner for Anouk's birthday on Friday, five days from now, and he'd promised faithfully to try to keep that evening free for her—not just so that they could spend some time together, but also to stop Anouk from inviting Guillaume as Cassie's "date."

They went up to the room, and Bas ordered a pot of boiling water from room service.

"Don't tell me you're fasting," Cassie scolded, going into the bathroom and coming out a minute later in one of the fluffy bathrobes. "You need to put weight on, not take it off."

"Not quite." He winked at her as he hauled his bag onto the luggage rack and began rummaging inside, triumphantly pulling out a small box of PG Tips.

"From our favorite little shop in the Village," he said, as she jumped up and down with excitement.

She brewed up a perfect pot, and they drank it happily, stretched out on the bed and watching the lights flicker on the Eiffel Tower.

"So, you happy, Teabag?" Bas asked her.

"I am now," she sighed, before slurping her tea noisily.

"Really, though." Bas was looking at her with concerned eyes.

Cassie took a little breath. "Well, getting happier . . . I'm more solitary here than in New York. Back there, you and Kelly just completely adopted me and I scarcely had a moment to register my sadness, I was so busy. And then when I got together with Luke, that was . . . a big milestone for me in so many ways. But coming over here meant leaving all you guys. I don't know, I think in some ways I arrived in Paris even sadder than when I arrived in New York. I wanted to *stay* with you, whereas I came to New York because I wanted to get *away* from Gil."

"And now?"

"Well, I think I've grown up some more. I can get dressed on my own and walk better in heels—though they still hurt like hell." She waggled her feet as if they were hands. "I do a lot of cycling around the city on bikes and sitting alone in cafés reading my newspaper. It's the hair, you see—it lets me blend in more."

"You got a European version of me here?"

"Don't be silly, I could only ever have the original," she grinned, resting her head on his arm.

"Glad to hear it," he replied, looking visibly relieved. "For my part, I've not met any other girls asking for yellowish hair and wearing numbered clothes either."

Cassie burst out laughing. "My God, I was a disaster, wasn't I?"

"You were, but I loved you for it. You're an original, Cassie Fraser."

"I'll tell you what else *I've* got that's original," she said, looking at him slyly.

"What?"

"A really grumpy Frenchman who looks like a bear."

Bas grimaced. "He's your French *Luke?* Honey, you could do a lot worse than go back to that man. God knows, *I* wouldn't have left him."

"No, no, nothing like that." She looked over at him, disconcerted by the unexpected mention of Luke's name. "Have you seen him at all, since I . . . you know?"

"What? *Didn't* stay?" He shook his head at the memory of the disastrous Stay party. "No. No. He's been keeping clear of all of us. Kelly and Brett haven't seen him once. I expect he's been traveling a lot, though—there's been the couture, campaigns . . . you know."

"Yes, I know," she murmured. "Is he seeing anyone?"

"Not that I know of, but like I say—I haven't seen him."

Cassie twitched her mouth anxiously. She hadn't mentioned his name once since he'd changed his number. It had been an abrupt and very clear message that he was moving on, but she couldn't help wondering—when she was in the bath, on the bike, scouting locations for the party, or standing in the bread queue at Poilâne—whether he actually had. She'd resolved not to mope, but that didn't mean he'd quit his lodgings in her head.

"So tell me about the bear man," Bas said quickly, taking in her sad expression and obviously regretting bringing Luke's name into the conversation. Cassie smiled again. "Well, his name's Claude and he's appalling in every way. Rude, obnoxious, abrupt, always got to be right, arrogant, imperious . . ."

"Wow, dream guy," Bas drawled sarcastically. "I can see why you like him."

Cassie turned her head on the pillow and looked at him dreamily. "He's utterly, utterly brilliant. He's the one making me happy out here."

Bas sat bolt upright at her limpid expression. "Don't tell me you're serious!" he exclaimed. "He sounds like a walking disaster—the last thing you need."

"He's a *chef.*"

"I don't care if he's the freaking president," Bas cried. "He is no good for you."

"No, no—I mean, he's a Michelin-starred chef. He's teaching me to cook."

Bas stared at her, trying to fathom how that could make her so happy.

"So you're not sleeping with him?"

"God, no!" Cassie chuckled. "I think he's probably got hair growing behind his knees."

Bas laughed, a little more relaxed now. "Well, that's okay then. Because I know what you're like. You've got no shit-o-meter. You'll just go headlong into more heartbreak."

Cassie put a hand on his and smiled. "You're so protective. But there's nothing to worry about. It is strictly pleasure."

He sank back into the pillows. "Huh. Cooking. Who knew."

"Yup, we did a tart last time I saw him and we had to boil the butter mixture in the oven, can you believe it?" she trilled.

Bas shook his head, completely baffled. "Not really."

"I see him on Saturdays. We go to the market on boulevard Raspail together and *shop*. Buy everything really fresh, and just the very best, you know? He's shown me all the best stalls—who to go to for truffles, who for olive oil . . . It's like being part of a club. It would feel like treason now if I walked into a supermarket." She looked at him, utterly earnest. "Do you know, I don't think I'll *ever* walk into one again, for the rest of my life?"

"The zeal of the converted," Bas muttered, pouring them each more tea. "So what you're telling me is you like this hick town?"

"Bas, how can you *not* like a city that has cooled sparkling water in the drinking fountains?"

He raised his eyebrows, impressed—as she'd known he would be—by that little nugget.

Cassie nodded.

"Hmmm, well I guess that's *something* in its favor." He looked at her. "But you're going to come back, right? I'm not losing you to this place for good?"

Cassie stared out of the window, focusing harder on the night-lit Eiffel Tower, which was beginning to blur from the condensation on the windows. "Do you know what I think," she mused. "I think that this city isn't so much telling me about *where* I want to live, but *how* I want to live. Does that make sense?"

"Not really."

"Well, I mean . . . I scarcely know anyone here, my job is basically paid tourism, there's no man on the horizon . . . and yet the quality of life out here is making me happy even without those things. I always used to think happiness depended upon them, but cycling about, shopping at the markets, cooking with Claude, unwinding at the hammam . . ."

"The what?"

"There's just an indolence here that makes my bones buzz."

"Well, now, I like the sound of *that*," he said, sliding further down the bed, his hands clasped behind his head. "But I guess I'm gonna have to meet your bear man and make sure he looks after you for me."

"He'll just snarl at you," she warned.

"No he won't," he replied confidently. "I'll know how to sweet-talk him. Everyone knows bears love honey."

Chapter Twenty-Seven

Cassie smiled brightly as she shook hands with the agent and started walking briskly away down the street toward the golden dome of Les Invalides. The strident pace and chic ensemble—navy beret and belted camel coat—helped hide her mounting panic. It was three in the afternoon, the last week in February, and there were only seven weeks to go till the party. The guest list was in the final edit stage as the powers-that-be ruthlessly whittled away the numbers to leave only the biggest spenders standing. The problem was, until they knew the venue, they couldn't confirm final numbers—it wouldn't do to have too many people crammed into a tiny space; and even worse, to have too few in a large space. Not to mention the fact that the printers needed a location to put on the copperplate.

Cassie had put various deluxe options in front of Florence—most of which were from Suzy's list—but they'd all been rejected as too "straight". It wasn't that the venues Suzy had given her weren't beautiful or spacious or historic, but none of them stood out—not at an international level anyway. This party was for people who spent half a million euros every six months just on their clothes. What did they care about a chateau? It was just a cottage in the country to them. The Eiffel Tower? A garden ornament, no doubt.

"The thing is, Cassie," Florence had explained patiently, "this party is about what Monsieur Westley has brought to the company. It is not about the tradition and formality of the legacy he inherited. Monsieur Westley, he is a rebel. He used to be called the "bad boy of fashion." And our customers love that. They like the frisson of excitement that comes with the renegade, with breaking the rules. For most of our customers, they are constrained by appearances, there is a level of decorum that must be maintained. But they like that Monsieur Westley can undercut the stiffness, take a bit of air out of the pomposity. He delivers a little bit of the punk into the couture—and we must do the same for his party."

Cassie had nodded enthusiastically, as though that speech were going to somehow translate into a solution, but two weeks later she still had nothing suitable to show Florence. This building—a converted prison that was, ironically, too luxurious now—had been her last option and they were due to have a final-decision meeting tomorrow.

Cassie rounded a corner, and as soon as she was sure she was out of sight, slowed to a dejected shuffle, her shoulders slumping, hands now clasped behind her back, her bag swinging into her knees. She blew out through her cheeks and came to a stop in the Esplanade. She sat down on a bench, knees knocked together, stumped. In her heart, she knew there was nothing for it—she'd have to come clean. She'd asked Suzy, Anouk, and even Bas, and had spent weeks cycling and walking all over the city taking photographs of interesting-looking buildings, but to no avail. She was all out of ideas.

Even on a day as bleak as this one—the sun had called

in sick—Rollerbladers raced past and elderly gentlemen convened for games of *pétanque* between the trees. At the steps of the Dôme church, noisy school groups in matching sweatshirts and baseball caps goofed about on the statues making bunny ears for each other's photographs, and every twenty yards, street sellers heckled the passing pedestrians, trying to flog tacky snow globes of the Arc de Triomphe and mini replicas of Notre Dame.

She looked away, trying to avoid their gaze, and caught sight of a man sitting on the bench diametrically opposite. He was staring at the ground directly in front of his feet, utterly oblivious to all the noise and movement around him. He looked like he'd been cast in stone. He didn't even seem to blink.

Cassie hesitated for a moment, wondering whether to intrude. She knew from bitter experience that he was graceless at the best of times, but something made her get up and walk over anyway.

"Claude?"

He looked up at her slowly, as though disoriented by the sound of his own name.

"Hi," she smiled as his eyes focused on her. "I was just passing . . ."

He looked back down again.

She knew she should probably go, that she'd regret it the second he opened his mouth. But it seemed so . . . extraordinary to run into him out here, so far from their usual meeting place in the quatrième arrondissement. Shopping and cooking with him had rapidly become the high point of her week, something she counted down toward like a child at Christmas, and she couldn't bear to pass him by on this bonus encounter. He was never going to win any charm awards, but his manner had begun to approach a pale shade of cordial in recent weeks, and she sensed that deep, deep down, under all the hair and gruffness, he maybe even, perhaps, liked her—a little bit.

"May I join you?"

He sighed heavily, as though waking from a deep sleep, flicking his index finger ever so lightly. She took it to mean "possibly," and sat down.

"Shitty weather," she muttered, instantly regretting it. He wasn't a man for small talk at the best of times, much less when he looked like this. Hunched, frozen, desolate.

"What are you doing here?" she asked instead.

Nothing.

She looked away, watching a group of pigeons fighting over some cake the schoolchildren had left in a wrapper on the wall. She ought to go back to the office, see if anyone else had any last-ditch offbeat ideas . . .

A bus stopped a hundred yards away, the Bebe Washington campaign slapped to its side. She'd seen it a few times now and the shock was beginning to wear off. She studied the glowing image that stared back at her—heady and enigmatic; watched as people in the queue stared at it. Kelly had told her the red top had already sold out (and that some late orders had come in for the collection as a result of the campaign) as other women tried to be her. But even she couldn't do that now. That girl was gone already, replaced by another. She was just a golden phantom.

"Did Henry tell you about me?" she asked quietly. "Did he tell you what happened?" She stared at the bus as the passengers climbed on, her voice little more than a murmur. "I think he did. I think he told you."

The bus closed its doors and pulled away. "Because I keep

wondering—why did he put us together? Why did he get me to ring you? He couldn't have known how I feel about cooking. *I* didn't know how I felt about cooking till I met you."

Silence.

She shot him a sideways look and gathered up her courage as if she were making a snowball. "I think he's put us together for another reason," she said bravely. "I think it's the thing that made you stop cooking."

Nothing. Not a muscle-twitch or blink.

She sighed and they sat awhile in the cold, their breath hanging like baby dragon puffs in the air before them. Her bottom started to go numb from being still for so long, and her nose tingled with the cold, but she sat on.

Eight, ten minutes passed and he didn't once move, stir, twitch, or even register that she was sitting there.

Finally she got up, feeling sad not to have made any progress. He had, quite literally, frozen her out. Clearly, whatever they shared in the kitchen stayed in the kitchen.

"Well, I'll see you on Saturday, then, Claude," she said, putting a gentle hand on his shoulder. "Usual time. I won't be late."

She walked away and had just reached the rue Saint-Dominique when she heard heavy footsteps behind her. She turned.

"It's cold out here," he said, as though he'd only just noticed.

"Yes." She was too surprised to comment further.

He looked at her for a moment, then gave a nod, as though agreeing with something. "Let's go and warm up."

She had been intending to go back to the office and admit her failure to Florence, but she didn't dare disagree with him. He took her by the elbow and led her toward the rank of scooters all parked askew farther along the road. His—a dusty gray model with bald tires—looked far too small to transport such a big bear of a man, but he handed her a helmet and she climbed on behind him, not quite able to get her arms around his chest.

He drove slowly, although without much care, totally disregarding one-way signs and dawdling pedestrians, until they stopped ten minutes later outside a green-paneled shop on the corner of rue Bonaparte. Its windows were stacked with boxes that looked like they would house scented soaps, and they came in every pastel color—baby pink, mint, sky blue—with chicks and bunnies alongside, motifs to bring the promise of spring to gray days. But she peered closer and saw it wasn't soaps they were selling.

Claude led her in and the bell above the door jangled merrily. Cassie marveled at the pâtissiers' treasures stacked in color-coded rows beneath the glass-covered cabinets that looked like they'd been sourced from an old apothecary. On the far wall, streams of ribbons in pink and mint hung down from their reels, fluttering gently in the breeze created by clamoring customers.

He led her toward the far end, past conical towers of pistachio and chocolate macaroons that defied gravity as well as belief, and into a small café. A baroque chandelier glinted roundly in the encroaching dusk, and they sat on a Napoleon-blue velvet sofa. Claude ordered for them without looking at the menu. From the speed and deference with which they served him, they seemed to know exactly who he was.

"What is this place?" she asked, shrugging off her coat and shaking her hair out from under her beret. "It's amazing."

"This is Ladurée." He said it with the same authority he'd said "I am Claude" at their first meeting.

"Ladurée? I've heard of that."

"I should hope so. This is the home of the most exquisite macaroons in the whole of France." He pinched his fingers to his lips. "You cannot claim to be a lover of French food—of Paris—if you have not been here."

A waitress quickly brought their orders—jasmine tea and a tiered cake stand piled with macaroons in pistachio, raspberry, rose petal, violet cream, orange blossom, and crème anglaise.

Cassie's eyes widened with delight.

"Try one," Claude said, pushing the stand closer to her.

She picked one up and took a small bite. The outer pastry was so light it was like biting into a cloud puff, and the cream filling was so rich, so intense, she had to close her eyes. "I feel like I'm Marie Antoinette," she sighed.

Claude smiled with his eyes, watching her intently. "We shall make these next," he said, holding one between his fingers and looking at it like it was a jewel. He dropped his voice. "There are two secrets to making them. One is to cook them on double trays, the other to let the dough form a shell *before* you put it in the oven."

She smacked her lips together. "Very, very good," she said, wiping her fingers with a napkin. God knows she could never let Suzy in here. She'd seen what that woman could do to a cupcake.

"Well, at least now Henry's list is making more sense. He told me not just to come to Ladurée . . ."—she took a sip of tea—"but to make *a habit* of coming here." She picked up an orange blossom macaroon and sighed happily just looking at it. "And that I shall do gladly."

She took another heavenly bite.

Claude watched her.

"He is a good friend to you."

"Who?" Cassie had to put her hand over her mouth. She swallowed quickly. "Henry?"

"Yes."

"Well, technically speaking, he's my friend's brother. We're not that close. I hadn't seen him for ten years before this summer."

"And yet he has done this *list* for you."

"Yes, well, he's a man of the world, isn't he? He goes to places where no one's ever been before. I think it was just unthinkable to him that I didn't have any ambitions about getting to know the cities I was living in."

"And why didn't you?"

Cassie looked at him. It sounded like Henry hadn't told him her backstory after all. "Because I didn't leave my home out of choice. I had made a life for myself. I had roots. I wasn't looking to suddenly rip myself away from them and start exploring the great cities."

Claude looked out of the window, nodding to himself again as though reading between the lines.

"Well, he has never suffered loss, Henry," he said. "The world is still straightforward to him. Still a present to be unwrapped. I suppose he is trying to make you a gift, to let you see the world through his eyes—something to be enjoyed and discovered."

"I guess I'd have to say it's working, then. All the greatest moments I've had since . . . leaving have come to me through his lists."

"Yes?"

"Meeting you, for example," she said, trying not to feel shy about it, just presenting it as the truth it was. "And when I met his friend Robin in New York . . . Do you know Robin?"

She wondered whether this network of men was all intercon-
nected.

Claude shook his head.

"Oh. Well, Robin let me read from a first-edition copy of *A
Christmas Carol* that had belonged to Charles Dickens!"

Claude gave what Cassie took to be an impressed nod.

"And he arranged a gift just for me under the Tiffany
Christmas tree on Fifth Avenue. It's been things like that, you
know—moments of rarity in the middle of the mundane."
She sighed happily. Then stopped. "Although I wouldn't
want you to think it's all been sweet consideration."

"*Non?*"

She shook her head. "He made me run round Central Park
on half a case of Château Margaux."

"*Non!*"

"Yes." She paused. "I mean, the Château Margaux bit
might have been my fault, but still . . ."

Claude laughed—the first time she'd ever heard it—and
she stared at him as his face crinkled stiffly with amusement.
He looked so young, like a little boy being tickled by his
mother.

"I think you are probably as bad as each other," he said,
shaking his head.

"Probably," she said, picking up the last violet cream macaroon.

"Do you have to call any other strangers in Paris?"

"No, thank God! It's now completely apparent to me why
my parents always told me not to speak to strangers. You've
put me off that for life." She laughed. "But I do have to somehow get myself invited onto some secret picnic society. I don't
suppose you've any contacts on that front?"

Claude shrugged and looked at her blankly.

"And I've got to go to the catacombs."

"Oh, *mon Dieu*," he said, giving a shiver.

"What?"

"Four hundred miles of tunnels that go down over seven levels below the city. Most are unmapped." He looked at her. "They are very dangerous to explore alone."

Cassie stopped eating. "And my night vision is appalling."

"Well, there is a short section open to the public. It is well-lit and clean there. You will be fine." He looked at her. "So long as you're okay about bones."

"Bones!"

"Yes. The walls down there are built from human bones and skulls."

Cassie paused. "Why?"

"Because by the end of the eighteenth century the cemeteries in the city were completely full and there was nowhere left to put the bodies, so they exhumed the human remains and relocated them to the limestone quarries that Haussmann had mined. They say there are over six million bones down there."

Cassie grimaced. "Oh, great. It'll be a party," she muttered.

"For sure," Claude smiled, motioning for the bill and bringing the waitress racing over.

They settled up—Claude insisted on paying—grabbed their coats, and walked back out into the chilly evening air with their cheeks pinked.

He pulled the hood of his parka up and turned to her, and for a second she thought how very frightened she'd be to pass him on a quiet street. He looked so menacing and dark, and yet for all his growling and sneers, there was something of the child about him, something vulnerable. Anouk was by far the more scary to encounter, especially at the moment. "I have been thinking—if you would like, we could meet more often. On Tuesday evenings, per'aps? And Thursdays too?"

"If I would *like*? I would love!" she squealed, hugging him hard, determined to make their good-bye on fonder terms than their hello. Claude stood like a plank in her embrace, but she didn't care. If they were meeting three times a week then some barriers had to start coming down between them. He was rapidly becoming one of the most important people in her life, and she'd be damned if she couldn't call him a friend too.

Claude nodded, embarrassed. "Okay. I see you tomorrow night, then." And he turned away without further ceremony.

Cassie shrugged happily and watched him shuffle off. She put on her beret and belted her coat tightly before turning and walking in the opposite direction toward the river. She didn't feel like cycling tonight—she didn't trust herself to keep her hands on the handlebars, for one thing—and she was close to home here anyway. But there was something else, something else Claude had said, that was knocking about in her head and giving her a plan.

Chapter Twenty-Eight

Cassie glanced around anxiously, wondering if this still counted as Paris at all, or whether she was in the suburbs now. She was only in the quinzième arrondissement, but whereas the buildings in the first, fourth, and fifth were built of limestone and decorated with pretty lead roof tiles, here they were square concrete tower blocks. The balconies had bikes and washing on them, and there wasn't a gargoyle or tourist in sight.

The park was easy to find, though, and she jogged through the gates, aware that the heavens were about to open, past two giant bull statues, beyond the old vineyards where the Pinot Noir grapes still grew and toward the pavilions she'd been told to head for. In their previous life they'd been the sheds of the old horse market, but now they housed the antique book market, and that was the reason she'd come.

She stepped under the roof just as it began to spit and she looked back up at the sky crossly. It was menacing and heavy, with billowing black clouds—the last thing she needed when she had a long bike ride home, freshly done hair, and ten people for dinner tonight. It was Anouk's birthday, and she was jangling with nerves, not only because this was her second attempt at making friends with Anouk's circle, but also because somehow she had persuaded Claude to help her cook for it.

It had been Bas's idea for her to check out the book market. He'd overheard a famous designer saying that it was one of his secret stops for design inspiration, but she didn't have much time to browse—Claude was coming over at three.

She dived straight in, weaving in and around the trestle tables laid out with ancient tablecloths and laden with boxes filled with musty old books. Pure heaven! There were occasional modern books in the mix, but almost everything she picked up was at least fifty years old and quite a few three hundred or more. They were generally arranged with their spines up, the titles picked out in gilt lettering against the fraying leather covers.

Every time she picked up a book she couldn't stop herself from smelling the pages. What was it Robin had called them? Volatile organic compounds? Well if this was decay, they could bottle it up and sell it to her. She smiled lightly as she recalled that newborn memory, sitting in the dark underneath Manhattan, reading from Dickens's very own book. She wondered what the stallholders here would think of *that* story.

Cassie moved slowly from one table to the next, not entirely sure what she was even looking for. A small emerald-green leather notebook caught her eye, and she picked it up. It was filled with black-and-white photographs of a woman, and from the way her hair was done and the clothes she was wearing, it looked like they were taken in the 1920s. The first photographs showed her fully clothed, hatted, and demure, but as she turned each page an item of clothing was removed until, at the back of the book, she was naked, her modesty gone with her clothes. There were a good few pages left at the back after all her clothes were shed that testified to that. It was early porn, but no less shocking. She put it back quickly, aware the vendor was watching her.

Some stalls specialized—in philosophy, or poetry, or military history, or history of art—and the haggling was done in low, intense voices, far more so than at the food market, where buyers used their hands, eyebrows, and smiles to try to drive down the price of sweet onions. Most of the browsers were solitary, like her, wrapped up against the midwinter chill, and were it not for the sound of children playing in the nearby playground, it would have been just like being in a library, the sound of pages flicking and turning, coughs muffled behind scarves, eyes down.

She made a purchase for herself—an early edition of *Larousse Gastronomique*—but nothing suitable to give to Anouk, and she was scanning the last row, about to give up, when a title caught her eye. *Bijoux des Anciennes*. She picked it up and began looking through it—it was all about the jewelery of the Egyptian and Roman empires, and showed jade necklaces, pearl-drop earrings, hammered gold cuffs, lapis lazuli and onyx rings, emerald and peridot collars . . . The illustrations were full-color and beautifully rendered, showing how they would have been worn.

It was perfect! Anouk would love it. The materials they'd used were precious yet rough still, not whittled to cultivated perfection like modern jewelery but retaining that guileless rusticity that Anouk managed to make so luxurious.

She bought it quickly, eager to get back, even though it was still raining. Pulling her beret out of her pocket, she tucked as much of her hair as she could into it, and trotted quickly toward the park gates. It was raining too hard to cycle now. She would have to catch the metro.

Everyone was jogging, dodging puddles, trying to get to cover. She saw a man ahead of her. He was walking briskly, the collar of his coat turned up and obscuring his face, but still she recognized him.

"Jacques!" she called, waving her arm to get his attention. "Hey, Jacques!"

But he was already out of the park and onto the streets. By the time she passed the bull statues and got to the pavement herself, he was gone.

She had just finished chopping the tarragon when she heard the curt rap at the door and felt her heart give a startled leap in her chest—even his door knock managed to sound stroppy. She wiped her hands on a tea towel and went to let him in, casting anxious eyes over the apartment as she passed through. Everything was immaculate—the table was set for ten, the crystal gleaming, the wine chilling, and all the guests' flowers, sent in advance, as was polite in Paris, decanted into vases of every shape. She'd even managed to save her hair from the worst of the rain. Now all she needed was the Michelin-starred chef.

Anouk was still detoxifying at the hammam—the worst of the crisis appeared to have blown over with Pierre but she was still on edge—and wouldn't be back till after five. Cassie was hoping all the food prep would be done by then and they could enjoy a quiet glass before everyone else arrived. It was usual for gifts to be opened in front of the giver, and although Cassie was pleased with her purchase, the book, at over one hundred and fifty years old, was in poor condition with its flapping spine and yellowed pages. It was a thoughtful gift, but probably not a *Parisian* gift. She'd prefer to present it to her privately.

"Claude." She smiled, letting him in and leading him through to the kitchen. She hoped he would comment on her outfit, or the way she'd laid out the kitchen utensils like his. But he walked straight through, his nose in the air, nostrils flaring like a bull about to charge.

"That's the reduction," she said, watching him sniff the air like a tracker dog.

"I know," he said tightly, walking over to the pan on the stove and immediately inspecting the bottle of Cabernet Sauvignon beside it. He tilted his head to the side for a second, inhaling deeply, then sliced off a tiny cube of the chilled butter, whisking it quickly into the red wine sauce. He tested it with the taster spoon. "Better. It needed more butter."

She nodded, picking up on his tension as he inspected the kitchen with a professional eye, seeing where the oven was in relation to the sink and fridge, assessing the weight of the pans, the sharpness of the knives . . . She could tell from the set of his shoulders that he was tightly coiled, and she wondered again whether it had been a mistake inviting him tonight, a mistake to try to move their relationship from purely culinary interest to wider friendship. They enjoyed a graceless, intense camaraderie in the kitchen, where neither thought about anything other than teaching and being taught, but step into another room and his composure collapsed quicker than a soufflé. She really wasn't sure how he was going to "transfer" from the kitchen to the table, and Anouk's circle was a sophisticated one.

She went back to peeling the egg for the sauce *gribiche* as he began to fillet the fish, her mind marveling at how he'd been able to tell by smell alone—"*au pif!*"—that the reduction needed more butter.

The pastry mix was boiling away in the oven when they heard Anouk's key in the door an hour later. She drifted in, wearing layers of pebble-colored yoga kit and not a trace of makeup or tension for once.

"How are the workers doing?" she asked, peering into the pans as though she knew what to look for, and Cassie noticed Claude stiffen at the gesture; his arm froze in midstir.

Cassie quickly poured her a glass of the wine and placed it in her hand. "Be gone," she said, shooing her out. "Get ready. Your guests will be here in a little over two hours and you look a state."

"I do not," Anouk protested vehemently.

"No. Of *course* you don't," Cassie smiled. "But I do need you out of this kitchen."

Anouk made a faint attempt at resistance but quite happily let Cassie push her toward the bathroom. The door clicked behind her and Cassie breathed a sigh of relief, happy to see that Claude had started stirring again and dinner was still on track.

"So, Anouk, did you hear about Cassie's fantastic idea for the party?" Florence asked. She was wearing a black draped Victoria Beckham dress that fitted like a second skin, and had a string of black pearls around her wrist.

"No," Anouk said, looking over at Cassie, who was red-faced from running between the kitchen to help Claude and refilling everyone's glasses.

"You'll never guess. Monsieur Westley just *loves* it."

"Enlighten me. Please."

Florence paused for dramatic effect as Cassie came over with the wine bottle.

"The catacombs," she said, leaning in. "Isn't it brilliant?"

There was a weighty silence as the women contemplated partying in a crypt.

"Well, it certainly sounds atmospheric," said Victoire, eavesdropping from her conversation with Jacques, Marc, and Pierre by the windows and turning to join them. It was the fourth of March and the French windows were open fractionally, allowing the chug of the boats on the river to serve as a bass beat to their conversation.

"It was the bones that clinched it," Florence said. "The Corsair collection three seasons ago was one of Monsieur Westley's most iconic collections and a big commercial hit for us. It drew heavily from pirate culture, and we did particularly well with a nebulous crossbones motif printed on to chiffon."

"Really?" Victoire asked. "You'd never have thought . . ."

"Oh yes. It did for us what the Stephen Sprouse leopard print has done for Vuitton. In fact, Cassie suggested relaunching the print for a limited-edition run to make up some scarves for the goody bags."

Anouk, who was looking especially ravishing tonight in a black lace dress overlaid on ivory silk, with a deep scoop neck and tight sleeves, squeezed Cassie's arm proudly. "Well, I knew Cassie would come through for you," she said, and Cassie beamed, almost faint with relief not to have embarrassed Anouk the way she had Kelly.

"Well, that's more than I did," Cassie demurred, smiling modestly. "I only thought of it the morning of our meeting. It was a lucky break, that was all."

"No, no, no," Florence protested, watching the two friends. "I knew all along you were the right person for that job. Everyone else in the department is too close—they don't see Paris with new eyes the way you do. It is always the person on the outside who sees things most clearly."

The words seemed loaded, but Victoire stepped in diplomatically. "Not that Florence means to suggest you're an outsider, Cassie."

"I do not think it is any bad thing to stand apart from the crowd. In fact I rather envy it. I wonder what else you see about Paris that we have become blind to?"

Cassie laughed lightly, but she definitely detected a frisson in the air and was relieved to hear a knock at the door.

"Bas, I'm so pleased you made it!" she said, hugging him as he stepped in. "I was so sure something would come up and you wouldn't be able to get away." True to her fears, their meetings had been sporadic and brief, and the days were rushing away from them.

"It did, and I nearly didn't," he said, shrugging off his coat. He looked exhausted, a paler shade of walnut. "Selena was up to her usual tricks again."

Cassie froze. "Selena? She's in Paris?"

"Yes, of course. You knew that."

"I guess so. I just forgot, now that I'm not at the coal face any more." She took his coat for him. "What's she been up to, then?"

"Oh, just refusing to have even so much as an aloe vera mask, much less a red rinse. Sonia's threatening to leave her out if she doesn't do it. All the girls are going red—it's to pay homage to her thirty years in the business—but Selena's booked for Balmain two hours later . . ." He threw his hands in the air. "Honey, I just left them to it. They'll still be going by the time I get back. And a boy's gotta eat, right?"

She patted his arm fondly. "Well, thank God you're here. I was feeling totally outnumbered. Come on. I'll introduce you to everyone."

"Wait," he whispered, holding her back by the door. "Give

me a quick run-through from here. You know I'm a disaster with names."

They looked in toward the assembled party. "Well, that's Victoire in the patterned dress. She's Anouk's closest friend and a textile designer. That print is one of her own. Don't you just love it? She does a lot of stuff for Dries Van Noten." Cassie sighed.

"Mmmmm."

"Florence, another close friend, and my boss at Dior, is in the tight black dress and pearls. She's married to Jacques— he's the tall, well-built fellow by the window. He's in antiques. And—"

"Way-hey-hey," Bas murmured. "Who's the stud-muffin he's talking to?"

"Which one? The one in the striped tie is Marc, that's Victoire's husband—"

"No, no, the lanky boy with the face of an angel."

Cassie burst out laughing. "You've got no hope there, I'm afraid. That's Pierre, Anouk's man."

"Get out!"

"Oh yes. And I wouldn't try to take her on if I were you. Just look at her in that dress."

Bas narrowed his eyes. "True. I can't pull off lace like that," he murmured.

"Come on. Let's go to the kitchen first. I want to introduce you to Claude. He's better one-on-one. Remember this is a big night for him . . . Bas?"

She turned back, but he was still leaning against the door frame, lost in thought.

"Hmmm? Oh yeah, right." He stood up and walked toward her.

"And remember, you promised honey . . ."

*   *   *

Jacques smiled appreciatively as he took a sip of the Sauternes Cassie had spent hours choosing to complement the pear tart sprinkled with hazelnuts and lavender honey.

He held his glass up to the light. "Soon you will be more French than any of us," he smiled. "Your choices tonight have been superb."

"Thank you," Cassie said, smiling radiantly. This dinner had been as much a success as the first had been a disaster. Everyone had steered well clear of controversial topics, and it didn't hurt that Cassie had unearthed, in the meantime, a talent and passion that was even more French than an affair. "I think I'm in danger of becoming a Francophile after all."

She looked down the table at Claude to check that he was okay, feeling like an overprotective mother. He was nodding as Victoire spoke to him in confiding tones, and her heart lurched a little. She could see on his face the effort it took just to smile and not speak with a growl. Anouk, on the other hand, was being haughty with him. In spite of the fact that he had masterminded a triumphant birthday dinner for her, she still hadn't recovered from his failure to fall at her feet, and was deep in conversation with Guillaume instead.

Cassie watched them for a second, feeling guilty that she couldn't entertain the idea of a romance with Guillaume—not even to be French. But Guillaume didn't seem too upset about it, despite what Anouk was saying to the contrary. On the occasions when they had met up as a foursome, they'd all had a great time together. She found him charming, intelligent, and easy to talk to, and if everyone would only let them, they could become good friends.

A sudden rip of laughter alerted her to the fact that things were a lot more lively at the other end of the table. Florence and Pierre were listening intently to Bas, who was in what he called full "fashionating" flight, wheeling out anecdotes about the week's histrionics, which might have driven him to the brink of madness while they were happening in real time, but made for fabulous dinner-party talk afterward. His listeners kept bursting into loud laughter and clapping their hands merrily.

Jacques followed her stare. "He is very much fun, your friend."

"Bas? Yes. Not at all French, of course," she said, aware he was breaking all the rules of conventional dinner-party etiquette. "But I don't know what I'd do without him. He's got a heart of gold, he really has."

"It must be nice for you to have him here."

"Yes. I just wish it was for longer," she sighed, running her finger round the top of her wineglass. "I've not really got anyone like him here in Paris. He's like a big brother in lots of ways: nonjudgemental, fully supportive, *great* shopping buddy." She laughed.

"And protective? He works with your ex-boyfriend, does he not?"

Cassie tensed. Oh no, not again. "Occasionally. They're both freelance, so . . . it's random when they meet."

"And is he over too?"

Cassie gave a small sniff. "Yes. I think so."

"But you have not seen him."

Cassie shook her head. She was still shocked by just how disappointed she was that he hadn't called. Fantasies of a reunion at the George Cinq, or wherever he was staying, had run through her head during unguarded moments, and she had hoped that at the very least they might meet for drinks and a talk. It had been two months since she'd left now; she was halfway through her Paris visit, and she wasn't going to be in London as long as she'd expected. In theory, they could be together again within weeks. At least, that was what she'd thought. But his silence was extinguishing that hope.

Jacques rearranged his napkin on his lap and changed the subject. "So tell me about Claude. It is an exceedingly rare privilege that he should be cooking for us tonight."

"Yes. I think I would gladly devote my life to learning from him. I'd give up my job and sleep on the kitchen floor," she said, before realizing her blunder and quickly recovering herself, remembering that she was talking to her boss's husband. "I mean, obviously I love working at Dior."

"But it's not your passion," Jacques said, cutting to the chase.

"No," she shrugged. "It's not. But it's only since coming here that I've realized what my passion actually *is*. I never knew before now."

"I had heard he was a recluse."

"He is very closed. Very private," Cassie confirmed.

"He must see something special in you to accept you as a friend. Perhaps you are the one to break him free."

"I'm not sure about that. We have virtually no social contact. Just a conversation once at Ladurée, but even that was only to introduce me to macaroons before we made them." She shrugged. "I doubt he considers me anything more than a bothersome, overenthusiastic student."

"Well, he came here tonight."

Cassie looked down the table at Claude. He was staring at his hands. "Yes. He did."

She suddenly remembered something. "By the way, were you at Vanves this afternoon? At the antique book market?"

"Vanves?" He shook his head. "No."

"Really? Because I thought I saw you coming out of the park."

Jacques shook his head again. "I was at the gallery all afternoon."

"Oh. Strange. I could have *sworn* it was you. Well, you must have a twin, then."

"I do. His name's Gabriel Byrne."

Cassie chuckled. "I had noticed the resemblance actually." She shrugged. "I guess there are a lot worse people to be likened to."

"Try telling that to my wife," Jacques said, rolling his eyes and looking over at Florence. "She would rather I was more like Robert Redford."

"Oh, there's definitely only one of him in the world," Cassie smiled.

"Luckily for me," Jacques laughed and gazed down the table at his beautiful wife.

"How long have you two been married?" Cassie asked.

"Seventeen years now—and counting."

"And counting," Cassie echoed, as she remembered yet again that she hadn't made it a single day past ten.

Chapter Twenty-Nine

Cassie nestled further into the deep red sofa, the color as warming as any fire. Bas was late, but that was to be expected. The schedule was out of his control—out of anyone's control, it seemed. The Valentino show was supposed to have started at two-fifteen, but allowing for the usual delay, plus twenty minutes of actual catwalking, another twenty afterward to pack up . . . She checked her watch. It was quarter past five now. He should be here at any moment.

A waiter came up again and asked if she was sure she wouldn't like something while she waited.

"Actually, I think I'll have a coffee," she said, and he nodded with a smile of satisfaction, as though it really mattered to him that that she should not be empty-handed.

A group came into the room—loud, young, fiercely chic—and everyone looked up at them. The girls were clearly models. Cassie noticed a sweep of red hair and did a double-take—was that Bonnie?—just as someone did the same to her.

"*Cass?* Is that *you?*"

Cassie looked up. Luke was staring at her, his camera in one hand as ever.

"Luke!"

"I'll be over in a second," he said to the group, and they

floated off to a far corner. He walked toward her, taking in the change in her appearance. "Jesus . . . look at you."

She got up from the sofa and obediently looked down at herself. She had come straight from the office, wearing an ivory silk floppy blouse, Anouk's red tweed jacket, and black cigarette pants.

"Hi." She smiled shyly as he took in the transformation, and she could actually see the conflict of wounded pride trying to assert itself over the happy surprise in his face. He was tanned, of course, wearing jeans, a pale khaki desert jacket, and a navy scarf.

"Hi," he said finally, no hint of a smile as wounded pride won the battle.

"How are you?" she asked, trying in turn to hide his effect on her, closing her eyes momentarily as his scent drifted over to her. She might not be able to detect a lack of butter in the reductive air, but she could still identify Tom Ford's Grey Vetiver in a crowd of thousands.

He just nodded.

"You've been away," she said, indicating the midwinter tan.

"Yeah, Turks and Caicos, for the Pirelli shoot. I probably told you about it."

"Yes," she murmured, thinking how strange it was to be greeting him so formally, in the middle of a hotel lounge, when eight weeks previously they'd have been running upstairs to bed.

A small silence began to push between them. "So . . . you're staying here?"

"Yeah. I always . . . do."

"I take it you've just been to Valentino?" As at the Bebe Washington show where they'd met, he got front-row status and was a VIP guest at every top presentation, a world away from the catwalk photographers crammed sardine-style into their taped box.

"Sure. I saw Bas was doing that one."

"Yes. I'm just waiting for him, actually." The waiter came back with her coffee. "Do you want to join us? He'd love to see you."

Luke hesitated. "No . . . I've got some stuff on that I need to deal with." He jerked his thumb back toward the group, and she saw, for the first time, Selena, staring at them, her hair still pulled back in a tight chignon, her lips pillar-box red. Short of the ubiquitous ruffled scarlet gown that accompanied such a high-fashion look, she was exactly the sort of creature who should be stalking these gilded halls.

Luke saw her stiffen and turned around. His shoulders slumped at the sight of Selena. "Oh."

Cassie looked back at him. "You're together?"

He shrugged. "Yeah."

"Right." She looked down at her coffee.

"Hey, look," he said, moving toward her, and she felt the heat coming off him, the intensity of his stare as he tried to absorb her dramatic new look. "You were the one that left, remember?"

"That's right."

"So don't get all . . ."

"I'm not getting all anything on you," she said quickly. "Like you said, I was the one that left. It's your prerogative to pick up with . . . with *her*." She looked away. Why did it have to be her, of all women?

"I'm not going to apologize for it," he said, his voice tight.

"I'm not asking you to," she said, whirling around quickly. "God knows you're not capable of it."

"What does that mean?"

"Well, your behavior has made it pretty clear just how limited your emotional span really is," she said angrily. She sank down into the red sofa again, the cushions mushrooming up around her.

He sat down next to her, just as quickly, just as furious. "Hey! *Don't* put all this on me. I was serious about you, I asked you to stay with me—and you just left without a second look."

"That is *not* how it was, and you know it," she hissed fiercely. "And besides, from the looks of things you didn't even wait long enough *for* a second look. I bet the bed wasn't even cold before you got her into it. I was probably still sitting on the tarmac, wasn't I?"

"You know, I don't know what the hell I was doing, thinking that maybe you . . ." He *tsk*ed and looked away, his jaw clenching and unclenching like a pulse. He looked back at her. "Well, it's clear that you've moved on anyway. Just look at you. It's like I've never seen you before—like the other Cassie, the one *I* loved, never existed."

She stalled at his mention of the L-word. "It's a hairdo, Luke. Not a personality transplant."

"Yeah, well . . . you look like you're doing okay from where I'm standing. Didn't get too burned after all, huh?"

"You don't know what you're talking about," she muttered, and looked away, her eyes prickling with tears, horrified to be having this argument in the middle of the Crillon. Quite a few of the other guests, also over for Fashion Week, seemed to recognize him, and were staring.

They sat in tense silence. She sighed—with exhaustion and disappointment. "You'd better go. Bas will be here any second."

He didn't reply, but also didn't get up to go, and the miserable silence stretched between them.

"So you're staying with Anouk?"

She nodded.

"Where does she live?"

"In the fourth."

"Nice." His voice was flat.

"Yeah."

Another silence. Where, oh where was Bas? She was going to need something stronger than PG Tips when he got here.

"Look, I'm here for two more days."

"Fine. I'm sure I can manage to keep out of your way."

"I don't mean that," he said, and she heard the frustration biting in his voice. He pulled something from his coat and handed it to her.

She looked down at it. It was a glossy invitation, printed with an image of Selena—who else?—reclining on a black suede sofa. His black suede sofa. She was nude, one arm slung casually over the side, the other resting against her temple.

"If that's supposed to be some kind of olive branch, you've missed the point."

"It's my new exhibition. It's tonight. It's called Muse."

"Congratulations." She made as if to hand it back to him.

"Keep it. You might want to come . . ." He stood up and shoved his hands in his pockets. "Seeing as you're in it."

"What?"

"Don't worry. You look beautiful. And anyway, no one's going to recognize you now." His hand instinctively lifted toward her hair before he pulled it away quickly. He stared at her. "Maybe we could have dinner after. Talk things through."

"I'm out tonight."

"Where? Who with?" he asked quickly, and her heart skipped at the possessiveness in his voice. "With Bas?"

She shook her head. "He's got a dress rehearsal with Isabel Marant tonight."

"So who?"

"Claude." She saw his mouth harden. "He's just a friend," she added.

"Yeah, right." His voice was instantly flinty.

"He *is*. He's teaching me to cook."

"You can already cook."

"No, I mean *really* cook—like professionally."

There was a short silence as he struggled to believe her.

"It's my thing," she shrugged.

"Really?"

She nodded. He cracked a relieved smile and she couldn't help her stomach turning over at how his eyes stood out against his tan, the way they roamed hers for the truth. "Well, okay then. So bring him too."

She paused for a second, not entirely sure that Claude was the best person to bring along to this. "I guess I could ask," she said finally.

"Okay." He gave a boyish grin. It was charming, infectious . . .

She felt her own eyes smile back. "So go."

"I'm going."

"Go then."

"I'm gone . . ."

Chapter Thirty

Cassie opened the door, beaming. Claude looked her up and down, gobsmacked surprise written all over him as he took in the vision of her. He was used to seeing her with flour on her cheeks, purée on her whites, and a hairnet on her head.

"What do you think?" she asked, planting one hand on her hip and posing. She was wearing nude stacked platforms so that she brushed the six-foot mark—his height—and a champagne-colored wool dress with a slash neck that fell into a deep V down her back. The front sections of her hair were tonged into laissez-faire ringlets, and she had a smudge of ruby-red lipstick on her generous mouth.

"*Mon Dieu,*" he murmured.

Cassie preened at his response.

"So you like it, then?"

"You'll freeze," he frowned. "And how are you going to walk in those?"

"Oh." She sighed. She supposed she should have known better than to expect any kind of complimentary response from Claude. Her text message, asking whether he'd come with her to the exhibition before their class, clearly hadn't infused him with the same excitement, as he was wearing dirty jeans and a dark brown parka with the hood up, and seemed to have steroid-boosted his stubble into an established beard that very afternoon.

She grabbed her coat.

"Thanks so much for agreeing to this," she said as they walked down the stairs, horribly aware that actually he hadn't agreed to anything. He'd simply not responded and she had bullishly decided to take his silence as an affirmative. Stopping by a photographic exhibition was most probably the last thing he wanted to do. If it had been a truffle convention . . .

The bracing air hit her immediately as they stepped into the courtyard, and she shivered. He had been right on both counts—she was going to freeze; and there was no way she could cross the cobbles in these shoes.

"Claude, would you mind?" She motioned for his arm.

It took him a moment to understand what she meant. His hands were stuffed deep into his pockets, but rather than pull them out, he swung his elbow out like a hinge. She held on, grateful.

"Thanks," she smiled.

They walked painfully slowly over the Pont Saint-Louis to the Ile de la Cité, where they could more easily catch a cab. They didn't talk. For once, she couldn't. She could scarcely believe the butterflies in her stomach. Of course, Bas had wound her up into a frenzy when he'd arrived just minutes after Luke had left, telling her that *of course* he wanted her back, but she had to play it cool, get him to dump Selena immediately, wear the stockings and suspender set that she'd bought with Anouk, tong her hair from *this* section . . . And Bas had promised to pop into the exhibition after the dress rehearsal so she wouldn't be completely at sea.

"So, this photographer . . . is he any good?"

"Yes, he really is. He's probably one of the three most influential photographers working right now."

"And he has taken pictures of you?"

"Well, we lived together in New York, so . . ."

"You did?" Claude stopped and looked at her. "But I thought your husband only just left you?"

Cassie cringed. Would she ever get it right here? Her walking away from the situation was regarded as an overreaction, and now it was being implied that her new relationship was considered too hasty . . .

She'd deliberately not told Claude about Luke as she chattered away prepping food. She had confined the summaries of her recent life history to the bigger events—cheating husband, backstabbing best friend, continent hopping to escape the pain . . .

"Yes, that's right," she said tonelessly. It was better not to pontificate on the matter. She sensed she'd disappointed him somehow, that she hadn't been victim *enough*.

They walked on slowly in silence, and Cassie began to regret the shoes. She began to regret bringing Claude along—he wasn't exactly a happy-go-lucky girlfriend interested in the on-off dynamics of her relationship with her ex. She began to regret saying she'd go to the exhibition full stop. If she could just go back to this morning, when everything had been simpler—a site visit to the catacombs with Florence, coffee with Bas, cooking with Claude this evening. Her disappointment at Luke's silence had gnawed away at her—silently, privately—but at least it had been manageable. It was so much harder trying to control her excitement, to stop her imagination from racing ahead to the what-ifs—what if he smiles with his eyes again, what if he pinches his bottom lip with his fingers while he listens to me talk . . .

They were over the Pont Notre-Dame and onto the voie Georges Pompidou before they caught a cab. Claude got in first—chivalry was completely lost on him—and she bent down to get in behind, leaning in to him.

"Look, Claude—are you sure you want to come with me to the exhibition? I don't want you to feel that you have to do this. You hadn't bargained on coming with me. I could always come over after if you prefer?"

"*Non*," Claude said, buckling up his seat belt. "I will come."

The driver—clearly suicidal—deposited them outside the gallery five minutes later, and Cassie anxiously checked her appearance in the window as Claude paid.

Inside, it was heaving. Every single member of the fashion glitterati was in attendance, and they were all in black—the men in sleek Armani suits, the women in architectural black dresses that owed more to Mies van der Rohe than to Yves Saint Laurent.

"Oh my God," Cassie said to Claude quietly as she recognized the impact her nude-colored dress would have amid the all-black crowd. "I not only stick out like a sore thumb, I *look* like a thumb." She had grown used to Anouk's sophisticated palette of "off" colors and had forgotten the uncompromising uniformity of the passing-through fashion pack.

Cassie noticed that Claude was regarding the crowd with even more unease than she was, and she instantly threw off her embarrassment. They couldn't both flounder. "Come on, let's get a drink and go and find me," she smiled.

It was Mojitos only, but Claude, not finding the ice crushed to his liking, asked for water.

They wandered around slowly, studying the pictures on the wall, though Cassie couldn't stop herself from scanning the room, trying to find Luke. After five covert scouting missions she found him leaning against a wall, a drink in his hand, his ankles crossed as he listened to a petite brunette in an Erdem minidress with ankle boots—Alexa Bourton, she realized with horror—extrapolating on something to do with the picture they were standing by. It was of Selena again, nude again. She was sitting up on the roof terrace, a large straw cowboy hat on her head, legs up on the wall as she lay back on the Adirondack steamer chair, her face basking in the sun.

Selena herself was only a few people away from him. She was still wearing her hair in the severe chignon she'd favored earlier. Quite how she could bring herself to be in the same room as all these people when they were looking at pictures of her *in the buff*, Cassie didn't know. She might as well walk around here naked.

She turned back to Claude. "So what do you think?" she asked, waving a vague hand around the room. "Do you think he's worth all the noise?"

Claude looked at her, and she thought that in spite of obscuring his face with hair—like reeds over a pond—he looked like he'd lost weight. "Do you?"

Cassie shrugged. "Well, I can't claim to know much about photography. I'm of the 'point and click' school myself—"

"*Non.* I mean do you think *he's* worth all the noise?"

"I don't understand."

Claude looked her up and down. "I see you dressed up like this for him tonight. Not like you have dressed since I have known you in Paris."

"I dressed up for Anouk's birthday dinner," she contradicted.

"Not like *this*, you didn't. Tonight, you dress for a man. That night you dressed for friends."

Cassie paused, then shrugged. She supposed it was true.

Her lingerie tonight was certainly making her feel different, stand differently. At Anouk's dinner she'd just been wearing a T-shirt bra and Spanx.

"I see you dressed up for him," Claude continued. "But I see on the walls a man who has many women dressing—or, more to the point, *un*dressing—for him."

Cassie stared at him, not much caring for his point. "He's a photographer, Claude. They're models, not lovers."

"But you're on the walls somewhere in here."

"Well, that's different. We lived together. 'Muse' was his nickname for me. And that's what he's called the exhibition. It's just about inspirations, not women he's taken to bed."

She saw Bas clock the two of them and make a beeline across the floor. He shook Claude's hand and flirtatiously ran a ticklish hand up her bare back. "You look divine," he said proudly. "How could he possibly resist you?"

Claude gave her a pointed stare, but she looked away, pretending to study the picture in front of them instead.

"So have you seen yourself yet?"

"Only in the mirror."

Bas chuckled. "Well, come this way," he said, guiding her by the elbow. "I must say, it's very clever of you to hide in plain sight."

"What do you mean?"

"Well, the contrast dress, the dark hair. Nobody would guess you're the girl in the pictures."

"Is that a good thing?" She was amused.

"Well, your modesty, your naïveté—and I say that with love, dear thing—are among your most defining characteristics."

"And . . . ?" The three of them plaited their way through the crowd.

"And there's no trace of them here," he winked.

What did he mean? Cassie felt her blood begin to pulse at her temples. She stepped around some large columns, and as she saw the run of huge black-and-white prints, she stepped straight back in time. It was early morning; the leaves were still on the trees but turning coppery, hinting at their intention to fly; sleep still rested upon her like a sheet—light and warm; Luke was straddling her, she could feel his weight, pinning her down. And she was as naked as a baby.

Bas turned back to her—and the smile slid off his face like jelly off a plate. "Oh God, Cass!" he said, in horror. "Don't say you didn't *know*?"

She shook her head, her eyes shining with tears as she took them all in, snapshots of their brief happy life together—sexy, vital, and deeply private. Her eyes rested on the one he'd taken of her running toward the bathroom. Her butter-blond hair was lifted and dynamic, her legs long in midstride, her breasts partly obscured by her arm, an impish smile on her face as she made eye contact through the lens . . . She looked down to the ground, feeling humiliated and every bit as exposed as she had expected Selena to feel.

Bas rushed to her, throwing his arms around her like a blanket—protective, covering, warm.

Claude didn't move. His face was as set as concrete, and his eyes burned darkly from beneath his shaggy hair and furred hood. Then suddenly he moved forward, put his arms around the nearest print and lifted it off the hooks. He pivoted it around and set it down on the floor, facing in toward the wall.

Then he walked down the length of the wall doing the same thing to all the other pictures of her, regardless of whether she was clothed or not.

"Hey!" Luke called out furiously as someone alerted him to what was happening. "What the hell do you think you're doing?" he yelled, running toward Claude looking threatening, even though Claude was taller than him by several inches. Luke didn't seem to care, but perhaps he should have, for as Luke reached him, Claude landed a powerful left hook on his jaw that sent him sprawling at his guests' fashionable feet.

"Claude, don't!" Cassie cried, just as Luke got back up and Claude sent him flying back down with another punch to the nose.

Claude didn't hear her. He was bent over from the effort, his breathing heavy with adrenaline, his expression lightening as he vented some of the anger that consumed him. He dragged Luke up by the collar of his navy shirt.

"She was a gift to you," he growled contemptuously. "A rare bird to cherish. Not some *thing* to humiliate by parading her naked like a slave."

Luke put his hand to his nose to try to stop the blood. "You don't know what you're talking about," he spat. "I loved her."

"*Non.* You love how she made you feel—important and central and needed. It is different. If you knew her at all, you would not have done *this*." He released his grip and let Luke fall to the ground.

A bundle of security guards—overweight and too late—ran up, clustering around Claude and trying to manhandle him into a headlock, but he was too big. One of them managed to pinion his arm behind his back, and they rushed him toward the doors. He put up no resistance. Honor had been satisfied. The crowd—scandalized and delighted—parted as they passed.

Luke, still on the ground, looked up at Cassie, who was still being held by Bas. She was pale with shock. "That's your *friend*?" he spat. "Gimme a break!"

The security guards started replacing the prints on the walls, some of them off-plumb, ruining the harmony of the severe lines.

"He was defending me, like any friend would do," she said quietly, trembling as she felt everyone's eyes make the connection between the nude blonde on the walls and the sophisticated brunette in the standout dress. "You have no right to use these pictures."

Luke stood up, putting a handkerchief to his nose to stem the blood. "On the contrary, I have every right. When you signed the contract for the Washington campaign, you signed your image rights over to me."

Cassie looked at him in horror. "But that was for the campaign *only*."

Luke shook his head. "You should have read the small print. And you can thank your friend for helping me make up my mind to tour with this exhibition after all. London and New York want it. There have been enquiries from Moscow too, so I'll make a point of returning those calls." His eyes glinted bitterly and she saw that whatever had once been between them had been buried by his pride. He pulled the cuffs down on his shirt. "*And* I've just been talking to Alexa. She's theming an entire issue around "The Muse." You may as well know I'm giving her the exclusive on them."

Cassie looked at the floor for a moment, and then back up at him. She took a deep breath, drawing her own line in the sand.

"Then I guess you'll be hearing from my lawyers," she

said, before shaking her head sadly and walking away. She could hear Bas's footsteps right behind her, and as she pushed through the doors—just in time to see Claude's taxi pulling away—she wondered why her relationships with the most important men in her life always ended by being signed off with legal letters.

Chapter Thirty-One

"Still no word?" Suzy asked.

Cassie shook her head, eyes down. She didn't need to look at the Skype screen to know that Suzy had her head tipped to the side, as she always did when she was concerned.

"Nope. He's not returned any of my calls. I don't know what else to do."

"Well, have you been over to him? If he's not picking up, he might let you in."

"I guess. I'm just so worried about him. You didn't see him, Suze . . ."

There was a pause. "Well, for the record, Mummy thinks it sounds hilarious."

"Sorry?"

"Yeah. Bailey photographed her when she was our age, and she said you should enjoy your moment in the sun."

"This is completely different! They were private pictures, Suze. He has no right to show them publicly."

"That's exactly what Henry's been shouting about."

"Henry? Shouting?"

"Oh yes, he's been in a terrible rage about it all. But then, he's in a foul mood about everything at the moment. Stress. Nerves." She waved her hand dismissively and rubbed her tummy. "God help him if he ever gets pregnant, that's all I can say!"

Cassie chuckled. "Well, you're not the only one nurturing new life," she quipped. "Tell him my seeds have grown into little buds. That should cheer him up." The seed tray had sprouted not grass this time but a mass of tiny buds with shiny leaves.

"Shall do."

"Everything going okay with the baby, though? Stand up so I can see your bump."

Suzy stood up and presented her miraculous profile. "To be honest, I wouldn't be surprised if I was growing a cupcake," she said, patting it tenderly. She was not yet five months gone and she already had an impressive bump.

Cassie sighed enviously. "You are so lucky. I suppose Archie's just mooning about with happiness, is he? He's been trying to breed mini-Suzies for years."

Suzy pulled a face as she sat back down. "Eww. Don't mention Archie and mooning in the same sentence! A big white bottom just flashed in front of my eyes."

Cassie giggled. "You two are too happy. It's hateful."

"Ah, but your time shall come," Suzy sighed, head tipped back to the side again.

"Oh, I shouldn't count on it, Suze."

"Hey, you can't let a little international incident like pictures of you naked being toured around the world and printed in the most prestigious glossy magazines stand between you and Mr. Right. I still say Luke Laidlaw's the man for you."

Even Cassie had to laugh at that. If there was anything to be salvaged from the situation, it was that it had successfully pressed the delete button on her lingering feelings for Luke.

Claude had been right that night—Luke had exploited and humiliated and traded upon her, all in the cause of boosting his various reputations. All that was left between them now was litigation.

"I think you're right," Cassie said as she heard Anouk's footsteps in the hall outside. "I think I should go over there and *make* Claude let me in. I mean, he surely can't hold me responsible for the whole fracas?" She sighed. "I just don't think I can bear it if he stops teaching me, Suze. I think I'd have to leave Paris. I honestly do. It's become the defining reason for being here."

"Well, the sooner you get here the better, as far as I'm concerned. I need someone to talk some sense into Kelly." She shook her fists in the air. "You know she asked for a gun salute?"

"No! But Brett's not army."

"I know. And I tried telling her you cannot have guns going off in SW3. Just think of all the pigeons you'd take out! It'd be horrific."

Cassie chuckled again just as she heard Anouk's key jingling outside the door. "I'd better go. Anouk's not up to par at the moment either." She wrinkled her nose. "Very tense. I think there are big problems with Pierre."

"Oh no." Suzy tipped her head again.

"Mmmm. She won't talk about it, of course, but it's all been rumbling on for weeks now. I'd better go pour her a glass of wine."

"Well, give her a hug from me."

"I will. And big hugs to you two," she said, flicking her eyes down to Cupcake.

The screen went black, and Cassie turned with a sigh from her happy friend to her sad one.

347

*   *   *

She knocked again. She'd been out here in the drizzle for fifteen minutes but he was refusing to answer. She pressed the intercom buzzer and spoke into it with more bullishness than she actually felt.

"I know you're in there, Claude. You're *always* in there. Please let me in. I just want to talk to you." She paused. "I'm worried about you."

Nothing. Silence was very loud when you didn't want to hear it.

She turned around in a restless circle, debating what to do next. Pitch a camp? Starve him out? Smoke him out maybe?

"Cassie."

She looked up. Claude was standing at the top of the alley, a huge brown paper bag filled to overflowing in his arms.

"Claude! Oh, you're there!" she said, relief flooding her as she ran toward him. "I've been trying to . . . well, I thought you were . . ." He flipped off the hood of his parka and looked down at her, and she stopped short at the sight of him. He had shaved off his beard and had a haircut. He was wearing clean navy chinos instead of his grubby old jeans, with a white shirt and gray sweater. He even had a scarf twisted around his neck, in that way that only Frenchmen can pull off. He looked really . . . *good*. The revelation was startling.

"God, look at you," she said, astonished. "You ought to punch people more often."

He laughed his rare crinkly laugh and walked past her, and she noticed that even his walk had changed—his usual shuffle had been replaced by a casual, loping stride. He got out his keys and opened the door.

"Coffee?" he asked.

Cassie could only nod.

They walked into the apartment and she gazed around in yet more amazement. During all her visits, the kitchen had never been anything less than spotlessly clean and sparkling, ever-ready for culinary action. But the rest of the apartment . . . mmm, not so much. The blinds were always down, with never a window open or a fire set, a bed made or a cushion plumped. Dirty clothes infused the apartment with a dank, musty smell that made you feel like you were living in a shoe, but today . . .

"And to think I was worried about you," she muttered, going from room to spotless room without even bothering to ask permission while he unpacked the bag. The Muse fracas clearly hadn't just signaled the end of an era for her relationship with Luke.

She saw that the gray duvet on his bed was clean, ironed, and pulled up. She even spotted a bunch of freesias in a vase on the bedside table. Did he have a woman?

The thought jolted her as she felt the jealousy switch on in her like a light, her territorialism springing from the only child's delight of having enjoyed his undivided attention until now. Was "enjoyed" the word? Sometimes it had felt like standing in front of a firing squad, but she would have willingly put up with worse just so long as she could carry on sharing this huge passion with him. Rightly, wrongly, selfishly, she liked having him all to herself.

Maybe it's because I'm giving all of myself to him? she wondered as she wandered back into the kitchen and watched him in uncharacteristic silence. She had no job that she cared about, no man to divert her from this big new love. She'd found her path, here in Paris, and the idea of its becoming diluted or lessened through *sharing* filled her with horror. Suzy had said come to London if Claude cut her out, but by the same token, if he invited her to stay, would she? Could he succeed where Luke had failed? Could she really turn her back on this and move over to London—to another makeover, overhaul, revamp?

He set a coffee on the table, smiling at her benignly.

"Are you going to tell me what's going on?" she asked, walking over to pick it up. She perched on a tall stool and watched him begin to chop onions and garlic with speedy grace. "You've not returned any of my calls. And I couldn't get hold of you last week for our lessons."

He looked up. "I know," he smiled.

She watched him. No apology. No explanation. The man was infuriating.

"That's all?" she asked, irritated. "*Hmmph.* I think I liked you better before."

Claude gave a low chuckle and shook his head. He didn't believe that for a second.

"I have been very busy," he said, smashing the side of the knife down with the heel of his hand on a clove of garlic.

"I can see that," she said crossly. "Just getting a brush through your hair must have taken a week."

He chuckled again.

"Shaving that beard off must have required a small army."

He laughed out loud, and she rolled her eyes in defeat, losing inspiration and the desire for insults in the face of his laughter.

He put his knife down and stared at her, fixing her with his black eyes. "I have a job."

Cassie gasped. "A *job?*" She repeated it with the same awe as if he'd said he'd communed with Elvis.

She noticed his knuckles were still reddened and swollen from when he'd hit Luke.

"I have a new backer. We are opening on the old site of Maxim's in the premier." One eyebrow was arched ever so slightly, betraying a well-suppressed desire to impress her. "My backer has given me carte blanche—my team, my budget, my menus, my rules."

Cassie gawped at him, both delighted and horrified at the same time. This would surely mean an end to their lessons? "When?" she asked, managing to keep a ghost of a smile on her face.

"We launch in May. Once the refit is completed."

May? So she wouldn't even be here to see it. It was the third week in March now, and spring was definitely on the march to Paris, but she wasn't scheduled to see summer.

"I can't believe it," she murmured, shell-shocked. "It's such great news. The best."

He looked up, smiling. "Yes, it is. And it is thanks to you."

"To me?"

"Taking me to the exhibition. It woke me up. When I saw those pictures of you . . ."—she instantly blushed at the thought that he'd seen her naked—"it reminded me of what passion can do. The greatness we can achieve. I had forgotten that. I had been immersed in misery for so long that misery itself had become my pleasure. It was all I knew how to be."

She stared at him, puzzled. He was essentially saying that the photos were great. "But . . . but . . . you punched him."

"Yes, of course. Because he did not have your permission to show them, he violated your trust." He shrugged as if to say "I *had* to punch him." "But the photos themselves? They are beautiful. You are beautiful. It is clear the passion he has for you. Anyone could see it. They were able to touch even a man steeped in misery like me. It made me want to bring that vigor back to my life, so I said yes. It is time to live again."

Cassie watched in silence as he went back to the chopping board. She wanted to kick herself for ever having texted him that night. She should have just stood him up—or better still, not gone to the exhibition herself. She sighed heavily. It seemed her loss was Paris's gain.

"What are you making?" she asked, baffled by the mix of ingredients, but her voice sounded strained.

"I'm trying a new recipe—*feuille* and red wine–poached pear with a mint salad and pomegranate reduction. You will be my guinea pig?"

"Sure," she said vaguely, wondering how long this proposal had been in the offing. Heading up a brand-new restaurant didn't happen overnight. He must have been in negotiations for months—and he'd never said a word.

She realized, dejectedly, that the store she placed by their relationship went one way. She was just a student, a wide-eyed, overawed pupil with a crush on her teacher's talent. Claude Bouchard was the real deal, a big name in professional kitchens and someone with more to prove and more to do than simply give pastry tips to a spinning divorcée with nudity clauses. She'd been naïve to think that her offer of friendship had meant anything to him, or that shopping together at the market in some way enriched his life in the way it enriched hers.

Hadn't she seen for herself for these past few months how morose and depressed he'd been, living at that level? Whatever his reasons for stepping back from the Michelin stars three years ago, he was a different person back under their twilight. It was where he belonged. This was what he needed, not her friendship.

She took a deep breath, scared to ask the question, but

knowing she couldn't leave without an answer. "So when will we stop, then? You and me?" Her eyes widened as the next thought hit her. "Or have we already?"

Claude glanced up at her. "Well, we shall do this for a few more weeks, *oui*? Going through recipes. We can prepare the menu together."

Cassie nodded, devastated. What he meant was—I'll come up with the ideas and cook them—you watch and eat.

"But then I think we need to concentrate on your desserts."

She nodded. He had quickly honed in on her favorite discipline, making puddings and trifles, cakes, macaroons, cookies, and so on.

"Because you are very good at those, but if you are going to be my pastry chef then you need to be absolutely—"

"*What?*"

He wiped his hands on a cloth and faced her, hands on hips and a smile all over his face. "I said if you're going to be my pastry chef, then we need to bring you up to speed on filo and—"

Cassie was off the stool, across the kitchen, and into his arms in a shot. "Oh! Do you mean it?"

He nodded awkwardly, looking comically constrained by her physical gesture.

She looked up at him again in sudden alarm, dropping her arms. "Oh, but—I surely can't be ready, can I? I mean, it's one thing to work with you here. But in a kitchen with other professional chefs . . ." Panic swept over her features.

"Ordinarily, I would say no. It is early days for you. But . . ." He smiled down at her. "I see you work, I see your passion for this. You have much natural talent, Cassie. We just need to build your confidence. This is what you should be doing.

It is very clear to me. *Nobody* I have ever taught has had tears in their eyes like you when I show them how to let the knife sink into the apples for Tarte Tatin."

"But it was an emotional experience. I don't understand how other people can't feel that."

"That is what I mean. You are a natural. You have the passion. And I have the expertise, the time and the . . . inclination to train you. I will be there to lead you every step of the way."

Cassie threw her arms around him again, pushing her cheek up against his chest so that she looked like a Cabbage Patch doll. "Thank you, thank you, thank you—oh, thank you," she whispered. "I won't let you down. I promise I won't. I want this more than anything."

"You'll have to call me 'Chef,'" he said, trying to be stern but failing with the ridiculously crinkly smile on his face.

"Of course."

"And no hugging in the kitchen."

"Fair enough." She chuckled, dropping her arms. "When shall I hand in my notice to Dior?"

"Not yet. I have lots to do still, and you have to get the party out of the way first."

"I guess so."

Ever since she'd come up trumps with the location, Florence had given her more and more responsibility for the night. Her burgeoning passion for cooking—which had come to Florence's attention at Anouk's birthday dinner—meant she was now overseeing the menu for the canapés as well as the goody bags. For someone who was working simply to pay the rent, she'd netted herself an increasingly fancy job.

"So we'll work on the menus together and train you up in the recipes. Then from the end of April you can come and work with me, full-time."

Cassie clapped her hands together gleefully, scarcely able to believe that she was going to work properly in a kitchen with Claude Bouchard. It was the most perfect ending! She'd found her way at last! Life was going to be in Paris. Here was her Happy Ever After, and it didn't include a man. At least, not in *that* way.

There was only one small blot on her perfect happiness—having to tell Suzy (and Henry) that she wasn't going to get to London after all.

Chapter Thirty-Two

Cassie sat with the French windows open, her feet propped up against the railing of the Juliet balcony, and a fresh coffee steaming in her hands. She had to enjoy the river views while she could—she had, just this morning, paid a whopping deposit she could scarcely afford on a grotty bedsit in the treizième, and was going to be moving in in just over a fortnight. She felt like a proper grown-up, with a job and a home of her own, and a divorce on the way.

She wanted to tell someone, but it was Easter weekend and Anouk was away with Pierre, staying at a small chateau (hopefully sorting things out between them), and Claude was on the Normandy coast, trying to tie a noted fish supplier in Le Havre to an exclusive contract.

The Bateaux Mouches were filling up daily now, after months of sailing past with just a few intrepid tourists braving the river chill. But after such a bitter winter, spring had hit the city like a flood. The trees were stubbled with leaves, and tulips and narcissi swayed from every flower bed. The sun had impressive focus now too, leaving behind its cold, pale, wintery color wash and tinting everything with a thick yellowish hue instead.

It beamed down on Cassie like a spotlight; she could feel

the fresh air regenerate and revive her. She knew that soon enough she was going to see only the four walls of the restaurant kitchen and hear nothing other than the frantic shouts of the line cooks, and she would look back on this leisurely period—working in the glossy LVMH offices with little more to stress her than sorting out a party, and sleeping late on weekends—as a purple patch in her life, the last dreamscape before reality hit.

A sudden knock at the door startled her, and she whipped her head around questioningly. Who could that be? She got up to open the door.

"Henry! What are you doing here?" she exclaimed.

"Charming!" he replied, grinning, from the steps. "Is that any way to greet an old friend?"

"You know what I mean." She smiled, holding the door wider to let him in. "Come in. Are you alone?" she asked, peering out into the hallway.

He kissed her lightly on each cheek. "Yes. It's just me." He inhaled deeply. "Oh, that coffee smells good," he remarked subtly.

Cassie laughed. "Would you like one?"

"If you insist," he replied, following her into the kitchen. "Anouk's got more space than Kelly, I see."

"Yes, thank God! At least here I can get a coffee without having to walk a block and a half to buy it."

She looked back at him as he wandered over to the windows and looked out. "So . . . you leave next week?" she asked.

"Yup." He turned back and smiled at her. He was thinner than when she'd seen him last, and there were dark purple shadows beneath his eyes.

"You've lost weight," she said.

"Have I?" he asked, looking down at his blue shirt and jeans.

"Aren't you supposed to . . . I don't know, feed yourself up before you go, to compensate for what you'll lose out there?"

"Easier said than done," he replied, giving a slight shrug. "There's been a lot going on."

"Yes, Suzy said."

He looked at her, his blue eyes paler than she recalled.

"And you've had your hair cut, I see," she continued, beginning to cluck like a mother hen beneath his gaze. "At least you've done that in readiness."

"Yeah." He was still staring at her.

She sighed. "Henry, you're staring at me."

"Am I? God, sorry! It's just that . . . you know . . ." He waved his hands at her. "You look so different . . . *again*."

Cassie's hands flew up to her hair. It had grown out a bit since January but was still several inches shorter than when he'd last seen it, and, of course, many degrees darker. "Oh, of course, you haven't seen it," she said shyly. "I forgot. I'm so used to it now . . ." She shrugged, letting her hands fall back to her sides. "So what do you think, then?"

Henry nodded as his eyes traveled over her. "Well, yeah . . . I mean, you can carry it off, definitely." He continued nodding, and she knew he was trying to find the right words. "It's just really different, that's all. I don't think of you as . . . dark."

"It's been weird, that's for sure," she said, turning back to the kettle as she heard the switch click off. "I had to change my makeup—none of my usual colors suited me. Suzy's desperate to get me back to blond."

"She's gutted you're not going over," he said softly, and she felt a collective weight of disappointment bear down on her. Her decision had had far wider ramifications than she had foreseen—Suzy was upset because she had been waiting "her turn"; Kelly and Bas were upset because they took her adoption of Paris as a rejection of New York . . . She didn't want to think about what Luke's reaction would have been.

"Added to which, of course, you're contravening the terms of our lists," he said with a lighter tone. "I take it those are the seeds I sent over," he said, jerking his chin toward the small pale gray ceramic plant pot on the counter into which Cassie had transplanted the seedlings the previous week.

Cassie nodded, running a light hand through the tender shoots. Pink buds, still tightly wrapped, were popping up daily, and she expected them to be in full flower within the next few weeks. "I'm diligent about watering them. What are they, anyway?"

"Ah, that would be telling."

She raised an eyebrow. "You mean I've got to wait till they flower and then *identify* them?"

"Something like that," he nodded.

"Why?"

"Why not?"

Cassie rolled her eyes heavenward. "So you sent me chamomile in New York—"

"How did you know it was chamomile?"

"Your sister tripped and fell face first in it, and promptly asked me to make her an infusion."

Henry laughed. "Gotta love her."

"So chamomile in New York, and anonymous little pink flowers in Paris . . . hmmmm. I reckon I'll just take them to the flower market and ask someone there to ID them for me."

"Go for it," he replied.

"Urgh," she groaned as he called her bluff. "I don't see

what the big deal is. Why can't you just save me the bother and tell me yourself?"

"It's no big deal," he said, taking a sip of the coffee and moving out of the kitchen. "But rest assured, there is always method to my madness."

Cassie followed him out of the kitchen and sat on the arm of the sofa, watching him as he stood next to the French windows looking out on the river. He leaned an arm against the window jamb and her eyes absentmindedly followed the triangular shape of his back.

"Like introducing me to Claude?" she asked. "Were you intending to bring method or madness into my life with him?"

Henry turned and looked at her. "A bit of both. I thought you could probably help each other."

She mused on his comment. All things considered, they probably had helped each other—he'd unearthed her life passion; she'd given him back his passion for life.

"How are you getting on with the rest of it? The list, I mean?" he asked.

"Okay, I guess. Point Zero, Ladurée habit, and Claude—all done. And I've arranged a *party* in the catacombs, would you believe?" she giggled.

He shook his head in wonderment. "No, I wouldn't."

A beat passed between them and Cassie felt herself shift beneath his scrutiny.

"So why are you here? Has Suzy sent you on a mission to convince me to get to London no matter what?"

"No," he replied. "I came to see Anouk. It's my last opportunity to get the rings before the expedition."

"Oh. But Anouk's not here," she said.

"Where is she?"

"Away with her boyfriend for the Easter weekend."

There was a short silence. "Bugger."

"She didn't mention anything about seeing you."

"No I . . . well, it was a spontaneous thing." He gave a rueful grin. "I guess I should have called first, huh?"

Cassie shrugged. "I guess so. It's a long way to have come for a wasted trip."

He looked out of the window, as though thinking about something, then looked back at her. "Well, it doesn't have to be wasted," he said. "What are you doing for the rest of the afternoon?"

"Uh . . ." She hesitated, racking her brains for something to wow him with. It wasn't very impressive for her to announce she was staying in Paris because she was so content here, and then show him she had nothing to do. "Well . . . actually I'd planned to visit the Rodin Museum today. Strike off the last thing on the list I actually have any control over."

"Great," Henry beamed, draining his cup. "I love it there. We can go together, then."

"This is very tactful of you, Henry," Cassie quipped, staring up at the huge marble sculpture.

"What do you mean?" He was standing with his hands behind his back, his face upturned to the sun.

"Well, it's beautiful and everything. I totally get why you wanted me to see it, but a statue that celebrates adultery? I mean—come on! Could we not see *The Thinker* instead?"

"Ah, but you see, that's where you're wrong. Everyone thinks this statue is about adultery. But it's not."

"It isn't? Because I'm pretty close to where the guy has his hands, Henry. There's nothing platonic about it. Look!" She tried to pull him to where she was standing.

"You have to know the story."

She crossed her arms, bemused. "Then tell it to me."

He paused as if debating the request. "Okay. It's based on the story of a young wife entrusted to the care of her husband's brother. They fell in love, and the sculpture depicts the moment they realized their true feelings for each other and went to act on them."

"So far, so adulterous, then," she said, rolling her eyes.

"No. Because, you see, the woman's husband surprised them at the moment they went to kiss and killed them both. They never became lovers." He gave a small cough. "Most people don't realize this, but *The Kiss* is actually the ultimate representation of unconsummated love."

Uncons—? A faraway memory of their teenage kiss over ten years earlier flashed through her mind and she looked up at him, startled. But Henry was staring fixedly ahead at the thwarted lovers.

He took a few steps away, as though to appraise the statue from other angles.

"You know, he kind of looks like you," Cassie said after a while, squinting at the statue's profile and then his.

"You think?"

She nodded.

"Nah. I reckon I've got better hair. The chest's quite accurate, though," he said, pushing his out to force the point.

"I'm not seeing it," she laughed, smacking him playfully in the stomach. He instinctively caught her arm before letting it go as if she'd burned him. He stared back up at the statue.

Cassie stared back at it too, holding her wrist where he'd grabbed her. His hands had been big and rough, but also surprisingly hot, and she distantly remembered a conversation she'd overheard between Hattie Sallyford, his mother, and her own—"Honestly, one moment he was holding a bag of Maltesers. By the time I'd moved into fourth gear it was like he was having his very own fondue party on the backseat . . ."

She chuckled lightly at the memory.

"What are you so amused by?" he asked.

"I was just remembering something your mother said to mine about your hot hands."

He considered for a second. "I feel like there's a punchline in there somewhere."

"If there is, leave it where it is." She laughed, just as her foot caught in the strap of her handbag and she fell sideways into him. He caught her easily, and for a second the world contracted to the diameter of his bright blue eyes. There was nothing else except the slow spreading of his irises as he held her in his arms, his eyes boring into hers.

And then the world suddenly exploded around them again, dazzling her with color and noise and light as he pushed her away from him—actually *pushed* her, as if she were a drunk who'd fallen asleep on his shoulder on the Tube.

Henry's reaction had been like a slap in the face.

"Sorry," she said quietly, her cheeks flaming.

"No, Cassie, *I'm* sorry. I didn't mean to . . ."

She put up a wan hand, warding off his apologies. "It's getting late anyway. I really ought to head off . . ." she said, walking quickly toward the exit.

"Hey, Cass, look . . ." He called after her, but there was a thick stream of German schoolchildren coming in and it was difficult for him to wade against the flow. He caught up with her outside, at the bike rack.

"I'll let Anouk know that you came by to see her," she said lightly, keeping her eyes down as she unchained the bike.

"Look, Cass . . . about what just happened. I'm sorry . . ."

"There's no need for you to apologize, Henry," she said quickly.

"But there is! Look, Cass, I'm an idiot. You just startled me, that's all . . ."

"I need to get back."

"No you don't," he said in a tone that made her look up at him.

"Look. Let's just forget all about it. I'm a stress cadet at the moment. Please? I was a complete jerk."

She sighed and looked away again. She didn't want to go. She hadn't realized, until he'd turned up, quite how lonely she'd been feeling. It was one thing sorting out the direction your life should take, quite another taking it alone.

"Look," he cajoled, "why don't you show me something that *you've* discovered over here? If this city is good enough to keep you in it, then the least you can do is let an old friend in on the secret." He nudged her with his elbow. "Let's go off-list. Come on. What do you say?"

She stayed resolutely silent for a minute.

"Off-list, huh?" She looked at him out of the corner of her eye.

Encouraged, he moved closer and put his arm around her, resting it on her shoulders so heavily that she sank a little beneath the weight. "See? I really don't have some strange phobia about touching beautiful women," he grinned.

She chuckled and jabbed him in the ribs. "Fine—*weirdo!* I know somewhere."

She hopped on her bike and glided away. "Keep up!" she called over her shoulder.

Henry was after her in a second and she led him expertly through the warren of narrow streets that ran east from the museum, behind the Musée d'Orsay, and alongside the Sorbonne, eventually coming to a stop fifteen minutes later outside an innocuous-looking grocer's.

"What are we doing here?" Henry panted. She'd led him a merry chase.

There was no Vélib docking station nearby. "You just hold the bikes. I'll be back in a sec," she said, darting inside.

She reappeared a moment later holding two ice-cream cones.

"Ice cream? Really?" He took the cone she held out to him. "No wonder you and my sister are friends," he said, shaking his head.

"Shut up and try it," she said.

Henry took a bite out of the top, his eyes blinking rapidly as the tartness of the orange mixed with the chocolate that was so rich and creamy it was more like a ganache. "Bloody hell!" he exclaimed as soon as he was able.

"You see?" she smiled, taking her own bite. "That's worth staying for, isn't it?"

"Suzy would *kill* me for saying it," he said, looking at it as if it held magical powers. "But yes. What *is* it?"

"Berthillon ice cream," she said, beginning to wheel her bike away. "It's made on Ile Saint-Louis, a family-run business. Widely regarded as the best ice cream in Paris."

"The best in France, I'd say. I've never tasted anything like it."

They walked along slowly, their bikes resting on their hips as they ate their ice cream. They hooked a left, and Henry could see the river ahead of them.

"I know where we can sit," he said, pulling forward slightly.

They stopped at the lights and waited to cross.

The pedestrian lights flashed green and they crossed over,

wheeling straight on to a footbridge. Unlike all the other grand and flamboyant bridges in Paris, this one, the Pont des Arts, wasn't embellished with gargoyles or gilded statues or hewn from limestone. It was a humble footbridge with wooden planking and black wire sides, and all the way along brass padlocks had been fastened to the links by lovers as tokens of commitment.

"Been here before?" Henry asked, as they laid the bikes down next to a bench. It had a great view upriver to the Eiffel Tower.

"Of course. It's the only bridge on which you can sit down and not get hit by a bus."

They sat on the bench together, eating the ice cream in happy silence, watching a barge sail beneath them. It had a shiny red Fiat Punto parked on the back.

Henry eyed the huge bike padlocks. "Hey, you still wearing your Christmas present?" he asked.

"Of course." She fingered the necklace delicately. It had become her soothing habit here, much like brushing her palm over the chamomile lawn in New York. "I love it. I never take it off. But it really was way too much, Henry. I mean—a Tiffany's necklace, for heaven's sake!"

"It's not like it was gold or diamonds or anything," he shrugged. "Can I see it?"

"Sure." She leaned forward slightly, holding it out toward him.

"No, I mean—can I . . . hold it?"

Cassie hesitated. "Sure."

She unclasped it and handed it to him. It had such a comforting weight, it felt strange taking it off. It was warm from her body heat.

"I don't understand what the message on the back means, though. What's 'Maiden's Blush'?"

Henry raised his eyebrows at the question as he read the words on the back. "You mean you don't know?"

"Uh-uh."

He tipped it in his hand slightly so that the charm slid off the chain. "Hold that for a sec, will you?"

She took it as Henry stood up and walked over toward the railing.

Cassie laughed as he turned his back to her, fiddling about in his pockets, and she realized the intention of his joke. "Oh, stop being such a copycat, Henry! Even you wouldn't put a Tiffany's charm on this bridge!"

He looked back at her and winked, attaching the locket to one of the links. "There!"

She stopped laughing as her eyes confirmed her worst suspicion, and she ran over, horrified. "Henry! It'll fall! The lock doesn't work! I've been keeping it on the . . ." She stopped and stared down at it. The arm was fastened shut and supporting the full weight of the dangling pendant.

She touched it lightly, terrified of knocking it into the river below, but to her amazement it was locked solid. She turned back to him. "How did you get it to lock?"

He shrugged. "With my supernatural strength, clearly," he quipped, flexing his arm and showing off a mighty impressive biceps.

"I'm serious, Henry. I've never been able to lock it. I was supposed to change it in New York before I left, but then Luke . . . the point is, it was broken."

"Oh. Well, get it fixed here, then. There's a Tiffany's in the deuxième." He took another bite of his ice cream.

"Well I was *planning* to, smartypants, but that's going to be tricky now that it's welded to a bridge," she said sarcastically.

"Do you not know how to use a key?" he asked slowly, as though she was stupid.

"There is no key!" she cried, exasperated.

"Huh?"

"It never came with a key. I wore it on the safety chain, and somehow you've managed to secure it to a bridge!"

"No key?" He looked back down at the tiny pendant fastened to the side of the bridge. He planted a hand on his hip. "Huh."

Cassie groaned as words failed her. He was beyond aggravating. Sometimes it was as if he were still sixteen.

She crouched down and peered closer at the pendant, trying to fathom a way to unlock it, but though it was tiny compared with the huge bike padlocks covering the rest of the bridge, it was still solid silver and not giving an inch. She looked back up at him. "I'll have to contact the head office and get a key for it. There must be a serial number or something. I'm sure someone in the office has contacts at Tiffany's."

"Well, you don't need to worry about someone coming along and nicking it. If we can't get it off, no one else can either. Not without taking wire-cutters to the bridge."

He went to sit back down next to the bikes. Cassie stomped after him.

"I can't believe you just did that!" she said sulkily, refastening the silver chain round her neck. "I loved that necklace."

"How was I supposed to know it didn't . . . Hey! Have you got a sister I never knew about?" he asked.

Cassie turned just in time to see a bus stopping on the Quai Malaquais. She turned back. "Oh, that. It was a favor to Kelly," she said flatly. "I kind of owed her."

"You're a *model* now?"

Her eyebrows shot up. "What are you saying?"

He blanched at the indignation in her voice. "I don't mean that you couldn't be a model, Cass. Of course you could. You're a babe! But it's . . . well, it's . . ."

"Yeah, yeah, yeah, don't hurt yourself," she muttered, giving a heavy sigh. "Luke took them. The model was high as a kite and they needed someone and I was there and Luke . . . just insisted."

"Oh, I bet he did," he muttered stonily. He cast her a sidelong glance. "He really likes taking photographs of you, doesn't he?"

Cassie bit her lip, a furious blush running up her cheeks. "Mmmm." She didn't want to go into it. It was bad enough going through a divorce, let alone this litigation as well.

They sat in silence for a minute. "You got an injunction, though, right?" he asked.

"For here, yes."

"What do you mean—for here?"

"He's got copyright for the pictures. Technically he can use them. But French privacy laws protect the individual, so he can't show them in the exhibition over here."

"But he can elsewhere, is that what you're saying?"

"Theoretically. And he's touring the exhibition worldwide. I'll have to go to court in every country he shows in and get individual injunctions if I want to stop him."

"Sonofabitch!"

"Yeah." She shrugged, the crisis over the Tiffany's pendant

now forgotten as the full strain of this more pressing situation bore down on her again. The simple fact was that she couldn't afford to keep hiring lawyers to stop him. Her savings had been all but used up. "And that's not even the worst of it."

"It gets *worse*?"

"American *Vogue* wants to publish them—the editor is finally getting her revenge on me for the whole show fiasco. I take it you heard about that?"

Henry nodded.

"Well, they're doing a 'Muse' issue, and Luke's kindly telling her I'm his."

His eyes narrowed. "I hated him on sight."

"Yes, I know. I don't blame you. He was a prat toward you."

"Glad you noticed. I was worried I was growing a sensitivity gene."

Cassie chuckled. "Do you know what he thought the padlock was for?"

"No."

She looked at him. "A chastity belt."

Henry went still at this. Then he held his hands up. "Okay, I admit it. I'm a spy working for your mother."

Cassie burst out laughing. "You are a ridiculous man," she giggled, elbowing him in the ribs.

"Ah well, you're not the first to have said it." He smiled, watching her before frowning a little and looking away.

"What?" she asked, feeling his attention drift.

"Nothing."

"No, tell me. What?"

"Well, it's this . . . this whole Paris Cassie look you've got going on. It's freaking me out."

"I *knew* you hated my hair," she muttered, holding her hands over it defensively.

"No, it's not that per se . . . Well, okay, yes it is . . ."

She tutted, annoyed.

"It's more that you've done precisely what I told you not to do—tried to reinvent yourself when there is absolutely nothing about you that needs to be fixed."

Cassie froze at his words. "Well, sorry to have been so disobedient," she wisecracked finally.

"In fact, the only good thing about your hair is that it's right for Venice." He shook his head and looked upriver.

"Venice?" She turned and looked at him. "What are you on about? I'm not going to Venice."

"No, but you should."

Cassie blinked at him. He had an ice-cream mustache across his top lip. "You've got a . . ." she indicated to her top lip. He put his finger to his own and found a smudge of ice cream.

"Mmmm, bonus," he quipped.

"Don't tell me there's a list for Venice too," Cassie said.

"Well, there's going to be. I'm taking Lacey there for our honeymoon."

Cassie slumped down a bit. "Venice. For your honeymoon. That is so romantic." They sat there for a moment, then she turned to him, perplexed. "But what's that got to do with my hair?"

"Don't you remember? You told me in New York that you thought you might be a brunette there, with a bob. And you'd wear flat shoes like Audrey Hepburn and eat prosciutto for lunch and read the papers on a balcony at breakfast."

Cassie stared at him in amazement. "I can't believe you remembered all that!" she exclaimed.

Henry shrugged. "Eidetic memory."

"That figures. So what's your Venice list going to say, then?"

"I don't know yet. That's why I'm going out there—to draw it up."

"You are? When?"

"Tonight."

"Tonight!"

"Mm-hmm."

"Oh." She immediately tucked away her growing idea of cooking him dinner—the duck Claude had done with her last week.

She felt him sit up a little, then sink down again.

"What?"

"No, nothing."

"Go on—say."

"Well, I was just thinking that you should come with me."

"To Venice? Don't be mad!"

"Why? I've never been there before either, so I could do with a bit of help."

"I don't think Lacey would be too happy about it."

"I don't see why not. Why's it any different to being out here with you right now?"

She tipped her head to the side. Good point.

"We're old friends, Cass." She felt him grin. "Unless of course you're worried you can't trust yourself around me."

She gasped and gave him a sharp jab in the ribs with her elbow. "Dream on!"

"Right, then." He laughed, thoroughly amused by her indignation. "Well, that's settled. We'd better get you packed."

"But wait . . . I can't just . . . *go*."

"Why not? It's Easter weekend. It's only an hour and a

half's flight from here and you don't have to be back at work till Tuesday. What reason do you have for not enjoying an adventure in Venice?"

Cassie shook her head. She couldn't think of one.

"So come on, then," Henry said, picking up their bikes. "Come on!"

Chapter Thirty-Three

They touched down at Marco Polo just before nine and caught a water taxi across the lagoon. The sun had set less than an hour earlier, and the sky was still alight with flaming clouds along the horizon. The silhouette of the city was instantly recognizable by the grand domes of the basilicas, which glowed like celestial orbs in the sunset, and candy-striped canal poles threw long, rippling shadows onto the water.

Cassie tipped her head back and let the wind blow her hair off her face as they sped over the water. She had no idea where they were going to stay and she was already starving. Henry had waited—until they were safely flying over the Alps—before he told her that he hadn't booked a hotel, having guessed correctly that she wouldn't have dreamed of coming if she'd known that little nugget.

"I never do," he'd protested as she started to huff and puff. "It's all part of the adventure."

"But it's Easter weekend! Everywhere will be booked up."

He'd just shrugged. "So much the better. It means we'll find a real jewel hiding away somewhere."

Cassie had rolled her eyes huffily. "A word of advice—don't try that on your honeymoon. Lacey's going to have packed nice shoes and pretty dresses and she's going to want to go on a gondola. Trekking around Venice trying to find a bed for the night with her luggage on her back is not going to be the best start to married life. Trust me."

"You're speaking from experience?"

"I'm speaking as a woman."

The boat docked at a taxi stop alongside St. Mark's Square and Henry jumped out, offering her his hand before the driver had even turned around. He had thrown a sweater over his shirt but he had no jacket, and no bag.

"Are you really saying, Henry," Cassie said, walking alongside him as he carried her bag, "that you just carry your wallet and passport? You don't pack *anything*?"

"Nope. I don't do luggage if I can help it. I'll buy some toiletries in the first chemist I see," he said, his eyes scanning the perimeter of the square, though it was hard to see anything beyond the crowd. It was heaving with tourists. And pigeons. "And other bits and bobs. Don't worry. I won't smell and embarrass you."

"You don't need to smell to embarrass me," Cassie quipped, just as a pigeon dive-bombed her. She ducked low. "That looked personal," she muttered, turning round to make sure it was still flying on and not making a U-turn for another go.

They stood in the middle of the square, hemmed in on three sides by imposing buildings and flanked on the fourth by water. The Doge's Palace was to their right, the basilica straight ahead. That was two of the five Venetian landmarks she knew off the top of her head. She'd only taken ten steps into Venice and she'd already practically exhausted her knowledge of it.

"So. Where to now?"

"Hmmmm," Henry said, watching the flow of pedestrian

traffic. The main current seemed to work from the front to the back of the square. "Come on. We'll go this way," he said, heading left.

They walked out of the square and straight into a labyrinth of winding alleys, some so narrow Cassie felt she could stretch her arms out and brush the walls on both sides. Through the open windows she could hear the canned laughter of television shows, and a couple were shouting to the backdrop of a violin being played elsewhere. A stocky woman was beating a rug from a top-floor window and plumes of dust cascaded down, forcing Cassie and Henry to break into a jog to escape it.

They turned left and right at random, so that within twenty minutes Cassie didn't know which direction she was traveling in; but Henry seemed to. This was probably nothing to him, she thought, hiding in the Venetian maze. He was used to hacking his way through jungles and rain forests and jumping off icebergs, not just water taxis.

They found an overpriced boutique where Henry got ripped off on a shirt, two pairs of socks, and some boxers; there was a small drugstore farther along and he darted in there too, emerging minutes later with a toothbrush, toothpaste, deodorant, razor, shaving foam, shower gel, and shampoo.

They passed an *osteria* where two off-duty gondoliers were drinking espresso. Henry clocked their eyes following Cassie as she passed, and he moved in a step closer to her.

She looked up at him. "You know, we're going to have to find somewhere soon, Henry. It's getting late and you must be frozen without a jacket on."

"I'm fine," he said, giving her a wry smile. "Trust me, I know frozen."

By the time they had been walking for forty minutes, Cassie half expected to see the hills of Provence around the next corner. They came to a tiny crossroads, where their path bucked up to an ornate minibridge. A small canal passed beneath, but there was a path that ran along one side of it. They—meaning Henry—decided to follow it, turning right.

Cassie glanced at the water nervously. It was dark and slapped the sides noisily, agitated by activity farther along the canal, and she could see puddles where it had slopped up onto the path. Around the bigger waterways, she had noticed that profuse flower baskets and parked gondolas provided a barrier between the water and the streets, but here, it was just a straight drop in. She moved in closer to the wall and was so busy eyeing the dark water that she didn't notice Henry had stopped walking. She bumped straight into him. He'd dropped her bag and was trying to peer over the top of a wall.

"What are you doing?"

"Hear that?"

She listened and heard the babble of conversation over the wall, music playing softly.

"So?"

"It sounds good, don't you think?"

"Well yes, but . . ." She looked at him, trying to guess his intent. "No, Henry! It's someone's *garden*. They're obviously having a party."

"Maybe, maybe not. Venice is famous for its walled gardens—at the very least you should see one. Here, I'll lift you up. You peer in."

Cassie took a step back. "Absolutely not," she hissed, worried someone would overhear their plan. "I'm not going to snoop on someone's party like a Peeping Tom!"

"It's not snooping. We're just seeing if it's a private residence or not."

Cassie planted her hands crossly on her hips and tilted her head.

"What?" He held his hands out. "You wouldn't want to stay there if it was a hotel?"

The sound of laughter gurgled over the wall.

"Yes, *of course*," she said.

"So?"

"Ugh," she said crossly. "You know, you can't do this with Lacey either," she went on, as he bent down and picked her up, holding her around her knees as if he were about to toss a caber.

He walked backward toward the wall so that she could see over, and a little gasp of excitement escaped her. It was just like a hanging garden, with potted orange trees dotted around a small courtyard, a small vine draped across a trellis, and espaliered peach trees against the walls. Six or seven small round tables, covered with white tablecloths and candles, were evenly spaced around a firepit, which burned in the middle, casting a gentle heat and flattering light.

"What's it like?" Henry asked, loosening his grip so she slowly slid down to the ground. He didn't seem to notice that he was holding her in an embrace, their bodies touching, their faces just inches apart.

She pushed back a little. "Yes, well . . . ," she said, playing with her hair and fidgeting restlessly. "It seems very nice."

Henry blinked at her. "And? Is it a hotel?"

"Yes, yes . . . I think it is."

"Great." He beamed. He picked up the bag and strode ahead. Cassie lagged a couple of paces behind, inexplicably cross and bothered. She *had* to get some food.

They followed the wall around, turning into a narrow deadend street. There was a small café at the far end on the left, with several metal tables pushed against the wall and some dogs sleeping next to them. On the right, an illuminated black-and-white sign, HOTEL CAPRESA, hung above the cobbles like a lamppost.

"This'll be it," he said, pushing open a wrought-iron gate and walking into a small garden, different from the one Cassie had just spied on, with a fountain gurgling like a baby and clumps of hibiscus and petunias everywhere. The building was a tall villa, ocher-yellow with white-trimmed windows and small balconies decked with rattan-seated dining chairs. Two olive trees flanked the front entrance, and the light shining from within was the color of amber.

"I feel like Mary at the inn," Cassie sighed as she took in the sight.

"Well, let's just hope they've got rooms," Henry said, crossing his fingers at her as he walked into the hotel. It was cavernous inside, with high ceilings and an intricate parquet floor, but scarcely furnished except for a giant chandelier twinkling overhead, a desk to the left with an open newspaper on top of it, and, opposite that, an enormous oak daybed, the size of a half-tester, with a foot-deep mattress.

"If they're fully booked, I'll sleep there," Cassie said, motioning to the daybed. "I can't go another step."

"If they're fully booked, we'll both be sleeping there," Henry replied, just as a man came out of a room at the other end of the hall, looking Lilliputian as he came through the door, which must have been fifteen feet tall at least.

"*Buona sera.*" He was wearing faded black trousers, bunched at the waist, and a white undershirt beneath his shirt. He was unrolling the sleeves from his elbows.

"*Buona sera, vorremmo prenotare due camere, per favore,*" Henry said in flawless Italian. "*Per due notti.*"

The man looked first at Henry, then at Cassie, seemingly baffled by the request. Then he shook his head. "*No.*"

"No?" Henry repeated. "*Non avete camere libere?*" He was going to have to plead for the daybed then.

"*Ho due stanze libere per stasera,*" the man said, holding up his fingers. "*Ma solo una domani.*"

"Oh." Henry turned and looked back at Cassie. "He says they've got two rooms tonight, but only one tomorrow."

"Well then, I guess we could stay here tonight and maybe try to find somewhere else in the morning?" Cassie said.

Henry nodded. "We could do that." He looked back at the man. "Could we do that?"

The man shrugged, uncomprehending, although from the way he looked from Cassie back to Henry, Henry could tell that if it were his decision, that wasn't what *he'd* be choosing.

"Okay," Henry smiled. "*Cominciamo a prenotare le due stanze per stasera e in mattinata decideremo cosa fare per domani.*"

The man opened a small cabinet on the wall behind him and grabbed the only two keys from the hooks. They followed him up a winding staircase with gray marble treads, and along a wide corridor that had demilune tables set with lamps between every doorway.

He stopped outside one room and unlocked it, turning on all the lamps and walking to the far end to open the doors onto the balcony. Cassie remained at the doorway, blinking. The walls were set plaster with a delicate *trompe l'oeil* mural, and a pair of mint-green silk curtains fluttered in the night breeze. A regency wardrobe and escritoire stood against the far wall, opposite the bed, which made the daybed downstairs look like a footstool by comparison. It was high, princess-and-the-pea style, with a luxurious pocketed head-board and footboard, both of which curled around the ends like little walls, and sheets that were white and crisply ironed with a handmade lace trim. The bathroom, leading off from the near corner, was, from what she could see, utilitarian, and all the more chic for it.

There was nothing else. There didn't need to be. It was perfect, even better than she had imagined. Cassie walked slowly through it toward the balcony, which overlooked the small canal and the gardens she had peeped at earlier. She couldn't see much through the canopy of trees and vines, but the music was still playing and she could hear women's laughter carrying into the night.

"*Signore, la sua stanza è di fianco.*"

"I'm next door," Henry said. His room was set out as a mirror image of hers, except that his curtains were ivory silk with a velvet stripe, and the bed was a Napoleonic four-poster with a pleated-silk tent effect that fell from a corona in the ceiling.

"Wanna swap?" he asked with a twinkle, clocking the majesty of his bed.

"No," she said smartly. "I like the roundy bits on my bed."

"*Roundy* bits?"

"Roundy bits." She giggled. "And I'm going to *die* if I'm not eating within twenty minutes. I'll come and knock for you when I've freshened up," she said, walking toward the door.

She threw her bag onto the bed and tried to make sense of the jumble of clothes she'd thrown in several hours earlier. Everything had been so rushed, so last-minute. She rifled through, trying to pull together an outfit, which was easier said than done with one pair of white city shorts (an accidental choice—she'd thought they were a shirt), a Fair Isle cardigan, her black biker jeans, a butterscotch silk blouse, one pair of narrow khaki trousers, and a pair of camel Tod's moccasins.

She looked down at herself. She was wearing her favorite blue jeans (about to die on the right knee but now exquisitely soft), a black and ecru fine-striped silky top that gathered at the bust, a pair of Superga sneakers, and a burnt orange hacking jacket. There was no getting away from it—even Kelly wouldn't be able to number this lot into some sort of order.

She jumped into the shower first, letting the limited options settle in her mind, and hurriedly washed her hair with the complimentary shampoo. The advantage of having a bob meant her hair dried within minutes, and as the Brazilian perm had long since given up the ghost, it settled into a casually disheveled style all its own.

As she put on a spritz of makeup, she could hear Henry clanging about in his own bathroom on the other side of the wall. It sounded like he was digging himself out of Shawshank.

Five minutes later, she was knocking on his door. "You still there?" she called.

He opened it, toweling off his hair. He had a towel wrapped around his waist. "Where else would I be?" he asked, letting her in.

"Well, from the racket you were making, I thought maybe the mob had caught up with you," she said.

She felt his eyes drag up and down her.

"What?"

"Look at you," he said. "You look Italian now."

"Don't be absurd," she said, embarrassed. "It was the best

I could cobble together, given the limited time I had to pack in. Seven minutes, wasn't it?"

"You need to learn to accept compliments. You look great," he said, walking back into the bathroom.

Do I? she thought, checking her appearance in the mirror. She'd teamed the khaki trousers with the Tod's shoes, the butterscotch blouse, left artfully disheveled, and the orange jacket.

She removed a smudge of mascara from beneath her lower lashes and twirled the front strands of her hair around her finger, the way Bas had taught her to. She heard a clatter in the bathroom and automatically looked over, about to ask if he was all right. But she didn't. He had kicked the door with his foot, but it hadn't closed fully and his reflection bounced from the mirror within next to hers. She could see perfectly well that he was all right. In fact, she could see he was more than all right. He was spraying on some deodorant, standing in profile to her, every bit as naked as she was in Luke's photos. She knew she should look away *right now*, but . . . his body, just as a physical entity, was extraordinary—the way his upper back sloped down to the tight hollow in the small of his back, the dig-in of the muscles between his shoulders and biceps, and the color of his skin, like honey . . . He turned to grab his boxers off a hook on the door, and as he did, he looked up and his gaze swept into hers.

And just for a moment, before the shame and humiliation came crashing down upon her, she felt a current pass between their reflections, a power-surge that threatened to slam her against the wall and knock all the air and sense out of her.

And then he blinked, and Cassie's hands flew to her flaming cheeks. Henry knew before she did what was coming next, but his wet towel—flung carelessly on the floor—was lying in front of the door, and by the time he'd ripped it out of the way, she had run from the room.

"Cassie!" he cried, running out into the hall just as her door slammed shut and she turned the key. "Dammit!" he shouted, and she heard him running back to his room, no doubt to grab some clothes.

Within a minute he was rapping on her door again. "Cassie, let me in," he said. She heard the elevator door open and Henry saying "*Buona sera,*" in an excessively formal voice, compensating no doubt for the fact that he was clearly half-dressed and on the wrong side of the door. "Cassie, look, you have to let me in," he said, whispering through the door. "People think I'm a nutter standing out here like this."

She said nothing.

"We'll get thrown out," he said.

Still nothing.

He moved in closer, and she heard him put a hand against the door. "Look, it doesn't matter Cass," he said quietly. "It was nothing. I'm not embarrassed. I don't want you to be."

She remained silent.

"It's different for blokes. We're not funny about that the way you girls are. I've grown up walking about in the nod in front of forty-odd blokes, for God's sake—and they *were* odd, I can tell you." He patted the door with his palm. "Come on, let me in. You can't stay in there forever. You'll die of hunger, remember? The sooner you look at me, the better you'll feel. We can forget all about it."

She paused—she knew he was right—then took a breath and turned the key. Slowly she opened the door. She was staring at the floor. "I'm so sorry," she whispered. "It was just an accident. I didn't mean to . . ."

384

He pushed the door open gently so that she had to step back. He walked into the room and stood in front of her, his arms wide.

"Hey, look, I'm not scared. See? I'm fully clothed now. My virtue is safe."

She shook her head, a mortified smile breaking out. "I don't want you thinking I'm some kind of pervert or . . . or desperate woman who has to—"

"Honestly, Cass, this happens to me all the time. *All* the time. Really. I'm used to it," he said with a grin, wrapping his arms around her and stroking her back soothingly.

She closed her eyes for a moment, feeling his heartbeat next to her ear, so grateful for his humor.

"You weren't joking about the chest," she said after a moment, pulling away from him.

"No. No, I never joke about that," he deadpanned, patting it fondly. "Want a go?"

She burst out laughing, the ice well and truly broken. "No thanks. I want to eat."

"So then, let's eat," he said, stepping back to let her lead the way. He watched her go ahead and she felt his eyes on the back of her neck as she walked. Then he closed the door behind them and on everything that had just passed.

Chapter Thirty-Four

Cassie didn't sleep for anywhere near as long as she would have liked, not because she was woken by the sounds of the water pipes rattling and shaking into life, or the shouts at the vegetable market that was apparently in the next piazza, but because Henry was on a mission.

She opened the door to him at 6:30 A.M., too sleepy even to muster a look of thunder. They had laughed and chatted by the heaters in the garden till two, and four and a half hours of slumber did not cut it in her world.

"If there's one thing you need to know about me, Henry—and I'm only telling you this with your safety in mind—it's that I *need* to sleep," she slurred. "I'm famous for it. It's non-negotiable. Not a luxury—a *need*." She went to shut the door on him. "I'll see you for elevenses."

Henry put his foot in the door. "We've got two days here and we are *not* going to spend them in bed. Come on," he said, pushing the door wider, going straight to her French windows, and flinging them open. The Venetian sunrise burst through with all the power of a Canaletto, and Cassie winced at the apricot light.

"Where are we going?" she groaned, slightly knock-kneed as she pulled her T-shirt down over her knickers.

"You're going to love it," he said confidently, sitting in one of the rattan chairs on her balcony, his face glowing in the rising sun, his arms behind his head.

"Ugh, that's not an answer," she muttered, but gave up and walked toward the bathroom.

An hour later she had her answer. She'd thought that maybe—since it was Easter Sunday—they were going to an early mass at St. Mark's, but no, that was too obvious for Henry. Instead, they'd taken a mini vaporetto over the Bacino—the spray from the boat spritzing her wide awake once and for all—and zoomed across to the island of San Giorgio Maggiore. The boat had docked at the foot of a majestic church whose reflection had quivered in the still-quiet water, and now they were leaning from the bell tower, the *campanile*, Henry told her, and looking down upon Venice, at the tiny bridges and watery lanes, just as the city tore itself from sleep and launched into celebration of its most revered of holy days. All across the city, church bells pealed and swung in their towers, out of sync with one another and hitting different notes, but their exaltations as clear as any choir's.

Cassie watched the water begin to rock as boats and vaporettos filled it as steadily as the bodies filled St. Mark's Square.

"It's just amazing," Cassie murmured, "to sit all the way up here and see a city wake up like this. It's . . . it's like a heart that's just started beating again." She caught herself and looked at Henry, embarrassed to have said that out loud. "Sorry. That was a bit much."

Henry shook his head. "On the contrary, I love it. I think that's exactly what it's like," he said, looking out over the water. "A heart that's come back to life."

They sat there for over an hour, but soon the hordes started making their way over to the island and intruded upon their solitude. They made their escape again, catching a boat back to the Grand Canal. In spite of Henry's determination to avoid anything that catered to the tourist market, Cassie was equally determined to tick several of the hot spots off her own list, and they ended up compromising—visiting first one of Henry's choices, then one of Cassie's.

Thanks to Cassie, they bought Grand Cru Easter eggs at VizioVirtù Cioccolateria and ate them for breakfast. Thanks to Henry, lunch was eaten standing up in a dark *osteria* frequented entirely by Venetians, where they feasted on tomato and melon soup and squid risotto, and drank *lo spritz*, a local sweet, fizzy wine that was so delicious they got through two bottles.

Thanks to Cassie, they visited the Guggenheim Museum and stared in bafflement at Vorticist art; thanks to Henry, they found a fabled *enoteca*, where Henry charmed the owner into selling him a bottle of his famous vino fragolini bianco, a dessert wine made from strawberry-shaped grapes, which was kept under the counter.

And it was thanks to Cassie that they found themselves on the Grand Canal—in a gondola.

"You realize the local children call these Japanese boats," Henry muttered, embarrassed that *anyone* should see him as they sat in a traffic jam behind five other gondolas, all filled with Japanese tourists singing at the tops of their voices.

Cassie sighed, nonplussed, and slid slightly further down the black leather cushion. It was heart-shaped and edged with the thick bullion you might expect to see in a Victorian rectory rather than an Italian "love" boat. The early start was catching up with her—and they'd been on their feet all day.

She didn't care about the Japanese; she cared about stretching out and stopping just for a moment. Touring with Henry was exhilarating but also exhausting. They had walked for miles, chatting away, nipping into quiet, dark churches to stare up at the gilded frescoes, trying to find dead ends that walked straight into the water, and marveling at the cascades of laundry and bed linen that were strung from the windows above them, crisscrossing the alleys like bunting. They had sat cross-legged beneath a bell tower, eating Gelateria Nico ice cream—Venice's equivalent to Berthillon—as they watched the gondolas go by; and later on they had sat at a deserted café in Campo di San Giacomo dell'Orio—"one of the prettiest squares in all Venice," Henry had said proudly—sipping hot chocolate that was so thick and glossy, it was more of a pudding than a drink.

But now—for forty minutes—they could do nothing. They *had* to sit down. It felt exquisite to let her limbs go heavy and to feel the late-afternoon sun beat down on her, its heat sinking into her black jeans and warming her aching thighs. Henry was snapping away on his phone (hers had died the day before and in the rush she had forgotten to bring her charger), ignoring the Rialto Bridge altogether and taking pictures of interesting-looking Venetians, carved details on the boats . . .

"I'm going to need a sleep before we go out tonight," she murmured.

"You know, there are other places to get a Bellini than at Harry's Bar," Henry said, scowling up at the tourists on the bridge taking photographs of them as they sailed past like newlyweds.

"Yes, but it's *Harry's*," she protested, her words slurring a little. "It's an institution."

"I tend to make it a point of principle never to become an

inmate of any institution," he drawled, but his words fell on deaf ears. Her eyes were closed, a soft smile curving up her lips as she sighed. She was fast asleep.

They walked back slowly, only finding the hotel by identifying the thick swath of wisteria that fell, Rapunzel-like, over the garden walls. Neither had bothered to actually note the address before they'd left that morning. They also remembered, but only as they asked for their room keys, that they hadn't bothered to check out.

They looked at each other in horror. They would have to spend hours traipsing around with their bags trying to find another hotel!

The owner's wife, who was on duty and spoke English, shrugged apologetically—the first of many apologetic shrugs—as she led them upstairs. "We had to get the room ready before the other guests arrived," she said, putting the key into Cassie's door and opening it. All of Henry's belongings—not sizable, admittedly, given his aversion to luggage—were neatly folded and stacked on the floor. "And is after check-out now," she said, pointing to her watch, "so you must pay for this room tonight, even if you do not stay." She shrugged apologetically again.

"Of course," Henry said, nodding honorably to the wizened old woman. "Of course we shall stay."

Cassie looked at him. What was he saying?

The woman walked away, shaking her head and muttering to herself in Italian.

"Are you mad?" she asked as Henry shut the door.

"She's just running her business," Henry said appeasingly. "It's not her fault we shot off at dawn and didn't confirm our plans about leaving. And it's too late now. I don't want to have to pay for a room twice tonight, do you?" Cassie shook her head and looked around. The room seemed smaller than it had yesterday. Henry walked over to the windows and leaned against the frame, one arm above his head. "Anyway, it's fine. I'll sleep on the floor."

Cassie looked at the floor. Bare, unyielding, wooden parquet. "You can't sleep on that."

"It's amazing what you can do with a rolled-up towel," he smiled, looking back over his shoulder. "Just don't use them all up when you have a bath."

Cassie chewed her lip for a few moments. "No. No, I can't let you do that. You can't sleep on a towel while I sleep in that thing," she said, pointing to the luxurious bed. "It's massive anyway. There's plenty of room in it. It's fine."

Henry looked dubious. "Honestly, Cass. I sleep in snow holes and hanging from ropes sixty foot up a tree. I'm fine on a towel. I really don't think—"

"I insist," Cassie interrupted. "There's no way I can sleep easy knowing that you're on the floor."

Henry sighed, but her tone was final. She sank onto the edge of the bed and pushed her sneakers off with her feet, the laces still tied. She fell back, arms outstretched. A bath really seemed like a good idea, actually. Tiredness was stalking her. The nap on the gondola had been as brief as her night's sleep—Henry had jogged her awake after a few minutes, telling her that if they were spending a hundred pounds for the privilege of starring in thousands of strangers' photograph albums, the least she could do was be conscious for them.

"I think I might have a bath, actually," she said.

"Go ahead," Henry said, turning back and walking toward the small escritoire. There were some tourist pamphlets and a map on it. He picked them all up and reached into the bag he'd left on the floor when they'd come in. "Fancy a glass of this?" he asked, holding up the bottle of vino fragolini.

They had been drinking wine pretty much all day—but what the hell! "Oooh yes," she said as she went into the bathroom and opened the taps. She retrieved a small travel bottle of Anouk's Nina Ricci bath oil from her washbag and poured it all in, letting the scent perfume the air.

There was a light knock at the door and Henry's hand snaked around, holding a filled glass out to her. She peeped out and watched Henry take his drink over to the balcony and stretch himself over the two chairs, flinging open the map like a commuter reading the *Times*. Thirty-five minutes later she joined him, the white toweling robe tied tightly around her. He dropped his feet and poured them each another glass as she sat down on the chair and they both angled their legs up onto the balcony. The *signore* was lighting the candles on the tables below and the firepit was already flaming, gathering heat.

"According to the guides, Calamari Griglia is supposed to be good, and Spaghetti alle Vongole is a local favorite."

"I could eat them all," Cassie smiled. The sky was turning lilac, silhouetting the last of the day's pigeons as they flew home to roost for the night.

"I was just looking on this map," Henry said with the same shame that men reserve for asking for directions. "Figured I'd better try to memorize where north is, at least. But it says Campo San Polo is just over there," he said, pointing over the rooftops just to the left of them.

"What happens there?"

"Well, in the summer, you can watch movies *sotto le stelle*," he smiled. "Under the stars."

"Oh wow, how gorgeous. I bet that's just amazing," she

sighed, before suddenly exclaiming: "Oh! That will have to go on the list, won't it!" She picked up the pamphlets he'd left on the floor and started flicking through them.

"That's what I thought. We could come back and see it then."

We? Cassie looked at him. "You and Lacey, you mean?"

There was a short pause as he took a sip of his drink. "Yeah. That's right."

"She'll love that," Cassie said, holding up a leaflet. "And look at that—the Lido di Venezia. It's the beach where all the locals go. You could take her there too."

"Mmmm." He gave the leaflet only a cursory glance before looking back out across the garden.

"Should I start writing things down?"

"Hmmm?"

"For the list. You don't want to forget. I mean, whether you'll ever *find* Campo Whatsit or that tiny *enoteca* again is a different matter, especially with your sense of direction," she teased. "*Tch.* A map. I don't know. I feel like my world's been tipped off its axis."

Henry chuckled and Cassie stared at his profile as he followed the sun's tired trajectory.

"How long did it take you to do my lists?" she asked, taking a sip of her drink.

He shrugged. "Not that long. I know those cities pretty well."

"Well, I can't *wait* to see London's."

"You're not going to now, remember?" he reminded her.

"Oh yes," she sighed. "What a shame. It would almost have been worth going just to see what you'd have dreamed up for me over there."

"Glad to hear you've enjoyed them so much," he said,

stretching back in the chair. "Which were your favorite bits, then?"

"Good question. Let's see." She chewed her bottom lip for a while. "Well, in New York it has to be Christmas at Tiffany's. I don't think I've *ever* been so excited as when I saw my name on that box!"

Henry chuckled, clearly delighted.

"But the dinner party was special too, so much greater than the sum of its parts. I think I'll always remember it . . . ," she murmured, a smile softening her expression as she remembered that night. "What made you put it on the list, though? It's hardly specific to New York."

"No." Henry shrugged. "But it just forced you on to the next level of living there. Moving off the surface of things."

She raised an eyebrow. "So—what? The tasks had meanings attached?"

Henry gave a small shrug, his eyes set on the horizon. "Something like that."

"Then why did I have to run around the park?"

"It calms the mind," he said, looking over at her. "And I reckoned yours must have been pretty insane at that particular point in your life."

"*Hmmph,* that's an understatement."

"Not that I mean to suggest you aren't *still* completely insane." He laughed, and she reached over to give him a playful slap, almost missing and falling off the chair. The wine and exhaustion were beginning to overtake her, and Henry laughed even harder.

"How about for Paris?" he asked, helping her back up.

Her smile brightened instantly. "Claude, definitely," she nodded. "He's changed my life. But I'll be honest—I thought you'd put him in as some kind of practical joke when I first met him—like maybe I had to shave him for charity, or get him to say a kind word . . ."

Henry laughed.

". . . Ladurée I just *adore*," she said, clasping her hands above her heart.

"Well, you're friends with my sister for a reason," he said, getting up and walking across the room. He pulled the other bottle from his bag. "Shall we?"

She hesitated fractionally. They had plowed through the first bottle in no time—not to mention the *lo spritz* at lunch— and it was already going to her head. She needed to eat.

"Don't you want to keep it? Drink it with Lacey?"

"No. It'll only get confiscated if I take it through as hand baggage."

"Oh well, in that case . . ." She smiled, standing up and holding both their glasses out. From the small canal outside, they heard a gondolier singing. "It's so strange to think that this time yesterday we were in Paris. Now we're here in Venice."

"And this time next week I'll be on an icebreaker in the Bering Sea," Henry added. "Weird."

"And then a couple of months after you get back, you're getting married. Even *weirder*. I so can't imagine you as someone's husband," she teased.

He shifted his weight. "Can't you? Why not?"

"Well . . . I mean *you*, Henry! All grown up and responsible?" She laughed. "I just can't imagine you doing the whole pipe and slipper thing. You seem way too young to settle down yet."

"This from the girl who got married at twenty!" he shot back, his jaw clenched as he looked at her. She felt the atmosphere change in the room. "I'm thirty years old, Cass. I've met the girl I want to spend my life with. Why *would* I wait?" He looked at her, their easy conversation of moments before now tinged with a sharp edge. "Do you think that I haven't seen the world?"

She shook her head. The suggestion was ridiculous. "Of course not!"

"Do you think that I haven't played the field, taken advantage of *every single one* of the opportunities that have come my way, is that it?" The way he said it suggested there had been many opportunities.

"N-no," she stammered.

"But you still think of me as the bumbling schoolboy you knew as a teenager?"

The image of his powerful physique reflected in the mirror flashed across her mind. The idea of him as bumbling almost made her laugh out loud. Almost.

"Of course not," she said, shaking her head.

"Then why are you so determined to keep me in that box?"

"I'm not. I mean, I'm . . ."

"Yes. You are," he contradicted, his tone brooking no further argument. He walked toward her. "For some reason, you have to keep me one step removed all the time—I'm just *Suzy's* brother, *Kelly's* friend. Have I not proved my friendship to you over the past few months?"

"Of course you have," she said hurriedly, taking a step back onto the balcony. "You've been one of the best. I don't know what I'd have done without you." Her hand found the balustrade behind her.

"And yet you always have to pigeonhole me." He shook his head and shrugged, advancing all the while. "Why is that?"

Cassie mirrored his body language, shaking her own head.

He was close now and she could see his breathing was rapid, his eyes burning at her condescension, fueled by the wine. He leaned forward, placing his hands on the balcony to either side of her. She had to lean back, but he wasn't deterred.

"I'm no boy, Cass," he said, his voice so low she could feel the bass in it vibrate through her body. "And I'm no angel either."

His lips were inches from hers, his eyes all over her mouth, and she realized she was holding her breath. Somewhere, a tiny red light was flashing in her brain telling her this was crazy, he was Suzy's little brother, he was like family to her, he was engaged to the girl of his dreams . . . And yet, standing inches apart, he was suddenly none of those things, and the urge to have him kiss her, to feel his hands upon her body, to mold herself to him, rose up like a wave and she felt instinct override logic, pushing her up slightly so that their bodies touched.

He dipped his head fractionally at the feel of her beneath him and she wet her lips, almost begging for his kiss; she closed her eyes, feeling like touchpaper awaiting the single movement that would set her alight.

But it didn't come. She felt the radiant heat cool and she opened her eyes. The lust in his eyes matched hers, but he was backing away from her as if she were dangerous, his chest heaving as if he'd just run up the stairs.

And then he turned and marched across the room in four strides and grabbed his sweater from the pile on the floor.

"H-Henry," she stammered. "Where are you going?"

"Out!" he said without looking back, and closed the door smartly behind him.

Cassie winced at the loud slam, her breath catching as she

heard his footsteps pounding down the marble stairs three at a time. She turned and saw him tear out of the courtyard beneath her, flinging open the gate angrily.

"Henry!" she cried out, but he didn't stop or come back. He didn't even look up.

He just seemed to want to get away from her as quickly as possible.

The clock read 3:43 when she felt the mattress dip behind her and Henry's body-heat gradually emanate across the white-sheeted expanse to her side of the bed. She had slept fitfully, dreaming too vividly, her brain feverish and revving too hard. She had got up at midnight to get a glass of water and had seen his side of the vast bed still cold and smooth. Where was he?

He wriggled into a comfortable position and she felt her heart punching against her ribs at his closeness, wondering whether he could feel it through the mattress, vibrating through the coils to where he lay. She shifted position slightly.

"Cass?" His voice was quiet and low—but even in that one word she could hear the slur of sambucas—and she heard his hair rustle against the pillow as he turned his head.

She froze. She knew he was going to apologize to her; he was that kind of man. It had been ungentlemanly to slam a door in her face, to leave her abandoned in a foreign city, to have advanced upon her like a lover when she was just an old friend, to have made her want him and then to have left her hanging . . .

His apology would cover all those things, she knew, though they'd both leave the specifics unsaid. But she didn't want it now. Not here, lying in the dark together, the smell of him covering her though his hands wouldn't.

He turned over fully and she could literally feel the weight of his stare. She wondered whether he could tell she was feigning sleep. She struggled to keep her breathing slow and steady, but it was tricky with her heart pounding like a jackhammer. A deafening silence stretched between them in the blackness. She heard him place his hand on the sheet behind her, and she could feel it glowing like an ember between them.

"There's no wedding. We called it off," he said quietly.

The news jolted her. It echoed through her like a slap, stinging and hot, but she willed her body not to flinch or start, not to betray her to him. Because if she turned around now . . .

"Cass? Did you hear what I said?"

He waited for a response—anything at all—but she kept up her pretense, playing dead, and after a minute or two he gave a weary sigh and turned away from her. She listened for the sound of his breathing to change, and within moments he succumbed to a deep, inebriated sleep.

She lay next to him like a piece of driftwood—far from home, wooden, and washed out—with just one thing running over and over through her mind. If there was no wedding or honeymoon, then what were they doing here?

Chapter Thirty-Five

When he awoke, she was already dressed and sitting at a table downstairs, drinking a cappuccino and nibbling on a cornetto while her mobile phone charged up at reception. She had resolved to continue as though nothing had happened between them on the balcony, and, more importantly, as though she hadn't heard a thing he'd said—after all, she'd pretended to be asleep and she couldn't very well bring it up now.

Not that she needed to worry about keeping up a pretense. One look at his face in the doorway—puffy and pale—told her his hangover was fairly monumental. He probably didn't even *remember* telling her the wedding was off. There again, it occurred to her, maybe . . . maybe it had all been a joke, a drunken lie? Maybe his resolve to stay faithful to Lacey had weakened with the drink, and the prospect of coming back to a sure thing was too much for him to resist. One last hurrah. After all, he was about to spend the next two months in the Arctic, and hadn't he said himself that he was no angel?

She stared at him as his bleary eyes sought her out in the empty room. She had no idea what the truth was. Everything he did and said was a riddle.

She smiled politely as he sat down, determined to recover the dignity she'd lost last night. "Good night?"

Henry arched one eyebrow at her to see whether she was being sarcastic, but she gave nothing away.

"Not really," he mumbled, wincing from the effort. "Bad idea."

Cassie said nothing, just looked out into the garden. A gardener was out there, pruning the bougainvillea.

"How about you?"

"Me?" She picked up her coffee cup, trying to look nonchalant. "Oh, I just had an early night."

He gave a small painful nod. "Did you get anything to eat?"

She shook her head, almost offended by the question. As if she could have eaten. "I wasn't that hungry."

"Ah."

A pretty young waitress came up, her dark hair tied back in a long ponytail, her pink dress straining slightly over the hips, and handed Henry a menu, her eyes sweeping over his lightly as she did so.

Cassie felt herself prickle. This was obviously one example of the many opportunities that Henry had been talking about.

"Is my phone ready?" she asked the girl, her voice tight with irritation.

The girl looked at her, a languid arrogance in her eyes. "I shall check." She smiled, giving Henry another glance before walking back to the reception desk, deliberately swinging her hips.

"Ugh, I can't believe I've done this," Henry said, pushing his knuckles to his temples. "Cass, I'm so sorry."

He looked up at her but it was impossible to tell what he

was apologizing for. Last night? Or the hangover? He clearly wasn't in any fit state to go sightseeing.

"Maybe you should go back to bed," Cassie said, watching him. "I can go out and do some sightseeing on my own. I'm sure I'll be able to find some good things for your honeymoon list." She watched Henry's reaction as she said this, but from his grimacing, it was hard to tell anything other than that his head was about to fall off.

The girl came back with her phone. "Full charge," she said, putting it down on the table.

"Thanks," Cassie said, not looking at her as she picked it up.

"Could I possibly have bacon and sausages and eggs?" Henry asked. "I know it's not on the menu, but . . ." He managed a smile.

"Of course," the girl smiled back. "Anything."

Cassie furiously jabbed at the buttons on her phone. She already hated today and they hadn't even had breakfast. The previous evening's humiliation, mingled with the confusion from his middle-of-the-night confession and now his debilitating hangover, meant he wasn't fit to spell his own name, much less explain to her what the hell was going on.

She turned the phone on and the message icon started bleeping at her. She dialed the voice mail and listened in.

"You have eighteen new messages . . ."

Eighteen? *Who the hell could need to get hold of her so urgently?* she wondered. She'd only been gone a day and a half. *". . . voice mail is full. Please delete any unwanted messages . . ."*

She suddenly felt a wave of horror flush over her. Suzy!

"First message . . . Message received . . ." She listened to it, her body tense.

"Cassie. C'est moi." She relaxed as she heard Claude's dis-

tinctive voice—probably ringing up to moan about the price of the fish, or the tablecloths coming in the wrong color. She just hoped he wasn't going to reschedule their lesson tomorrow. It felt like a long time since she'd seen him, even though it had only been Thursday evening. She pressed the next message.

"Cassie? Where are you? I need to see you. Ring me."

She blew out a breath, pressed delete, and held the phone up to her ear for the next message.

"Cassie, it is me again. You must ring. I do not understand. Where are you? Why do you not call me back? Call me. Please."

Cassie deleted again, somewhat annoyed by the instructions. She didn't have to answer to him if she wanted to go away with a friend—their mutual friend—for a weekend jolly. She put the phone back to her ear for the next message.

"Why are you are doing this to me? Is this funny to you? I thought we had an understanding? I thought you understood me?"

Cassie looked at the phone, a knot of nausea beginning to tighten inside her. This wasn't right. His voice was different— higher, faster. She pressed delete and listened to the next, aware that her hand was beginning to shake.

"Cass? What's going on?" Henry asked, holding his head between his hands, staring at her curiously. She didn't answer, just kept putting the phone to her ear, listening, and then pressing delete, and repeating the maneuver again and again and again. Henry grabbed the phone from her and listened himself, his eyes meeting hers as he heard the desperation building in Claude's voice. By message fourteen, Claude was manic, rambling and swearing at her—Cassie could hear his voice down the phone from across the table. Tears were streaming down her cheeks, and she held her hand across her mouth as she shook her head.

By message number seventeen, his voice had changed again—slow, dull, inert, rambling. Henry was holding her hand across the table, his eyes red-rimmed, as he pressed play for the eighteenth message. Except for a faraway *bang*, it was long and silent.

Chapter Thirty-Six

"You can't blame yourself," Anouk said, watching as Cassie paced the room. She hadn't sat down for days, a nervous energy keeping her moving at all times like a spinning top. She'd barely slept either, and she'd lost a ton of weight, seemingly overnight.

"I don't!" Cassie refuted, whirling around to stare down at her—stare her down. Her face was pinched white with anger and blanched whiter still by her harsh black mourning clothes. "Why would I? I did nothing wrong. I went to Venice to help a friend. What, in that setup, could possibly have prompted Claude to kill himself?"

Anouk swallowed in the face of her fury. Cassie's shock had gradually settled in the past few days since arriving back from Venice, but today, the day of the funeral, it seemed to have been replaced by a molten anger that was stoked by grief. She didn't want platitudes. She wanted answers.

"It wasn't jealousy, I know that much," she muttered as she lapped the room. "I'll scream if one more person looks at me as if my loss is more than the loss of a friend. He'd be so furious at them, you know he would." She balled her hands into little fists as she stared over at Anouk. "I know you believe me . . . that it wasn't like that between us."

Anouk nodded. She didn't dare not to, even though she knew people had been asking why he'd left the messages on Cassie's phone, why he'd been so unbalanced by her trip with another man.

"What we shared was a passion, a calling. There was no expectation, no drama. Just conversation and cooking and making up recipes and plans for working toge—Oh God!" Her voice broke and she collapsed suddenly into a heap on the floor, her face burrowing into her hands. Anouk dropped her cigarette into her coffee and ran over to her.

"Why?" Cassie cried. "We had all these plans, Nooks! Everything had just come right for him. At last! He'd been unhappy for so long, and then all of a sudden there was this huge change in him. He just suddenly *got happy,* overnight."

"Maybe that was the warning sign," Anouk said.

Cassie went stock-still. What had she missed? She peered up at Anouk, and Anouk noticed her hands were trembling. "What do you mean?"

"Maybe it was his final, last-ditch attempt at normality, a desperate lunge toward happiness. You know—fake it till you make it?"

"No. No." Cassie shook her head. "He *was* happy. The restaurant . . . he was so fired up . . . it was real."

"Maybe he was never going to be able to find lasting happiness," Anouk said quietly, rubbing Cassie's back. "After what had happened to him, I don't know how anyone could bear it."

Cassie looked at her. "So you know too, then? About his wife and child?"

"Henry told me," she nodded. "In the church."

"Last week was the anniversary of the crash." Cassie's voice was flat now. Henry had told her too, but only afterward, at the airport. Why hadn't he told her before? If she'd only known . . .

"I know," Anouk whispered. "Three years. That's what I mean, Cass, when I say you mustn't blame yourself. This wasn't about you being in Venice with Henry. He wasn't sensitive—he was broken. I think he was always trying to run away from this."

"But why all the phone calls? Why to me?" There was a tremor in Cassie's voice. For all her defiance, she was plagued by the fear that she had unwittingly driven her unstable friend over the edge.

Anouk chose her words carefully. "Because you were the one who let him dare to hope that, maybe, things could be different for him. You brought him hope, Cassie, not despair."

Cassie stared at her, her eyes filling with tears. "But I let him down. I wasn't there when he needed me, when he needed some hope."

"There was no way you could have known. He lied to you—he wasn't even supposed to be in the city. He was supposed to be in Rouen."

"But . . . but if I had picked up . . . if I had been there instead of in Venice on some *masquerade*." She spat the last word out.

"Masquerade? What do you mean?"

"Henry told me that he needed me to help him research a list for Venice—for his honeymoon."

"So?"

"So there's not going to be a honeymoon—because there's not going to be a wedding."

Anouk stared at her, stunned. "*Non.*"

"Oh yes. They called it off, supposedly."

"Supposedly?"

"He was drunk when he said it. I don't know if it's on or not . . . I don't know anything about anything," she said vehemently, balling her hands into fists again and feeling the nails dig deep into her palms.

Anouk thought back to the funeral service that morning. Henry and Cassie had barely spoken, Cassie choosing to sit apart from them in the pews, tears sliding silently down her cheeks. Anouk had thought it strange, given that they'd been together when it had happened, and she had caught Henry glancing at Cassie worriedly several times during the service. He had delayed the departure of his expedition by three days in order to attend the funeral, but he'd had to leave immediately afterward to catch a flight late that afternoon.

"You sound angry with him," she said quietly.

"With Claude?"

Anouk shrugged. "Yes, with him too. But I meant Henry."

There was a short pause. "Well, I am," Cassie muttered. "I've had enough of all his games. I don't know which way is up with him. I feel like he's got me on some kind of treasure hunt, some quest he's devised for his amusement." She smacked her chest with her open hand. "But it's my life he's manipulating, Nooks."

"He's just trying to help you, Cass. From what I've seen, he seems to be trying to give you goals and focus and direction. It's sweet. I mean—wasn't he the one who introduced you to Claude in the first place?"

"And the one who kept me from him in the last," Cassie said bitterly.

Anouk patted her hand. "You can't think like that. Claude made his decision for his own reasons. I don't think there's anything you could have done, even if you'd known. I honestly believe this would always have happened, regardless of whether you were in Venice with Henry or standing with Claude in the kitchen . . ."

"Well, I've still had enough. Henry can take his bloody list and take a running jump as far as I'm concerned. I'm not having anything more to do with any of it."

Anouk paused for a moment. "Well, that's a shame."

Cassie looked at her. Her voice was odd. "What do you mean?"

Anouk stood up and walked over to the table in the hall. A small pile of unopened cards—from Bas, Kelly, Suzy, and others—was stacked up on it. Cassie was resolutely refusing to accept any sympathy or kind words from friends. She was determined to punish herself.

Anouk picked up a thick white envelope.

"This arrived for you the other day."

Cassie took it. It had been opened.

"I accidentally opened it without looking. I'm sorry."

Cassie pulled out the stiff card inside. It was a startling white, with a smart cream script across it. In the top left corner, someone had written her name.

She looked up at Anouk in amazement. "When did this come?"

Anouk shrugged. "I don't know. Yesterday? The day before? Why?"

"Because that's Claude's writing," she said, pointing to her name. "But he died last week. Are you sure it didn't arrive sooner?"

"No. Definitely not."

"So then *who* sent this to me? And why?"

Cassie got to the bus stop ten minutes early. She'd had to factor in extra time getting there as the list of extras she was required to bring—tablecloth, tealights, glasses, a bottle or two of wine, and a small hamper—made it difficult to walk.

She put her bags down with a clatter, feeling both conspicuous and ridiculous among the homebound commuters in her all-white outfit—after all, it was only the end of April and still far too early to be wandering around the city in summer clothes. She had settled upon a white pantsuit in the end, worn with a pale pink silk shirt of Anouk's and a wide-brimmed floppy white hat, and now she leaned against a wall, keeping her head down as bus after bus arrived, disgorged and swallowed up passengers, and drove off again.

After ten minutes exactly, a string of buses pulled up in front of her and, as she looked up, gathering her bags protectively as passengers got off, she noticed that everyone on board looked just like her. In fact, the bus almost seemed to shimmer from the inside out, like a glowworm in the dusk.

"Come in, come in," they cried, recognizing her as one of their own. She had her invitation in her bag, but clearly no invitations were necessary. The distinctive dress code and being in the right place at the right time were all that was needed to show that you were on the guest list.

Cassie climbed on, stepping cautiously around hampers and crates and cardboard boxes, instantly enveloped by the party atmosphere on the bus. The doors closed behind her and they pulled off along the rue de Rivoli. There were no seats left, but Cassie preferred to stand anyway, looking at the different interpretations of the dress code. Some people had come as Pierrots with whited-out faces, others in their wedding dresses, a few had copied the pantsuit Bianca Jagger had worn to marry Mick; someone had even come swaddled in bandages as a mummy. Her chic suit felt dull and uninspired by comparison.

The buses swayed around corners and ornate landmarks picking up more and more guests—Cassie glimpsed at least five other buses in their convoy—eventually coming to a stop outside the Opéra. The doors folded back on themselves and everyone rushed out like spilled buttons, seemingly with their own sets of orders about what to do next, be it carrying and opening picnic tables, shaking open tablecloths and napkins, setting up candelabras and tealights, or opening bottles of Sancerre and unpacking smoked salmon parcels. Cassie watched in amazement as every single bus disgorged its all-white load all the way down the boulevard des Capucines, so that within minutes the length of the pavement on one side of the street was cloaked in white, like a freak snowstorm.

She stood motionless, her bags hanging limply from her hands, not quite sure where to go. Everybody seemed to know somebody else, and although they were a friendly crowd, she felt distinctly alone. She asked herself for the hundredth time why she'd agreed to come. It was madness. Inappropriate.

"Your first time?" a woman behind her asked.

Cassie turned. A thin, ultrablond woman was giving her a half-smile. Cassie recognized her immediately, although of all the people she would have thought *wouldn't* be here, it was surely her.

"Mrs. Holland?"

"Katrina, please." The woman narrowed her eyes in concentration. "Cassie, yes? From Dior?"

"Yes." Cassie was amazed that Katrina should remember her name. Their meeting in Anouk's studio—brief and uneventful—had been three months ago now. At least Cassie had the advantage of society pages and Bas's outrageous gossip to prompt her memory.

"You seem surprised."

Cassie shook her head, trying to recover her manners. "Well, I'm surprised *I'm* here, to be honest. I have no idea how I came to be invited."

"No one ever does." She smiled. She was almost albino-pale, her hair Bas's special chamomile tint and not much darker than her ivory crêpe-de-chine jumpsuit, which did an impressive job of showing off her international-standard thinness. "Are you here with anyone?"

Cassie shook her head. "No, I uh . . . wasn't sure of the form."

"Well, would you care to join me? I'm alone too." She indicated a small table next to her. There was no handsome walker or miniature dog in attendance, but an all-white butler had smoothed a fine linen tablecloth over the table, and was laying white-gold cutlery settings with a porcelain dinner service.

Cassie nodded, relieved. "I'd love to," she smiled. "If you're sure I'm not imposing . . ."

"Of course not. Come, let us have some Salon. It's a blanc de blancs, the whitest champagne I could think of." She smiled, pouring them each a glass. "It's rarer than hen's teeth, with only two vintages since the millennium."

Cassie watched as the butler started unpacking an enormous Fortnum's hamper that two men had carried over from a limo parked by the curb. Queen scallops, moules marinières, oysters, foie gras, and sole meunière were placed on plates in front of them. Cassie discreetly kicked her hamper under the table, too embarrassed to hand it over to the butler. The cheese baguettes inside were wholly inadequate in the face of this blanched feast, and she didn't want to get into a discussion about why she'd lost her enthusiasm for cooking recently or how her appetite had diminished to the point that she could barely finish a slice of toast.

But as they sat down and Katrina busied herself with eating only the oysters from a solid silver oyster-shaped holder, Cassie realized no such discussion would be necessary—a top-tier socialite was her ideal dining companion while she was deep in the depths of grief. She managed a few of the scallops and some salad, as Katrina shared her deep fondness for Bas and her belief in his absolute *genius* with a hair-dryer.

Time passed and the noise levels ratcheted up quickly, not just because of the jubilation of the guests as they tucked into their picnics, or the passersby stopping to cheer and take photos, or the waiters from the "hijacked" cafés coming out to clap and smile, or the cars honking their horns at the spectacle, but also because a flatbed truck was driving by very, very slowly with a live jazz band playing on the back of it.

A few people got up to dance, igniting a round of applause and cheering that left Cassie feeling more and more uneasy. Since the funeral a fortnight earlier, she had closeted herself away, going out only to work or to take walks along the Seine so early in the morning that the only other people about were the tramps huddled beneath the bridges. And now here she was in the middle of music and feasting and champagne and laughter and dancing and the bright glare of an all-white guest list.

She closed her eyes for a moment. She shouldn't be here. It was too much, too vibrant, too alive. It was wrong to be here, at a party, when her poor dear tortured friend was so recently dead.

She opened her mouth to make her apologies to Katrina; she'd been a consummate hostess and Cassie knew that what she was about to do—abandon her halfway through the dinner—was unforgivable, when there was a sudden noise farther along the pavement, the distinct whine of a microphone surging up.

"Ladies and gentlemen," a man said, speaking as loudly as he could, for there was a fair distance to cover. He was wearing a white suit and fedora, and sunglasses obscured his face so that he remained anonymous. "Thank you for coming to the Dîner en Blanc tonight. For those of you who have been before, you know that the Dîner is only made possible by your discretion, *joie de vivre,* and great taste."

Everyone laughed except Cassie. She stared instead at the tablecloth, dismay and guilt written all over her.

"Tonight, of course, is about celebrating the very essence of Paris—good food, good wine, and good company—and we hope that by the time you leave here, you will have eaten well, drunk well, and made new friends."

A cheer rose up from the crowd—and not just from the ones seated in white. The spectators watching from the sidewalks were several deep now.

"But just before we go any further, I would like to take a minute of your time. As you know, we prefer to keep our identities secret, but a recent sudden event means that we have decided to break with that tradition, to honor the memory of one of our founding members—Claude Bouchard . . ."

Cassie's head snapped up. What?

She looked at Katrina, almost as though she expected this to be less of a surprise to her, but Katrina looked as distracted as Cassie felt. She had pushed her chair back slightly and was dabbing her neck with a moistened napkin. Cassie noticed her hands were shaking.

"Although you may never have heard it linked with this

organization, many of you will already know his name. Claude was a pioneering spirit in the restaurant world, one of the greatest chefs in all Paris. He made food that could bring tears to your eyes and heaven to your mouth. He believed that beautiful cuisine was an assault on the senses that no other art form could match. Some of you may have heard that—"

A sudden wail charged up the street, accompanied by whirling blue lights. The man shrugged nonchalantly and patted the air calmly to keep everyone in their seats.

"Just the annual police drive-by letting us know that they know we're here," he said, toasting them with his glass. A wave of laughter swept through the crowd as the police cars rolled slowly past and everyone raised their glasses in a toast.

"Uh, where was I? Oh yes . . . Well, some of you may have heard that shortly before his death, Claude was developing a new business venture. Indeed, his business partner is present here today . . ." A murmur went through the crowd at the suggestion, everyone searching vainly for the anonymous businessman. "And I have their assurance that C.A.C., the new restaurant, is still going to open as planned next month in the cinquième. Claude had drawn up the menus, hired all the staff, and developed every minute aesthetic detail with the architects, so that C.A.C.—even though it will open posthumously—is truly his flagship, the standard bearer of his vision, and it will be his lasting legacy. He will never be forgotten."

A cheer went up through the crowd, and the speaker took a sip of his drink, but Cassie sat as still as a stone. Was this why she was here?

"I have no doubt C.A.C. will open to accolades and acclaim, and will win the coveted honors that always graced

Claude's enterprises, but you know that Claude himself did not care for the glory of a Michelin star. He simply wanted great cooking and exciting new flavors to be available to everyone. In recent years he had stepped back from the professional kitchens to teach a few willing students his trade secrets. It is why he set up this underground picnicking society years ago, so that people from every walk of life would be brought together by food and its close companions, wine and conversation!"

Another cheer rippled through the diners.

"To those who knew him in recent years, he was a soul in anguish, but let us remember him for the zest and passion with which he pursued his art—for he always believed, even in the darkest days, that a love for food is a love for life. And so, before we continue our celebrations tonight, I would ask you all to observe a minute's silence as tribute to our dear and great friend, Claude Bouchard."

The man bowed his head and an extraordinary hush fell upon the crowd. Even the cars stopped hooting their horns as the drivers realized that the guests were all sitting as still and as silent as statues. Cassie looked around in awe. She had thought she'd been alone here tonight, the only person present mourning a dear friend, but she couldn't have been more wrong. In among the strangers everywhere were people who had known him longer, better, loved him harder, people who hadn't let him down the way she had.

This wasn't a party; it was a memorial. She looked up gratefully at the silent crowd, wondering who around her had known him. She looked at Katrina, alarm gripping her as she saw the beads of sweat rolling down her brow.

"Katrina, are you all right?" she asked quietly, leaning forward. "Your color's bad."

"Actually, I'm not . . . I don't . . . feel so g—" She clapped a hand across her mouth suddenly, her eyes wide with panic, as her body began to heave. Cassie looked around in horror. Oh God! Where was the butler? She looked for the limo but it was nowhere to be seen; the police must have moved it on from its illegal parking spot when they'd driven by a few moments before.

She looked back at Katrina, who now had both hands over her mouth. It was clear she was going to throw up, right here, in front of everyone. Without thinking, Cassie grabbed her bag—the beautiful, much-loved green Maddy Foxton bag that Kelly had given her on her first day in New York—and opened it. She passed it over the table, and Katrina—as discreetly as she could—vomited violently into it.

No one noticed. At that exact moment, the minute's silence was ended by the sound of the speaker clapping, and within seconds the noise had gathered crescendo until everyone was on their feet clapping their hands above their heads.

Cassie saw the limo come back down the street looking for another convenient illegal place to park, and quickly raised her arm to get the driver's attention. She helped Katrina up and, with one arm around her birdlike shoulder, guided her to the car.

She dumped the newly filled bag into a trash can as they passed, trying not to think about the three-thousand-dollar price tag as the driver opened the passenger door and Katrina almost fell in, grateful for the blacked-out privacy of the tinted windows.

"She's eaten a dodgy oyster, I think," Cassie said to the driver. "She might need to see the doctor."

The driver nodded. "Thanks."

Cassie watched the car roll away as the butler came out of

a café with a freshly replenished ice bucket. She shook her head at him and gave a small shrug, but that seemed to tell him all he needed to know and he started packing the table away again, even though only a fraction of the food had been touched.

She stood with the passersby watching the diners tucking into their meals again, and saw she was no longer one of them. She was a spectator now, not a guest at her friend's picnic—and she had been, she realized, ever since his death. In losing Claude, she'd lost part of herself too—the part that had found confidence in her passion, the part that had found pride in her talent. He was gone, and he'd taken her dreams with him. She had a sense that Paris had nothing more to offer her.

Chapter Thirty-Seven

Cassie was rummaging through the bags like a bear in the bins. She was sure she'd seen one of the scarves in the blue-ribboned bags, and she'd expressly told Marina that they *only* went in the pink. "You can't let a captain of industry go home with a woman's scarf . . . ," she muttered.

"How is everything going here?" a voice asked behind her.

Cassie turned around. Florence was smiling at her, looking a vision in a red and white column dress appliquéd all over with chiffon flowers, which she had borrowed from the atelier's archives. One of the assistants had had to go through the accounts to make sure that none of the guests who'd RSVP'd yes had ordered it. It wouldn't do to have another Holland-Bruni fiasco.

Florence's beatific face revealed none of the stresses that had accompanied the run-up to tonight, unlike Cassie's, which had hard grooves of shock and grief worn into it. Her skin was thin and papery, her lips pale, her hair lank, and her eyes almost opaque from the tears. She had done her best for tonight: while Anouk had made a beeline for the hammam, she'd tried to draw herself a happier face with her now extensive makeup range, but when she looked in the mirror, she thought she just looked clownish. Even the four-thousand-euro dress—hers was borrowed from the pret-à-porter collection: cranberry chiffon with a crossover neckline and feather fringing—made her feel like a little girl in her mother's clothes.

Florence peered into the bags. They were bulging with gifts that money literally could not buy—a copy of the book, which had a print-run of only one hundred; a cashmere scarf produced in the specially reissued skull-print, of which, again, only one hundred had been made; for the ladies a bespoke "bounty" necklace by Anouk with tiny gold bones and dubloons threaded onto leather, with a hammered gold locket filled with solid perfume, a "private" scent that Monsieur Westley had developed especially and only for the anniversary party. For the men, Anouk had made gold cufflinks shaped like tibias, skulls, and ribs.

She nodded at the small but exclusive cache. "All of these were your ideas, Cassie," she smiled. "As was this." She held her hands up at the crypt, flickering with Diptyque candles. The bones in the tunnels here were actually arranged decoratively—the femurs laid out end first, so that the "knuckles" created the wall's dimpled surface, and the skulls interspersed among them at regular intervals, some tracing crosses, others hearts.

It wasn't creepy. It was almost beautiful, a bit like a shell grotto. Extravagant profusions of blood-red—almost black—velvet roses had been placed around the walls, and the music echoed with eerie exaggeration into the black abyss beyond. Some of the tech guys who'd been setting up the sound systems earlier had been messing around and daring each other to go farther into the unroped areas of the tunnels, but their shouts had quickly lost bravado, and when they'd eventually found their way back, they were pale-faced and quiet.

For Cassie, this place was yet another reminder of Claude. He'd been the one who'd told her about it. It was as a result of *their* conversation that this party was happening here at all.

"He should have been here," she thought, and the anger ricocheted around her again like a whip.

"You know, Cassie," Florence said, looking at her pinched expression with concern, "if you felt like perhaps you didn't want to leave after all"—she looked down for a moment—"and no one could blame you for wanting to think twice, you know we would be delighted to keep you on the team." She held her hands up before Cassie could protest. "I know. I know it is not your great love . . . but still you are very good at it. I think maybe you do not realize how much you have helped us these past few months." She tipped her head to the side, the way Suzy always did when she was concerned. "I admire you, Cassie. And if tonight really is your last night with us, well then . . . tomorrow I shall miss you very much."

Cassie looked at her and realized, for the first time, that perhaps she had missed a trick with Florence. She'd just gone through the motions the entire time she'd worked with her— she'd used her job here as rent money, nothing more—and it was only now that she saw it could have been so much more.

"Thanks, Florence." She smiled, genuinely touched. "I'll give it some thought. I have been . . . having doubts." She didn't mention the nights spent staring up at the ceiling, bathed in sweat at the very prospect of heating a pan without Claude. She gave a little hopeless shrug. "I'm not ready without him. He was going to mentor me, and . . ." She trailed off as the tears threatened.

Florence nodded. "You don't need to decide tonight. Take some time off after this anyway. Rest a bit. We'll still be here if you do decide you want to stay."

"Madame Lazartigue," a harried voice called behind her. It was one of the girls from the press office, looking flustered and brandishing a clipboard like a hand grenade.

"Excuse me." Florence smiled, rolling her eyes and going off to deal with the next crisis.

Cassie watched her go. There were legitimate reasons to stay here, not least that she could afford a better flat with the salary Dior paid her. The thought of the dingy bedsit she'd lined up lying there empty, just waiting for her to move in, made her shiver.

She heard the music volume rise just a little—telling her that the first guests had arrived—and took a deep breath. She was going to be everyone's first port of call. Initially, Florence had wanted her to take more of a leading role in the night's events in recognition of her contribution, but in the wake of Claude's death, Florence had agreed she could hide out here and man the cloakroom instead.

Space was tight, but still they had managed to create a glamorous cloakroom where the tunnel bellied out a little. Three high walls had been erected to enfold hanging rails behind them, and a specialist team from De Gournay had been shipped in to create a specially commissioned historic cityscape of eighteenth-century Paris. It was a lavish and luxuriant commission for something that was only up for one night, but as the candlelight flickered on it, it brought back to life the Paris that had existed when the bones down here now had been its citizens.

The guests arrived quickly through the tunnels, their slightly pensive expressions softening into relief and then excitement as they descended the stairs from the pavement above and took in the moody lighting and murals and flowers. It had enough of what they knew—and needed—to make them feel secure, but the shock factor gave them an added thrill. The atmosphere switched on, and it rapidly grew louder and warmer.

Within half an hour, Cassie was rushed off her feet as wave after wave of fur coats was tossed toward her. She had a split second with each to find the owner's face and name on her list and write it down on a labeled hanger—it was considered far too vulgar to hand out numbered tickets—and Cassie had been sure to study the "who's who" list for this event.

Anouk, Pierre, Guillaume, and Jacques arrived together shortly after nine, once the party was gearing up to full swing. The initial VIP rush was over and Florence had arranged for Stephanie, an office junior, to relieve Cassie from her post once everyone was in.

"You look sensational," Cassie gushed as Anouk shrugged off a black taffeta belted trench coat to reveal a tight black satin dress with long sleeves and a lace spiral that started at her collarbone and spun all the way around her, narrowly missing strategic anatomical points, but making it clear nonetheless that she was wearing nothing underneath.

It wasn't her usual style—much more provocative and outré than usual—and from the looks on the guys' faces, they all thought so too, clearly wondering whether the spiral might snake up when Anouk walked.

The place was packed and people were leaning casually against the stacked bones as if they were library shelves. Across the crowd, Cassie could see Florence introducing her bosses to the distinguished guests. Cassie grabbed herself a drink, feeling assured that she could relax a little, and went to join her friends.

The champagne fizzed lightly on her tongue and she closed her eyes to savor the first hit of alcohol in her system for weeks. Since Claude's death—and especially after the aborted Dîner en Blanc—she had stopped drinking wine in the evenings, preferring to sit alone in the dark in her room, suffering a punishing asceticism that seemed to satisfy her guilt at not having picked up . . .

But tonight she felt an overwhelming urge to let go—of her sobriety, her dreams, her inhibitions. Tomorrow was supposed to have been the first day of the rest of her life proper, the life *she* had chosen for herself: living in Paris, following her dream with Claude. It wasn't going to happen now, at least, not the way she had dreamed it would, and in the morning she was going to have to start facing up to the options that remained open to her—walking into the kitchens without Claude's protection and guidance, or staying on at Dior and trying to pursue a valid long-term career in marketing.

Neither one appealed—for different reasons—but she figured she'd probably make just as good a decision on a hangover as not, and she took another sip of her drink. She swayed softly to the music. It was ambient and indistinct, echoing in the subterranean caves, and she wondered what Gil would think if he were to see her here, at this party *she* had organized—dressed in not-in-the-shops-yet Dior, her body supple and gleaming with oils, her hair chopped off and darkly glossy in the candlelight. Would he want her? And more to the point, would she want him? For all the self-assurance and genteel manners that had swept her off her twenty-one-year-old feet, had he really been such an unbeatable proposition? She had grown up more in the past six months than in the entire decade preceding them, and in lots of ways now, she had slipped out of his league.

She felt an arm slide over her shoulders, and from the smell of jasmine in the air, knew that Anouk had come to dance with her. They swayed in time, eyes closed, Anouk humming gently in her ear, and Cassie was surprised to see the covetous glances bouncing their way when she looked around her a few minutes later. Jacques was watching intently, a barely disguised film of lust on his face; Pierre had moved away slightly and was talking to an older woman in another group.

Florence came over and joined them. Her cheeks were flushed—with champagne *and* success, for there was no doubt the party had really taken off. She looked radiant, and Jacques must have thought so too, for he snaked an arm around his wife's slender waist and kissed her adoringly in the crook of her neck, making her giggle ticklishly.

"Congratulations, *ma chérie*," he smiled.

"You should be congratulating Cassie," Florence protested. "All this was her idea."

"Then my congratulations to you too," Jaques said, giving Cassie a little bow. "It seems you have shown us all a new way to party in Paris."

Guillaume and Anouk concurred, holding their glasses up to her in a toast.

"Fresh eyes," Florence smiled. "Such a privilege."

"Well, I do believe it was *my* idea for you to bring Cassie on board in the first place," Anouk said, a tone of petulance hanging off the words. "A little gratitude might be thrown my way too." She planted an indignant hand on a narrow hip.

Florence's smile froze slightly at the flash of tantrum, and Jacques and Guillaume nodded their heads obligingly. Pierre, having overheard, leaned in quickly and kissed Anouk's neck the way Jacques had just done to Florence.

"*Bien sûr, chérie,*" he crooned, rubbing her arms lightly. "All the very best ideas spring from you."

A stiff silence permeated the encompassing din, and Cassie saw for the first time that something about Anouk was "off" tonight. There was a bitterness in her smile, a sour edge to her comments, a competitiveness in her dress sense that she rarely felt obliged to enter into. An air of desperation clung to her, Cassie realized. Anouk was making a point. She was being provocative, clearly *trying* to provoke some kind of re-action. But from whom? Pierre? He seemed as languid and unruffled as ever. Cassie noticed Guillaume's eyes on Anouk as she looked around the room, but why would Anouk possibly want to provoke him?

"Have you tried the sesame tuna canapés?" Florence asked lightly.

The men shook their heads. "The waiters aren't getting to us," Guillaume smiled. "We are too far from the kitchens."

"Well, you must. They've been such a hit. In fact, I shouldn't say it because it'll only confirm her decision to go, but they're another of Cassie's . . . suggestions," she said, trailing off as she realized she was complimenting Cassie again.

Everyone tried not to look at Anouk, who was rolling her eyes with unconcealed irritation.

"*Alors*, I'll go and find a waiter to bring some over to you," Florence said quickly, making her exit.

Anouk gave a heavy sigh. "Well, it really is your night, Cass," she said with a smile that didn't quite reach her eyes, though the champagne clearly had.

"I don't think so, Nooks," she said. "I wouldn't have known about this place if it hadn't been for Henry and Claude; and the same goes for the food. They're the masterminds behind it all. I just implemented their ideas."

"To Henry and Claude then," Jacques said merrily, clasping a warm arm around Cassie's shoulders and toasting them jovially.

Anouk fidgeted with her clutch bag, swapping arms as a waiter sped over with the promised tray of canapés.

"So this is your last day at Dior?" Guillaume asked, changing the subject completely.

"Yup. I was hired on a project basis really, and now that this is done . . ." She shrugged.

"I know Florence is desperate to keep you," Jacques interjected, and she noticed Anouk bristle again.

"She did mention I could stay on," Cassie replied, keeping it light.

"But you are determined to go?" Pierre enquired.

"Well . . ."

"Oh yes. Everything's sorted. Flat. Job. Cassie's going to stay in Paris, but under her own steam from now on, isn't that right?" Anouk said with a brittle smile. From the way Anouk put it, she sounded delighted finally to be free of her.

Cassie paused. "Yes."

"Is that so? You are still going to work as a chef?" Guillaume asked.

"I'm not sure about that, actually. I need to sit down and really think things through. But whatever I decide workwise, I've found my own apartment and I'll still be moving there at the weekend." She was packing tomorrow.

It was late now and the catacombs were very warm. Florence hadn't returned and Anouk jiggled restlessly, fiddling with her dress, which seemed to get less saucy and more slutty the more everyone drank. Eyes were brazenly resting upon the intriguing lace spiral and the flashes of peachy flesh that winked from beneath. She tried smoothing the dress back over her hips, but it was difficult with a glass in one hand and a clutch bag pinned under one arm.

"You look like you're struggling," Cassie said, smiling sympathetically. "Why don't I put your bag in the cloakroom for you?"

"I'm fine," Anouk said tersely, just as the bag slipped from beneath her elbow.

Guillaume caught it gallantly and handed it back to her. They'd all had too much to drink, but whereas everyone else was feeling relaxed and loose-tongued, Anouk was getting more and more uptight. Pierre made a polite excuse and left the group, but Anouk didn't seem to care as Jacques started regaling them with the story of how he'd almost induced a heart attack in an elderly lady earlier in the week when he'd moved the giant polar bear that stood in his gallery window.

". . . I had to give her a *verre églomisé* mirror to stop her from suing," he chuckled, but this time Cassie didn't join in. The mention of the bear had made her think about Henry in the Arctic instead. He had been away for almost three weeks. She'd heard from a round-robin e-mail Suzy had pinged through that they'd arrived at "base camp" the previous Tuesday, and that aside from some frostnip to his little finger when he hadn't got his gloves on quickly enough, all was progressing well. There were fourteen other scientists in the team, and they had a nine-week window in which to collect their data before the weather started to close in again and the ice floes made it impossible for them to get out.

Anouk's bag slipped again and this time Guillaume nearly missed it.

"Here, I insist," Cassie said, taking it from him. "It'll only take a moment. I'll put it with mine."

"Fine," Anouk snapped impatiently, as though it were the only way to stop Cassie *going on.*

Cassie raised her eyebrows at Jacques as she passed, sharing an "Oh lawd!" moment.

It was slow going through the crowd. There was very little available space in the main room—and absolutely nobody appeared to have left yet. She tried pushing through, but when one body moved over, another filled its place. Then she remembered the roped-off tunnel on her left that looped around in a long cut back toward the main entrance. The waiters had been using it all night.

She slipped past the twisted red rope and made her way down the tunnel. It was darker down here, lit not by flashy Diptyque candles but by large yellow plastic torches positioned on their ends that cast unflattering white light up onto the walls. Underfoot, the pathway crunched slightly with shards of bone that hadn't been swept back.

Ahead, in the gloom—the torches were spaced only every fifty yards—she thought she could see a junction. She moved nearer. There was movement ahead. Although only one of the paths was lit, a waiter was clearly going down the other one. She hesitated. She'd overheard some of the techies joking earlier about putting lighting down the wrong tunnels just for a laugh. They knew none of the guests would come down here, only staff, and she'd seen for herself earlier that it wasn't beyond them to play a joke on the "pretty boys" working here tonight.

She stood for a moment, trying to work out which way to go. It seemed more obvious to follow the torches, but this was the waiters' tunnel and she'd seen one of them come down here. She listened for sounds. The music behind her was distant now, and she could clearly hear movement in the darker tunnel. It had to be this one.

She started walking down it. There was no light at all, and within a hundred yards she was in almost total darkness. Dammit! Wrong call! What had she been thinking? It seemed she couldn't even trust her eyes and instinct anymore.

Slowly, her senses began to attune to the darkness, and although there was nothing to see or hear, there was something to feel. Quite suddenly she knew she wasn't alone.

"Hello?" she said quietly. She didn't need to call out—the silence was resounding. There was nothing to hear—but not nothing at the same time. She could feel the person's presence, the way she had felt Henry's stare in the dark. She felt frightened immediately, sheer terror flooding her. Even her breath shivered.

She put her hands out to turn and get the hell out of there, but instead of the reassuring cold hardness of bone, she touched something much more terrifying, something soft and warm—flesh. She was about to scream when a hand went over her mouth, and an arm clasped her to the warm chest she'd just touched.

"Sssssh!" it whispered. "It's okay, Cassie."

He knew her name?

"There is nothing to be frightened of. You have just taken a wrong turn, that is all."

The hand was still over her mouth, and she was trembling all over with fright, but the man rubbed his other hand down her arm in a comforting gesture, and she managed to give a little nod. He uncovered her mouth. "Ssssshhh," he said in the darkness.

"Who are you?" she asked, immediately taking a step back.

"It doesn't matter. Just go back," the voice said. "You should just go back."

"What are you doing down here?" she asked, but as she said it, she heard another sound like someone fumbling behind them only a few feet away. "Who's that? Who else is here?" she asked, her voice rising again.

"It is okay," the voice said, gripping her arm firmly again and forcing her to turn. "Just go back now."

Pointlessly she nodded in the dark and turned around, treading carefully on the bone shards that littered the floor. It was easier now that she was following the light that shone dimly in the distance, and she began to calm down as she got closer to it. Her brain began to work again. He had known her name, this man. He must have seen her—been watching her—from the moment she'd stepped into the tunnel. And there was something about the way he'd rubbed her arm. She'd seen him do it before—just moments before, in fact, when Anouk had been upset.

She was only a few feet from the lit tunnel now. Everything was still silent in the blackness behind her, even though she knew there were two people still in there.

She turned.

"Pierre?"

"*Oui?*" came the voice in the darkness, the small gasp of surprise that followed it audible even from where she was standing. He had responded to his name on impulse.

"*Merde!*" Another voice—male—hissed and then she heard the rustle of fabric, harried whispers as the lovers clashed in the dark.

"Wait!" Pierre cried. The clatter of loose bones falling to the floor echoed down to her, but Cassie had already fled. She was back in the light and running down the torchlit passage.

She ran toward the cloakroom, out of breath and panicking. Would Pierre assume she'd run back into the party?

"Hi, Stephanie," she said, her eyes darting up and down the corridor distractedly. "I'll take over for you now."

"You are sure?"

"Absolutely," Cassie assured her, nodding hurriedly, eager to get rid of her and just shut the door, shut the world out so that she could have a minute to think. How on earth could she tell Anouk what she'd just discovered? Was this what had been making her so unhappy?

She paced the room, her hand absentmindedly brushing the furs as she deliberated how to tell her friend, for she instinctively knew she *had* to tell her. Anouk deserved to know the truth.

Cassie tried to consider the facts: she had just caught Pierre with another man. In the best-case scenario for Anouk, it meant he was bisexual. At the worst, it meant he was gay. But no, no . . . that didn't make sense. Would he be able to hide his sexuality from her so convincingly? Anouk was highly tuned in to her sexuality, and they met up for a rendezvous every afternoon. There was no way he could maintain that kind of pretense with her.

So then, if he was bi, did Anouk know about that? Were his affairs with men an agreement between them, or was it his secret?

Oh God, her head was spinning, and not just with what-ifs. Cocktails, secrets, and shock were not a good combination. At the very least she was going to have to sober up before she said anything to Anouk.

She perched on the small table and took some deep breaths. Pierre would be desperate for her to keep his secret, at least for tonight, and the safest place for her to be, she realized, was back out there, in company. He couldn't get to her with Anouk and the others around.

She opened the small drawer beneath the table to hide Anouk's clutch bag, but the door opened in the same instant, and she looked up in alarm, sending the bag flying onto the floor.

"Oh Jacques, thank God it's only you!" she exclaimed, slapping her hand across her chest as he peered round the doorway.

"Thank you very much," he said, smiling wryly as he came in.

Cassie dropped to the floor and began picking up the bag's contents as he leaned against the wall.

"We were wondering where you had got to. Pierre thought you might have taken a wrong turn in the tunnels. I have been sent as the search party," he said as she retrieved a lipstick, an atomizer, and a tube of Touche Éclat that had rolled under the tables.

"Is she there?"

Cassie looked up as she heard Anouk's voice coming down the hallway, and then saw her pretty toes by the door. She pulled back to get out from under the table when she saw a small hairbrush under the coats, as well as a small notebook. She felt the hairs on her arms stand on end as she picked it up. She didn't even need to flick open the pages to know what was inside it. She'd have recognized it anywhere.

Suddenly, everything had changed again. She stood up slowly, like a sunflower stretching toward the light, the book resting on her open palms, and she saw that Jacques and Anouk were watching her in silence, a protective silence that was trying to pull itself like a sheet over what was really going on.

Cassie looked from Anouk to Jacques.

"It was you at the park," she said to him. Not a question. A statement. A fact.

"I don't know what you—" he began in protest, but his voice died away as Cassie looked back at Anouk, ashen-faced.

"*Him?*" Cassie was so shocked she could hardly speak.

"No." Anouk shook her head firmly, walking farther into the room and shutting the door.

"Yes!" Cassie contradicted. "No one else would give you a book like this," she said, flinging the emerald-green leather notebook onto the table. A loose black-and-white photo fluttered out from the pages and the naked woman within it stared up at them all from the floor—as much a player as any of them in this unfolding drama, as her spread legs and hungry eyes exposed the carnal intimacy between the two secret lovers in the room.

Anouk swallowed hard and fell back into her defensive silence. Disgust simmered in Cassie's eyes as the parallels of the deception began to dawn on her.

"To think that I trusted you," Cassie muttered, her cheeks beginning to redden, her voice to thicken. "To think that I actually put myself in your hands, actively sought out your guidance, accepted your advice, happily remade myself in *your* image . . ." She gave a small, bitter laugh. "When all along, you were doing exactly the same thing to your best friend as was done to me. You're exactly the same as *her*. And *I* was trying to be *you*."

Cassie shook her head—incredulous, stunned, her eyes swimming with tears at the thought of being so close to that dreadful scenario all over again. She looked back at Anouk. "Do you have *any idea* what it's taken for me to get through this? Of how tortured I've been by the lies and the not-knowing what was real and what wasn't in *my own marriage*?"

Anouk only blinked.

"I'll tell you what's been getting me through it—the complete and utter belief in our friendship. I looked at you and Suzy and Kelly and I saw these crazy, full, chaotic lives that were all about glamour and the right jeans and good haircuts, and I thought *that's* where I've been going wrong. It's my fault he looked elsewhere. I'm too dowdy, too parochial, too unsophisticated to keep a man. I need to be more exciting, more mysterious, more sexy . . . I need to be more like *you*, I thought to myself. So I left *me* behind that night. I'm still upstairs in the Faerie Room somewhere, wearing a Laura Ashley dress and a saggy gray bra. I'm not *really* standing here, in a bony crypt, wearing a dress that costs more than a car, with brown fucking hair! I mean, if only you'd told me that being like you would involve becoming an unscrupulous, conniving bitch, it would have saved me thousands in airfares."

There was a heavy pause and Cassie realized she'd started to shake.

"A *bitch*?" Anouk whispered, her usual *froideur* replaced now by a white-hot anger. "After everything I've done for you, this is how you repay me? I have been nothing but a friend to you. My relationship with him has nothing to do with you. How dare you stand in judgment of me! You know nothing about the situation."

"There's nothing to know. You're fucking your friend's husband. It's as simple and final as that. You chose him over her. You chose yourself over her."

"It is not like it is in—"

"Oh, please—spare me!" Cassie cried. "Don't try to justify

this with your crackpot explanation about how *relaxed* you all are about affairs over here, about how they don't matter, they don't mean anything."

"It *doesn't* mean anything," Jacques interjected, a note of finality in his voice.

The makeshift room fell into a trembling silence and Cassie felt as if the walls might collapse in on them all, the opulence and extravagant excesses burying them alive.

"It is merely a convenient arrangement, Cassie. Pierre has been very kind to step in and deflect attention away from us—and I pay him handsomely to do it—but nobody is going to get divorced as a result of this. Anouk knows I will never leave Florence, and if Florence knows about Anouk, well . . ." He shrugged his huge shoulders. "She knows Anouk is no threat."

Cassie looked between the two of them. Anouk was staring at him, her eyes unblinking.

"Florence will feel as devastated about the affair as I did," Cassie said finally.

"*Peut-être*," he conceded. "But only if she finds out." Jacques put his head to the side questioningly. "You know, when Anouk came back from staying with you last year, she asked me the same question. Should she tell you? But she said you seemed happy enough in your ignorance. There was no point in you being hurt needlessly."

Cassie felt the walls shift, the floor begin to slide as she realized what he was saying. Anouk had *known*?

"But even when you did find out, she said you could have carried on happily enough too. There was no reason for you to make such a fuss the way you did."

"A fuss?" Cassie echoed, looking over toward Anouk, who had grown visibly paler throughout the conversation. "I don't remember raising my voice, throwing anything, hurling an insult even."

Anouk didn't reply. She seemed frozen.

"*Non,*" Jacques said, fighting her battle for her. "She said you went for quiet hysteria. I suppose you imagine it was dignified, flouncing out like that and breaking up the party."

"Breaking up the *party*? That's your concern? I find out my husband has another family and you're both more worried about keeping up appearances?" She gave a laugh of disbelief, of bitterest despair to think that her friend could have thought all this about her while living with her. She thought back to their dinners in the apartment, sharing bottles of Beaujolais while the sun went down, relaxing together in the hammam, and laughing at themselves in their endermologie stockings, when all this time Anouk had not only kept the worst of secrets, but had been mirroring it herself.

Cassie slowly picked up her own coat and moved past them, toward the door. She stopped just beyond Anouk and turned to look back at her.

"I never thought I'd say this—to you of all people, Nooks—but I pity you. I do. You've lost your way. I used to think you knew everything. I wanted to be *just* like you—sophisticated, enigmatic, alluring. But now that I see your life close up, I realize you're none of those things. You're just hollow and cold and cheap. And you're no friend of mine."

And she turned on her heel and stalked down the tunnel, tears streaming down her cheeks as she climbed up the steps and emerged for the last time into the nighttime shimmer of the City of Light.

LONDON

Chapter Thirty-Eight

The knocks at the door grew louder, but Cassie just dived further beneath the duvet.

"Come on, Cass! You have to speak to her sometime!" Suzy called loudly, knowing full well that Cassie was burying herself under ten-and-a-half layers.

Nothing.

"*Tch.* She can't keep this up forever. I'll get her to call you back, I promise!" Suzy said just as loudly into the phone, so that Cassie could hear.

She opened the door without knocking and sat down on the bed so heavily that Cassie felt a draft blow between her and the mattress. "Cupcake" was nearly fully baked now— only seven weeks to go—and Suzy looked like she was having twins. Or at least a large fruitcake.

"You're going to have to talk to her sooner or later."

"No I'm not! Not after what she's done."

"She hasn't done it to *you*, Cass."

Cassie poked her head above the duvet, outraged, and cried, "Oh yes she has!" but immediately regretting it.

"What does that mean?"

Cassie didn't say anything. She hadn't told Suzy the full story about that last night in Paris. It was so damning, so devastatingly revealing of Anouk's twisted priorities, that she felt the damage to the four of them, to their group, would be irreparable if she told the girls everything that had been said, and she wasn't sure she wanted to be responsible for that. History counted for a lot. Weren't your friends the family you got to choose?

"Cass!" Suzy said in a warning tone. "What else happened out there? What haven't you told me? I know there's something. I've never seen you like this before."

"I'm fine."

"You are not. You listen to your friend kill himself over the phone, have a fight with your best friend, leave all your new shiny dreams behind, and turn up, unannounced, in the middle of the night, crying and shivering on my doorstep, and then don't leave your bed for three days. That is *not* fine."

Cassie sighed and sat up higher in the bed. There was little use in trying to keep Suzy in the dark. It wasn't as if there was any way back for her and Anouk now. Too much had been said and done.

She took a deep breath. "Anouk knew about Wiz and Gil. She knew and she never told. She *kept* their secret for them."

Suzy's eyes widened in horror. "No! She couldn't have!"

"She did."

Suzy stared at her in shocked silence. "*How* could she have known?"

Cassie shrugged. "I don't know. We didn't get into specifics. She came to stay for a long weekend last year. She must have seen something then. She probably saw the signs because she was in exactly the same position, having an affair with *her* friend's husband."

Suzy shook her head, aghast. "I just can't believe it," she

murmured. "That she would do that to you and put Gil first."
Her face darkened suddenly. "Besides which, I sincerely
doubt your situation was exactly the same. Yours was a lot
worse. There was a child involved."

The mention of Rory made Cassie crumple suddenly, and
she hid her face in her hands as the tears rushed out again.
They just wouldn't stop now. It was as if all the bravery she'd
been showing as her public face had been nothing more than
a wall that simply dammed the tears, until eventually just
one little crack had made the whole edifice crumble, and all
the grief and anger and betrayal was now spilling out from
her all at once and was completely unstoppable.

She had spent the past nine months trying to avoid precisely this moment. She'd worked and played and dressed
up with the girls, found love (of a sort) with Luke, and found
her "path" with Claude. But now they were gone, all of them,
and all she had to show for her adventures was chopped off,
dyed hair, toned, moisturized skin, and a macaroon addic-
tion she could only satisfy with daily trips to the Ladurée
salon at Harrods, which wasn't the same thing at all.

Suzy gave a sad little sigh. "God, the shit just keeps on
coming," she said, rubbing Cassie's arm protectively as her
sobs settled down a bit. "No wonder you won't talk to her. I
don't blame you."

Cassie looked up quickly. She knew that tone. "Look, Suze,
I don't want you to feel like you have to . . . you know, take
sides on this. It's between me and her."

"I don't think so!" Suzy retorted angrily. "After what she's
done, exactly what kind of friend is she supposed to be? Not
one I want, that's for sure, and I think I can speak for Kelly
on this too."

"Wait, Suzy. Just let it settle, at least. I don't think we should mention this to Kelly. You know those two have always been close . . . *Tch*, I shouldn't have said anything to you."

"Oh? So you want Anouk on the phone and getting her side over to Kelly first? As soon as she realizes you and I aren't budging, she'll go straight for Kelly, and you know it."

Cassie dropped her head. It had been exactly as she'd feared. More splits and recriminations. When would it ever end?

"God, I bet Gil would be delighted to know that he's split us up at last. He was always jealous of our friendship, you know," said Suzy.

"I didn't know that," said Cassie, looking up in surprise.

"Oh yes. Kelly and Nooks and I used to joke that he looked at us as if we were the Witches of Eastwick or something, there to corrupt you and steal you away from him. He was always so *nervous* when we were around. It always gave me the impression that he felt he had won you falsely, you know?"

"Not really."

"Must have been the guilt, of course. He probably knew that we'd strip and flail him alive if we ever found out. Wasn't he lucky that Anouk was the one to uncover his little secret?"

"Mmm." It was shocking to hear how much her friends had hated her husband. Ten years, and she'd never known.

"God, he really was a shit," Suzy continued. "I should *never* have let you kiss him that night at the ball. You'd have been far better off with Henry."

"Henry?" Cass echoed in alarm, the tears coming to an abrupt standstill. Surely she wasn't referring to their drunken embrace behind the curtains ten years ago? She was certain that had gone unnoticed. "You know about that?"

"Oh, give it up, Cass! Of course I do! What do you think Henry yawned on about while you were on your honeymoon? Drove me round the bend."

Cassie shook her head. "I had no idea it was common knowledge. I mean, it was just a drunken teenage thing. You know what it's like—drunk on a hip flask and desperate to snog someone and not be deemed totally unfanciable."

"Henry's never looked unfanciable," Suzy muttered. "*He's* got great hair."

"Yeah, I know," Cassie concurred, before comprehending the veiled insult. "Hey! What're you saying?"

"No, no—you're right. You give good hair too."

Cassie chuckled lightly.

"I have to say, though, I never thought I'd see the day my brother became the condemned man. He just didn't seem the type. He was always so restless."

"Condemned?"

Suzy rolled her eyes. "Now that he's a few months off getting married."

Cassie gawped at her. "But . . . I thought the wedding was off?"

Suzy gave her a quizzical look. "No. What on earth made you think that?"

"He told me. Henry did. Horse's mouth."

"Oh, classic Henry windup. Can't believe you fell for it. Honestly, Cass, how long have you known him?" she laughed, shaking her head.

"Ugh, he's incorrigible!" Cassie exclaimed, diving back under the duvet again. "I'm *always* falling for his tricks."

"Come on," Suzy said, getting up and patting her prone form beneath the duvet. "Cuppa downstairs when you're ready."

Cassie grunted, but her thoughts had already flown far away. She was remembering something she'd been determined to forget—lying in bed in Venice, in that golden window of time after his drunken revelation and a few hours before Claude's death had broken upon her. He'd been fast asleep, his lips ruby red and parted, his heavy, honeyed arm slung over her like a strap. She'd watched him sleep for almost an hour, too scared to move lest he should wake, and then . . . well, what then? She hadn't known what to think, dared to hope . . .

It was all irrelevant. Whatever fanciful daydreams she might have allowed to peek through in the Venetian dawn were dead in the water now. She'd been too scared to stay and had made her escape downstairs as soon as he'd turned over. And now that he and Lacey were getting married after all, it looked like he'd made his.

In contrast to Anouk's, which was sleek and minimal, and Kelly's, which was so minimal it wasn't even there, Suzy's kitchen was as chaotic as a teenager's wardrobe. Everything was towered in perilous stacks—white cups that sagged forward like old women, mismatched plates from great-aunts and charity shops—and the warped wooden worktop looked like it had been mined from the Tudor Rose.

Cassie sat up on it, still in her pajamas. She hadn't changed out of them since arriving from Paris. They comforted her, even if Suzy was beginning to wrinkle her nose and look around suspiciously for dead mice whenever she walked into the room.

Suzy was sitting at the enormous farmhouse kitchen table, Mothercare and JoJo Maman Bébé catalogs at one end with Post-its fluttering from the pages. All around there were ring binders full of other people's weddings, other people's happiness.

"So . . . this week's bride. Do we like her?" Cassie asked, wrapping her cold hands around the mug. She wasn't eating enough to keep warm.

"Hate her!" Suzy said vehemently, sloshing tea all over her paperwork. "As soon as she's paid me, I forbid you to even so much as smile at her."

"Okay." She waited for the dramatics to be revealed.

"Her theme is 'Outback,' right? Groom's an Aussie. *I* said, 'Let's take a cricketing angle'—famous link between the two countries, no? And I can see the best men in cricket jumpers, can't you?"

"Totally!" Cassie agreed.

"Just think, you could have the bride's party as fielders; groom's as batsmen; red and ivory color scheme. And they're getting married in St. John's Wood, for heaven's sake—Lord's country. Lovely."

"Lovely."

"Does she think lovely? She does not! She wants Crocodile Dundee, gold and green."

Cassie waggled her head from side to side, considering the colors. "Not a *disaster* for a spring wedding. Bridesmaids and flowers should work, no?"

"Aside from the fact that I hate anything gold at a wedding, in theory, yes, it should. But it's got to be *Australian* gold, see? Any old yellow tulip won't do. I'm having to color-match marquee ribbons and buttonholes to some manky old rugby shirt I'm carrying around in my bag."

"Dead glamorous, your job," Cassie said, giggling, as Suzy opened another file. She looked around the kitchen-office. Cuttings from magazines showing dress necklines and hairstyles were pinned to a corkboard; swatches of fabrics for tablecloths and napkins were overspilling from the drawers of a dresser, and at least twelve different styles of wineglass were stacked on a slightly off-plumb shelf. It was mad to think that there'd be a high chair by the table and a bottle sterilizer by the sink in a couple of months' time—and of course a cherub of a baby gurgling in a bouncy chair amid it all.

Cassie had fallen in love with the little mews on sight, albeit through tears. It was her idea of a proper home—messy, noisy, and bursting with the full-to-bursting lives of the people who inhabited it. Unlike her life—transient, rootless, undefined, lost again. She hadn't even been able to consider what she was going to do now that she'd left Paris and turned her back on the opportunities at both Dior and C.A.C. All she'd known was that she couldn't stay. She'd thought it was where her future lay, but too much had gone wrong, soured. Claude was dead, and one of her oldest friends in the world had been revealed as a stranger to her. There'd been nothing to stay for.

"I don't suppose . . . Henry left anything here for me, did he?" she ventured. She hated herself for asking. She'd been adamant that she'd wean herself from his influence.

"Like what?" Suzy replied without looking up. She was scribbling some notes down in a book.

"I dunno. A list? Or . . . a packet of seeds maybe?"

Suzy looked up at her. "You mean more chamomile?"

"Yes, like that—except not. He changes it each time."

"Different herb, different city?" Suzy said, amused.

Cassie rolled her eyes. "I don't think the last one was an herb, actually. It had tiny pink flowers—you know, kind of spriggy."

Suzy shook her head. "My God, my brother's rock 'n' roll! Live fast and die young, that one."

"So no ideas what it could be?"

"Afraid not," Suzy said.

"You are *so* not your mother's daughter."

Suzy put down her pencil to rub her tummy. "Nope. But I sure am Cupcake's punching bag." She smiled. "Ooooh, feisty today." She rifled through a stack of books on the floor that was so high it was acting as a fifth table leg. She grabbed one, a thick hardback volume, and pushed it toward Cassie. "Here. Have a look in there."

Cassie hopped off the worktop and picked it up. It was an encyclopedia of flowers. She thumbed through it slowly, getting more and more confused. There seemed to be hundreds of pictures of pink spriggy plants.

"Does the world really need this many identical plants?" she muttered, before stabbing the page suddenly. "Oh! That could be it."

Suzy looked up and read the words upside down. "Sweet Alyssum. Huh."

"Heard of it?" Cassie asked hopefully.

"Nope." She went back to her writing.

"Hmmm. Well, I'm pretty sure that's the one."

"Yeah? And what's the point of that plant, then?"

"Your guess is as good as mine," Cassie sighed. "I just don't know why he sent them to me. Can't you ask him for me? He won't tell. I mean, the lists are just guides to new cities, but—what's the link between New York and chamomile, or Paris and Sweet Alyssum?"

Suzy scrunched up her face in concentration. "Maybe he . . . knew you wouldn't be able to get a decent cuppa at

Kelly's . . . and that . . ." Her shoulders slumped. "No, I don't know. I can't make any connection. Sorry."

"Bizarre. And there's no list or seeds here?"

"Well, I suppose you *had* said you weren't coming . . ."

Cassie narrowed her eyes. "I *knew* I was imposing on you. I'm in the way, a burden—"

"Oh, be quiet! You're not a burden, you silly moo. I'm delighted you're here. Completely thrilled. It was what I wanted all along." She gave a wicked grin. "Because now it means it's my turn to play with the Cassie doll."

Cassie looked back at her nervously. "Come again?"

"Go get dressed."

"No. I'm not—"

"Get dressed! We're going out." She got up slowly from the chair, moving like a stately galleon in full sail.

"But where are we going? What are we going to do?"

Suzy patted her arm. "Oh, I think you know!" she winked.

Chapter Thirty-Nine

Cassie eyed herself suspiciously in the chair as the hairdresser performed acrobatics behind her with the mirror to show that—yes—look!—she really was blond all over again. It wasn't a trick of the light.

"What do you think, Suze?" she asked anxiously, whirling around in the chair as she pulled off the gown. She'd lost all perspective about what she was even *supposed* to look like anymore.

Suzy looked up, and, for just a second, Cassie noticed how tired her friend looked. She made light of her workload and her clients' neuroses, but Cassie knew Suzy fell over herself to deliver exactly the wedding they wanted. No request was too obscure for her to deliver on no matter what she might have to do to make it happen, heavily pregnant or not.

"Oh, Cass! You're you again!" Suzy exclaimed happily.

Cassie looked back at the mirror, her hands patting her head hesitantly. "Yes. I think I might be."

They admired her familiar reflection. There had been no chopping this time. The stylized bob from Paris was growing out into a flattering midlength cut that she really liked, and, more importantly, didn't have to think about. Surprisingly, Suzy had been with her on that one. "There are enough things to think about without adding hair to the list," she'd said dismissively while texting a soothing assurance to her current bride that the colors of the dessert mangoes had been cross-matched with the napkins and approved.

"Of course, you realize Kelly's going to kill me now," Suzy said, pressing SEND. "She's ordered the taupe bridesmaid dress because you told her you'd be brunette."

"But that was when I was intending to stay in Paris."

"Yeah, and who can keep up? She's going to need to go for butterscotch now. *You* tell her."

"I'll Skype her tonight. She can see for herself. She'll probably be pleased anyway," she said, bouncing her hair up with her hands. "Back to Manhattan Cassie."

Suzy stood up and squinted at her reflection. "That's not Manhattan Cassie," she drawled, resting her head on Cassie's shoulder. Cassie squinted too. Suzy was right. Manhattan Cassie's hair had been a sunny, buttery color. It had been a high-maintenance Disney princess look that Bas had lovingly tended on a round-the-clock basis and that Luke had fallen for, hook, line, and sinker. This dye-job was darker, less flashy. It allowed roots.

"This is London Cassie, a bit . . . slummier," Suzy said, nodding. "I like it. Feels real."

"Mmm," Cassie said, not quite sure what to make of being called "slummy" when she'd just spent two hundred quid for the pleasure. Her bag began to vibrate across the floor and she picked it up, rooting around for her mobile. She checked the caller as they walked over to the reception desk.

Anouk. Again. She let it go to voice mail.

"So what now?" she asked casually as she handed over her credit card. God, she needed the divorce to come through soon. She pledged to ring her solicitor for an update when she got back to the house. She was racking up a horrific over-draft.

Suzy shrugged. "What d'you feel like?"

"What?" Cassie gasped, slapping a hand above her heart in mock horror. "You mean you're not going to insist I have every hair on my body waxed off? Or soak me in oil until I feel like a chip? Or have my fat bits vacuumed up?"

Suzy gave a squeamish look. "Why on earth would I do any of that?" she asked, opening the door and walking out into the Pimlico sunshine. Cassie had scarcely recognized the place when the taxi had dropped her off from Waterloo. The last time she'd been in Pimlico—nearly eleven years ago—it had been a ghetto of dry-cleaners and tailors. Now, antiques boutiques, interiors shops, upscale organic markets, and chi-chi delis littered the pavements, and it could rival St. Tropez for café culture.

Cassie decided to bite her lip rather than spill the beans on what their friends did in the name of beauty. She thought they were nuts, both of them, but they had shared these in-the-know rituals with her as favored intimacies, and it would be a breach of their trust to publicly satirize them. "God, listen to yourself," a voice in her head jeered. "You won't even breach someone's trust over a *beauty procedure*. Little wonder you're such easy pickings."

She closed her eyes instead, letting the sun do what the tea had tried to do earlier—warm her up. Spring was blossoming nicely now. It was early May and the trees were fully laden with leaves again, beautifully maintained flower beds blooming almost garishly against the muted colors of the area's unofficially adopted Farrow & Ball palette. The birds were back too, tempted by the sunny skies, which even managed to make the Thames a shimmering blue.

But it wasn't the sights that made her feel she was in London Town. With her eyes closed, she could hear its distinctive soundtrack. New York's had honking cab horns as its brass section; Paris had the tinny percussion of whining brakes; and London had a phlegmatic woodwind chorus, courtesy of the chesty engines of the iconic black cabs and red buses.

"Hungry?" Suzy asked, clocking the newly carved hollows of Cassie's cheeks. She'd not put more than a dab of tinted moisturizer on, and it was clear that the months' stresses had taken their toll on her.

"Nope. But let's eat anyway," Cassie smiled, sensing that the question had been rhetorical.

They linked arms and walked slowly along the sidewalk, letting other pedestrians swerve around them. Pregnancy gave you that prerogative, and absolutely no one was going to confuse Suzy's condition with indigestion.

"Had an e-mail from Henry this morning."

"Oh yeah?"

"Mmmm. Sounds a bit low. He says they're having a bit of difficulty getting the ship past west Svalbard—too many polynyas, whatever they are. Anyway, he sounds pretty pissed off. For once, I get the impression he really doesn't want to be there."

"Oh. That's too bad."

"Mmmm. Can't usually stop him going on these adventures."

"Well, it is his work. He's not just a Boy Scout shinnying up a tree for fun."

"No, I guess not. I think he just wants to get back. Probably missing Lacey."

"Yeah, I bet he's *gutted* to be missing out on the wedding-hysteria countdown. How is Lacey, anyway?"

"I think she's all right. I've not seen her for a while. She's been working on contract in Bristol for the past few months."

"What does she do?"

"Private wealth manager at Cazenove."

"Really? Huh." That figured—gorgeous *and* high-powered.

They carried on walking, eventually stopping at a little shop painted all around in pale turquoise with bold white polka dots and chocolate lettering above the door: KISSES FROM HEAVEN.

"So this is where you come to worship?" Cassie asked, eyebrows raised as Suzy practically butted the door open with her tummy.

"Oh yeah," she nodded. "I'm a devout disciple. Go grab the table by the window. I just need to talk to Julian about Saturday's wedding."

Cassie took a seat as Suzy started talking to a small, slim man behind the counter. He had a thatch of dark brown hair and really dark eyes. He looked up and waved at Cassie as Suzy pressed her nose against the glass counter, looking at the day's fresh offerings.

Cassie looked around her at couples and small groups, mothers and children, all huddled at their tables, laughing and gossiping and chatting among themselves, picking at their cupcakes, which were whipped and frothed dashes of whimsy, iced in all the colors of the rainbow. It was a world away from the pared-back, biodynamic vision Claude had had for C.A.C., where the food was to be served up on sheets of slate and oiled slabs of balsam wood, and flowers were intended for ingestion, not just decoration. In fact, she almost smiled at the thought of his bearlike reaction to this den of kitsch; he was, after all, the man who'd introduced her to the elegance of Ladurée (well, Henry too). And yet, nonetheless, the ambitions of both places were the same—to bring people together through a love of food.

She sighed again at the thought of what she'd lost. Not just a friend, but a path—for she knew she was too green to go it alone. Under Claude's tutelage, she might just have been able to wing it, but only thanks to some rampant nepotism. His huge reputation would have shielded her from the accurate, inevitable accusations that she was nothing more than an enthusiastic amateur, but without him, she was just a lamb for the slaughter.

Suzy came back a few minutes later with a tray laden with tea and two enormous cupcakes covered in an intricate lacework of spun sugar, like gold thread, cupped around a glistening cherry on top.

"It looks like a bird in a cage," Cassie trilled delightedly, aware of the covetous glances of their neighbors.

"I know," Suzy beamed. "This is an exclusive. We're doing them for Saturday instead of a big cake."

"Can I crash it?"

Suzy rolled her eyes. "Trust me, you wouldn't want to. I'll be so glad when I've put this wedding to bed, I tell you."

Cassie laid her hands on the table. "I'm worried about you."

"And I'm worried about you."

"No! *Please* let's not go on about me and my woes anymore. I'm so bored talking about my problems. I mean it, Suze. You look exhausted. I think you're doing too much."

Suzy paused for a moment, and Cassie could tell she was wrangling over whether or not to concede defeat. "Well, it's only in the last couple of weeks that I've started to notice it."

"So let me help you. I'm here till the baby's born, anyway. Put me to work."

She had no idea where she was going to go after the baby

was born. Suzy would need the spare room, and having forefeited her savings on the deposit for the bedsit in Paris, and with no decent paid job here, she wouldn't be able to afford anything in London, unless the divorce suddenly, magically happened. She could go back to New York, perhaps? Kelly and Brett would be married by then, so she couldn't stay there, but Bas might put her up . . . ?

Suzy looked at her. "I assumed you'd want to find another chef's position. I was going to ask Julian whether . . . that's why I brought you here."

Cassie shook her head vehemently. "No. I couldn't do that. Not yet, anyway. I think I need to step out of the kitchen just for a while. Regroup. I was punching above my weight for a bit there."

"But it made you so happy."

"Yes. And then it didn't. I don't know if—well, it was so tied in with Claude." Her voice trailed off.

"Sure. I get it," Suzy said, patting her hand. "Well, if you're sure . . . I really could do with a girl Friday."

"Great! So let me have it." She reached down into her bag and pulled out a notepad.

"What, now?"

"No time like the present."

Suzy sighed and pulled her BlackBerry from her pocket. "Well . . ." she mused, scanning her lists. "If you could swing by Elizabeth Street to pick up the favors for the Aussie wedding . . . then on your way back stop in at the printers—I'll text you the address—to approve some invitations for a couple wanting a 'summer of love' wedding in Primrose Hill—honestly, why they don't just hold it at Glastonbury, I don't know. Anyway, the theme is 'festival' and the invitations have to look like tickets. Get them to give you a proof to bring back to me. Oh God, and I need to audition some bands for Kelly's wedding, so be back with me by four and we'll road-test them together. Should be a laugh. Hmmm . . . oh, and . . . oh, no. No. That's all."

"No, what is it?"

"Honestly, Cass. I'll deal with it."

"Please tell me. I want to do it."

Suzy shot her look. "Trust me, you don't."

Cassie shot a look back.

"Fine. I was going to ask you to go to New Covent Garden Market tomorrow to check Dean's got the order in for Aussie bride's bouquet. I have a face-to-face with him every Wednesday."

"That's fine," Cassie shrugged. "What's the big deal about that?"

"You need to go at five."

Cassie looked at her blankly. Then twigged, nearly choking on her drink. "In the *morning*?"

Suzy nodded. "See why I said I'd do it?"

Cassie swallowed bravely. She couldn't believe she was going to say this. "Suze. You are almost eight months pregnant and run off your feet. You and five A.M. are going to be good pals in a few weeks. *I'll* go. I can do it. How hard can it be?"

Chapter Forty

"Famous last bloody words," Cassie fumed as she tried for the fifth time to parallel park Suzy's shiny new red Fiat 500 across from the giant gates of the market. It was like stepping into a parallel universe. The sky was still dark, with just a chink of light peeping over the rooftops as the sun made a dozy ascent into the sky, but within this gated community bright halogens were on, dimming the backup lights of lorries filled with tulips from Amsterdam, which were *beep-beep-beeping* away over the cheery shouts of the dawn workers.

Cassie walked in slowly, stunned that there should be— *could* be—this much life so early in the morning. She checked, for the third time, that she wasn't still in her dressing gown and slippers. It was hard to tell when her eyes wouldn't focus and her hands defiantly refused to perform any micro-dexterous activities like opening doors or turning on the ignition.

She checked the note Suzy had given her. *Dean Marshall, Marshall and Son, Door 4, N12.*

She walked into the lights, feeling like she was entering the final frontier. The harsh light was shocking to her dormant body, but not as much as the drop in temperature and the heady scent of millions of flowers in one space. It was like several slaps in the face, and she woke up properly. How the heck did Suzy find her way around here?

She couldn't see above most of the stalls, and many of them were so deep it felt like wading through meadows. Some stalls had tables laid out with elegant arrangements for inspiration, others had giant glass globes or antique Portland stone urns frothing with flora, and many just had long flat pallets with stems laid out, or deep plastic buckets with thick bunches of flowers propped up in them.

There was a bonhomie among the traders and customers, most of whom seemed to know each other well. They were all wrapped up in Puffa jackets, hats, and fingerless gloves, clasping steaming cups of tea in polystyrene cups as they chatted and laughed and haggled.

Cassie shivered a little, regretting her choice of waffle-knitted grandad top and jeans. It was May, but still the middle of the night. Almost.

Bright plastic banners stretched between steel poles or tied between buckets proclaimed the names of the stallholders, and she began to move more quickly, finding Marshall and Son thanks to a bright blue banner with yellow letters strung from the metal rafters above.

A plump man in his midthirties, wearing a black beanie and green jacket, was sitting on an upturned bucket, writing notes using a wooden plank as a makeshift table. A royal blue thermos flask sat to his right, and he was slurping his tea from the red plastic lid.

"Mr. Marshall?"

He looked up and gave Cassie a great big smile.

"Hello. Who's asking?"

Cassie held her hand out. "Hi. I'm Cassie Fraser. I'm working for Suzy McLintlock."

"Suzy! Well any friend of hers is a friend of mine." He stood up and leaned across the plank. "Dean. Pleased to meet you." He looked at her more closely. "Blimey. You look perished. Fancy a cuppa?" He pulled a thick china mug from behind a bucket of petunias. There was a big chip at the rim and it looked like the handle had been glued back on.

"Ooh. That's the best offer I've had all day," she said and smiled.

Dean poured her a cup and she let the steam warm her face for a moment. "Brrrr. I should have realized it would be chilly in here."

"Oh yes. All year round."

"Do you ever get used to it?"

"I don't know no different. Worked here all my life. I'm the son in the 'and Son' bit."

"Oh. So I guess you're used to the early starts as well, then."

Dean smiled. "Oh yes. Although my wife isn't, bless her."

"What time did you get here this morning?"

"The usual. Three."

For the second time in two days, Cassie choked on her tea.

"You're not a lark, then," he chuckled.

Cassie shook her head. "No. Famously not, actually. You might need to keep your thermos filled up. I don't think this is going to get any easier for me."

"Done," he said, toasting the deal with his plastic cup. "So, I 'spect Suzy's sent you over to check on her order for Saturday's job," he said.

"Yes."

"Lemme see," he murmured, pulling out a ring binder. "Yeah, she's got that yellow and green theme this week, don't she? Right, well, the Green Goddess Calla Lily's fine. I get those daily from Holland, no problemo. And the orchids . . ." He looked up at her. "She did settle on the dendrobiums in the end? Not the cymbidiums?"

"Uh . . ." Cassie quickly checked the wedding file she'd brought with her. "Yes. Yes the den . . . dendrib . . ."

"Dendrobiums," Dean said, grinning. "Good. That's just as well, because they're coming from Thailand and they've already been shipped. They should arrive day after tomorrow." He looked up. "So everything's bang on schedule. No worries."

"Thank goodness for that."

"Oh yeah," Dean said seriously. "I've seen Suzy on the warpath before. I ain't letting *her* down! How's she doin', anyway? Baby must be getting big."

"There's a few more weeks to go, but she's getting pretty tired. I've had to force her to let me help."

"I bet she'll be one of them mums that's up and working the next day, like ain't nothing happened."

"Oh, I hope not. She needs a proper rest. As well as having a baby and doing her usual workload, she's also organizing our best friend's wedding two weeks before the birth, and her brother's a month later."

Dean gave her a funny look. "Really? I thought that had been canceled."

"Sorry?"

Dean checked his book. "Yeah, look, there it is." He pointed to a big red line through the Sallyford name. "Shame. They'd asked for Himalayan blue poppies. Dead rare they are. I've only been asked once before to order those in. Still," he shrugged. "Can't have 'em getting married just 'cos the flowers is right."

"No," Cassie murmured. "Not because of the flowers."

*   *   *

When she got back, Suzy was still in her dressing gown, which barely closed around her, brewing some coffee.

"And how was that? Find him okay?" She set a cup in front of Cassie.

"Oh yes, yes. Once the halogens had burned through my retinas it was fine."

"It's not that bright in there."

"And I'm just about back to body temperature," Cassie said, continuing her moan.

"I'd have thought it was obvious it'd be cold. Flowers don't look their perkiest in the heat. Talking of which—that came for you." She pointed to a small potted rose standing on a wonky round table by the window.

"Ooh, who's it from?" Cassie asked, darting over and looking for a card.

"Doesn't say. Don't worry, I've had a good look. Luke, per-haps?" Her toast popped out from the toaster and she put it on a plate and walked over to the table.

"Hardly! Unless the thorns have been dipped in poison. The last communication I had from his lawyer was that the *Vogue* story was going ahead."

"No way! I thought you'd got it all stopped."

"In Paris, yes. But they've got different privacy laws in the States, and he's got copyright." She gave a defeated shrug.

"Well, can't you fight it?"

"I could—if I had more than eighteen quid in my bank ac-count."

"No! You don't—"

"Not literally, Suze! But not far off. I'm just going to have to get my head around the fact that most of the Western world is going to see me naked." She was silent for a minute, and then a slightly hysterical laugh escaped her.

"What's so funny about that?" Suzy asked. "I'd be topping myself. I have to whistle just so that Archie can brace himself for the sight of me coming out of the bathroom."

"It's not that," Cassie sighed. "I was just remembering how terrified I was of Gil's reaction to me in the *nightie* dress. I mean, it was because of that that I was trying to find him that night. If I'd just worn the velvet one, I still might not know about him and Wiz, even now. Instead, half the world's going to see me in the buff! How ironic is that?"

"That's mad karma, babe. You must have done something really bad in a previous life!"

"I'm beginning to agree." Cassie smiled, brushing the tops of the rosebuds. They hadn't opened yet, but she could tell from the buds that the petals were a delicate pink.

Suzy looked over at the rosebush. "Hey, that couldn't have come from Henry, could it? Didn't you ask about flowers from him?"

"No. The others came as seeds. I had to grow the damn things. Why suddenly send me a plant?"

Suzy shrugged, and Cassie remembered what Dean had said.

"By the way, Dean said something."

"Oh yes? Dean says a lot. Trust me. Can't stop him."

"He says Henry's wedding *has* been canceled."

"Yes, he just rang. I've put him straight, don't worry. There had been a query over the reception venue's availability and I'd forgotten to cancel the first date option, that's all. It's all sorted."

"Oh. Good," Cassie said flatly.

"Is that disappointment I hear in your voice?" Suzy asked, a small smile twitching her lips.

"No, not at all," Cassie replied, sitting back in the chair.

"I was just getting fed up with being told first one thing and then another. I mean, hello? New hat? Should I get some new shoes? And dresses need to be sorted . . ." Her voice trailed away.

Suzy pulled herself up to standing. "Well, worry no longer. It's all on. I spoke to him this morning, actually. He sounds a lot happier. They've broken through the ice and reached the Gakkel Ridge. I think he'd rather be swimming with seals than examining the new anthropogenic pressures on the pristine Arctic ecosystems, but . . ."

Cassie shot her a look. "You have *no* idea what you're talking about *at all*, do you?"

"None whatsoever," Suzy agreed as a big, noisy yawn escaped her. "Lawd, I'm tired."

"Go and have a nap," Cassie said. "I'll take over whatever you were doing here."

"Oh, would you? I was just looking through the brochures to draw up a short list of dresses for Miss Second-Weekend-in-September-Chiswick. She says she wants something modern and simple. No hoops or ruches or anything that makes her look like an Austrian blind."

"Sure thing," Cassie smiled. She'd gone from girl Friday to girl Monday-through-Friday in the blink of an eye, but she kept the smile on her face until Suzy had shuffled out of view. Then she laced her fingers around the warming cup and gave a weary sigh, eyeing the happy-ever-after brides on the table as if they were the enemy.

Chapter Forty-One

The days began to pick up the pace as Suzy's various deadlines loomed ever larger and Cassie attuned herself to the neurotic, just-below-hysteria pitch that most brides-to-be operated at.

"God, tell me I wasn't like that," she muttered to Suzy as they came out of a meeting with a prospective bride who wanted the cast of Riverdance to perform at her reception.

"Some hope. You were so dreamy you could have got married in a trash can and thought it was romantic."

Cassie pulled a face. "Was I really that bad?"

"Worse. Nothing would have stopped you," Suzy said, opening the car door. Cassie was doing all the driving now, as Suzy had to struggle to get Cupcake behind the wheel. She clicked her seat belt on. "What did make you fall for him, anyway?"

"You mean apart from the voice?" Cassie asked, throwing her bag into the backseat. She'd bought a pleather Topshop one to replace the Maddy Foxton bag she'd ended up giving to Katrina Holland. Not exactly a fair swap.

"Fair enough. I get that."

Cassie turned on the ignition and pulled out. "I don't know that it was one thing, really. Just the package, I guess. He was older, confident, self-assured. Dry sense of humor that I like. I was far from home and he just . . . made me feel safe." She gave a shrug as they pulled onto the Fulham Road.

"You never saw the boring, pretentious, affected arrogance that we all saw, then?" Suzy asked innocently.

Cassie gave a startled laugh. "He's not that bad!"

"You're defending him? What on earth is wrong with you? You're supposed to curse the very mention of his name."

Cassie sighed. Being so busy for the last few weeks had had a positive effect on her mood, but she still felt she was barely more than sleepwalking most of the time. The divorce proceedings were dragging—her solicitor seemed unable to get through to Gil's; she'd had to suspend her litigation against Luke due to insufficient funds; and all hell had broken out among the girls. Suzy had told Kelly everything that had happened in Paris, and Kelly had sided with the two of them immediately, to the effect that Anouk found herself sacked by e-mail as both Kelly's bridesmaid and Suzy's baby's godmother. Cassie was grateful for the support, but also depressed by it as the girls' exhortations breathed fire into the new enmity and made it a living thing.

"It's too exhausting. I can't live with that much hate inside me, Suze. I'm just not made that way."

"*Don't* tell me you're going to forgive him?" Suzy asked, indignation pulsating all over her.

Cassie paused. "Forgive, no. But I just don't want to keep it with me." She swung the car through amber lights and Suzy grabbed the handrail. "I want to keep on moving—physically, geographically—until the hurt is so far in the distance, I can't really remember it anymore."

"So what are you saying? What about Wiz?"

"What about her?"

"Don't tell me you're forgiving her too."

"I'm not forgiving either of them," Cassie said sharply, and there was a brief silence between them. "But at the end of the day . . . she's a mother," she shrugged. "Once she fell pregnant with Rory—even if it was accidental—she must have had a deep need to keep her son with his father. You can't blame her for that."

"You most certainly can!" Suzy said crossly. "Gil was not hers to take."

"No . . . But he was Rory's."

"Ugh!" Suzy exclaimed, crossing her arms petulantly over her belly. "I don't know what to do with you, really I don't. You're far too soft. I worry about you, Cass. I fear you haven't learned anything this year, that you'll let someone else use and abuse you, just like they did."

Cassie didn't say anything. True, she might be soft-hearted, but Suzy must know after all these years that if she believed something, she stuck to it.

They sat behind a bus chugging along the King's Road.

"Of course, I don't suppose it's ever occurred to you that there could have been a different way to play all this?" Suzy said in a lighter, more playful tone.

Cassie arched an inquisitive eyebrow. "That being . . . ?"

"Why, to seduce Gil one last time, get pregnant, bear the rightful *legitimate* heir, get the entire estate passed over to your child, kill Wiz, and adopt Rory as your own, of course. Not considered that option?"

Cassie burst out laughing. "No. But now that you mention it, I'll keep it as my Plan B. It's a good backup. Modest. Achievable."

They pulled up outside the mews. A blacked-out top-of-the-line Range Rover with all the toys was parked opposite.

"Hmmm, swanky," Suzy muttered, trying to get herself elegantly out of the tiny car. Not easy when she was—as she kept saying—as full as an egg.

They were just through the front door and kicking off their shoes when the bell rang.

"I'll get it," Cassie called to Suzy, who had made a beeline for the bedroom and an elasticated waistband.

Cassie opened the door.

"Katrina!"

The older woman smiled. She was wearing sunglasses and a Hermès scarf wrapped around her hair as though she were Grace Kelly and had traveled here in a sportscar, not—Cassie could see the chauffeur standing by the car opposite—in an armored tank.

"You are a difficult woman to keep up with," Katrina said, smiling. "Almost as many air miles as me."

"How did you find me?"

Katrina dipped her chin. "Anouk," she said, with a look that suggested she knew something, if not all, of what had happened at the Dior party. "May I come in?"

"Uh, yes, yes, of course," Cassie replied, holding the door wider. "Suze! We've got a guest."

Suzy walked back into the sitting room, rubbing Cupcake. She'd changed out of her chic Diane von Furstenberg pregnancy dress into one of Archie's tracksuits, and a vast expanse of tummy was now on show.

"Katrina, this is my friend, boss, and landlady, Suzy McLintlock. Suze, this is Katrina Holland." She stalled. It didn't seem right to call her a friend. "We met in Paris. Mrs. Holland is one of Anouk's clients."

"Katrina, please," Katrina said, shaking Suzy's hand lightly. "And I'm one of Bas's clients too, don't forget."

"Of course," Cassie nodded.

"It's a pleasure," Suzy said, trying to suck her tummy in—a totally pointless exercise. She recognized her guest instantly from the gossip pages. Everyone knew Katrina Holland was a serial bride, and Cassie watched her friend thinking how *great* would it be to get her on her client list! "We were just making tea. Would you like some?"

"Thank you. That would be lovely."

Suzy nodded and dashed out, and straight back into her DVF dress. Cassie wondered whether she'd be able to cobble together a matching teacup and saucer from her lovingly mismatched collection. She wasn't sure Katrina Holland would ever have put anything other than Limoges to her lips.

"Please, won't you take a seat," Cassie said, indicating the patchwork linen sofa. She sat down opposite on a calico-upholstered wing chair.

Katrina swung a large bag over to Cassie. "I wanted to bring this to you," she said quietly, her eyes flicking toward the kitchen door to make sure they were alone. "And to thank you for what you did for me in Paris."

Cassie peered in, hoping to God Katrina wasn't giving her her old bag back. Even if it had been dry-cleaned, she wasn't sure she could feel the same way about it, knowing that it had been used as a receptacle for something other than chewing gum and Biros.

But it wasn't. It was a replica, but one size up and scarlet. Cassie gasped as she pulled it out.

"I'm afraid Maddy didn't have any green leather left. I hope you like it?"

Cassie looked at her. "I *love* it! But you didn't have to do this. Honestly, I was perfectly happy to . . ." She kicked the Topshop bag beneath the sofa with her foot.

"I know. That's what made your gesture all the more generous."

Cassie gave a small, embarrassed shrug. "I can't believe you've come out of your way like this to find me."

"It was the very least I could do, Cassie. You don't understand how devastating that incident could have been for me. For my reputation. The press would have had a field day. I would have been humiliated, and most probably libeled."

"I can imagine."

"You are very discreet."

"Soft and wimpish is usually how my friends describe me." She grimaced.

"Well, I came today because I wanted to know how I can thank you properly."

"Oh no, really!" Cassie said. "This is *more* than enough. There's honestly no need—"

"Ah, but there is." Katrina's gaze was firm and insistent. "I insist. There must be something I can do—a little influence I could wield for you?"

Huh, if only. Cassie gave a polite smile, trying to deflect the offer, but Katrina's gaze was firm. Cassie held her palms up, vainly searching for something to offer. "Well, uh . . . maybe . . ." An idea came to her. "Maybe you could buy one of Maddy's bags for yourself? She's found it difficult to get any publicity since her alliance with Oscar de la Renta . . . broke off, and you always get photographed such a lot."

"Done," Katrina said without missing a beat. "And what else?"

Cassie's eyes widened. Wasn't that enough?

"Really Katrina, I'm not—"

But Katrina was still staring at her expectantly, insistently.

The favor Cassie had done her obviously carried more weight than she'd realized.

Katrina leaned in. "I'll cut to the chase. I thought that there was probably one way I could *really* help you." She flicked her eyes down at the floor and then back up at Cassie. "It's to do with Paris."

"The Dîner en Blanc?"

"*I* sent you the invitation, on Claude's behalf."

Cassie's eyes grew wide. "You knew him?"

"Very well. We had grown very close."

Cassie couldn't hide the shock on her face—Claude had been sleeping with Katrina?

"I'm his backer," Katrina smiled, reading her mind. "A package arrived at my home the day after his death. One of the things it contained was your invitation to the Dîner. He implored me to make sure you attended."

"But . . . why?" This was so much to take in. "Because of my list?"

List? Now it was Katrina's turn to look baffled. "I think he wanted us to meet. He knew I could help you."

Cassie sat back, blowing out through her cheeks. "Katrina, I'm sorry, but you've completely lost me."

"I was there the night Luke Laidlaw had him thrown out into the street."

"At the exhibition?"

Katrina nodded. "He told me all about what Luke was threatening to do to you—giving the pictures to *Vogue*."

Cassie nodded, looking away. "I see."

"He loved you, Cassie. You were a dear friend to him. He wanted to protect you. So I've done what I think he would have wanted."

Cassie looked at her in alarm. "What's that?"

"I had lunch with Alexa Bourton. She's agreed to pull the pictures. They're not going to be a problem for you anymore."

Cassie sank back into her chair as if she'd been pushed. But her overwhelming relief was mingled with suspicion. "How did you convince her?"

"Partly because her boss is a . . . *friend* of mine, and partly because I pointed out that you probably aren't the only former girlfriend he's photographed nude." She gave Cassie a pointed look.

"He has photos of her too?"

"Most likely." Katrina nodded. "It's in Alexa's best long-term interests not to give him too much power."

"I should say."

"But it's left something of a hole in the magazine, which is why I'm here. They're going to press next week, and Luke's exhibition pictures were the holding piece for the issue. They need a muse."

Cassie wondered why Katrina was looking at her so intently. "I'm afraid I don't know any muses."

"I've offered them Claude's."

"Claude had a muse?" Jealousy reared up in her.

"You, Cassie."

Cassie laughed suddenly, shaking her head. "No! No! I'm not. For a short while I was going to be the pastry chef, but he never interviewed me for the muse position. No."

Katrina paused for a second, then reached into her bag, looking for something. "The restaurant already has an eighteen-month waiting list. And we've pushed the opening back by three weeks to coincide with the date *Vogue* hits the stands." She pulled out a proof of the wine menu and handed it to Cassie. "Now do you believe me?"

Cassie stared at it, the hairs on her neck standing on end

as she read the name for the first time. "I thought it was an acronym," she frowned, staring at the name written in pistachio script across the top and realizing her schoolgirl error. "I heard it in French but translated it in English."

"'*C et C*'? Yes. It stands for Claude and—"

"Cassie."

Chapter Forty-Two

"There you go," Dean said, loading the last of the flowers into the back of the car.

"It's beyond me why Suzy didn't get a minivan, or at least an estate," Cassie said as she fiddled with the catches to drop the backseats down. She was fairly expert now, having done little else for the past month. "I'm getting RSI constantly pulling these seats up and down."

Dean clapped his hands together. "Well, another weekend, another wedding," he said. "How many more to dispatch before the hatch?"

Cassie blinked at him for a moment before she got his meaning. He was always falling into rhyming slang and confusing her. "Oh, you mean . . . uh, well, it's Kelly's wedding next weekend. And the baby's due a fortnight after that. It's all planned like a military procedure."

"Yeah? Well I hope everything goes according to plan. Never work with animals or children, innit? I'm sticking to flowers." He shut the door firmly. "Righty-ho. I'll see you Wednesday, then, and we can go through the checklist. Ranunculus roses, right?"

"Yes, but in that particular color—"

"The one that only two growers in the world produce?

Yeah, yeah, yeah, got it," he said, shaking his head as he walked off.

Cassie was just opening the door when she saw the Post-it she'd stuck to the glove compartment, reminding her of what she'd been meaning to show him for weeks.

"Hey, Dean!" she called, jumping back out. "Before you go, you couldn't have a look at this for me, could you?"

Dean turned back, amused. "What's that, then?"

She showed him the picture on her phone. "Any idea what that is?"

Dean raised a cocky eyebrow. "It's a rose, innit? I'd have thought even you could tell that."

"Ha-ha," Cassie said, rolling her eyes. "I mean what type of rose is it?"

The buds had opened two weeks earlier into multilayered heads of a dusky powder pink. Even to her untrained eye she could tell it was a show specimen.

"Hmmmm, looks like an alba to me," he murmured, holding the phone to the light to get a better picture. "Oh, yeah—yeah, it is, definitely. It's what we call an 'old rose.' The type you used to find before they imported all them china roses and cross-bred them all. You can tell because of the frothy petals and the scent. I bet it smells gorgeous, dunnit?"

"Like you wouldn't believe."

"Where'd you get it? That's a beauty."

"A gift. D'you know the name of it?"

"Do I kno—*Please!*" He puffed out his chest. "*That* is the Cuisse de Nymphe." He said it with a slightly camp, lispy accent and Cassie tried not to smile. Dean was sweet, but always hopelessly showing off in front of her.

"Thigh of the Nymph?" Cassie translated.

Dean's face fell as his moment of glory was stolen from him. "Yeah. You speak French, then?"

"Oh, you know . . . a bit. Well, that's great, Dean. Thanks so much. There are so many different types of roses—"

"Over two thousand and counting," he said, quickly restoring his pride.

"Right, yes. Two thousand—no wonder I didn't know how to start identifying it. I should have just come to you in the first place."

"Always come to me first," Dean beamed, punching himself on the chest and marching off proudly. "Dean's your man."

Cassie was just packing the last of her things into a blue plastic Ikea bag to stack behind the sofa when she heard Henry's triumphal return—the thump of bags and kit hitting the floor, a ballyhoo cry that sounded like the love child of a hunting horn and a rugby song, and the pounding of feet down the hall as Suzy ran like a baby elephant toward him, her tummy acting as a rebounder between them.

Cassie peered nervously around the doorway. Archie was tossing the car keys onto the hall table and Henry was bending forward in a comical manner to accommodate Cupcake as he hugged his sister.

"Someone's come between us," Henry laughed, rubbing her tummy affectionately. "I can't believe how much Cupcake's grown!" Suzy pushed it out even farther.

He pushed his hair back from his eyes—it was so long now—and looked up. He saw Cassie leaning awkwardly against the door jamb and just for a fraction of a second she saw her own hesitation mirrored in his face. But only for a moment.

"Hey!" he said with an easy smile. Except for the vast white patches left by his goggles, his face was nut brown, making his teeth look glaringly white. But that wasn't the biggest change. Apart from the long hair, he must have lost nearly ten pounds, and he had grown a beard. He looked older than when he'd left.

"Hi, Henry," she said tentatively, walking down the hall and greeting him with a brief hug. "You made it back safely, then."

"Yes."

"Arch, cava!" Suzy ordered, walking back to the kitchen. Archie followed obediently, a giggle in his eyes.

"So . . . how was it?" Cassie asked him stiffly, wishing Suzy hadn't left her alone with him like that. Henry shrugged off his massive red quilted jacket to reveal yet more layers—a navy turtleneck, thermal waterproof trousers, and heavy boots. She felt awkward and tongue-tied. The last time they'd been together, they'd listened to Claude's messages together, his hand on hers, just hours after a near-miss seduction, and then he'd been gone for two months and . . . well, what was normal now? Did they talk about the things that had happened—and hadn't? Or just carry on like they'd never been to Venice?

From his easy body language, Henry was clearly taking the latter option.

"Chilly. But good," he said, bending down to unlace his heavy boots. "We got some really good data. The Russians were putting flags down everywhere we stopped, of course—trying to expand their continental-shelf claims."

He pulled off his boots and straightened up, staring down at her, his eyes all the more piercing thanks to the Grizzly Adams beard. There was a short pause between them as they took in the changes in each other's appearance. "And so you made it here after all," he said finally.

"Yup. Paris was . . . too much . . ." Her voice trailed off. She realized he didn't know about everything that had happened with Anouk. But then he didn't need to; what had happened with Claude would have been enough to make most people run.

"And you're back to looking like you again."

"Finally." She primped her hair self-consciously.

"And are you going to stay as you now? Or have you got some other versions you want to debut this year?"

Cassie narrowed her eyes at the humor in his. "No. I think I'm done."

"Glad to hear it," he said, pulling off the turtleneck. He was wearing a navy Helly Hansen thermal grandad shirt underneath, which did a fine job of tracing his muscles. She tried not to look. "Did it work?" he continued.

"What?"

"Your search for the real you. Were you supposed to be a brunette living in Paris and working as a chef? Or a man-eating fashion bunny in Manhattan? Or are you really a blond wedding-planner in London?"

"I'm a little bit of all those girls, I guess. Brunette, no; Paris, not any more; chef, ideally; man-eating? I don't *think* so; fashion bunny—never; blond—definitely; London, New York—perhaps."

He nodded. "A process of elimination, huh?"

"That seems to be the way it's working. But I'm getting there."

"And how are you finding London?"

"You mean, without a list?" She shrugged. "Okay. I'm traveling all over sourcing churches, reception venues, bands, caterers . . . It's been a baptism of fire, really, but I'm trying to take as much pressure off Suzy as possible. She's getting really tired."

He nodded, smiling casually.

"Shall I, uh . . . run you a bath?" she asked, jerking her thumb toward the bathroom and beginning to move away. "I expect you can't imagine anything greater than hot running water right now, can you?"

"Well, if you want the honest answer . . . ," he said with a wink, and her stomach somersaulted at the very thought of his intimation. She remembered Venice again—the bathroom, the balcony, the bed. Why wouldn't the memory die? Just leave her be? Was she going to go back there every time she saw him? He was *engaged*.

A cork popped in the kitchen. "But we should probably have a drink," he said. "Suzy will insist."

They walked up the hallway together.

"I've cleared your room for you," she said.

"You didn't need to do that," he protested.

"Honestly, it's fine. I've got the sofa-bed. I'm very happy," she assured him.

"But . . . well, I'm staying with Lacey this week."

There was a short pause. Of *course* he was. "Oh, right. Yes, of course. That makes sense," Cassie said quickly.

"Sorry. I hope you haven't changed the sheets and all that stuff."

"Had to be done anyway." She smiled as they walked into the sitting room and Archie handed them each a glass.

They all stood in a group and held their drinks aloft, like Morris dancers about to smack batons.

"It's good to have you back, Henry old boy," Archie said with a broad smile. He paused meaningfully. "Nothing lost to frostbite, I hope?"

"No!" Henry laughed, shaking his head. "Everything's secure."

"Marvelous!" Archie boomed, much reassured. "In which case, I should like to toast our intrepid explorer's safe return."

"*Your safe return!*" Suzy and Cassie cheered.

They all collapsed onto the sofas. "What did you miss most while you were gone?" Suzy asked, putting her feet up on the coffee table.

"You mean apart from s—"

"Don't say that!" Suzy hollered.

"I was going to say your shepherd's pie," Henry quipped. "Well, let's see . . . a cup of tea not made from melted snow was up there. My daily pat with Cupcake, *obviously*. The sight of Archie's boxers drying above the bath." He looked at his brother-in-law. "Strangely comforting, Arch . . ."

Archie nodded earnestly. "Yeah."

"And of course I missed the ever-changing carousel of Cassies. How many others have there been since I've been gone?"

Cassie rolled her eyes as they all burst out laughing.

"So tell us all about it, then," Archie instructed. "I want to hear about at least one wrestling bout with a polar bear."

"And I want you to tell me that you sank all Japanese whaling boats on sight," Suzy said.

"I see," Henry said, grinning. "Well, seeing as I'm taking orders for my memoirs, what about you, Cass? What do you want to know?"

She shrugged helplessly, her mind a blank. All she really wanted to know was whether Venice haunted his dreams too. But his easy smile wasn't that of a man on the run.

"Put a porpoise in there somewhere for me," she smiled.

Chapter Forty-Three

Cassie's mobile *beep-beeped* under the pillow and she turned over, frowning in her sleep. Her body clock, highly advanced in matters of sleeping as long as possible, told her it was nowhere close to getting-up time. From behind her welded-shut eyelids, she could detect sunlight. That meant dawn had passed, so it was definitely after five. Still . . . she drifted away again.

Beep-beep. Another message. She sighed. If it was a damned bride having an early-morning freak-out, she'd have one of her own back. Sliding her hand under the pillow, she found the mobile and, with Herculean effort, opened her eyes to read the display.

"Get dressed. I'll be over in ten."

Huh?

She opened the next one. *"I mean it. Get up."*

Oh God, she moaned. She knew that tone from Venice. Henry was on the march.

Eight minutes later there was a discreet rap at the front door. She was already there, leaning against it, eyes closed, trying to doze upright but keen not to have him disturb Suzy and Arch. God knows, they needed to hoard all the sleep they could.

"Shouldn't you have jet lag or something?" she muttered, looking at him through bleary eyes. Henry looked back at her, his hands in his pockets and laughter in his eyes. He clearly found her morningitis amusing.

"You've got a bit of toothpaste . . . ," he said, pointing to the corner of her mouth.

"Oh." It hadn't quite dried yet and she rubbed it away.

"It's been bothering me that you didn't have a London list."

"Has it now?" she deadpanned.

"Yeah. So I've devised an abridged version for you. A one-day London extravaganza." He looked her up and down. She had pulled on cut-off jeans, a yellow T-shirt, and sneakers.

"Okay, you're suitably dressed. Let's go."

They shut the front door gently.

"Your carriage, m'lady." Henry smiled, holding open the passenger door of a tomato-red Mini—the old, tiny version.

"How the devil do *you* fit into *that*?" She chuckled, sliding into the seat.

Henry came around and opened his door. "I'm double-jointed," he joked, curling himself in.

"How old is this?" she asked, her hands lightly fingering the ridges and piping of the leather upholstery.

"Nineteen sixty-six," he said proudly. "It was Mum's when she lived in town. It's still got the original Webasto sun-roof and reclining seats." He gave her a cheeky look and she blushed slightly.

She noticed, with alarm, that the Bakelite steering wheel was held together in one section by masking tape.

"And that's original too, is it?" she asked, nodding toward it.

"Yes," Henry said wistfully. "It snapped in the last cold

spell. I've been hunting around for months trying to find an original to replace it."

He turned the ignition on and they bounced comically along the cobbles and out of the mews. The streets were still deserted, but then Cassie had known they would be. She was up at this time or earlier every Wednesday morning to have her confirmation meetings with Dean.

She sank her head back against the headrest and closed her eyes.

"You really don't like mornings, do you?"

"Nope. And the urge to hurt you right now is overwhelming," she muttered. She heard him chuckle beside her, and she liked the sound of it—playful, joyous, full of life. They whizzed along the embankment in companionable silence—her exhausted state of semiconsciousness meant that for once she didn't care about filling silence with nervous chatter—and she slowly woke properly to the icons of London flashing past the window: the Houses of Parliament and Big Ben, the Eye on the opposite bank, the strange MI5 building, the glorious dome of St. Paul's bulging against the morning sky.

She knew these landmarks, of course, but still as a tourist. This wasn't the area of London she was currently calling home. For her, that was Battersea Park just over the river, where she'd started running again, Kisses from Heaven for constitutional cups of tea and chats with Julian while she sorted through Suzy's brides' escalating demands, the Tachbrook Street Market for fish and Kentish meats, the Saturday farmers' market just around the corner in Orange Square where she'd found a fascinating grocer who sold multicolored carrots and stripy beetroots (what Claude could have done with those on a plate!), and the Italian deli and fromagerie in

Upper Tachbrook Street whose owners she had become very friendly with. She had recently banned Suzy from shopping at the new, controversial Sainsbury's and had made a point of introducing her to all her stallholder friends.

She looked back at Henry. He had shaved and had a haircut since she'd seen him four days ago, and he was back to looking exactly as she remembered him, albeit thinner. "Where are we going, anyway?"

He raised his eyebrows a touch and she sighed wearily.

"Don't tell me. It's a surprise. I have to work it out for myself."

Henry flashed her a devastating grin and she looked away quickly. It was too early for her to deal with that.

"What does Lacey think about all this? You're scarcely back and you're already sloping off on adventures."

"She doesn't mind."

Cassie nodded—bully for her! she thought—and looked back out of the window. She didn't want to dwell on his reunion with Lacey or the fact that he'd come from her bed this morning.

He turned in toward the City, darting and wheeling around the curved medieval backstreets so that the only direction she could be sure she was facing was forward in the car.

Eventually he stopped and parked at a meter, feeding it with change from the deep and many pockets of his cargo shorts. She stood on the pavement, trying not to stare at the shape of his back in his navy T-shirt. The street was so narrow it was almost Venetian in scale, but here the buildings were gray stone, not terra-cotta and pink plaster, and it wasn't washing that hung above their heads, but telephone wires with pigeons sitting on them.

"Come on," he said, grabbing a bag off the backseat and

bounding over to her, taking her by the hand, and leading her around the corner.

St. Paul's jumped out at them like a mugger.

"Oh my God!" she exclaimed, stopping dead and taking in the dramatic facade. She was used to identifying the cathedral by the great dome, but down here, by the steps, it was all about the pediment and the colonnades and the solid towers flanking them. "How could I not have noticed it before now?"

They walked up to the huge doors set back in the portico, and Henry discreetly rapped.

They waited a moment. Cassie noticed a sign with the opening hours on it. "Oh. Henry—look, we're too early. It doesn't open till eight-thirty." She checked her watch and groaned. She'd been trying not to know the time. It would only make her feel worse. "It's only seven-thirty."

Henry looked over at her just as the door opened. "Yes, but they open for matins now. And Richard here"—a smiling man in a cassock shook her hand—"said it would be okay for us to come in. I've promised we'll be quiet." Henry looked over at Richard and pumped his hand gratefully. "Thanks, mate."

Richard smiled and nodded once again. "If you're sure you know where to go, then I'll leave you to it," he said in a quiet voice. "Duty calls."

"Sure."

Richard hurried off.

"Libraries, cathedrals, Michelin-starred kitchens . . . is there *anywhere* you don't have contacts?" Cassie whispered, looking around. Farther down she could see a good few worshippers sitting in the pews and the choir sitting in their white-topped cassocks, lamps lit to illuminate their scores.

The dean's words—deep, rhythmic, slow, and pious—drifted in fragments toward them.

Henry shrugged. "He's not a professional contact. Rich and I were choirboys together back in Gloucestershire. I've known him since I was four. Hey, we'd better move out of eyeline. Richard's done this—"

"As a favor. Yes, I guessed that."

He led her behind some pillars and toward a door that had a red rope barrier slung across it. Henry stepped behind the rope and tried the door.

It opened and he smiled. "Come on."

They started climbing and climbing . . . and climbing.

And climbing.

"Oh, Henry—wait," she puffed finally, sitting down on one of the steps, thinking how much Kelly would *love* to run this tower.

"We can't," he said, looking back at her. "There's a very short window of opportunity for doing this."

"What do you mean?"

But he just walked off. Sighing, she got up and followed him, resisting the urge to cry as they bypassed doors that would lead to lower galleries.

Eventually, just as Cassie thought she might have to be winched to the top, the steps ran out and she saw exactly why Henry had brought her here. London lay spread out before them, giving her an overview of its own gray, stubby beauty, so distinct from that of Manhattan, Paris, or Venice.

"A lot of people use the Eye for panoramas of London, but I still think this is the best," he said, leaning his chin on his hands, which were folded over the railings—his token nod to the effort required to climb all 528 steps.

"It's stunning," Cassie wheezed, looking behind and

up and around. Above her stood the famous lantern, ball, and cross that were so fundamental to the London skyline. "Wow," she whispered.

Henry followed her gaze. "Yeah. Do you know you could fit ten people inside the ball?"

"Seriously?"

"When I was younger I used to think it would be a great bedding lair for James Bond."

Cassie giggled and smacked his arm. "I don't think that's what Wren had in mind," she chastized.

Henry put the bag down on the floor and unzipped it. He took out a thermos of boiling water, premixed with a little milk. Pouring it into a plastic camping cup, he took a teabag from a secret compartment in the lid of the flask and proceeded to dunk it. "Say when."

Cassie smiled and waited until it achieved the perfect color. "When."

He passed her tea over and repeated the method for himself. Then he fished out two large parcels wrapped in tinfoil. "One for you, one for me."

Cassie opened hers. Inside was a steaming roll filled with two slices of bacon, a fried egg, and a dollop of ketchup. "Ah! You read my mind!" she gasped, now ferociously hungry as the shock of her early alarm call and climbing hundreds of steps ebbed away.

"So you have breakfast here every morning, do you?" she teased after a while, scooping up a bit of ketchup that had fallen on her wrist.

"Of course. It's important to have a view while you're eating."

Cassie giggled and shook her head. He was joking, but she knew he meant it too—that it was all about *savoring* experience, not just going through the motions, be it munching toast mindlessly while reading the paper or exploring a city on a tour bus. He always seemed to get to the heart of a situation, to see it from a different angle, from the inside. Or, in this instance, from the top.

"Well, it was very brave of you to put your life in your hands and bring me here this morning. But wake me up like that again and it won't be polar bears you should watch out for."

Henry chuckled.

"The view's worth it, though," she conceded.

"It is. But that isn't why I brought you here." He checked his watch and started packing up the breakfast things.

"It isn't?"

"Nope. But I thought you'd appreciate breakfast."

"What are we doing here if not admiring the view?" she asked, knowing as she did so that he wouldn't do anything as straightforward as simply *tell* her.

"We'd better hurry. There are only a few minutes before they start up again."

"Start what?"

"The Eucharist," he said over his shoulder, opening the door and leading her back down the stairs. Her muscles felt weak and ticklish, as though someone were squeezing them, but Henry showed no mercy.

Halfway down, he stopped at one of the doors and gingerly opened it.

"Where are you going?" she hissed.

"In here."

She followed him through and gasped at the sight. If she'd thought the exterior views were impressive, what was happening inside the dome was even more phenomenal. Below,

the black-and-white mosaic floor was decorated with a mag-
nificent star; above her were grisaille murals of St. Paul and
mosaics of the prophets and saints. She stopped and leaned
against the gilded balustrade.

"I've never seen anything like—" she started, but Henry
rushed over and clamped his hand over her mouth, pulling
her back toward the walls.

He placed a finger to his lips before dropping his hand,
and she looked at him, open-mouthed with outrage. "What
the . . . ?"

"This is the whispering gallery," he whispered. "And we're
not supposed to be here. They're starting the service in a few
minutes and I don't want them to see us before we've done
what we came to do."

"And what *is* that?" she hissed back.

"You've got to whisper a secret."

"What makes you so sure I've got any secrets?" she whispered, one eyebrow arched.

"Everybody's got secrets, Cass. Now, I'm going to go
round to the other side of the gallery, and I want you to whisper a secret to me, okay? Wait till I'm all the way around or I
won't hear it."

She looked over at the opposite side of the gallery. "But
that must be a hundred feet away. You'll never hear it."

"Oh yes I will." He turned to go and then turned back
again. "And make it a good one, okay? I haven't done all this
just to listen to you admit that *Pretty Woman* is still your favorite film."

Cassie gasped. How the devil did he know that? She always told people it was the *The English Patient* when the topic
came up. Henry grinned and jogged off.

She walked back toward the balustrade and looked over tentatively, worried lest someone should see her and throw her out. She watched Henry moving around so effortlessly, his arms pumping lightly as though he hadn't really climbed a vertical mile, or however it translated.

Everything about him was extraordinary. Not just his fitness or his looks or his contacts book, but the way he lived—it was so dynamic and fresh and vigorous. Life was so exciting with him around. Never pedestrian, never dull. She could only imagine what sex with him must be like.

She caught herself and slapped her hand over her mouth as though she'd actually articulated the thought. She watched him approaching the point that was exactly opposite, and before she knew what she was doing . . .

"Don't marry her," she whispered, sending her secret floating across the sacred air, ferried by angels, carried on the wings of destiny, to where he was positioning himself.

The very second she said it, she regretted it. She wanted to pull it back in like washing on a line. Her heart lurched. Oh God, what had she done? She stared at him, stunned and horrified by her recklessness. Until that moment, it had been a secret even to her. Why had she said it? Where had it come from?

Henry looked up and smiled at her. With a nod of his head, he beckoned for her to begin.

What?

He nodded again. "Go on," he mouthed.

She couldn't believe it. He'd been so nearly there. He must have missed it by millimeters, her secret slipping past like angel's breath and absorbing itself into these thick walls that held the secrets of so many other saints and sinners.

Her eyes shone with unshed tears—relief and regret mixed together. She had been right all along. There was no such thing as destiny. It was all about timing.

She opened her mouth to speak. What could she say?

"I'm secretly frightened of cats," she whispered.

Henry paused, waiting for the words to come to him. He frowned as they landed.

"Seriously?" he whispered back.

"Yeah, retractable claws . . ." She gave a small shudder.

Henry pursed his lips in consideration. He seemed disappointed that that was the best she could manage. He shrugged.

"Now you," she whispered.

But he just shook his head. "It's your list," he whispered, walking back to her, completely unaware of how close he'd come to discovering the deepest and darkest of her secrets.

They walked back to ground level and emerged into the bright sun, both muted. Henry smiled at her but didn't say anything as they walked back to the little Mini, and she wanted to kick herself for having been so uninspired.

He threw the bag onto the backseat while she fastened her seat belt.

"I'm not even going to ask where we're going next," she said, resting her head against the headrest.

"Well, it's going to be a bit of a drive," he said, turning on the radio.

Traffic had built up quickly during their hideaway breakfast at the cathedral, and it was well over an hour before they parked at another meter at the foot of some green, sloping hills.

Henry opened the small trunk and took out a much larger bag and a hamper.

"Are we having a picnic on these hills?"

"This is Hampstead Heath, Cass."

"Is it *really*? I've always wanted to come here." She looked up. Trails and paths crisscrossed all over it. Bicycles, baby buggies, and dogs jostled for space, and there were already lots of picnic rugs spread on the lawns and people playing Frisbee. A game few were trying to fly kites, but there was scarcely any breeze today, and no matter how fast they ran, the kites weren't airborne for more than a few seconds.

Henry led them up the hill.

"Where shall we sit?" she asked, amazed that this pastoral scene could be in the center of London. Central Park had been an impressive "cultivated wilderness" in the middle of Manhattan, with its high banks and clumps of trees, and Paris's parks, of course, were beautiful exercises in symmetry, with long, straight avenues where people could sit and watch, or gently stroll in neat lines. But this was genuinely wild and untouched heathland.

"I know the perfect spot," Henry replied, without slowing down.

"Of course you do," she muttered, panting slightly. "Won't you at least let me carry one of those bags?"

"Nope."

He seemed to know his way around the paths expertly. Cassie lagged a few bedraggled steps behind, and before long they arrived at a small gateway with various black noticeboards posted on it. HAMPSTEAD HEATH MIXED SWIMMING POND.

Cassie looked at him, a small feeling of anxiety beginning

to eddy in her stomach. "Tell me we're not," she said as he paid the entrance fee.

"I'm afraid I can't do that," he replied, leading her down a narrow dusty path with rickety wooden fencing on either side. It opened out onto a pond surrounded by thick woods and tall trees, with uniformly straight platforms floating above the green water and steps placed along it at intervals.

It was already filling up and it was still only ten in the morning.

"We're just going to have a picnic here, right?" Cassie asked, warily looking around for nudists as Henry threw a large blanket on the ground.

"Nope."

Cassie planted her hands on her hips. "Well," she said, exhaling patiently, "as much as I would love to get in the water, I can't, see? I haven't got any swimming kit with me. And before you say it, no, I am not going to swim in my underwear."

"I wasn't going to say that, actually," Henry said, leaning down and picking up the bag that had held the blanket and shaking it out. Two beach towels, a pair of palm-leaf–printed shorts, and . . . she reached down in horror.

"You're not serious?" she gasped, holding a tiny gold swimming costume between her fingers.

Henry just nodded.

She held it from different angles and stared at it from every which way. It appeared to be cut out at the sides so that only a thin strip at the front connected the bottom to the top. "I'll look like Paris bloody Hilton!" she protested. "What were you thinking, buying *that*? What's wrong with Speedo, for God's sake?"

"You'll look great in it."

A thought occurred to her. She pulled a face. "Is it Lacey's?" She knew for sure it wasn't Suzy's.

"No! I bought it for you especially. I was in a rush and it was just there and . . ."

"And you thought it would be funny to make me wear it!"

"You can get changed over there," he said, indicating a block of toilets.

Cassie didn't move.

"Or you can wear your underwear if you prefer," he shrugged, reaching down for his trunks. "I was just trying to be helpful." He straightened up. "But we're not going till you've had a swim."

Cassie tried to remember what underwear she'd pulled on in the dark reaches of the morning. A white mesh bra and matching thong. Even less of a goer than the gold thing.

She grabbed a towel from the ground and stomped over to the loos, muttering to herself crossly. Much as she loved his lists, they always seemed to involve an element of sacrifice on her part.

When she emerged five minutes later with her towel clutched fiercely round her, she was no happier. Henry was walking just in front of her, having changed out of his shorts into his trunks, and was pulling his T-shirt over his head. She stopped walking, mesmerized by the movement of the muscles across his back, until she noticed two teenage girls giggling at her.

Blushing, she met him back at their blanket. He was rubbing lotion onto his shoulders.

"All okay?"

"Oh, tickety-boo," she said, holding the towel even tighter around her. "I'm delighted to be dressed as a Vegas showgirl in the middle of Hampstead Ponds."

Henry chuckled. "Here, let me put some lotion on you."

Cassie took a step back. "I don't think so."

"Why not?" he frowned. "It's seventy degrees already. You'll burn otherwise."

She hesitated for a moment, then turned her back to him. "Fine."

He squeezed some lotion out. "Uh, can you . . . lift your hair up a bit so I can do your neck?

She reached an arm up but couldn't grab it all in one clutch.

"No, there's a bit over there," he said.

She tried reaching it with her fingers, but it just wasn't long enough. Hurriedly she tucked the top of the towel in on itself and held up her hair with both hands, but the movement released her makeshift knot and the towel fell gracelessly to the ground.

"Oh, for God's sake," she muttered, reaching for it, but Henry grabbed her by the elbow and stopped her.

"It's fine, Cass," he said, beginning to rub the lotion on her shoulders with his other hand. "We'll be in the water in a minute anyway. No one's looking."

"They definitely wouldn't be if I was in a proper swimsuit," she mumbled, less aware now of his eyes on her than of his hands.

His fingers slipped beneath the straps of the costume and she felt herself catch her breath. Then, from behind, they spread over her collarbone and beneath the plain silver necklace—all she had left now of her Tiffany Christmas present.

"Hey, did you manage to release the padlock?" he asked, leaning over her shoulder to see if the charm was there. She was vividly aware of his lips just inches from her neck.

She closed her eyes and shook her head. She still played

with the necklace absentmindedly when she was reading or concentrating on something, but her fingers couldn't get used to the missing padlock. "No. I forgot. Because of Claude."

"Yes. Of course," he said, moving back and sliding his hands down her arms. "Well, I expect it's still there."

"I know it is. Nothing will get it off."

"You could still contact Tiffany's and see if they can issue you a replacement key. Did you find out the serial number?"

Cassie shook her head.

"Well, Anouk can always get it for you," he said, smiling, as he finished, and she remembered that he still didn't know what had happened between them. "Come on, then."

Cassie went to pick up the towel again.

"Leave it!"

"But Henry," she hissed. "I do *not* want to walk in front of everyone in this thing."

"We're here for some wild swimming. Towels are not allowed."

Cassie narrowed her eyes, but he just grabbed her hand and towed her along like a tugboat. She could feel absolutely everyone's eyes on her.

"Now, do your best not to swallow the water, okay?" he said as they walked onto the floating platform.

"You mean the water's not *clean?*" She looked down into the dark water.

"Clean enough, but it's not chlorinated or anything like that."

"I rather like my swimming pools chlorinated," she mumbled nervously. "Preferably with bright turquoise water and Roman statues all around the sides. You know, properly fake."

Henry chuckled.

"Is it cold?" she gasped. She'd been so preoccupied with the swimsuit and dark water, she'd forgotten all about heat.

Henry turned and dived in. Just like that. No preamble. No psyching himself up. Just did it.

He surfaced with a smile on his face, his hair slicked back and eyes closed. So that's how he looks in the shower, her mind flashed. "Not too bad," he called up. "You try."

Cassie bit her lip and stood at the side, looking down into the depths. She couldn't see the bottom. She shook her head. "I . . . I don't think so."

She looked back at Henry and found him staring at her, his eyes walking up and down her body with blatant masculine interest, and she was so panicked that she jumped in too. Just like that. No preamble. No psyching herself up. She needed to hide and she hadn't brought the towel. When she broke the surface, though, she was gasping with shock from the cold, and all thoughts of what had made her jump in fled. It was *freezing*.

"Oh. My. God," she chattered, treading water as Henry swam around her.

"The only way to warm up is to move," he called over. "Come on."

He set off, his powerful arms like rotary blades cutting through the water. She swam in his slipstream and quickly realized she was easily able to keep up for once. It was years since she'd last swum, but she'd been in the swim club at school and had a natural style that made the years fall away. She quickly found her rhythm, synchronizing her breathing with her arms, and crossed the water effortlessly, happily.

Within a few minutes, she didn't care about the temperature or the fact that she couldn't see the bottom—a growing exhilaration built within her as she swam nearer to the banks beneath the willow trees that dipped their tendrils into the water and near the reeds. Then she turned and swam in the opposite direction, out of Henry's wake now, lost in the moment and her own body's rhythm. She liked the peace that came from controlling her breath, the heat that came from pushing herself, and she wondered why she hadn't come back to swimming sooner. Possibly because Gil couldn't swim, she supposed.

After a while, without particularly noticing where she was in the pool, she turned onto her back and just floated, forgetting everything—even Henry. She let the other bathers' exertions in the water rock her gently, and she basked in the sunlight, unaware of the way it caught her costume as she bobbed along.

"You never told me you were a mermaid," Henry said quietly, and she opened her eyes to find him floating next to her.

"You don't know everything about me," she replied enigmatically.

"Clearly not," he said, staring at her, and she remembered how his eyes had scoured her when she'd been standing on the side. She stared up at the sky, watching the clouds drift, aware of a change in the atmospheric pressure between them. There was a subtext to their words, questions in their eyes. She was beginning to wonder whether he hadn't forgotten Venice after all, whether what *hadn't* happened had stayed with him as it had with her. And yet neither of them said anything. He was engaged to be married, and only a missed whisper testified to the ambiguity of their friendship.

"You're a natural. Some people really don't take to wild swimming," he said after a while, and she could tell that he too was staring up at the clouds now.

"I didn't think I would. I'll never forget the time I was

swimming in a river when I was about nine and a snake skimmed past me."

"I can see how that could put you off," he conceded.

"I'm loving this, though. I think I could definitely do this again."

"I know some great ponds farther up the Thames in Berkshire that would blow your mind."

"Well, I'm game for that. We could take a picnic and see if Suzy and Arch want to come too. And Lacey too, of course," she added hurriedly.

"Yes."

An older woman in a sturdy turquoise costume and pink swimming hat with rubber flowers glided past doing a majestic breaststroke and gave Cassie a sniffy up-and-down with her eyes as she passed, and Cassie realized that, as she floated on her back, her golden breasts rose out of the water like queenly treasures. So much for hiding in the water.

She ducked her legs down so that she was treading water again. Henry looked across at her.

"What are you doing?" he asked, his voice deep and relaxed.

"Racing you to the bank," she replied, and set off in a sleek crawl.

"Hey!"

He raced after her, but her refined technique meant he couldn't close the gap between them and she kept her lead. She wanted to giggle with delight, but she kept her composure and sliced through the water. She was just about to put a hand to the steps when she felt his fingers close round her foot and drag her backward through the water toward him so that she slammed against his chest.

She could feel his heart hammering behind her.

"That's not fair," he panted in her ear. His breath felt warm against her neck. "You had a head start."

"Maybe," she said breathlessly, "but you've got a height advantage."

Stretching past her from behind, he had one hand on the handrail of the step, and one arm clasped round her stomach, which was practically bare. She suddenly grew very aware of her body's movement against him. She felt his fingers spread against her skin slightly, and her muscles tensed beneath them. She was just wondering how it was possible to feel so hot underwater when a yell alerted them to a teenage boy running down the platform, closely followed by four others, and then he made a flying leap and did a bomb entry into the water.

"Time to get out," Henry muttered, releasing her.

She climbed the stairs as quickly as possible, horribly aware that he was probably staring at her bottom, and that the teenage boys had stopped their charge down the ramp and were noticing her barely there costume.

"You have some not-so-secret admirers," Henry said, nodding toward them as she clutched her arms across her chest, as much to hide herself as to keep warm.

She got back to the blanket as quickly as possible, almost diving under the cover of the towel again, while Henry just stretched out and air-dried in the sun. He closed his eyes and was asleep within moments, just like he had been that night in Venice.

She watched him for a bit, nervously, worried he'd suddenly open his eyes and catch her out, but he was properly asleep. She gazed at the slow rise and fall of his chest, remembering how it had felt pressed to her back in the water, at the way he slept with his palms up, his body language utterly open.

Life felt so easy and charmed and golden with him, somehow. To hell with it! She threw off her towel and lay down next to him in the ridiculous costume. She closed her eyes as the sun pounced on her like one of its golden maidens, and felt herself finally succumb to the other thing she'd been resisting all day—sleep.

Chapter Forty-Four

It was midafternoon when they woke, and she was immediately grateful for the sun lotion Henry had insisted upon slathering on. The pond was absolutely jam-packed now, with hardly a patch of grass free and scarcely a cubic inch of water either.

"We'll get going after we've had lunch," Henry said, opening the hamper and passing over one of the distinctive vintage china plates Suzy had been collecting for years and some mismatched silver cutlery. He handed her a small wineglass and poured some red wine from a half-bottle.

"Aren't you having any?"

"Can't. I'm driving," he said.

Then he opened a parcel wrapped in greaseproof paper and string and took out some rare fillet of beef, presliced, a small waxed cardboard box of potato salad (wrapped in what appeared to be vintage wallpaper), and a cloth-covered jam jar filled with beautifully pink beetroot horseradish.

"Are you serious?" Cassie gasped as the chic little picnic was revealed. "Whatever happened to soggy sandwiches and a Twix?"

"I'm afraid I can't pretend to have made it myself," he admitted.

"Don't tell me—you've got a friend . . ."

"Yeah, Zara. We were at university together."

"For which -ology?" Cassie teased.

Henry grinned. "She's just set up a vintage catering company, so I asked her to do this hamper for us. She left it in the car at about five this morning, on her way to Wimbledon."

"It's beautiful," she murmured, taking in the lovingly prepared spread. She looked up at him. "It never ceases to amaze me what people can do with food. I mean"—she held up the jar of horseradish—"this just makes me so *happy*. Crazy, right? To be made happy by a sauce."

"Not in the least," Henry replied, watching her. "Zara would be delighted to see your response. She could have just packed it all in Tupperware with paper plates and plastic cutlery, but she's got a bit of style, a sense of ceremony about things. I think you'd like her."

"I *know* I would," Cassie said, cutting the beef. It was cooked to perfection.

They ate happily, ignoring the covetous glances of their neighbors stuck with packets of potato chips, and then packed up to get ready for the "final leg of the list," as Henry called it.

The Flying Tomato—his name for the car—stayed north, taking them past high stuccoed townhouses, through Regent's Park, and across the top of Hyde Park before finding a tiny parking space that only a classic Mini, motorbike, or cat could have fit into.

They were in Notting Hill now. She'd been here several times before, meeting prospective brides with Suzy, but had only ever passed through. They ambled lazily down the Portobello Road. The wine, sleep, and sun (not to mention climbing all those stairs and the wild swimming) had left her deeply relaxed. She was in her element, talking first to one stallholder, then another. Henry tagged along, thoroughly bemused.

"You're not a department-store shopper, are you?" he asked as she deliberated over a vintage flour sifter, even though she had no kitchen of her own.

"Nope. I've not set foot in a supermarket since cooking with Claude. I think it's really important to support independent enterprises. I'll take it, thanks," she said to the stallholder, handing over the cash.

"Mmmm," Henry hummed thoughtfully, as they started walking again.

"What?" she asked, her curiosity piqued by his tone.

"Well, I just wonder whether it would be worth you meeting up with Zara."

"Your vintage catering friend? Sure, I'd love to."

"No, I don't just mean as a social thing." He stopped walking and looked down at her. "She needs someone to come in on the business with her. It's too much for her to cope with on her own, and you'd be perfect."

Cassie's eyes widened. It would be a dream opportunity! And a lot more realistic than the one Claude had proposed for her. Catering for picnics—albeit fine ones—was much more within her capabilities. At least to begin with.

"Oh, but I don't . . . well, I can't bring any financial investment. At least, not *yet*. And she'd need that, wouldn't she?"

Henry shrugged. "I don't know. I'm not sure. She only mentioned it to me the day before yesterday when I placed the order." He narrowed his eyes slightly. "What about the divorce settlement?"

Cassie looked away. "Oh . . . it's not finalized yet."

"What? Ten months later? I thought you weren't contesting anything?"

"Not the estate, no. I had to sign a prenup, and I'm very happy to receive what it states. It'll be more than enough for me to start up somewhere."

"So what's the problem, then?"

"Gil won't back down on the reasons. He doesn't want it to cite his 'unreasonable behavior.' He wants it to be 'irreconcilable differences.'"

"What! Are you bloody kidding? He does what he did to you and then refuses to admit what he's done?" Henry had gone red in the cheeks and his jaw twitched angrily.

"It's fine—really, Henry. I'll sort it out. My lawyer's on the case."

"Oh, I'm sure! And meanwhile it's costing you three times what it should, all because he doesn't want it written down in black and white for the world to see."

Cassie sighed and looked down at the sifter in the brown paper bag. She understood why her friends got so agitated about this. Kelly, Suzy, and Anouk had all reacted in the same way. But they didn't seem to see that their reactions upset *her* even more.

"Unless . . ."

She looked back at him. "Unless what?"

"Unless he's just using that as an excuse."

"What do you mean?"

"Maybe it's the ideal stalling tactic. He knows you're not driven by money, but that you do have a strong sense of justice. Maybe he's using it as an excuse to stop the divorce going through."

"He wouldn't do that."

"Why not? Have you spoken to him? Have you seen him since that night?"

"Well, no. I . . . There's nothing to say."

"Not for you, maybe. But what if you read it wrong? What if he never wanted to leave you?"

Cassie fell silent. There was a strange logic to his words. She'd assumed Gil's bullishness on this point stemmed from pride, from not wanting to sully the family's good standing. Was Henry right? Had she left before Gil could explain? Could there be another explanation?

She swallowed hard, determined not to relent now, not after everything she'd done to get over him. And it didn't seem likely, anyway. He and Wiz had a child together. There was nothing ambiguous about that. "I'll get my lawyer to step up the pressure," she said finally.

Henry look unconvinced.

"Are we going in here?" she asked. They had stopped outside a building with a vertical blue sign and ELECTRIC written on it in dot matrices.

"Yes."

"It's a cinema?"

"The oldest in London. And unlike any other."

He picked up the tickets he'd reserved earlier and, having bought another bottle of wine—"I can have two glasses now," he said—they went through to the auditorium. She saw what he meant as soon as they walked in. The white walls with blood-red plaster panels and velvet curtains were familiar enough, but she hadn't expected the wide leather armchairs with footstools and tables instead of the velour flip-up seats that made your head itch.

"Where are we sitting?"

"Over here."

He led her toward the back of the theater, beyond the back row to a nook where a couple of small sofas were nestling.

"Cozy," she said approvingly.

They sat down, the lights still up. The film wasn't due to start for another few minutes and he poured the wine. "If I start to snore, just jog me awake," she smiled, looking at her large glass before taking a sip.

"So, have you enjoyed your London list?" he asked, stretching his long legs out, and she felt his thigh muscles relax and rest against hers.

"Yet again, you managed to put a twist on everything. I don't know how you do it." She put a hand on his arm. "Thank you. It's meant the world to me."

"Glad to have been of assistance," he said.

"But will you write it down for me?" she asked. "Only I've kept the other ones. I reckon I'll get them framed, ready for the day when I have a downstairs loo to call my own."

"Sure. I'll do it now. You got any paper?"

"Uh . . ." She looked around her. "Oh, use that." She handed him a white napkin from the table.

He raised an eyebrow. "You're going to one day frame *that*?"

"Well, it's not as if the other lists were particularly illustrious. New York's is on a piece of notepaper and Paris's is a postcard."

"Okay," he said, sitting up. "Excuse me, have you got a pen?" he asked an attendant who was showing people to their seats in the row in front. "Right . . . so, first one: '*Whisper a secret in St. Paul's Cathedral.*' It's cheaper than seeing a shrink, and you can unburden yourself of any secrets that are making you unhappy." He looked up at her with a sardonic expression. "Such as your pressing and debilitating phobia about cats."

Cassie gave an embarrassed shrug.

"'*Two, go wild swimming ut Hampstead Heath.*'"

"Dressed in a gold swimsuit. Go on, add that," she ordered. "That was the worst bit of all."

"You looked like a goddess." He laughed. "They'll be talking about you there for years—the golden mermaid in Hampstead's sylvan glades." Cassie smacked his arm and he laughed even harder. "You did, though."

"'*Three, buy something vintage at Portobello Market.*'"

"I love my sifter," she cooed. "I've been looking for one of those for years."

"'*Four, catch a classic at the Electric, and five . . .*'" He stopped speaking but carried on writing.

"What are you writing? What else have I got to do? I thought this was it."

She leaned over to see what he was writing, but the lights went down and music blared from the speakers and she looked up to see the red curtain reveal the screen, which was flickering into life with the film board's ratings certificate.

He handed her the napkin and she squinted to see what it said.

"*Stay in London, no matter what.*"

It was close to midnight by the time Henry dropped her at the door, and the combination of a nineteen-hour day, too much sun, and far too much wine had had a soporific effect on her. She yawned as Henry put his key in the door.

"Henry, you are truly exhausting to be around—but also the most fun I know," she smiled, resting her head against the wall.

"Fun?" He looked down at her, his expression intense and as inscrutable as ever. "You make me sound like a Butlin's rep."

The thought of Henry in a colored coat dancing onstage

with foam dinosaurs made her giggle lazily, as if her body was too tired to find the energy to laugh.

"Okay, okay then—you are the most . . . *exciting*," she giggled, leaning in toward him teasingly. But as she did so, she saw something flash in his eyes—determination, desire, recklessness. It was a look she'd seen before, in Venice, and a current charged between them, pulling them inexorably toward each other so that she suddenly found herself in his arms, their mouths open, their bodies desperate. He rolled her against the wall, pushing up against her, pinioning her with his arms, his leg pushed between hers as they tried to push their bodies into one.

It was nothing like their first kiss ten years previously. It was the kind of kiss that stripped away inhibition and fear, the kind of kiss they'd spent all day avoiding, the kind of kiss that had spent ten years on simmer and suddenly shot past boiling point, the kind of kiss that left her panting and wet and desperate for more.

But she wasn't going to get more. Henry suddenly let her go, just as the door opened and Suzy flung it wide.

"Oh, it's you two!" she said, not appearing to notice that Cassie was holding the wall for support, her breath rapid and her lips a crushed, wet pink. "I thought I heard the keys in the door. What are you doing standing out here?"

There was a pause as Cassie tried to catch her breath, her cheeks flushed not with embarrassment but desire. Henry was looking at her as if he were Samson to her Delilah—shocked, weakened . . .

Suzy rolled her eyes impatiently at their silence. "Have I interrupted something?"

"No!" Cassie said quickly.

"Fine, so are you coming in, Henry, or what? Because Archie wants to you to listen to him do his reading for the wedding. He's got no idea what he's saying."

"Uh, no," Henry murmured, his eyes never leaving Cassie. "I should go. I just wanted to . . . drop Cassie back. It's been a long day."

"You're telling me. What time did you sneak out? I was up at half six, thanks to Cupcake using my bladder as an exercise ball, and you were gone by then."

"Yeah, well . . . I'll see you tomorrow," he said, bounding down the steps, making his escape again.

Cassie watched him curl himself into the Flying Tomato like Houdini.

"And are you going to stand out there all night too, or are you coming in?" Suzy asked, holding the door wider.

"Yes, yes, uh . . . ," she murmured, shuffling into the hall. She could scarcely believe what had just happened. She had just had the kiss of her life. He had literally taken her breath away, and then just taken off. He was driving back to his fiancée at this very moment. How could he kiss her, *like that*, and then go back to Lacey? What was wrong with him? What was wrong with her? Why did he always end up rejecting her?

"What were you two talking about, anyway?" Suzy asked, watching Cassie shake her head mutely.

"Just this and that. Not much—you know."

Suzy hesitated. "Are you all right?"

"Tired."

"Sure. Do you want a cuppa?"

"No, I think I'll just go straight to bed," Cassie murmured, picking up the mail on the hall table and walking off toward the bedroom. "See you in the morning."

"Yes, see you," Suzy said, watching her go.

Chapter Forty-Five

Suzy was distracted when Henry knocked just after ten o'clock the next day.

"Morning!" he beamed, kissing his sister on the cheek and loping down the hall toward the kitchen. He noticed the spare-room door—his room, Cassie's room—was still shut. "Has Arch left yet? We can go over his reading now, if he likes." He poured them each a cup of tea from the pot that was brewing on the table.

He handed one to her, noticing for the first time how pale she looked. "Wassup? Hey, are you all right?" he asked, suddenly concerned. "Is it Cupcake? Have things started?"

"No. It's not me," Suzy said, shaking her head. "It's Cassie."

"Cass! What about her?"

"She's gone."

"Gone? What do you mean she's *gone*? Gone where?" he repeated, putting his cup down on the table and rushing through to the bedroom.

The bed was made, the curtains drawn so that the sunlight was puddling in pools on the floor. He saw that some of her clothes were still draped across the back of the chair. And then he saw the note on the pillow.

I have to see Gil.
Cassie xxx

"No!" he shouted angrily.

"I know," Suzy said, pacing anxiously. "And she's not picking up her mobile. I just don't understand it. She's spent the best part of a year avoiding any kind of contact with him. Why would she suddenly go and see him now, without any kind of notice?"

Henry didn't reply, and Suzy narrowed her eyes at him. She knew her brother too well. "Henry?"

Henry slumped down on the end of the bed, recalling their conversation at the market. "I told her he was probably stalling because he doesn't want to divorce her."

"You said *what*?" Suzy screeched. "Henry! How could you?"

"I didn't mean to . . . I didn't bloody intend for her to go running after him. I was trying to help."

"How? By giving her false hope? It'll send her straight back to square one again," she countered crossly. "This is the last bloody thing I need," she said rubbing her tummy. "Cassie falling apart again, just when she was pulling her life together."

"I wasn't . . . Shit!" He dropped his head into his hands. "We were just talking, and I couldn't *understand* why he should be delaying it. *He* was the one tarting around. You'd have thought he'd be happy to simplify his life." He gave a shout of exasperation. "What a total fuckup!"

Suzy sank onto the bed next to him. "It's that all right. You've sent her straight back to him."

Cassie stood in the room where her marriage had ended, waiting for her husband to appear. The housekeeper,

Mrs. Conway—delighted and then panicked by Cassie's surprise arrival—had sent word to the estate that she was back and Gil was to return to the house.

She stood by the desk, a stranger now in her own home. She didn't like to sit in the chairs to wait, or to read a magazine. She just traced the tartan wallpaper with her eyes and rehearsed the various speeches she'd run over and over in her head on the train up.

But the voice—when it came—wasn't the one she'd been expecting.

"Cassie."

She looked around. Wiz was standing in the doorway holding a vase of freshly cut flowers. She was wearing skinny blue jeans and a red silk camisole—*the* red silk camisole Cassie had worn in the campaign for Bebe Washington. The color clashed slightly with her hair, and Cassie could see the white elastic strap of a very plain bra beneath. Cassie knew she'd worn it better, and that it would be improved immeasurably with a black or pink satin bra strap on show.

"Nice top," Cassie said quietly.

"Thanks. Gil bought it for me when we went to New York," Wiz replied breezily. If she was shocked by Cassie's surprise arrival, she didn't show it.

"You went to New York together?" Cassie asked, determined to keep her composure, to keep her voice level, her eyes clear. Wiz was not who she wanted to see; Wiz was the *last* person she wanted to see. Where was Gil?

Wiz walked farther into the room and set the flowers down on the desk. "Yes. For Valentine's Day. It was just a weekend," she added airily, knowing full well Gil had never taken Cassie farther than Perth. She fiddled with the flowers casually before straightening up and regarding Cassie more closely.

"And you look . . . well," she said in a flat tone that passed as polite, but barely.

Cassie looked down at herself and shrugged. She was wearing the same cut-off jeans and yellow T-shirt she'd been wearing yesterday and looked more like an au pair than the wife who used to drift around the house in tatty sweaters and velvet. But she also knew she looked five years younger and ten pounds lighter—like a completely different person.

"Thanks," Cassie replied, pushing her hand casually into her pocket as she caught the flash of jealousy in her former friend's eyes.

She looked around the room slowly. All the same photographs were in the same frames in the same places. The place mat for Gil's cup of tea was still positioned just below the telephone, and the annual burgundy leather desk diary was still opened to the left of the computer. The volumes of his law journals were freshly dusted in the bookcases, and this week's copy of *The Field* was fanned with *Country Life* on the side table. "I see everything here looks exactly the same."

"Not *exactly* the same," Wiz replied quickly, her eyes flicking toward a box of toys in the corner, and making it clear that this was a family home nowadays.

Cassie followed her stare and gave a bright smile of acknowledgment, determined not to show her pain. "And how is Rory?"

"Enjoying nursery." Wiz nodded briskly. "He's reading already, and they're just about to start him on Mandarin. All the experts say the earlier they learn another language the better."

"Yes. I heard that." Poor child.

Wiz was wearing a barely there smile, her head tilted slightly as though *baffled* that Cassie should be here, and they stood in silence for a second—all small talk exhausted—the tension between them as thick as mud.

As ever, the silence made Cassie nervous and she fidgeted on her feet. It was clear that neither tea nor an apology was going to be forthcoming.

"Well, it was Gil that I came to see," Cassie said finally. "Mrs. Conway's gone to find him for me."

"She won't find him. He's in Edinburgh today."

"Really?" Cassie was surprised. "But this is peak season for the grilse. They're making their first runs up the river just now, aren't they?" Salmon fishing was Gil's favorite sport, and over the course of the past ten years, Cassie had learned never to try to impede his instinct to stand waist-deep in freezing, rushing water.

"I'm quite sure they are," Wiz replied tightly. "But I told him there's simply no time for that kind of leisure activity now. Gil needs to bill more hours if we're going to get the extension built by Christmas."

"You're doing building work?" Gil had always said the house had more listings on it than a phone book.

"Yes. It'll pretty much double the square footage. Rory's going to need more space as he gets older." She narrowed her eyes slightly. "And of course, if we choose to have more children . . ."

Cassie gasped reflexively. It was a blow she couldn't absorb, and she looked away quickly, biting down hard on the inside of her cheek. She blinked several times, determined not to let the tears fall, but she knew Wiz was watching her and could see everything. It would always be the trump card. She knew just how badly Cassie had wanted children—Wiz had been the person she'd confided in, after all.

There was no point in staying any longer to be used as

Wiz's punching bag. It was absolutely clear that the friendship between them had been a myth, a convenient alibi to keep Gil as close to her as possible.

Cassie reached into her bag, pulling out the large brown envelope that she'd opened the night before. "Well, if Gil's not coming, perhaps you'd like to give this back to him. He seems to have *forgotten* to sign the Decree Absolute."

She stared straight at Wiz, and she could see this was all news to her.

"Which is a strange oversight for a barrister," she continued, an idea suddenly coming to her. "In fact, if we're being honest, he's been peculiarly reluctant to sign off on anything in this divorce. People are even joking that perhaps he doesn't *want* to divorce me."

Cassie didn't believe it for a minute, but it was a line of attack every bit as biting as her opponent's—and she savored the tiny wave of triumph that rushed up inside her. This woman might have taken her husband from her; she might remodel her home to her own specifications; she might even bear the large family Cassie had dreamed of having; but she didn't have all the boxes ticked, and the revenge tasted sweet.

"Maybe *you* can convince him," Cassie smiled, pushing the papers toward Wiz, who was pinched white with anger. "And then we can all move on with our lives."

Chapter Forty-Six

The taxi sped off the M4 and onto the country lane and Kelly grabbed the handrail as the driver took a hairpin bend in fourth gear. "Jeez-us," she muttered. "It'd have been safer coming by missile."

She patted the thick garmet bags on the seat next to her and checked her watch. She'd landed at Heathrow three hours ago. Hopefully, she might make it for afternoon tea—Hattie's scones were one of the abiding memories of her childhood. She texted another *"missing you"* message to Brett, and his return message *beep*ed just as they drove into the tiny Cotswold village where Suzy and Henry had grown up. It had been years since she'd been here. In fact, not since Suzy's eighteenth, if she remembered correctly—a big black-tie do with a marquee in the garden. God, it had been a blast. Everyone wasted on Lambrini and Beck's and dancing to Prince. She vaguely recalled Henry trying to hypnotize Cassie into taking her clothes off.

They clattered over the cattle grid, where Kelly had once broken a heel on the way back from a secret mission to the pub, and past the gateposts where West Meadows was carved into the stone; the gate itself hadn't hung for at least thirty years, but the cattle grid was enough to keep the Sallyfords' livestock in and the neighboring dogs out.

Hattie was in the garden when the taxi pulled up. She was kneeling on a gardening pad next to a Sussex trug filled with cut stems, a huge linen hat flopping over her brow. Behind her sprawled West Meadows, a small sand-colored manor with an ancient white-flowering wisteria fluttering like eyelashes at the windows. It sat squatly in the middle of its own grounds like a hen on her nest—protective, settled, not going anywhere.

Kelly gave a happy sigh. It was just like coming home. Every weekend leave from school had been spent here. She, Suzy, and Cassie had piled into Hattie's long-wheelbase Land Rover, which usually stopped off to collect Henry and a friend from his school twelve miles away, before hightailing it back to West Meadows for a weekend of home-baked cakes and lie-ins.

"Oh, Kelly! Our beautiful bride! You're here!" Hattie cried, dropping the pruners as Kelly emerged, tall and willowy, like a black orchid amid the blowsy heavy-headed blooms that swayed in the late June breeze. "It's a joy to see you!"

"Aunt Hats, it's so great to see you," Kelly cried, throwing her arms around Hattie and squeezing her tightly, then pulling back to look at her. "And thank you so much for hosting this for me. I am forever in your debt. I can't tell you how lovely it all looks—it's even more beautiful than I remembered. Brett will just die!"

Hattie planted her hands on her hips and looked around contentedly. "Well, Suzy's been working me to the bone to get this place ready for you." She nodded. "But I have to say, it's been wonderful waking the old place up again. I hadn't realized how neglected it was getting." She smiled. "It's delightful to be having such a happy occasion here. I feel greatly honored that you chose West Meadows for your wedding."

Kelly shrugged. "All my memories here are happy ones. I couldn't think of a more perfect setting."

"And is that your dress?" Hattie asked, looking at the voluminous garment bags.

Kelly pressed down on the small plastic window of the biggest bag so that Hattie could peer in. "Ivory duchesse satin. I think you'll approve."

Hattie clasped her hands together. "I simply can't *wait* to see you in it."

"Well, wait till you see the bridesmaids. They're a symphony in caramel and butterscotch." Mocha had fallen by the wayside with Anouk.

"Good heavens, they sound like an ice-cream sundae." Hattie tittered. Then she stopped. "Did you double-check the sizes for Suzy? Because I don't know when you saw her last, but—" She puffed her cheeks impishly and Kelly burst out laughing. Hattie didn't pay any attention to political correctness, and not even her children were immune from her keen wit and sly humor.

"She's getting big, then?"

"Oh, darling, she's blocking out the sun. It's absolutely killing! She's like a balloon ready to pop, honestly. She's just having a lie-down at the moment."

"Good for her." They walked into the hall. It was cool and shaded, with an extravagant display of roses on a table in the middle, and threadbare rugs criss-crossed over each other on the flagstone floor. It was utterly silent.

"Who else is here?" Kelly asked, turning to her. "Don't say I'm the first?"

"No, no. Suzy and Arch came up this morning, and Cassie's due here any minute." She lowered her voice conspiratorially. "She's on her way back from Scotland, you know."

"No, I didn't know," Kelly said, alarmed. "*Don't* tell me she saw Gil."

"That's what her note said," Hattie said, wringing her hands. "But nobody knows *why* she went."

"You surely don't think they might have got back together?"

"Who knows? We didn't know if she was coming back at all until she texted Suzy earlier. Everyone's been in a terrible dither."

"Why did no one tell me about this? It's *my* wedding." She didn't like the sound of this. She'd already sacked one bridesmaid, one was heavily pregnant, and now the other was missing in action. What the hell was going on?

"It all happened so quickly. She just took off at first light yesterday, and I expect you were already traveling by then. There was no point in worrying you until we knew exactly what was going on," Hattie said, starting up the stairs briskly. She was in her late sixties but still as lithe and wiry as a hare. "Anyway, tell me, when do I get to meet your lovely boy?"

Kelly snapped back into focus. "Brett? Not till tomorrow. He and my dear friend Bas are on the flight after me, and they'll be going straight to the Rose and Crown this evening. Brett's very superstitious. Point blank refuses to see me on English soil till I'm walking down the aisle."

"I love him already," Hattie trilled, opening a bedroom door. "Now, I've put you in here, darling. I remember you always loved the views on this side."

"I love them on every side," Kelly said, walking in and dropping her bags. "But thank you. It is my favorite room."

"Well, hang up your things and have a rest. Come down when you're ready for some tea."

The door shut gently and Kelly walked over to the windows. Everybody stood at the windows in this house. In fact, Hattie always said West Meadows was only built to frame the views out onto the gardens. And she had a point. The gardens here were simply breathtaking. From the terrace, a formal garden lined with topiaried birds opened out onto a two-acre silver lake and distant views over the Slad Valley; to the left of the house, there was a pleached-lime-tree walk leading to the massive greenhouse and the acclaimed sunken rose garden where Hattie cultivated obscure and ancient species. To the right was an immaculate grass tennis court. And encircling all of this, beyond the clipped lawns and vibrant, fiery borders that teemed and buzzed with life, were the wildflower meadows where they'd all loved to play as children and where a single track was mown through in curvaceous sweeps. From the window, she could just make out the tip of the Big Top.

She unpacked quickly—she was a mistress of the capsule wardrobe, and her honeymoon bags had already been sent ahead to the hotel—and took a shower, sitting down on the bed afterward to towel-dry her hair. She felt the mattress sink beneath her weight and she lay down—just for a moment—to relax her body. She'd had no rest at all on the flight. Thanks to the socialite Katrina Holland buying up the entire Maddy Foxton collection and flaunting it around town like her prize shih tzus, Hartford Communications' star was rising again. Tory Burch had asked her to deliver a pitch when she came back from her honeymoon and, accordingly, Kelly had worked from wheels-up to touchdown. She felt shattered, and the bridesmaid situation wasn't doing anything to relax her. If she could just lie still for a moment . . .

A sudden shriek pierced her calm, and she sat bolt upright, dislodging the towel turban on her head. What was that?

She waited, tensed. Then she heard it again. It was coming from down the corridor.

Throwing her legs off the bed, she raced down the hallway, coming to an abrupt halt outside Suzy's old bedroom. She put her ear to the door. There were sounds of movement inside.

"Suze! It's me, Kelly. Are you awake? Is everything okay?"

There was no reply. She opened the door

"Suzy . . . ," she faltered as she saw her lying on the bed with Archie sitting beside her.

There was a big splash of water in the middle of the carpet, and Kelly scanned the room for an upturned jug or something. But there wasn't one. Then Suzy started panting and Archie started counting the minutes on his father's temperamental watch.

"Oh my God!" Kelly cried as she took in the situation. This couldn't be happening—it couldn't. She wasn't due for another week. The wedding was in eighteen hours.

Archie looked up at her and broke off from counting. "Kelly, get Hattie quickly! Suzy's waters have broken."

Kelly dashed off to get some towels from the airing cupboard, then ran down the stairs two at a time, her heart pounding nineteen to the dozen. She raced into the kitchen but there was no one in there. Just a large tray laid with scones and jam covered in cling film, and a giant pot of tea. Where was Hattie?

Maybe she should get a doctor first and find Hattie afterward? Kelly looked around for a phone, but Hattie only had the old-fashioned wall-mounted kind with curly cable, and she had no idea how to work it.

She ran through to the drawing room, but that too was empty and silent, except for the steady beat of the carriage clock on the mantelpiece. Her phone rang and she answered it automatically.

"Yes?" she shouted, panicking as she wondered where to try next. Knowing Hattie, she'd still be in the garden, but there were twenty-two acres to cover. She ran out to the front drive, to where Hattie had been when she'd arrived, but it was deserted.

"Kelly? Thank God you've picked up! I just want to talk. Please! No one will even speak to me."

"*Nooks?*" Kelly stopped dead and looked at the phone in horror. She and Suzy had made a pledge not to *hear* her voice again. Not after what she'd done to Cass.

Kelly closed her eyes, summoning up resolve. "I can't talk to you, Anouk. You know what you did."

"But if I could just explai—"

"No! There is no explanation that excuses it! And I cannot deal with this right now! Suzy's in labor and I have to get a doctor. Good-bye!"

She hung up just as she heard a car rattling over the cattle grid and saw Cassie's smile through the back window.

"Oh, thank God you're here!" Kelly cried dramatically, clutching her in a ferocious hug before she'd even shut the car door.

"What's wrong? What's the matter?" Cassie asked her, shocked by the welcome.

"You're the last bridesmaid standing," she said. "Suzy's gone into labor! And I can't find Hattie. The whole thing's a calamity!"

The clatter from the cattle grid alerted them to the arrival of another car, and they both turned. Kelly refixed her turban and pulled her dressing gown tighter around her. A small tomato-red Mini was roaring up the drive, sending gravel flying behind it like the spray behind a speedboat.

They watched as Henry unfolded himself, cricking out his neck as he straightened up. He was in jeans and a pink-striped polo shirt, and Cassie felt her stomach flip again at the sight of him. She hadn't been able to stop thinking about him, her fingers constantly brushing her lips at the memory of the kiss. Okay, so he had cut and run instantly, leaving her alone again, but it was tangible proof that she hadn't been imagining what was happening between them.

He grabbed an overnight bag from the passenger seat and she swallowed hard, waiting for the look in his eyes that would confirm to her there was something going on. They could neither of them deny it anymore.

But Henry strode toward them in ominous silence, a thunderous look upon his face. Cassie felt her blood pool at her feet.

"Hi, Henry," Kelly said, turning with him as he marched past, eyes on the door.

"Yeah. Hi, Kelly," he muttered, not bothering to pause. "Congratulations for tomorrow."

There was a moment's silence.

"What was *that* about?" Kelly whispered finally as he disappeared inside the house. "I've never seen him like that before."

Cassie couldn't utter a single word.

Chapter Forty-Seven

They paced around the waiting room like stressed lab rats—repetitively.

"It's been five hours now," Kelly cried in exasperation. "What can be taking so long?"

Cassie shot her a look. "Hello—did you see the size of her tummy? I'd be hesitant about pushing out a baby that big too."

"Archie looked sick, did you see him?"

"Men always do," Cassie replied blankly, collapsing in a heap on a cold plastic chair.

Henry, who was reading an old copy of *National Geographic* and turning down the corners of the pages of all the places it featured that he'd been to, looked up at her coldly, unimpressed by the sweeping statement. She felt herself chill beneath his gaze, before he looked away and went back to his magazine.

Cassie looked over to check that Kelly hadn't seen the silent rebuke, but she was smacking her fist against a vending machine trying to release a can of Coke that was stuck on the coils. Cassie looked back at Henry again, his cheeks a deep red as he concentrated on reading the magazine, his eyes like lasers on the words. She couldn't understand what was going on, could scarcely believe it was only two days since they'd swum in the pond together, his body pressed up against hers, his breath against her ear And their kiss, *that* kiss . . . quite possibly the kiss of her life. *He* had instigated it. Not her. And *he* was the one engaged. Not her. Why was he so angry with her?

She heard Kelly give up on the Coke and come over.

"You look tired," she said to Cassie as though noticing for the first time.

"Do I?"

"Yeah." Kelly sat down next to her on the hard plastic seat and gave a weary sigh. This was not how she'd envisaged her last night before marriage.

They sat in easy silence, Cassie trying very hard not to look at Henry. She noticed the nail polish on her toes was chipped, and she slid her feet beneath the chair in case Kelly should see. She hadn't had a professional pedicure since leaving Paris; Kelly's and Anouk's fastidious beauty routines were beginning to slip. Before she knew it, she'd be back to nails like rhino horn.

"Of course, I'm not the only one whose plans are going to be disrupted by the early arrival of Cupcake," Kelly said after a while.

"What do you mean?"

"Well, where are *you* going to live? Their place is only two bedrooms, right?"

Cassie shrugged. "Yes. But I was already on the sofa from Monday anyway. The decorators are coming in this weekend to turn it into a nursery."

"Timing!"

"Yeah."

"So what are you going to do longer term? You can't crash on the sofa every night, especially if they're going to be up with the baby—which they so will be!"

"I know." Cassie looked around the waiting room, at the NHS posters Blu-Tacked to the wall, and the gurney by the swing doors, ready for when Suzy came out of the delivery room. "I've got the money from my trust to put on deposit somewhere. I guess it's time to strike out on my own and get my own place."

"But where's that gonna *be*? New York? Paris? Or London? You've lived in them all now. You have to decide where you're going to settle."

"Well, not Paris." Cassie shook her head. "Too many bad memories. It's not as if Anouk and I would be hooking up for lunches, is it?"

Kelly shrugged and patted her on the arm. "So how about New York? You know it's where you were happiest."

Cassie furrowed her brow quizzically. From what she remembered, she'd spent much of her time there confused and crying as she struggled to come to terms with the end of her marriage. She knew what Kelly meant, though. They'd had happy times there. "I don't know," she sighed. "You and Brett are getting married tomorrow. I don't want to get in the way—"

"Hey! You're not going to be sharing a room with us, if that's what you're worried about," Kelly teased. "Anyway, I'm moving into his place. You could rent my apartment from me. I'll charge you nominal rent. And Bas is there. How thrilled would he be to get you back?"

Cassie gave a pensive smile. She had hoped to see Bas for drinks tonight at the pub on the market square where he and the groom's party were staying—she could have done with his advice on what to do about Henry. But that wasn't going to happen now. Not tonight. She would have to try and get him alone at the wedding.

"So it's between New York and London, then. That's the short list?"

"Here?" Cassie repeated, her eyes flickering up toward Henry. His mouth had set into an even grimmer line. "No. No, I don't think so," she said quietly. As much as she wanted to stay close to Suzy and Arch, she didn't fancy watching Henry and Lacey settle down to marital bliss together. His behavior toward her—silent and scornful—was a categorical rebuttal of the kiss she thought had meant something. He hated her for it.

"Then it's New York, right?" Kelly exclaimed, delightedly holding her hands out wide. "You've chosen New York by a process of elimination."

"I have?"

"Oh, wait till I tell Bas!" she said, jumping up and grabbing her phone from her bag. "It's back to black, baby!" She looked over at Henry. "Hey! Did you hear, Henry? Cass is coming to live in New York! I won!"

Henry looked up at them and tossed the magazine scornfully onto the seat next to him. Cassie quickly put a hand on Kelly's arm as she began punching in numbers on her phone.

"Kell, you're not allowed to use your phone in here." She shook her head. "And I haven't decided properly yet. Let's just talk about it later."

"Well, I think it's great news," Henry said levelly, crossing his arms over his chest. "I'm delighted."

Cassie stared at him as his words floated over and punched her in the stomach. He was *delighted*? Delighted she was going? Well, of course he was! He didn't want to have to look at her and remember how he'd cheated on his fiancée. He didn't want his moment of weakness thrown in his face every time he popped in to see his sister and best friend, did he?

She felt her own anger stir and stood up suddenly, not trusting herself not to give away their dirty little secret. Because to him it obviously was that. He clearly couldn't even bear to look at her, to be reminded of what he'd done.

"Are you okay, Cass?" Kelly asked, looking between the two of them.

"I'm going to get a coffee," she muttered to Kelly. "Shout if the midwife comes out."

She marched down the corridor, following the green and yellow lines painted along it that would take her to X-ray and Haematology respectively. Turning left round a corner, she walked over to the coffee machine and leaned against it for a moment, trying to calm down. Her heart was pounding and she knew that if she felt her cheeks they would be hot to the touch. Salty tears stung her eyes, but she refused to let them fall. She'd had enough of being made the scapegoat. If Henry had issues in his relationship with Lacey, then he could bloody well take responsibility for them and stop dumping his problems on her.

She reached into her jeans pocket for some change and stabbed the buttons for a coffee. Behind her, she heard footsteps approach and stop a yard away, and she spun round, ready for the fight.

"It was just a bloody kiss! Get over it!" she cried.

"Hi."

She froze.

"Please. I just want a minute . . . there are some things I need to say."

"What are *you* doing here?" Cassie asked.

Anouk shrugged. "I rang Kelly. She picked up by mistake, I think. She said Suzy was in labor and then hung up. Obviously I knew you were all here for the wedding tomorrow, so . . . it was easy enough to find the nearest hospital."

"How long have you been here?"

"I've just arrived this minute. I came on the first Eurostar." She looked exhausted. Her hair was limp and lackluster, and there was no makeup at all on that beautiful face. She was pale and drawn, and she had also lost weight in the two months since they'd last seen—squared up to—each other. Her lips were cracked and she was wearing a shapeless . . . *fleece*. That was the most shocking thing of all.

"I'm sorry, but I don't think this is the time, Anouk," Cassie replied tersely, turning back to the coffee machine.

But Anouk grabbed her by the arm. "On the contrary, I think it is the *only* time. If you don't talk to me now . . ." Her voice cracked and she shook her head. "Suzy is having her baby; Kelly is getting married tomorrow. These are events we've been waiting our whole lives for, sharing our lives for . . ."

"Shame you forgot about that then when you decided to keep my husband's secret."

"I know, I know," she said, staring at the floor. "It was unforgivable. Everything you said that night, it was true. All of it." She gave a small nod. "I just didn't want to face it."

She looked up at Cassie, her pale face like a sad moon, her dark eyes like limpid pools. "The thought of being without Jacques, even the little bit of him that I got to have . . . I didn't think I was strong enough to bear it any other way. I can't remember a time when he *wasn't* in my life. Like you and the girls." She looked up again and Cassie saw the red rims of her eyes. She looked like she'd been crying for years. It occurred to Cassie suddenly that she probably had.

"He was the love of my life, Cassie. I had my chance with him, but I threw it away. I was *careless* about him. I thought I made things passionate and exciting. But he got bored with my games. So he married Florence. My friend Florence. He knew what it would do to me—what it did do to me—but I always thought he would leave her for me eventually. He'd loved me first, longest. I thought he'd loved me hardest. Only when I heard him dismiss me to you . . . well, it was the first time I realized I'm nothing to him."

Cassie stared at her, realizing that what she had taken for Anouk's Parisian cool had actually been the strain of living a lie—keeping up the pretense with a decoy boyfriend, her fragile self-esteem that Claude had shaken so easily, her near-neurotic emphasis on grooming and seduction. For the first time, Cassie saw her friend's pain written all over her as clearly as if it had been tattooed.

"Does Florence know?" she asked.

Anouk nodded. "I have not seen or heard from Jacques since, so I can't be sure." She gave a small shrug but it came out as more of a shudder. "I think she has probably always known. We will continue to be polite when we see each other. Of course she will have forgiven him."

Cassie raised an eyebrow. "*Of course,*" she echoed, unable to keep the sarcasm out of her voice.

Anouk looked up. "I didn't mean . . . I didn't mean to imply that you should have forgiven Gil too. I think you were right not to, actually."

"You do?" She well remembered the dismayed reactions at the dinner party, Jacques's scorn.

"Yes. He was never right for you."

Cassie stared at her. Is that what she thought? That she had left simply to find someone better?

"I didn't leave Gil for *my* benefit, Anouk," she cried suddenly, her hand smacked across her heart. "God knows it would have been easier to stay—to have just refused to leave, swallowed my pride, and thrown Wiz out—as was my right!"

Anouk looked confused. "So then . . . why did you go?"

"Because there was only ever one possible healthy outcome—the chance of a stable family life for a little boy every bit as innocent in the whole bloody charade as me! Rory's my godson, Anouk. I loved him. I was there when he was born! But my marriage stopped being about me the second he was born. Even if Gil and I *had* been able to patch things up, how could I have knowingly kept his father from him?"

Her voice choked and Anouk stared, horrified. "I didn't . . ."

Cassie looked away, staring at the far wall, blinking furiously.

"So I was wrong again," Anouk said quietly, in a small voice. "I . . . I am so sorry." She shrugged hopelessly. "I was so desperate to justify what I was doing. When I realized that Wiz was doing to you what I was doing to Florence . . ." She bit her lip. "I didn't want to see it. I couldn't bear to face it. I was so frightened of losing him. Then, when you found out and left Gil . . . it actually gave me hope. I thought maybe Florence would leave Jacques. Perhaps that was how it would work after all. He wouldn't leave her, but she would leave him. I could get him back again if I just waited." She shook her head. "I had lost sight of all reason, all friendship."

She raised her hand to touch Cassie on the arm, but Cassie flinched, and Anouk's arm hovered in the air instead. She dropped it and nodded defeatedly, understanding that words were not enough.

"I am truly sorry," she said, turning away. She walked back toward the doors, a tiny figure in the nighttime hospital lights.

Cassie looked down at her coffee still sitting in the machine, and heard her name suddenly echo down the hall. She looked back toward Anouk and saw that she had heard it too. It was unmistakably Kelly's voice. Anouk paused for a second, then carried on walking toward the doors.

"Oh God . . . be tough, don't crack," Cassie warned herself.

The doors hissed open.

"*Nooks, wait!*" she cried, running toward her.

Anouk turned.

"I just heard Kelly. I think the baby's here," Cassie gasped, reaching her.

The tears in Anouk's eyes spilled over and she placed a small hand over her mouth, nodding. "Will you send her my love?"

"No." Cassie said with impressive firmness.

Anouk gave her an anguished look. "Cassie, *please!*"

Cassie took her hand and started pulling her down the corridor. "You can tell her yourself."

"But—" Anouk dragged her heels on the lino.

"You were right, Nooks," Cassie said, turning to face her. "We can't be separated at a time like this. Suzy's just become a *mum*, for God's sake!" Her own voice cracked with emotion.

"But everything I did . . ."

Cassie sighed. Suzy would *kill* her for being this soft. "What's done is done. You acted out of fear. Don't you think I understand what it's like to love a man who doesn't love you enough? We're both on different sides of the same coin. At the very least we should be looking after each other, don't you think?"

Anouk nodded, beginning to cry again, but there was gratitude and relief in her eyes this time.

"So come on, then!" Cassie laughed, grabbing her hand and pulling her along the corridor just as Kelly called again.

Kelly's and Henry's jaws dropped as they saw Cassie skidding around the corner with Anouk in tow.

"I know, I know what you're thinking. You never thought you'd see the day when Anouk"—Cassie held her hands up as they arrived—"wore polyester."

There was a stunned silence for a moment, and then Henry and Kelly howled with laughter, Anouk too, as the tiny mewls of a newborn baby sounded through the swinging doors.

"A little girl!" Archie sobbed, falling through them. "I've got a little baby girl!"

Henry hugged him delightedly, tears in his own eyes. "Congratulations, mate!" he cried, thumping him on the back.

Kelly, Cassie, and Anouk all embraced each other, half sobbing, half laughing as they celebrated the recovery of their friendship as much as Cupcake's arrival. Archie came over to them openly crying, and Kelly and Anouk patted him soothingly, clucking around him like mother hens.

Cassie spun around, tearful and joyous. "Henry! You're an uncle!" she laughed, her anger forgotten as she rushed toward him, her arms outstretched in congratulations.

But Henry turned away at the sight of her, all his happiness suddenly evaporated.

Cassie stared at his back. It was like a wall. Defensive, defiant, protective. She couldn't get near him. Her anger shot through her like a bullet again. How *could* he snub her like that at a moment like this?

"What the hell are you so angry about?" she whispered, marching around to face him. "What have *I* done?" The unspoken reminder that *he* had kissed *her,* that *he* was the one engaged, hung between them.

But there was no time for him to answer. In the distance they could hear Suzy calling Archie back.

"Arch!" she hollered. "Get back here! I need some help with my boob!"

"Your sense of timing has something of the epic about it," Cassie murmured, not daring to raise her voice in case she should wake the baby sleeping in her arms.

"You're either born with it or not . . ."

Cassie smiled. "Will they let you out in time for the ceremony tomorrow?"

"It depends on how she feeds, I guess, and how our night goes, but they've said they'll do their best."

"That's great."

"Mmmm. I might have to come down the aisle in a wheelchair, of course."

"Why?"

"Hello? I've just delivered a bowling ball of a baby."

"*Tch.* How could you say that about her?" Cassie tutted, looking down adoringly at the little pink scrunched-up face.

"She was ten pounds, eleven ounces. It's a fact," Suzy said, inspecting a hangnail.

They carried on staring at the sleeping baby.

"I just can't believe she's here at last," Cassie murmured.

Henry and Archie had gone off to the pub to wet the baby's head with Brett and Bas and the rest of the wedding party. Kelly and Anouk were in the canteen, drinking bottles of sparkling water and catching up.

"Miss Clemency Velvet McLintlock. Gorgeous name."

"Yeah, but what's the betting we'll still call her Cupcake?"

"She's so beautiful."

"Hmmmm, I think she looks a bit like a baboon's arse, if we're being truthful. Look at her nose—it's all skew-whiff."

"Suzy! You are *so* your mother's daughter."

"I know." Suzy chuckled before her face softened into besotted adoration. "But she *will* be beautiful. The most beautiful girl ever."

"Yes, she will. And the most stylish." Cassie looked up. "You have reinstated Anouk as godmother, I trust?"

Suzy raised her eyebrows. "Not officially. Not yet. I wanted to speak to you first before I commit us all to a lifelong bond. It was quite a shock you lot coming in with her, I can tell you."

"Well, maybe it was a bit heat-of-the-moment. But I heard Kelly yell and I knew that meant you were through. I just couldn't bear for us to be warring at a moment like that. If you can't pull together in the good times, what hope is there for the bad?"

"*Tch*, I told you—you're too soft."

"She's been through enough, Suze. I think she's been suffering in that relationship for years. Honestly, she was so sad the whole time I was living with her."

"I still can't believe she wore a fleece."

"Me neither." Cupcake had fallen fast asleep in her arms.

"Hey, you're a natural," Suzy said, sinking back into the pillows. "Tell you what, enough already of the wedding. You can be my maternity nurse."

Cassie smiled but didn't say anything.

Suzy watched her, recognizing the longing in her friend's eyes. "Why did you and Gil never have kids, anyway?" she asked after a while. "You were married long enough."

The question took Cassie by surprise. "Oh . . . uh . . ." And then her shoulders sagged as Wiz's taunts rang in her ears again. What was she protecting him for? "Because he kept telling me that he didn't want to share me. That what we had was so precious. He said a baby would ruin it."

Suzy looked at her, shocked by his manipulation.

Cassie raised her eyebrows. "I know. Bollocks, right? But he said we could start trying after our tenth-anniversary party." She shrugged.

"Oh, that was good of him," Suzy drawled.

"Yeah," she sighed. "The last three years were just awful, to be honest. I was practically ticking off the days. It was the thing I wanted more than anything in the world. I was on my own all the time, but he just wouldn't listen. He wouldn't even hear of it. I had to get to ten." She nodded lightly.

"Cass, why didn't you say anything? I just assumed you and Gil weren't bothered about cracking on with a family. You never mentioned kids at all."

"He made me promise not to discuss it with any of you. Said it was our private business when and why we decided to start a family."

"The sneaky little shit. He knew we'd make you see sense if you repeated any of that baloney to us."

"Oh, he wasn't that bad, Suze! I guess Rory had been born by then, and . . . well, I think at the end of the day he just found himself in a situation he couldn't walk away from, even if he'd wanted to. He's fundamentally a moral man."

"Would you listen to yourself? What's so moral about shagging his wife's best friend?"

"I meant him sticking by Rory."

"I know what you meant. It just seems to me that he got to have his cake and eat it. And now you're being all understanding and forgiving." A look of horror crossed her face. "Oh no, you haven't found God have you?"

Cassie chuckled. "No."

"Good. Because I don't want Cupcake's godmothers being all godly."

Cassie arched her eyebrows at her and Suzy smiled wickedly, resettling herself in the pillows.

"So. Are we all set for tomorrow?" Cassie asked, changing the subject.

"Yup. I collected the cake today. And I took delivery this morning of the stemware and china for the caterers to lay out in the marquee."

"And the flowers—did Dean get the right color?"

"He didn't have them today. They weren't on the delivery."

"You've got to be joking!" Cassie cried.

"It's all in hand, don't worry!" Suzy soothed. "He said they are definitely arriving in the morning, and he's sending them up on the ten twenty-six from Paddington. He won't let me down. To be honest, I think he did it deliberately so that the flowers are extra fresh and perky. I think he's trying to impress Mummy."

"It's the bride I'm more concerned with impressing," Cassie said huffily before catching the look of concern on Suzy's face. They both knew Cassie's uncharacteristic touchiness wasn't due to flowers.

Cassie tried changing the subject. "I just can't believe the wedding's come around so quickly. I mean, this time last year they didn't even know each other. And now—"

"Now they can't live without each other."

"I guess there really is such a thing as love at first sight," Cassie sighed, remembering the night they'd first met Brett in the club. It had been just moments before Henry and Lacey had arrived. She stared down at her hands. "I suppose, when you know you've found The One, why wait?"

"Oh, I can think of plenty of reasons why you should wait," Suzy retorted quickly.

"What do you mean?"

"Sometimes the stars have to line up first."

Cassie looked at her in panic. "Are you saying you think they're rushing things? Because if you think it's too soon, we should be honest with Kelly."

"No. I think *they're* fine. I wasn't thinking about them."

"Who were you thinking about, then?" Cassie asked, puzzled.

Suzy stared at her for a moment, deliberating. "Well, it's funny, but I always kind of had it in the back of my head that you and Henry would, you know . . . get it together."

"Me and Henry! What on earth made you think that?" Cassie felt her customary blush light up the room. Had he said something? Had she seen them kissing after all?

Suzy shrugged. "I dunno. There's just something about the two of you when you're together."

"You're hallucinating," Cassie said, shutting the conversation down. "You've obviously been getting high on sugar. *He's* engaged, in case you'd forgotten, and *I* am categorically not looking for love."

"Sometimes love comes looking for you," Suzy countered.

"Would you listen to yourself?"

"Think about it! It's such a massive coincidence, you mugging him in the park that day."

"I did not mug him!" Cassie protested.

"But then Mummy said to me—and I think she's right in this"—Suzy put on a dramatic voice, eyes wide—"*Was* it a coincidence?"

"Huh?"

"Was it coincidence? Or was it, like I said, the stars lining up?"

Cassie rolled her eyes. "You should move into telephone horoscopes."

Suzy grinned, undeterred. "Well I've *always* thought that of the two men you kissed the night you met Gil—total slut, by the way!—you married the wrong one." She pushed herself further back into her pillows, bracing herself for Cassie's response, which was, as expected, open-mouthed, flaming cheeked, and stammering.

"Wha—? . . . Y-y-you do *not* think that."

"That you're a slut? No."

Cassie gave her a sarcastic look.

"Oh, you mean . . . well, yes I do, actually. Have done for years. Couldn't say it once you were married, of course . . ."

Cassie sighed and looked away. Why was Suzy saying all this? Henry was engaged to someone else. A very beautiful, enigmatic, willowy, stylish someone else. What did Suzy expect her to do? Hijack the engagement, all because they'd shared a few moments of desire that he'd walked away from every time? Besides, Suzy hadn't seen how he was reacting toward her now, after that measly, staggeringly incredible little kiss. It was as if he thought she was some devil-woman who'd stolen his soul.

"It was just a kiss, Suze. One kiss, a very long time ago," Cassie said quietly. "It was nothing."

"Mmm. You see, you say that. But then I see the two of you together and I can't help asking myself: what if it wasn't nothing?"

Suzy took Cupcake out of her arms and laid her down in the cot. She looked up at her friend, concern in her eyes.

"What if it was everything?"

Chapter Forty-Eight

Henry was tossing mushrooms in a frying pan, and Kelly was just finishing her toast—toe dividers on her feet, cotton gloves on her hands, and a moisturizing mask on her face—when Cassie walked into the kitchen the next morning. After three days' traveling up and down the country in the same clothes, she had finally showered and changed into a pair of white shorts and a khaki vest, no bra.

"Hey, sleepy-head! I'm supposed to be the one with the jet lag and dodgy body clock," Kelly joked, winking at her. Her eyes were as bright as buttons. "Are you ready to rock 'n' roll?"

Glancing over at Henry, who was still using his back as a wall, Cassie managed to arch an eyebrow to convey a sarcastic "Huh?" before slumping down at the table and pouring herself a cup of tea from the pot. She gestured vaguely at Kelly about a refill.

"Mornings still tough, then?" Kelly asked, looking her up and down. She leaned in toward Cassie and said in a quiet voice: "What's up? You look *awful.* I can't have you following me down the aisle looking like that. You'll ruin the pictures." She gave a little waggle of her head to show that she was joking—sort of.

"I didn't sleep that well. You know, with all the excitement last night . . ." Cassie murmured, keeping her eyes down. "Don't worry. I'll be fine as soon as I've had this." She brought the tea to her lips as Henry clattered about in the cupboards looking for a clean plate.

"Sure," Kelly murmured, peering at Cassie over the top of her own tea cup. "You should have joined the rest of us for a nightcap."

Cassie shook her head. "I think a pillow doused in chloroform would have been better."

"That bad?"

"Mmmm."

"Go back to bed for an hour. Everything's pretty much set to go."

"Can't. I'm frantic," Cassie replied, looking anything but. Henry dropped his breakfast on the table next to them and, covering it with HP sauce, started eating it obnoxiously noisily.

Cassie shot him a weary look. She couldn't believe he was keeping this up. What had happened to her funny, imaginative, exciting, worldly friend? The one who'd masterminded her recovery, putting all the fun and riddles into her explorations as she tentatively discovered the world all by herself? Had he really disappeared because of a momentary slip?

She watched him chew, cheeks full, his eyes steadfastly glued to his plate. She had to try to get him alone and talk to him before the wedding. Otherwise people were going to start asking questions.

She looked back at Kelly. "Where is everyone? It's suspiciously quiet."

"Hattie and Arch have popped over to the hospital to visit

Cupcake and see whether they can be discharged," Kelly said, pulling off a glove and stroking the deeply moisturized skin on the back of her hand. "They'll be back in about an hour. The caterers are coming at eleven, and Bas is upstairs setting up. He's desperate to see you. It was all I could do to stop him from interrupting your beauty sleep—and from the look of you, I'm glad I did. You needed every minute."

Cassie smiled indulgently at Kelly's fond barb. She couldn't wait to see Bas either. They had a *lot* to catch up on. "And how come you're so calm? I was expecting Bridezilla. Suzy's given me beta blockers to slip into your tea."

Kelly waggled her shoulders, shut her eyes, pushed her head back, and positioned her fingers into a yogic "om." "What's not to be calm about? Brett is on the other side of the market square, the sun is shining, Cupcake has been born, Anouk is forgiven, you've come back from your walk-about . . ." She opened her eyes and looked at Cassie. "We need to talk about that, by the way."

Henry paused, fork in midair, at the mention of Cassie's disappearance before collecting himself and resuming with even noisier gusto.

"Later," Cassie murmured, putting her hands on top of Kelly's. "Today's all about you."

"Yes, it is," Kelly smiled, and showed Cassie how she'd already moved her engagement ring to her right hand in readiness for receiving the wedding band on her left.

"Is Brett wearing a ring?" Cassie asked.

Kelly nodded. "Oh yes. I want the whole world to know he's taken." She looked over at Henry. "Are you going to wear a wedding ring, Henry?"

"What?" He clearly couldn't hear anything above the noise of his masticating.

"I said, are you going to wear a wedding ring?"

"No I'm bloody not," he said, dropping his cutlery and standing up so suddenly that the chair legs scraped along the kitchen floor and made the girls wince.

They watched him as he stormed out of the kitchen, doors slamming behind him in the distance.

"*What* is bugging *him*?" Kelly asked, palms up. "It was an innocent enough question. He nearly bit my head off!" She looked back at Cassie, who replied with a "Who knows?" shrug. "It has to be something to do with Lacey. Men only get like that over a woman," Kelly mused.

"Mmm, probably," Cassie agreed nervously. He looked ready to explode. "Don't worry about it today. He'll be fine. They've probably just had a fight. They'll patch it up."

"I guess. By the way, did you see Anouk when you were upstairs?"

Cassie shook her head. "No. Has she not been down for breakfast?"

"Not while I've been in here."

Cassie thought for a moment. Hearts didn't heal in a day—she knew that better than anyone.

"I think I might know where she is," Cassie said, getting up and pulling on a pair of wellies that were standing by the door. "Get Bas started on your hair and I'll bring her straight up to you."

"Would you? Because she hasn't tried her dress on yet, and if it needs to be taken in . . ."

"It'll be fine. Hattie makes all her own clothes—she can help with last-minute alterations, as long as she gets back from the hospital in time. I'll send Anouk up," Cassie said, shooing Kelly out of the kitchen.

She waited a moment before picking up the phone and

booking a taxi to deliver the flowers from the station. She didn't want Kelly overhearing her. The prospect of no flowers was up there with no groom in Kelly's perfectionist world.

Five minutes later, Cassie was wandering past the greenhouse and rose garden, up toward the small hillock that bumped up like a rucked-up rug in the far corner of the estate. There was an ancient oak tree at the top with a giant swing seat strung from one of the huge branches, which had been "their place" when they had escaped here for home weekends. It sat right at the boundary of the Sallyfords' land and swung out over a sudden drop that made you feel like you were being catapulted across to the other side of the valley.

She listened to the chatter of the swooping swallows above her, trying to talk herself into a lighter mood. Henry's coldness, Wiz's barbed comments . . . the animosity directed at her in the past twenty-four hours had sapped her, when all she really wanted to do was enjoy this day with her friends.

Everything else was in order. It was an idyllic summer's day, pale blue skies dotted with whipped clouds, and just a hint of breeze to make the women's skirts rustle and the feathers quiver in their hats.

As she approached, she saw Anouk's slight figure on the swing seat. She was leaning forward, her head in her hands, and looking just like Cassie felt.

"Mind if I join you?"

Anouk looked up and Cassie saw instantly that she'd been crying. "Oh, hi," she said, quickly wiping her face with her sleeve. "Sorry, I was miles away."

"Yes, I could tell," Cassie said, sitting down on the bench. "Kelly's sent me after you. She wants to check your dress still fits."

"Ah . . . I'll go in a minute. I just need to . . ." Her voice trailed off.

Cassie nodded, understanding completely. The tears hadn't dried yet.

"How is she this morning, anyway?" Anouk asked, dabbing her nose lightly with a tissue.

"Eerily calm."

"Scary."

"Yes."

They fell into rhythm, kicking their legs in unison, and the bench swung a bit higher.

"You will get over him, you know," Cassie said quietly after a while.

Anouk looked at her hopefully. "You think so?"

"I know so."

"Are you over Gil yet?"

Cassie hesitated. "Not fully. It's difficult not having answers to the questions in my head: When did it start? Did he ever love me? I only know what I've pieced together myself, and that's just assumptions. They leave room for doubt." She looked at Anouk. "Which is dangerous."

"What do you mean?"

"Doubt allows you to still have hope."

"And the only way to really get over him is to lose all hope?"

"I think so," Cassie nodded.

"Well," Anouk said in a flat voice, "I've definitely lost that."

Cassie looked away and they sat in silence for a few moments, watching a herd of Jersey cows grazing in a field on the opposite side of the valley. Low, intermittent moos could just be heard on the breeze.

Anouk's phone buzzed in her pocket and she checked the caller before pocketing it again.

"Who was that?"

"Guillaume." Anouk shrugged. "He keeps calling. He probably wants to arrange dinner, but I'm not ready to socialize at the moment."

Cassie shot her a look that clearly showed she disagreed.

"What?"

"Nothing."

"No, say."

"Well, maybe he's ringing because *he's* got a reason to be hopeful."

Anouk looked at her, puzzled.

"Haven't you ever noticed the way he looks at you? Whenever I looked at him he was *always* watching you."

"*Non!*"

"Oh yes."

"But we are just friends."

"Only because you've probably never given him a chance to be otherwise. You've been so hung up on Jacques all this time, you haven't noticed that Guillaume adores you."

Anouk looked at her in amazement. "But . . ."

"*And* he makes you laugh. *And* he's gorgeous."

Anouk stared at her, and Cassie could tell the idea had clearly never crossed her mind. Anouk reached into the pocket of her silk shirtdress and pulled out a slim packet of cigarettes. Lighting one, she blew out a plume of smoke, her eyes fixing on a blackbird in the branches above.

"Guillaume, huh?" she murmured after a while, the smallest of smiles beginning to play upon her lips, a pink tint warming her pale cheeks, a chink of light switching on behind her eyes.

She turned to Cassie devilishly. "Well, if we're going to share insights . . ." But her expression changed in a flash.

"*Merde!*" she murmured, looking past Cassie's shoulder.

"What's wrong?"

"Over there."

Cassie followed the line of her gaze. Henry was marching across the lawn toward them, his arms swinging like a soldier's. He seemed angrier than ever—and from the figure hastening to keep up behind him, she knew why.

Chapter Forty-Nine

"*Here* she is," Henry muttered as he showed Gil to where Cassie and Anouk were sitting. Henry was dressed only in his morning-suit trousers—no shirt, no shoes—though from what Cassie had seen of his mood over the past eighteen hours, she didn't think his temper stemmed from having been interrupted as he was getting dressed.

Cassie stood up abruptly. "Gil . . ."

"Cass," he said, his voice quiet and soft, his eyes skimming her like water. He was wearing his favorite charcoal suit and carrying a black leather briefcase. In contrast to Henry, who was unshaven, unkempt, and undressed, he looked immaculate, and not a little ridiculous to be suited and booted in the midsummer sun as if he was ready for court.

The four of them stood in awkward silence, nature making all the noise around them. All eyes were on Cassie.

"Well . . . I'd better get back to Kelly and try my dress on," Anouk said quickly, realizing that nothing was going to happen with an audience. "Are you okay if we leave you, Cass?" she asked, touching her friend on the arm.

Cassie didn't respond for a moment. She tried to focus. "Oh. Yes . . . yes, of course."

Anouk shot Gil a withering look and walked toward Henry,

who was still rigid and highly colored. "Come on, Henry." She took his arm but he didn't appear to notice. His muscles were bulging with tension—rigid and rock-hard. "Come on," she said, pushing him gently.

He looked down at her, then back at Cassie and Gil. "Right," he muttered darkly.

Cassie swallowed hard, clutching her arms around her as she watched them walk away and leave her alone with her husband. It had been one thing bracing herself to see Gil when she'd had an eight-hour train ride to gee herself up and the element of surprise on her side. It was quite another being tagged back twelve hours later.

"I didn't expect to see you," she said quietly.

"Wiz told me you'd stopped by."

Stopped by? A twenty-hour round trip wasn't what she called stopping by. "It wasn't a social call."

Gil looked away as though he hadn't heard. "Impressive view."

"Yes."

He turned back to her. "Could we possibly sit for a moment and just . . . talk?"

"Fine."

They sat down and watched the countryside play. The swallows were still diving through the sky, the cows plodding through the sweet grass, poppies and forget-me-nots swaying like hula dancers in the breeze.

"How did you know I was here?"

"I asked Mrs. Conway."

Cassie smiled. Of course! She had mentioned the wedding by way of excuse when the housekeeper had asked whether she'd be staying the night.

"I brought the papers with me."

"I guessed. But you didn't need to bring them yourself," she said. "You could have just posted the paperwork to my solicitor."

Gil looked at her, his usual cool scrutiny replaced with a kernel of panic. "I had to see you in person. I needed to be sure that you think it's . . . the right thing."

Cassie arched an eyebrow, quizzically. "Are you saying you don't?"

"I don't think it's straightforward, no."

She inhaled slowly. Henry had been right, then. "So you have been playing semantics with my solicitor."

"I had to. No one would tell me where you were. Kelly and Anouk and Suzy hung up on every call I made. And when you didn't contest the prenup . . ." He shrugged. "There was nothing to stop it all just going through. You never gave me a chance to explain."

"What possible explanation could there be?" Her voice had an edge to it.

He was quiet for a minute, the way he was in court when he stood to address the jury for his summing up. But there was no clever get-out.

"I know I can't justify what I did," he admitted. "There *is* no justification. But I never set out to hurt you. It was never planned. Not me and Wiz. Certainly not Rory." He put his fist to his mouth and cleared his throat.

"He's a glorious little boy," Cassie said quietly. "You're very lucky."

Gil nodded. "Yes."

"So when *did* it begin? You and Wiz."

He swallowed nervously and looked away. "When you went back to Hong Kong to stay with your mother."

"After Daddy's funeral?" Shock suffused her voice.

"Yes."

Cassie winced, doubly pained that he should have begun an affair while she mourned her father. "It was Wiz who encouraged me to stay out there," she said shortly, looking at him. "She must have known it was going to happen between you both."

Gil shook his head. "*I* never planned it. I swear. It just . . . happened."

"Isn't that what all adulterous husbands say?" she asked wryly. She was almost disappointed by the cliché.

"I took you for granted, Cass. I know that now. I underestimated what we had, and I neglected you." He looked at her meaningfully. "And it was deeply wrong of me to deny you the child you craved."

Cassie focused on a calf following its mother around the field, but her lip trembled at the admission. Cupcake's birth had brought all the old longings back to the surface again.

"I miss you, Cass."

She felt his fingertips brush her forearm lightly, so lightly it could have been a dandelion puff floating past on the breeze, and her skin goosebumped at the realization that she was back in the game. It had never occurred to her that he had seen her departure as anything but a relief, and her self-esteem had been obliterated as a result. So to discover that he wanted her still . . .

Henry had foreseen it, but she hadn't. She'd been so sure he'd delayed the divorce because he didn't want his "unreasonable behavior" on record, that the good Fraser name must be upheld above all else. Her taunt to Wiz had been nothing more than an opportunistic hit. She'd not for a minute thought there was any truth in it.

She looked over at him. His arm was stretched across the

back of the seat, and there was a gentle smile on his face. He wasn't some monster living a double life who'd crushed her with his careless appetite, as she'd preferred to believe during her darkest moments. He was the man she'd always thought he was—only fallible.

"You seem younger somehow," he said in a low voice, taking in the swell of her bare breasts beneath her vest.

"Do I?" She thought back to London and Henry—just three days ago they'd been eating bacon rolls at the top of St. Paul's as London stirred from its sleep, wild swimming in gold, kissing in the street . . . It was all behavior that you could classify as "younger." Or as more alive.

"You look incredible. So different."

"This is nothing. You should have seen me in Paris," she remarked, rolling her eyes.

"You were in Paris?"

She smiled at the way he said "Paris." Even if she ever got over him, she knew she'd never get over his voice.

"Are you with anyone?"

The question surprised her. She stroked the bare chain around her neck and wondered if he could sense her sexual awakening. Her relationship with Luke and her kiss with Henry had left her with a certain—if as yet unexploited— sense of her own sex appeal. "I was."

He fell silent.

"So then maybe I did you a favor after all," he said, the jealousy clear in his voice. "Paris, boyfriends . . . It sounds like it's been a good year."

Cassie looked at him. "The best and worst of my life," she said, confirming and confounding his fears all at once. "I've known much lower lows since leaving you. And higher highs than I ever knew with you. None of it's been easy."

She shifted position so that she was sitting side on, facing him. He was pushing them both gently with his feet, and she felt the breeze lift her hair off her neck. In the distance, on the up-swing, she could see the caterers carrying trays of glasses to the marquee, Anouk having a cigarette on the terrace. She could see Henry on the grass tennis court, still half-dressed, hitting the bejesus out of the tennis balls being pumped out of the serving machine.

She looked back at Gil—tailored, immaculate, and correct. "It's so strange," she murmured, taking him in. "My life has been turned upside down and inside out. But when I look at you, you're just the same. Same suit, same shoes, same shirt . . . I'll bet you're wearing the red-hooped socks, aren't you?" They both peered down and saw the red trim peeking beneath his trousers, and as she looked back up, she glimpsed a discreet newly bald patch through his hair. She couldn't stop a fond smile—absolutely everything Gil did was discreet. Even balding. "You're just exactly the same as I remember."

"I'm still the man you fell in love with." His eyes pinned hers, his voice laced with regret—and promise.

"What time is it?" she asked, quickly changing the subject. She felt unsure of herself, could feel herself inching toward forgiveness, back toward the comfort and safety of their old life.

"Nearly eleven. Why?"

She gave a little gasp and jumped up. "I have to get ready! Kelly will be going frantic."

"But we haven't . . . there's so much more we need to say." He grasped her hand in his. "We need more time, Cass."

Cassie looked down at his hand. It covered hers completely.

"I won't sign those papers, Cass, until I'm convinced that this divorce is what you really want. And at the moment—I'm not," he said boldly, encouraged by her hesitation. "We were married for ten years. We owe it to ourselves to keep talking."

Did they? Did she really owe him anything at all anymore? They had been married a long time, but what he had done could never be erased. Could she learn to live with it all—be stepmother, not godmother, to Rory, slip back into her old life and all its comforting familiarities? It wasn't as if there was anything in her new life to keep her away. No job, no home . . . no man.

She looked at him pensively. There wasn't time to discuss it further now; she had to get back to the house. She could contemplate her divorce during the wedding. "Well, you're pretty much dressed for the occasion," she said finally. "I'm sure Kelly won't mind if you come as my Plus One."

He clasped her hand even tighter. "Thank you," he said earnestly.

"Don't thank me yet," she said quietly, but even she wasn't convinced by what she heard in her own voice.

"Where have you been?" Kelly shrieked as she popped her head around the door. "We're leaving for the church in twenty minutes!"

"I keep telling her the church is ten yards down the lane. She'll be far too early," Bas muttered, putting down his brushes and coming toward her.

"Hello? Photographs?" Kelly rolled her eyes with her hands on her tiny hips. She was clearly in need of beta blockers now. She was wearing a tiny La Perla bra and flimsy knickers, and Cassie sent up a little prayer, hoping to God

Suzy didn't walk in. This was the last thing she needed to see a day after giving birth.

Bas took one look at Cassie's shaky expression and threw his arms around her. "How are you, Teabag?" he murmured, squeezing her tightly.

Cassie nodded into his shoulder and they both knew it wasn't good.

"Come," he said, propelling her toward a chair in front of the mirror and spritzing her hair. "First things first."

"What happened with Gil?" Anouk asked as Bas began tonging the back sections of her hair.

She was already wearing her mocha silk dress. It had a dropped waist and wrapped loosely around her, draping into soft, thirties-style folds. It had a Chanel chic to it, but equally was a forgiving cut for Suzy, who was still supposed to be filling it out with a bump. Suzy's was the next tone down in caramel, Cassie's down a hue again in butterscotch.

Bas stopped combing her hair and swung around to face her. "I can't believe he's *here*," he hissed. "What a nerve, gate-crashing your BF's wedding."

"You still haven't explained why you went to see him," Kelly said, walking around the mannequin her dress was hanging from and showing off her perfectly toned, run-every-day butt cheeks.

"You went to Scotland?" Bas gasped. "Why am I always the last to know everything?"

Cassie sighed wearily. "It was no big deal. I went up to get him to sign the divorce papers."

"What's wrong with the mail?" Kelly quipped. "You've waited nine months. What's a few extra days?"

"He'd returned the documents to my solicitors *unsigned.*

Henry said he was deliberately stalling, so I decided to confront him myself."

"That was brave," Bas said admiringly.

"I thought so—until I had to stand there and deal with Wiz instead."

"Oh my God! Tell me she threw herself on your mercy," Kelly commanded, daggers in her eyes.

"Not exactly. She said they were probably going to have more kids."

"The bitch!" Kelly and Bas hissed together. Anouk shook her head in sympathetic silence.

"I shouldn't have been surprised, really. It's only natural that they'd want to give Rory a sibling."

"Would you get over yourself?" Kelly cried, almost stamping her feet in frustration. "Stop being so goddamn reasonable!"

There was a slight pause. "Need a beta blocker?" Cassie asked.

"No. I'm fine," Kelly insisted, taking a deep yogic breath and shaking herself down. "Ask me again in ten."

"I *hate* that she's got away with it," Anouk said quietly, showing them all how far she'd come from being that very woman.

"Well, I'm not sure she has." Cassie bit her lip nervously. Here came the hard part.

"Teabag . . . ?" Bas warned.

She took a deep breath. "Gil doesn't want to get divorced." She cleared her throat. "He wants me back."

"*No!!!*" they all cried together, and Cassie winced at their vehemence.

"Don't do it," Kelly cried, running over and kneeling in front of her. "He'll just break your heart all over again."

"I'll disown you if you go back to that man!" Bas shouted. "I did not acquire a taste for black pudding for nothing!"

Even Anouk sat up to press her point. "You deserve better, for one thing," she said. "And the reason you walked away is still there," she murmured, referring to Rory. "It will always be there."

Cassie nodded. "I know. You're right. You're right. It's just that . . . it's *Gil*. The last time I was without him, I was a *child*. And this year's been so hard. I mean, there have been great moments with you guys, of course there have." She stroked Bas's hand, which was sitting heavily on her shoulder. "But it's been so tough too. I'm not sure, at the end of the day, that I'm any happier without him than I was with him." She shrugged.

There was no reply to that, but she could see that every person in the room felt somehow guilty for not having turned her new life into a fairy tale. Bas silently began pinning her hair with tiny cream rosebuds, Anouk lit a cigarette. Kelly stared at her, disappointedly, before getting up from her knees.

"I think I'll have one of those beta blockers now, please," she sighed.

Chapter Fifty

Hattie was in the hall, fixing her hat and pointedly ignoring Gil, who was sitting just feet from her, when Cassie skipped down the stairs fifteen minutes later. Suzy had made a last-minute appearance, having washed her hair at the hospital, and Bas was trying to style it while she stuffed breast-feeding pads into her humongous bra.

"You look beautiful, darling," Gil said, looking up from the copy of the *Times* he always had in his briefcase. She saw him catch sight of the champagne ribbon strap on her bra, but he didn't comment. "Thanks," Cassie replied shyly. The gang's collective rebuke upstairs was still with her. "And you look wonderful, Hats," Cassie said, smiling brightly, taking in the royal blue jacquard jacket and matching long dress that she remembered Hattie dusting off every summer for Glyndebourne. "I've just come down for the flowers. The photographer wants some pictures of Kelly by the window."

"Oh, the flowers didn't come," Hattie murmured, fiddling with a pin.

"What?" Cassie felt her heart rate accelerate to triple-time.

"The taxi man rang and said they weren't on the train. I don't know if the dozy driver forgot to leave them with the station manager . . . ," she murmured.

Cassie looked up toward the landing to make sure no one had overheard before running across the hall in horror. "But Hats," she whispered, "what am I going to tell Kelly? She can't walk down the aisle with no flowers!"

"It's fine, dear. I've already sorted it. I've cut some roses and made a bouquet for her. They're sitting in a bucket in the cutting room."

Cassie breathed a huge sigh of relief, smacking her hand over her tummy at the averted crisis. "Oh, thank God! It would have been a major crisis if you were an *interior* designer. I'd have had to give her some scented candles to carry," she laughed, running off to the room behind the kitchen where Hattie arranged all her flowers and potted seedlings over the winter. A red bucket was sitting in the butler's sink.

She picked up the bouquet inside it. The heads were thick with petals, the stems dethorned and wound with white ribbon.

"I've got some of these roses, Hattie," she smiled, holding them to her nose to catch the scent as she walked back into the hall. "Cuisse de Nymphe, aren't they?"

"Gracious, I haven't heard that name in years! That's not what they're usually called."

"I'm sorry?"

"Well, that's the Regency name, darling. I thought it had dropped out of usage." She lowered her voice. "It's considered somewhat affected to use it nowadays. Everybody uses the Victorian name."

"Oh." Flipping Dean, showing off as usual. "What are they normally known as, then?"

Hattie finished fiddling with her hat and turned away from the mirror, throwing Gil an icy stare en route. "The perfect name for a wedding flower: Maiden's Blush."

*   *   *

The photos took an age, and Gil had been cornered by two of Kelly's uncles when Cassie finally stepped onto the terrace, a drink in her hand. Kelly and Brett were running across the lawn for a supposedly "natural" shot, although Cassie had yet to go to a wedding where the happy couple spontaneously ran toward the horizon.

Suzy and Archie had disappeared off to the swing seat, ostensibly to feed Cupcake, but really to coo over her with abandon. Henry was standing by the steps, chatting to a pneumatic brunette, and Cassie watched how easily he made her laugh, one hand in his pocket, as he no doubt regaled her with one of his polar-bear-wrestling stories. It had been three days since he'd pinned Cassie to the wall, his body against hers. If someone had told her then that they'd be behaving like strangers at Kelly's wedding, it would have seemed ludicrous.

"Penny for your thoughts," Anouk whispered, sidling up to her.

"Huh? Oh, hi."

Anouk followed Cassie's gaze. "Why don't you go and talk to him about it?" she asked after a moment.

"No. I don't think . . ." Cassie turned to face her suddenly. "Talk about what?"

"The kiss."

Cassie gasped, checking around them suspiciously in case anyone had overheard. "How do you know about that?" she whispered.

"You said it, at the hospital—before you knew it was me."

Oh God. At the vending machine.

"It was just a kiss," Cassie said hurriedly.

"That was what you said at the time," Anouk smiled. "Although I don't think he is getting over it."

Cassie gave a derisive snort. "No? He looks fine from where I'm standing."

Anouk shook her head and took a sip of her drink. "She's ammunition, that's all."

"Well, I don't think Lacey would appreciate his behavior," Cassie mumbled.

"He's not doing it to her. He's doing it to you."

"It doesn't matter what I think. *I'm* not his fiancée. She is."

"No she isn't."

Cassie's glass slipped from her hand and the sound of crystal shattering on York stone made everyone—including Henry and the dollybird—turn around to stare. A waiter appeared out of nowhere and immediately brushed the glass away.

"He rang me after Christmas and canceled the order for the rings," Anouk said, once another waiter had handed Cassie a fresh glass and she'd shakily taken a sip.

"But why?"

Anouk shrugged. "I'm not his confidante."

The revelation changed everything. If he had called off the engagement after Christmas, then his trip to Paris hadn't been to see Anouk about the rings . . . and the trip to Venice hadn't been to organize his honeymoon. He had been telling the truth that night after all. "Does Suzy know?" she asked eventually.

"He told her when he was off on his expedition. Something about double-booking the flowers?" Anouk looked at Cassie. "You should talk to him."

But Cassie just felt even more confused. If his behavior

toward her wasn't down to feeling guilty about Lacey, then why was he so angry?

"Especially because you know Gil's going to want to pin you down for an answer."

"I know."

Cassie looked away. All through the service, while the twinkly eyed vicar joined Kelly in magical bliss with her soul mate, Cassie had tried to draw up a mental list of pros and cons for taking Gil back. She knew that he would continue to try to convince her as soon as they got to the reception, and she had wanted to be sure of how she felt before he talked her around, the way he did so cleverly, every single day in court. But try as she might, all she'd been able to think about were the flowers in Kelly's hand and what they had to do with her necklace, which was still hanging from a bridge in Paris.

"I know he will. And I know what you think—you don't need to tell me. I'd be going back on everything I said to you."

Anouk considered for a moment. "Well, I think it proves your point that a little hope is a dangerous thing," she said, smiling ruefully . . . "Oh no, don't look up. He's coming over."

"Hello, ladies." Gil smiled, leaning down to kiss Anouk on each cheek, a casual arm sliding around Cassie's waist. "I'm so sorry not to have greeted you properly earlier, Anouk. I was somewhat . . . distracted." He flashed Cassie a loving smile.

"Gil," Anouk replied through gritted teeth.

"I'm looking forward to catching up with you. I'm rather hoping you can bring me up to speed on everything Cassie got up to with you in Paris." He squeezed Cassie playfully and it seemed strange to have him behave like that with her. She was used to detached formality in public from him.

"Thank you for taking care of her for me. It's something to know that she had her friends looking out for her."

"She's always got that, Gil," Anouk replied, and there was no hiding the flinty tone of her voice.

Gil glanced, nonplussed, at the guests milling about the beautiful gardens.

"There are quite a few of the old faces here, I see," he said. "Henry looks as though he's all set for a good night."

Cassie and Anouk looked over toward the steps. Henry had moved down two, to counteract the height difference— even in heels the brunette was barely five foot five—and she was taking every opportunity to thrust her bosom in his face.

"There are some new faces here too, Gil," Anouk said quickly, aware that Cassie couldn't take her eyes off them. "See Bas over there in the purple shirt?" she asked, pointing him out. He was standing by a topiary dove, throwing his arms around and sending his companion—a middle-aged woman in garish colors, quite possibly one of Kelly's aunts— into fits of laughter.

Gil followed her finger. "*Him?* Who's he?"

"He was Cassie's best friend"—Anouk watched the horror cross Gil's face at the thought of his wife being friendly with a camp hairdresser—"when she was in New York."

"You were in *New York*?" Gil asked her, incredulous. "Any- where else I should know about?"

"London, Venice," Anouk replied for her.

Cassie was still staring at Henry. She didn't know him at all, she was thinking to herself—not in *that* way. He had proved himself a good friend to her, but as a lover, he was dangerous, untrustworthy. Hadn't he himself said he was no angel? A broken engagement behind him, playing games with her in Venice, then cutting and running after he did kiss her. And any man who kissed like *that* . . . he was a predator.

She took a step closer to Gil, and he smiled in surprise at her move, spreading his fingers up her waist so that they brushed the bottom of her bra. Sometimes it was better to trust the devil you knew.

"You seem down in the dumps my dear," Hattie said, coming to join Cassie at the empty table where she was slumped, watching a friend of Brett's do his best Mick Jagger impersonation. She had suffered through the speeches and dinner, which Gil had dominated with a rare bombastic bonhomie, triggering unimpressed expressions even from Arch, and now everyone had scattered. Kelly and Brett had danced their first dance, Gil was somewhere at the bar ordering himself a whisky; Anouk was dancing to Abba with Archie, while Suzy had gone off to change her bra after her boobs leaked during coffee. Henry was still with the Jessica Rabbit look-alike two tables away. Cassie had her back to them, so she couldn't see what they were up to, but from the nervous glances Anouk had been shooting her way, she was amazed they hadn't found a room already.

Cassie straightened up and gave a brave smile. "Not at all, Hats. I'm just waiting for my second wind."

"What you need is some chamomile tea."

"Chamomile? At a wedding?" Cassie grimaced. "That's not the form. It said on my bridesmaid enrollment papers that I'm supposed to get slaughtered and snog an usher."

"Well now, *that* probably wouldn't be such a bad thing! If you want my opinion, you could pick any man at random here tonight and you'd still make a better choice than that roué husband of yours."

Cassie nodded stoically. The verdict was unanimous, then.

Hattie jerked her chin in the air. "But you didn't, so I'll keep my opinions to myself. Anyway, chamomile's what you need. Energy in adversity. It's just the ticket." She smiled sympathetically, patting Cassie's hand.

She went to get up, but Cassie clutched at her. "What did you say, Hats? Energy in adversity?"

"Yes, dear. It's just the tonic for you right now."

"But why did you say those specific words? You could have just said it would revitalize me."

"Hmmm, yes, I suppose I could," she mused. "But I'm something of a stickler for being correct about these things. The language of flowers is open enough to interpretation as it is."

"The language of flowers?"

"Yes. The Victorians ascribed specific properties to flowers, and they attributed chamomile with 'energy in adversity.'"

Cassie let go of her hand. She knew those very words, of course she did. They had been written on the tag that came with the grass seeds. "Energy in adversity" had been Henry's "motivational" motto to her in New York. She thought about the list he'd given her: hosting dinner, running around the park . . . getting her going, getting her *living* again.

But there hadn't been a "motto" for Paris. And he'd been adamant she had to find out what the flowers were herself. Did he want her to decipher their identities . . . and then their *meanings*?

She felt her pulse quicken. She instinctively knew this mattered.

Hattie had moved on to the dance floor and was being twirled around by the vicar, who was more twinkle-toes than brimstone. Cassie stood up and stepped into the wriggling, giggling mass toward them.

"Hats . . . Hats," she called, trying to tap Hattie on the shoulder. "So what is the meaning for Sweet Alyssum?"

"What's that?" Hattie asked, cupping her ear and trying to hear over the drumbeat to Lady Gaga.

"Sweet Alyssum," Cassie called, running in circles with her as the vicar attempted to whisk Hattie's feet off the ground. "What does it mean?"

"Uh . . . ooooh!" she squealed as he achieved liftoff and she dissolved into a fit of girlish giggles.

"Hats! Please!" Cassie cried. She could see Gil paying for his drink by the bar.

"I'm not sure. It's been so long . . . 'worth beyond beauty,' I think!" the older woman called.

Cassie stopped running. Worth beyond beauty? Her motto for Paris, when she had lost all sight of who she was and no longer recognized her own reflection? She remembered sitting on the bridge with Henry just after he'd idiotically locked her padlock to the bridge. *You've tried to reinvent yourself when there is absolutely nothing about you that needs to be fixed* . . . Her mind slowed. He'd given her energy in New York, the will to fight back straight after her marriage had been dealt the knockout blow; tried to show her she had a worth beyond the cosmetic in Paris. So, then, for London . . . ?

She started chasing Hattie in circles again. "And Maiden's Blush? It's the last one, I promise."

"I'm sorry, dear. It's been years since I looked at that book," Hattie said, shrugging apologetically.

Cassie's face fell. "You really can't remember?"

"Check in the library. It'll be there somewhere."

The library? Gil was making his way back to the table; she could already see him scanning the marquee for her. She ducked down and moved across the dance floor, darting behind the DJ and running along the electrical cables until she found her escape through the caterers' exit, past the bottle bins.

She ran across the terrace, startling Suzy, who was rocking Cupcake in her arms, through the French windows into the drawing room and beyond, into the library.

It was dim in there. Only a table lamp was lit and she could feel the bass of the music vibrating through the old oak floorboards. Quickly she began scanning the shelves. Decades' worth of *Gardens Illustrated* magazines were lined up next to horticultural tomes and glossy coffee-table books paying homage to the gardening greats Bunny Guinness, William Kent, and Charles Bridgeman.

But the book she was looking for, and eventually found, was nothing like as grand. It was small and somewhat tatty, with yellowing pages and charming line illustrations. *Language of Flowers, illustrated by Kate Greenaway.*

She thumbed to the front page. It was a first edition—1884—and the pages gave off that wonderful smell she loved so much. She read a message that had been written in pencil in a young hand:

> Happy 40th, Mum.
> Love, Henry xxxx

She flicked through the pages. It was like an index, running alphabetically, and there were soiled thumbprints at the corners of the pages. A few pages had been marked, some by a felt-tip pen, obviously wielded by a very young child, but others were ticked in the margins with a pencil, firm and sure. Her answers were here, she knew.

With shaking hands she went to *M*.

"Madder; Magnolia; Magnolia, Swamp; Mallow . . ."

It wasn't there! She took a deep breath and tried to focus. Then she remembered Cuisse De Nymphe. She went to *C*.

No luck.

"Oh, come on," she murmured . . . *R*! It was a type of rose. It had to be subclassified under rose.

She flicked through the pages as quickly as she could, but it was tricky—the book, though small, was a hardback and the pages thick. But she knew she was on the right page before she even saw the letters. A tiny silver key was taped in by the spine, a miniature tag swinging from it that read:

"Yours if you want it."

It was the key for her padlock. It wasn't lost at all. Had never been lost, simply withheld, and she could have it back now—could get the necklace back—if she wanted it.

She pulled the tape off carefully and dropped the key into her bra. Well, why wouldn't she want it? Who in their right mind would willingly leave a solid silver Tiffany's necklace padlocked to a bridge in Paris?

Her eyes scanned the opposite page.

"Rose, Guelder; Rose, Hundred-Leaved; Rose, Japan; Rose, Maide—"

Her heart skipped a beat at the sight of it and she slid her finger slowly over the page, the slightly furred texture tingly beneath her skin.

"*Rose, Maiden's Blush . . . If you love me, you will find it out.*"

Words rushed at her, ghosts clamoring. If you love me, you will find it out. If you love me . . . Not nothing . . . Everything. Unconsummated love . . . Find it out . . . find it out.

The book fell from her hands and she was back in Venice that first night, checking her makeup in the mirror. *His gaze swept into hers. And just for a moment, before the shame and humiliation came crashing down upon her, she felt a current pass between their reflections, a power-surge that threatened to slam her against the wall and knock all the air and sense out of her.*

In a thunderbolt of realization, she suddenly understood that it hadn't been embarrassment that had made her run that day. It had been the look that had passed between them—it had been the moment of truth.

"There you are!" Gil said from the door, and through her shock she could hear the possession in his voice. "I was about to do a head-count of the groomsmen and start searching the camellia bushes."

Cassie heard him place his drink on the table and walk over to her, his eyes drinking her in before he placed his cool, smooth hands on her. Slowly, he turned her around.

"Darling, what is it?" he exclaimed, looking startled. "You're as white as a sheet."

She was quiet for a long time, and when she did speak, she felt dazed, remote. "You're exactly the same."

"I am," he soothed, rubbing her hands as though to warm her up.

"And that's the problem. You're frozen. Stuck. While you've been busy staying the same, I've changed every aspect of my life. It's been completely terrifying—but also exhilarating."

She looked at him, watched him balk at the pity in her

eyes. "You and Wiz gave me back my freedom, and, thanks to my friends, I grabbed it with both hands. You are the one left without choices in all this."

"I don't understand . . . ," he said warily.

"You're still the husband I knew, Gil. But I'm not your wife."

"You are in law," he retorted obstinately, too flummoxed by the turn of conversation to remember to tread softly.

"The law's an ass. Isn't that what they say?"

He stepped toward her, cupping the back of her head with his hand and gazing into her eyes passionately . . . but he saw that they weren't his anymore. They had belonged to him for the longest time, holding all the uncertainty and insecurity that he had fostered in her, the very thing Luke had first noticed and been attracted to in her. But all he saw now was purpose and confidence, a woman who knew herself. He pulled back, knowing somehow that, in the time it had taken to buy a drink, he had lost her.

"I don't want to be without you, Cass. I want you back." It was his final card—pleading, without pride.

Cassie looked at him, her gaze level. "But I don't *want* you to want me, Gil. The only thing I want from you is my divorce."

Chapter Fifty-One

Henry was sitting at the same table, his cheek resting on the palm of his hand, when Cassie walked back into the marquee. The brunette was chattering excitedly about something, but Cassie could see, now that she looked, that he seemed more bored than enthralled by her.

She watched for a moment, wondering how to cut in, how to start this . . .

Then she walked across the matting floor, weaving between the tables toward him. He saw her approach from three tables away, her eyes locked onto him, and he lifted his head automatically—just in time for the glass of water she threw over him, which drenched his hair and shirt and left the brunette squawking pathetically. Archie and Anouk, nearby on the dance floor, burst out laughing, absolutely delighted, but Cassie didn't stay to join in. As quickly as she'd soaked him, she turned on her heel and fled from the marquee, kicking her shoes off so that she could run faster, barefoot, through the meadow and down toward the lake.

After ten seconds, during which Henry sat there, stunned, he was up and straight after her. She could hear his outraged breathing advancing closer with every stride. She knew she could never outrun him and stopped abruptly, whirling around to face him so that he had to jump sideways to avoid mowing her down.

"What the . . . what the *hell* was that for?" he howled, regaining his balance, water still dripping from his hair.

"You deserved it," she panted, her heart hammering inside her ribs.

"For what?"

"For behaving like such an arse toward me since you got here."

Henry stared at her, flabbergasted. "*What?*"

"Don't try to deny it. Ever since you kissed me, you've acted like you hate me."

"I don't hate you!" he exclaimed, seemingly unaware that his hands were repeatedly balling into furious fists.

"Oh, I know that *now!*"

"Now that you've thrown water over me?" He was incredulous at her behavior.

"Now that I've discovered your secret."

There was a pause. "What secret?" He looked like she'd slapped him.

She took a deep breath. "That you love me."

It was an extraordinary statement to make out loud.

He was silent for a long time. His chest heaved with adrenaline, his eyes bored questioningly into hers. "And what makes you think that I love you?" he asked more quietly.

"I found out what Maiden's Blush stands for," she said, watching as he turned away from her.

He raked his hand through his hair. "Well, that was before."

It was Cassie's turn to pause. Had she misunderstood? "Before what?"

"What do you think?" he demanded, wheeling back and

staring her down again. "Before you decided to go back to that soft-bellied, manipulative, cheating husband of yours."

"Can you blame me? Ever since you jumped on me, you haven't been able to even look at me! You couldn't get out of there fast enough! I thought you were running back to your fiancée, which was bad enough! But *then* I learned you called off the engagement months ago. So why have you been lying to me about her? What is she? Your cover story for making a quick exit?"

"You don't know . . . you don't know the first bloody thing about it!" he countered in exasperation, pacing back and forth.

"So tell me then!" Cassie demanded. "Tell me what's going on with you. Because I can't keep up!"

"You really wanna know?"

"Yes!"

"Fine! I have been in love with you my whole life, okay? All of it! Even while you were married for ten years to *him* and I thought you were completely lost to me. I was convinced I'd never find any kind of happiness after y—" His voice broke and he swallowed hard, hands on his hips, as he stared down at the ground. "But I met Lacey and I thought maybe . . ."

He looked back up at her. "And then you came back into my life again." He gave a small, unamused laugh. "I couldn't believe it. I'd just got engaged and you were just getting divorced! It felt like some kind of fucking cosmic joke."

Cassie watched him, silvered in the moonlight, and she felt herself begin to bruise and ache at the heartbreak he had hidden so well.

"I tried to keep my life with Lacey on track, but I knew pretty much straightaway it was never going to work out between us. Not when there was a chance that you . . ." He looked away again.

"So why didn't you just tell me you'd called off the engagement?"

"Because for as long as you thought I was with her, I knew you wouldn't let anything happen between us. I knew *I* wouldn't be able to hold back from telling you how I felt, and I couldn't do that. Not then. It was the last thing you needed to hear. You couldn't go straight from a ten-year marriage into 'happy ever after' with me." He inhaled deeply, and she could sense the resentment building in him again. "So I kept quiet. I kept away. I watched while you got it on with Luke sodding Laidlaw. And then the second I *finally* showed you how I felt—when I couldn't hold back any longer and I thought maybe you could handle it—you went running back to Gil. One hint that he wanted you back, and you were right there, on his doorstep."

"But I didn't go to Scotland to get back with Gil," Cassie gasped.

"Oh no? So what's he doing here, then, hands all over you like you're newlyweds?"

Cassie rubbed her face in her hands. How could she explain it to him?

"After you kissed me, I knew there was no going back to him. I went to Scotland to make him sign the divorce papers, but he wasn't even there. I came back, hoping you would finish what you started, but you wouldn't even look at me, and when he turned up, asking for a second chance . . . I didn't think you cared."

They stared at each other, eyes burning, hearts racing.

"So . . . what are you saying?" His hands were jammed in his pockets, all his usual lackadaisical ease gone.

Cassie walked toward him, cupping his face with her hands. "I'm saying that I love you," she whispered, gazing into his blue eyes, which were as bright and clear as the Arctic waters he explored. "I have done ever since I . . . *mugged* you in Central Park."

He gave a sudden laugh, and she laughed too, but it quickly faded as he grabbed her by the shoulders and kissed her. She felt the weight of his words through his lips as ten years of yearning was released and he wound his hands in her hair, grazed his mouth on her neck, and raked his fingers up her body with an exquisite lightness that made her feel her skin must be sparkling beneath his touch.

His skin felt cold and damp, and she unbuttoned his sodden shirt, smoothing it off him as she felt him pull the ribbon-tie on her dress. It fell open, sliding off her shoulders with silky submission so that she too stood almost bare before him, in just primrose lace—the two of them marble-white in the moonbeams, like Rodin's lovers.

A sudden glint caught Henry's eye, and he reached down, pulling the Tiffany key from her bra. He raised a speculative eyebrow, and Cassie took it from him. She stared at it for a moment—the symbol of his secret seduction through three different cities—then, kissing it lightly, she threw it as far as she could over the glassy water, and the silver key flew through the night sky, like a tiny Cupid's arrow.

Epilogue

New York, six months later.

"You said you'd done all your shopping," Archie moaned as Cassie stopped outside Tiffany's giant door. "I need to get home and check I've still got ten toes. I think Suzy might have sliced some of them off with her skates just now."

Suzy walloped him in the stomach. "I am the wind beneath your wings, and don't you forget it."

"We should get back, Cass, if I'm going to get that turkey stuffed before midnight," Kelly chimed in reluctantly.

"I promise I'll just be a minute. I know exactly what I want to get," Cassie said, nipping into the store before anyone could protest further. Henry, Arch, Brett, and Guillaume groaned and loped in after the girls, accepting the complimentary champagne with deep suspicion, and blinking warily in the glare that comes from being confined in a small space with millions of dollars' worth of diamonds.

"It's my fault. I've told her we should spend every Christmas at Tiffany's," Henry said, leading them toward the towering Christmas tree at the back. "Start our own traditions and all that."

The men watched as their girls leaned over a small tray of

brightly colored enamel trinkets, champagne glasses in hand, Cassie picking out items with nimble precision.

"Look what I've got," Anouk purred to Guillaume a few minutes later, holding up a teeny pink shoe charm on a necklace chain. Kelly came over bearing a tiny shiny red apple charm on hers, and Suzy seconds later with a yellow cupcake charm.

"What are they all for?" Archie asked quizzically.

"It's my way of saying thank you to my best friends for getting me through last year," Cassie said, smiling around at them all. "Energy in the Big Apple, elegance in Paris, and cupcakes in London. It was a big year for me."

"Yeah, and what did you do with it—huh?" Suzy drawled. "You were the poster girl for a fashion campaign, Luke's muse in an exhibition, the muse in *Vogue*'s special issue, and Claude named his landmark restaurant after you in Paris. I mean, for God's sake, Cass, why didn't you *do* something with your life?"

Everyone laughed.

"Honestly, I love this, Cass. I'll treasure it forever, and I'm not giving it back," Kelly grinned, clutching her necklace more tightly. "But I think we all know who really got you through last year," she said, holding up her champagne glass toward Henry.

"To Henry!" everyone cheered, and Cassie reached up to him to show her gratitude—again.

"*Tch*, you're always falling onto each other's lips!" Suzy groaned as they kissed for slightly longer than was strictly necessary.

"Personally, I think he was a bit long-winded about the whole thing. Lists, flowers . . . ," Archie muttered. "I just got Suzy drunk."

"Aren't you having a necklace?" Kelly asked. "I think we should all have a memento of that year."

"Ah, but I already have one." Cassie smiled, fingering the bare chain hanging around her neck. "It's just hanging from a bridge in Paris."

"I'm telling you, I am going to take Archie's toenail clippers to it if you don't release that thing," Suzy warned.

"We don't have the key," Cassie said, her eyes twinkling at the memory of her and Henry's first night together, down by the lake. "Besides, Nooks and Guillaume check it for us, don't you?"

"Every Sunday morning," Guillaume nodded. "It's fixed solid."

"I'll never forget that moment," Cassie smiled, looking back up at Henry. "In fact, I was standing just there," she said, taking a step closer to the tree and pointing toward the mound of blue boxes clustered around the base. "Honestly, you should have seen my face when I saw my name . . ."

She fell silent.

"What's wrong?" Anouk asked after a moment.

Cassie was staring at the gift boxes, seemingly lost in the memory. But then she bent down and picked one up. It was tiny, and heavy, and written upon a dangling gift tag was her name.

She stared back at Henry in amazement. *"Again?"*

"Better."

The question was in his eyes.

The answer was in her hands.

"Yes," she smiled. "Oh yes."

Acknowledgments

My biggest thanks must go to my two boys, Ollie and William, whom I took to Paris to show the Eiffel Tower and Mona Lisa to, but who ended up showing me the Paris that is featured in this book. Much of what is included in the Paris section we enjoyed ourselves—Ladurée macaroons, gargoyle spotting, even the passing mention of the polar bear is true! But most particularly, it was with them that I discovered the Pont des Arts and, crucially, its love padlocks. This would have been a very different book without their sharp eyes and tired feet. Thank you, my darlings.

Also, Anders, my own bear of a man who keeps me safe, happy—and to my word count. This book made it in time for Christmas only because of you.

Thanks are always due, and never said enough, to my beloved parents who are my biggest supporters—in every way. You might even be allowed to read this book!

A massive thank-you to Jenny Geras who instantly knew how to shape this book—from synopsis to first draft (eek, the original ending!), from title to graphics, your enthusiasm and ambition for it has been infectious and galvanizing.

Also, Thalia (what would I do without you?), Ali, Eli, and Juliet Van Oss (thank you for your fabulous note!), Katie and the rest of the Pan Macmillan team who have worked so hard in positioning, branding, and finessing this book. I am genuinely so proud of it and deeply grateful to you all.

Amanda Preston, thank you so much for always being so calm when I am not, and for forever knowing the right thing to say. You are the only person I have ever met who can rival my husband for pulling statistics and percentages out of thin air. You should be on a pub quiz team together!